THE SALT GOD'S DAUGHTER

THE SALT

GOD'S

DAUGHTER

ILIE RUBY

Soft Skull Press

AN IMPRINT OF COUNTERPOINT

ISBN 978-1-61902-002-3

Cover design by Faceout Studios
Interior design by Sabrina Plomitallo-González, Neuwirth & Associates

Soft Skull Press
www.softskull.com
An imprint of COUNTERPOINT
1919 Fifth Street
Berkeley, CA 94710

Printed in the United States of America
Distributed by Publishers Group West

10 9 8 7 6 5 4 3 2 1

In memory of M.N., woman of the ocean

"When angels fell, some fell on the land, some on the sea. The former are the faeries and the latter were often said to be the seals."

—Anonymous Orcadian

THE SALT GOD'S DAUGHTER

Prologue
Naida, 2001

PEOPLE HAD BEEN calling me the Frog Witch for as long as I could remember. My mother, Ruthie, lied and told me it was because they envied the long wavy locks of jet-black hair that fell across my back, which I had inherited from my father. His pale green sea glass eyes were mine. My dark red lips appeared bloodstained just as his had, as did the skin between the toes on my left foot. I knew my mother hadn't wanted to lie, that we had to agree to pretend there was nothing special about me. Even though I remembered everything that had happened, even though I noticed the shape of his absence all around us, how it lingered at the foot of my bed at dawn, caught between darkness and daylight.

When my mother first discovered me, felt me start to crawl deep within her, she thought of how my father had left her and her breasts dripped milk. She didn't know about the seasons of living things, that they needed to settle like water, to find their right place on Earth so as to fall in step with the moon. She didn't know how fast I was growing inside her. In my mind, I was already three years old when I pushed out of her body and into her hands.

But now, at twelve, I wanted to believe there was nothing different about me. My mother had refused surgery on my foot when I was a child because she didn't want to cause me pain. Now I kept my foot hidden as much as I could.

"Hey, Frog Witch, catching any flies?" the kids would taunt me, before knocking into me in the hallways, causing me to drop my books. Sometimes, when I tired of the bullying and teasing, when the name Frog Witch made my skin burn like fire, I snuck out at night under the stars and dove into the water where there was solace, where there was peace. When everyone else was sleeping, I'd dive into the cool Pacific and swim among the three sea lions that sometimes lived under our porch. They were my companions, and this was my meditation.

But some people wouldn't let me forget the past. I knew all my classmates talked about it, not just the mean girls who called me Frog Witch. They liked to point to the raised pink scar on my forehead I'd gotten one night when I was four. I stopped trying to hide it with bangs when Sister Mary came to visit and told my mother that the Devil and God had wrestled for my soul and God had let go first. If I was damned I might as well show it.

Each day after school, I'd run up and down the bleach-scented, burgundy-carpeted hallways of Wild Acres, the retirement home where I grew up. I could knock on any door whenever I wanted. I visited Dr. Brownstein every afternoon because her soft brown eyes were always warm if not slightly hidden under heavy painted-blue lids, because she kept two plastic palm trees and a parakeet that would say, "Hello, sweetie" and, "Time to make the donuts." Also because she kept fistfuls of Tootsie Rolls and butterscotch candies in the pockets of her housecoat, which she'd drop into my outstretched hands.

My moods were unpredictable and changeable, my mother said, like the ocean. It was true. Sometimes when I thought of my father and how he left us, I became so full of rage that my mother sent me out to the beach to scream at the seagulls, and after, I'd watch them drift down through the air like white scraps of paper. The sea lions would start barking on the shoreline, causing my mother to rush out onto our overhanging porch, calling me inside.

Didn't I deserve a life? The girls in my grade were just discovering how mean they could be. I just wanted a boyfriend, to be loved, to be kissed in the same ways other girls my age were kissed. Boys chased me down Second Street after school, calling me names, forcing me to find new paths home. Soon, I would need protection. I thought that if my father came back, he could stop this. As much as my mother said she hated him, I knew she idolized him. And because she did, I did too.

People whispered when I passed by on the pier.

"There's a Frog Witch," I heard them say every word.

Once when I was buying milk at RiteAid, a girl pulled a few hairs from my head as she walked by. "Nice foot, Frog Witch," she said, excusing herself in a laughing tone. She was hoping to get a piece of me. The worst was when the girls my age pretended to like me. Friendships were a bit foreign to me, as much as I craved them. My only friends were my mother and Aunt Dolly and the residents of Wild Acres. I'd be on cloud nine for days when I thought I had made a new friend. Then I would find out that she only wanted to be told stories: that things would work out just as she'd planned, that she'd meet a true love while seeking shelter in a rainstorm, or that she'd get accepted into Dartmouth or Harvard, land a good job after that, get married and then have a baby. As if my being different still lent me some kind of secret knowledge. I knew people craved assurance. That life wasn't hard, or painful, or that they wouldn't have to face it all alone.

Many nights, I crept out onto the porch and watched my mother standing on the sand below, her nightgown billowing under the hem of a shiny blue raincoat as she doled out fish for the three sea lions that crowded around her, filling her loneliness. Even though she could not swim, they were hers and she was theirs. They were mine, too. They were my guardians. And I was hers.

After, she'd crawl into bed with me to tell me the stories of her life. Sometimes she'd weep, and I'd hold her and promise never to leave her. I coveted her midnight visits even though I had trouble staying awake the next day. Once or twice, I put my head down on my desk and broke into sobs. My teacher asked if it was due to the bullying, but it wasn't. It was the weight of her, the sheer weight of my mother's love for me, and mine for her, and the memory of our bodies curved inward, our knees touching, and the feel of her hands bracing my shoulders as if I could ward off harm for us both. "You are my life, Naida," she'd whisper, waiting.

My words "and you're mine" became like escaped birds that floated above me, irretrievable. I wanted to reach out and grasp them, to tell her she was mine, then to tuck my mother's hair behind her ear as I usually did. But I held my breath under the blue sheet, pretending to be asleep, listening to the waves crash into the space between her need and my silence, until one of us fell asleep.

There was no water that was too rough or frigid. I could swim in nighttime storms beyond the breakwaters, and had dozens of times that my mother did not know about, letting my fingers sift through the tips of the feathered sea grass near the oil rigs as barracuda darted around my legs in figure eights, and a swarm of fish swam in silvery bubbles as a sea lion crossed, the slip of its coat brushing against my arms as its dark eyes flashed in the water. I was a person who remembered. My mother understood this. She said my father had the same gift. The story of what happened to me when I was four years old would never go away. I didn't want to think about lying in the hospital bed with drool dribbling out of the corner of my mouth and an IV stuck in my arm. Humiliating—my aunt took pictures.

The attack on me would be the last straw, and I could feel it in the same way certain animals lay down before a storm. I knew it, just as I knew that my mother's eyes would tear up whenever she'd catch me staring out at the ocean.

I knew that soon it would be time to leave home. As much as I loved my mother, I knew it would no longer be safe for me to be here with her. I was almost a woman now, a nerd by all accounts, a solid competitor in the science club, a good and loyal daughter, a friend who remembered the residents of Wild Acres, and an impressive swimmer. My father needed to know me, and I to know him. I didn't have a name for what I was and what I could do. But I needed to save myself. There were things I needed to discover—about who I was, my mother's past, and even the woman who came before.

The attack on me would happen first, though. I could feel it coming.

PART ONE

Chapter One

Ruthie, 1972

W E RAN WILD at night, effortless, boundless, under a blood-red sky—to where and to what we couldn't have known. We craved it, that someplace. We were two little girls, sisters, daughters with no mother, distrustful of the freedom we were given, knowing she shouldn't have left. We tore across dirt campgrounds where we slept, naked but for our mud boots, letting the wind shiver up across our bare chests. We stole bags of chips from the canteen on the pier. Our feet pounded the crushed oyster shells in seaside motel parking lots when we'd search for drinking water, and we let calluses thicken up our soles to withstand the hot desert sand, or dash over a highway of broken glass, wherever we'd been dropped. We scampered across the foggy cliffs that separated Pacific Coast Highway from the ocean in old ballet slippers, as nimble as two fairies, our long red hair whipping into tangles in the wind. We bumped up against the night, without stopping. We stole wrinkled leather sneakers that were two sizes too big, and wore them until they fit. We raced in the sand, fought in the dusk. We knew we were not invisible. We tightened belts around our stomachs at night and bicycled unlit sidewalks and sometimes tucked up our knees and steered with no hands through the darkness. No one hit us. We believed we were unstoppable. We slept under sleeping bags, beneath trees, and pushed our backs against cliffs, our noses cold.

We waited for our mother to come back.

"Ruthie, do you miss her?" Dolly asked.

"No," I lied.

We talked of Cool Whip and ice cream, of warm apple crisp and salty Fritos. We dreamed of flying.

Then my mother came back. We'd crawl into our station wagon at night, trapped by her need for freedom, and then by her soap opera, General Hospital, which we watched on her portable television. Afterward, we listened to folk songs and Hebrew prayers as she'd strum a fat-bellied classical, knowing this meant that she was feeling fine, that she had acknowledged she had two little girls, whether she wanted us or not.

We used our fingernails to cut away ticks from our legs, and we cleaned up her empty bottles before she'd wake up. We bit at the skin around our nails, leaving it swollen and red.

If I told you that I ached for a different mother, I'd be lying. I ached for my own, every minute. As motherless daughters do.

She was our child. We didn't know anything different. Everyone knew a mother was a daughter's first love.

When she asked if we thought she was still beautiful, we said yes, because she was. We told the truth about the steely lightness of her eyes, how quickly they changed color with her emotions, from gray to blue, in parts. We lied when she asked if we thought she'd fall in love one day. We said yes.

It was as possible to miss someone who was right in front of you as it was to miss someone who had left. It was also possible to miss someone who had not yet been born. This I had learned. My mother had told us as much. We walked around craving everyone, even before they'd leave. We never thought it would end, our ache. Often, from the windows of my mother's speeding green Ford Country Squire, we shouted out the words to James Taylor ballads and motioned for truckers to honk on demand by pumping our fists up and down. We grew cocky, forgetting we were people who had been left.

We were already nomadic, and from the most primal of places, we had become hunters, always searching for someone or something we could lay claim to, hook ourselves onto, to quiet our trembling clamorous souls.

As long as she came back for us.

I HAVE FEW memories before I was six years old, but waking up hungry is one of them. In the white sky of a January night, under the glow of a Hunger Moon, I remember looking out of the rear compartment window of the wood-paneled station wagon my mother called Big Ugly. We had been kept warm at the campsite all night, body pressed to body, wet leaves under the orange sleeping bag.

We hadn't eaten since the night before. I knew this only because my job was to get rid of the trash. My mother had spent the evening grazing the tiny bottles of liquor on the flipped-down tailgate. Dolly and I had kicked around the canyon, making Jacob's ladder designs out of string and waiting for the portable television's batteries to die, which always brought on my mother's mood swings. Even as Dolly moved the television so as to get the best reception and I adjusted the antennae, my mother drank. She watched us now from the roof of the car as she paged through her Old Farmer's Almanac in search of the moon's clues, her legs tucked beneath her on a plaid blanket that spilled over the car windows, keeping it dark inside for us when we finally went to bed, keeping out the moonlight.

When I woke up, I thought Dolly was crying because of my mother's anger at the batteries, but it was the trees.

The trees were falling off the hillside.

We had never seen anything like it. I watched the blurred brushstrokes, the cascading sweeps of russet and umber tumbling beneath a blue-black sky. I had always clung to land, distrustful of the tide's obedience to an irrational moon. Now, even the land was giving way. Storms from one of the strongest El Niños in years lifted the top layer of earth like a fingernail, flicking it off, along with rocks and branches. Dolly had woken up first, and started screaming. She pointed to the river of mud rushing down the canyon toward us. Only months before, fire brought by the Santa Ana winds had cleared the hillside of most of the trees. Now that there was little to hold the earth in place, the winds ripped the charred remains from their roots, spilling them across our campsite. The roots had released easily, willing to be exposed after having been tugged at and battered for so long. I could not blame them.

"Dammit, where are my keys?" my mother said, climbing into the front seat. She skimmed her hand across the vinyl. "Where are those damn things?" Her hair spun in wild black tangles, along with her rage. Dolly and I scampered around the back, searching. My hunger turned to dust. I could not find my glasses.

"Hurry up, Mom! Will you get us out of here?" Dolly cried, as rain swept across the windshield in blustery sheets, smacking the glass with rocks. Patterns of flesh and green filled the windows. Dolly handed me my glasses. Clarity.

"My keys. What did you girls do with them?" my mother asked, as I climbed in front beside her. The river of mud was coming toward us.

January's Hunger Moon was supposed to keep us fed, or return my mother's lover to her. But it had not done either, so far. The moon was misbehaving, my mother said. Bad unpredictable weather followed the Child Theory of Planetary Creation. The moon was Earth's child, which meant that the moon's materials had originally spun off from the earth. The

Hunger Moon had conspired, teasing the storms toward the Pacific coast of California, bringing heavy rains and torrential winds, not at all following what she had planned.

I kicked a pile of clothes aside and shook out my coat, reaching under the seat, feeling the sharp teeth of the keys.

"I found them!" I cried, certain this would make my mother love me.

She took the keys from me without a flicker of recognition. She pushed them into the ignition, and waited. Nothing. She pumped the gas three times and then flooded the engine. We started moving. "Faster. Keep driving, Mom. Don't stop," said Dolly.

"Be quiet," my mother whispered. "Please, just be quiet. If you're not quiet I don't know what I'll do." We drove off, barely able to see the full moon amid the darkness. This unforeseen storm had her rattled, threatening her mastery. My mother had been playing a trick on the world by surviving on her own with two little girls. Without a man. Without family or friends, to speak of. With only her Farmer's Almanac and the full moons to guide her, she would do it on her own. But this storm had caught her off guard, and to boot there was hunger, which always made her anxious.

I heard howling. I watched the gray Hunger Moon sneaking behind the San Gabriel Mountains. I wondered if it might be willing to help us find a safe place. She had told me such things were possible, and I believed that the reason we were stuck, why the moon hadn't cooperated, had something to do with me, my behavior. Not being good enough, brave enough, like my sister.

"We're not going to die," I whispered as I turned back to Dolly, noticing her hair, a deeper shade of red than mine, smeared straight across her wet cheeks.

As Big Ugly spun onto the slick highway and skidded to a stop, shattering the air with mud, I wanted to disappear from the aftermath of her lack of control, which I could feel. Disheveled tree roots, cracked rocks, broken bumpers, and shards of glass littered the road. People were being evacuated. I could sense my mother's anger filling the car as she weaved through fender-bender crashes, drove up beyond the curve of sky, and then, once out of sight, pulled off to the side in a quiet and dark patch of mud. She reached across my lap and pulled the door handle, opening my door. "Get out, Ruthie. Don't make me tell you twice."

I hesitated, wondering if she would do this to me again. Why was it always me? She lit a cigarette and blew smoke out the window.

"Out. Get out," she said, hitting the steering wheel with the heel of her hand. I opened the door and got out. Standing in the rain, I watched her drive off, my hands balled into fists. My cheeks flushed, though I refused to cry, letting the rain soak my jean shorts and yellow tank top. I refused to bite my fingernails to the quick again. I looked around in the silence, wiping my glasses with the hem of my shirt. There was nothing but darkness and an occasional flicker of moonlight on the wet pavement. I stopped breathing, if only for a moment. I reached into my pocket and took out one of the smooth stones my mother had given me earlier. It felt warm in my palm. Somehow it anchored me.

There was that howling again.

I shivered, counting my heartbeats as I had learned to do. I wondered what it was about me that made her do this to me but never to Dolly. I stayed there for a minute, certain that my sister, who didn't care about being loved and who could look a person in the eye without flinching and tell them how it was, scared my mother a little. Dolly had said "motherfucker" to a park ranger once, when he ousted us from an illegal camping spot. My mother had pretended not to smile and told her to swear only in Yiddish.

My mother liked it, her courage.

Just keep breathing, I told myself. I imagined the fairies and gnomes that we had been talking about the day before, the ones in our books. The thought of them helped. I guided my breath, and I imagined a huge gnome reaching down to find me. There he was, grasping me with his big hands underneath my armpits. I stood on my tiptoes, my face held to the rain, lifting my arms up, imagining him pulling me up and out of danger. I opened my eyes once, staring into the spray of stars I imagined were there.

PEOPLE LIKE US, with no home to speak of, fell into the category of "in-betweeners," forced to weather the uncertainty of unknown lands, and thus, we were members of the community of eclipsed folk—fairies, gnomes, Finmen, water sprites, waterhorses, and other creatures that made themselves known only in shadows and could be found in our books, *Grimm's Fairy Tales*, and folklore dictionaries, stories she collected.

"There could be gnomes under the bridges of the 405 in Los Angeles," Dolly liked to tell me.

"That's magical thinking," I would reply, as if our entire lives weren't already guided by it.

My mother repeatedly adjusted the rearview mirror as we cased the Southern California back roads in search of work. Our Country Squire housed everything we needed—rolls of toilet paper, cans of soda, pieces of fruit, and the last frozen TV dinner, which we'd split, unheated.

Wherever we went, burning down one highway after another, she'd take us to job sites where we were expected to work. Strawberry picker. Housemaid. Envelope stuffer. Bread baker. Personal aide to the sick and infirm.

"There's nothing wrong with a fairy tale or two. Everything is useful. You need to know how to navigate, to see roads before they are built. Be creative. Girls, just keep your eyes open to the possibilities."

We memorized lines from great writers as my mother drove—Shakespeare, Thoreau, the Brothers Grimm, Judy Blume, Betty Friedan, all from the compartment of the station wagon as the windows filled with dust spun by the Santa Ana winds, or fogged up with morning dew.

There were too many possibilities, I thought, and yet never enough. We had no map. My mother navigated our life along the grid of intersecting weather patterns, moon names, and catastrophic events on *General Hospital*. The eclipsed folk, we speculated, liked to appear in the white spaces of the grids during the shifting times of twilight and daybreak, within the place between life and death, and most often, we would soon find, during the threshold years of adolescence, between child and adult.

It was reasonable to imagine that now and again, to make things bearable, Dolly and I would play our games, calling out fairies on the cliffs near the ocean and climbing in the canyons near the roads. My mother thought us clever when we spoke of gnome families and of waterhorses kneeling under Belmont Veterans Memorial Pier, after they'd swim out from their beds near the pilings. "Brava!" our mother would shout as we narrated the drive. She applauded us for adding some magic to our day and making sure that there was a bit of fun amid it all, our hunger, the moon, and its white empty skies.

THE ONLY THING I knew for sure from the backseat of our car was that if I pressed a can of Coke between my knees, I would not dwell on food. If this didn't work, the only thing left was to picture streams of light flashing across the stones where a waterhorse rested, licking the salt from its legs. Sometimes it helped; my mother was right.

"Who else watches the full moon like we do?" Dolly once asked my mother.

"Farmers do. Sailors and fishermen who need to rely on the ocean," said my mother. She said you had to know that which could save you, for it could probably also kill you. You had to know it better than anyone else, every inch of it.

I STOOD THERE in the rain, my arm muscles trembling under my yellow shirt as I kept my arms lifted high, waiting, promising myself I would stay like this until my mother came back for me.

Out of the ink spot in the distance, I saw two lights.

As they grew bigger, I knew I was being saved. My mother was coming back for me. She always came back eventually. The front lights glowed like two moons. I noticed the goose bumps on my arms for the first time.

"That'll teach you to be so proud," she said, as she opened the car door. "No, Ruthie. Stop looking at me like that. Do you think I could really forget you?"

The front headlights illuminated the tiny threads of rain that slanted toward what I could now identify as cliffs. My stomach lurched. I climbed inside, and we drove back onto the highway, following the moonlight. I did not dare look at Dolly through my tears, nor she at me, as the wind spun bits of rock from the cliffs and the machinations of young girls into the waves.

"I have a secret," she said.

"What is it?"

"You'll have to wait. It's a surprise."

The deeply hidden flaw about me, the one that made my mother leave me and not Dolly, had not been found. But it was irrelevant now. It stopped mattering as soon as my sister reached over and squeezed my hand. We pushed on through the rain, driving against traffic, heading for the ocean, where my mother said no one in their right mind would be going, which meant there would be a place for people like us. No, no, no, I thought. You said we wouldn't sleep near the ocean. You promised. For years, I dreamed of drowning.

I dug my nails into my palms. I squeezed my eyes shut, but the sound of the ocean filled me and forced my eyes open. As she pulled off Pacific Coast Highway and onto Ocean Boulevard, I could see the waves spilling over the Long Beach–San Pedro breakwaters, crashing against the coast. I searched for land, grateful for the oncoming curb as we neared the seaside community of Belmont Shore.

We sought refuge at the first place we saw, the Twin Palms Motel, a salmon-colored stucco building right on the sand, flooded in seawater and mud. There was a public parking lot to the right.

The sign out front swung from two thin chains. The black vinyl lettering said FREE AIR CONDITIONING.

The parking lot was a pool, with a few abandoned cars as islands. The first floor had been flooded, forcing a woman in a shiny red raincoat to the second floor to wait for help.

She stood on the balcony, trying to shut a window, the wind catching her short gray curls as she held a green plastic tarp over her head. She waved to us with her free hand. My mother rolled down her window and called out through the rain, begging her for a room.

"We've been evacuated!" the woman called back. "I'm closing up."

"I have two hungry little girls in my car!" my mother yelled, a statement she repeated whenever she was caught speeding or we needed to be gifted food.

I looked out the window, my knees already shaking. Out of the corner of my eye I spotted something moving, something massive and brown in my peripheral vision. Then it faded. When I looked up again I saw the shadow shuffling across the parking lot. I said nothing, wondering whether I was dreaming. It appeared as a boulder near a parked car. A few seconds later it moved again, but it disappeared under a cloud. No one else saw. I'm not sure why I didn't tell my sister. She would have already been out of the car, perhaps, and a few steps ahead of me. Or maybe I just wanted it all for myself, my quiet rebellion. My silence should have never been mistaken for compliance or naiveté. It had protected me, at least from those who threatened me. But I was more worried about my mother's rage than about something unknown, something I felt was just as scared as I was.

"Come on, then," the woman called, her green tarp letting go like a candy wrapper in the wind. "That's no place for those girls. Get out of danger!"

As we bumped against the submerged curb in the parking spot, my mother turned off the ignition and looked over at me. "Ruthie," she said. "I said I'd never forget you. One day you'll have a daughter of your own and you'll understand why I did all of this."

MANY YEARS LATER, my mother would tell me, after her first week of sobriety, that both Dolly and I had been her first love; that a person could, in fact, have two beginnings. She told me she had doubted it was possible. You never know how little or how much time the heart will take, she said.

I would feel guilty that I'd doubted her. I'd see that perhaps she had been telling the truth about her love for me, and about the moon, too. This made me ache for her.

For years, I would keep my mother's photograph in a frame above her guitar case in my living room in Long Beach. In the photograph she is sitting on our balcony overlooking the Pacific Ocean, playing her guitar and staring up at the moon. Her Farmer's Almanac is open, one page dog-eared at her feet.

It was the only photograph I kept from my old life.

A life before my Naida.

Chapter Two

M Y MOTHER, DIANA, ruled the universe. Steeped in her belief that the full moons were portentous, she liked to sit on the roof of our car at a parking lot, campsite, desert, beach, or wherever we had landed, paging through her annual Farmer's Almanac for clues to our future. She said if I was very good, the full moon would protect me, too.

The small paperback with the yellow cover was a yearly calendar of the heavens, created to help farmers with weather forecasts, those who planted by the moon, and those who lived and worked by the sea. For people like us, who lived free, sometimes under trees, we, too, would do best guided by the moon's calendar, she said. May was the Planting Moon. July's Hay Moon provided extra light to bring in the crops from the fields before the fatigue of nightfall. The Harvest Moon was closest to the autumn equinox. The Hunter's Moon followed, when the fields were cleared and prey could be spotted. My mother believed this could be applied to our lives as well. In January, the Wolf Moon, also called the Hunger Moon, would lead us back to her ex-boyfriend, a farmer she said still wanted her. The Hay Moon in July could appear red and would provide extra moonlight so we could trash-pick late into the night. The Hunter's Moon would push the sweet flesh of tiny red strawberries into our hands, as if our fingers were white petals. Each full moon had several different names, she said, depending on who named them. She'd mostly use names from the almanac, from people called the Algonquin. But there were other names, those used by the English, or from medieval times or Celtic folks, that could come in handy if she needed to adjust things to fit our lives, she said.

Night after night, my face pressed against the half-opened window of our station wagon. I listened to the warm Santa Anas howling through the canyons and passes, letting dust burn my eyes, settling on my cheeks like embers. My skin burned. Still, I forced my gaze on the full moon, daring it to tell me its stories.

"I know you're afraid of the ocean, Ruthie. The women in our family have fears when they're young. But this teaches them how to become strong. Your fears will go away in time, and you'll be just fine. Besides, we have this," she said, holding up the almanac. "Truth in books."

As we cased the dusty Southern California back roads in search of work, my mother's ideas formed a highly charged circuit of intersecting stories of the moon, reports on the weather, her love life of travesties, and tales of deception on *General Hospital*. I grew up figuring that relationships were always like those in the scenes I watched. Didn't people shoot those who threatened their love? Didn't rape victims fall in love with their attackers, as Laura had done with Luke? Weren't love triangles a normal part of life? Wasn't someone always faking her own death, impersonating a twin, having an affair, getting murdered with a paperweight, and then coming back years later with a secret that could ruin everyone?

I pretended to believe this was a good enough plan for us.

This was part of the deal I made with God. As long as we didn't have to sleep near the ocean, I would be okay.

Now, here we were at the Twin Palms, doing the very thing she promised not to. I didn't want to question her. One day, within the thick clusters of waxy bougainvillea, I would hear women's voices rising from the blossoms, and I'd remember.

On nights of the full moon, their chorus would wake me from sleep, wailing, weeping, speaking for me because my own voice was lost.

THE COAST OF Long Beach, had been flooded with animals—herons and parrots, stingrays and sharks. Marine animals, like sea turtles, liked the warm waters created by the power plant and had crowded into the harbor and the bay. Dolphins could also be seen there, jumping in the waves. A plethora of fish, sardines and white croaker, made their homes among the pilings of the pier, which had been filled in with concrete to create an artificial reef. At the end of the pier were piranha and stingrays. Sand sharks swam just beyond the harbor. Seals could get lost or caught in the canals. The Long Beach Breakwater, though it had its openings, kept out most of the larger sea mammals, like whales and big sharks, and created a safe haven for mammals like sea lions and seals, and other large fish. Sea lions, in particular, had become strangely assertive in the last few years, leaving the rookery at the southwest end of Catalina Island and crowding the marina and the oil rig platforms. Sometimes they would crawl right up on the docks, especially if they were used to being fed by people. They were noisy and would defecate all over the pier and sometimes the boats, ruining equipment and eating the fishermen's catches. Fishermen struggled with them; in this place, everyone and everything crowded and competed for space and food.

THE STORM WAS just getting started.

The Twin Palms' parking lot was just beyond E. Ocean Boulevard. Belmont Shore, developed in the 1920s, had been almost entirely underwater at one time. Developers had built up the land and filled the canals with sand. Bordered by Naples Island and Seal Beach in the south, and Redondo Beach to the north, it was now a thriving beachside community and a popular spot for boaters and beachgoers, with quaint shops, restaurants, and stores on popular Second Street. But the motel was blocks away from all that.

Most days at the motel, it was so quiet that all you heard were the gentle waves lapping at the shoreline and the rustle of branches of the palm trees. Now, there was nothing but rain. My knees shook as I sat in the car, trying not to look at the ocean as the windows vibrated from its roar. My heart pounded and sweat crept up my neck. I pressed my hands over my ears, trying to drown out the noise of the waves crashing against the coast. The latest El Niño, a warming climate pattern, which tended to come on in the winter months once every several years, had formed over the Pacific and caused flooding and heavy rains along the California coast. Though the breakwater kept out the biggest waves, the year Dolly and I were eight and six, the coastal neighborhood of Belmont Shore saw floods.

"What is it, Ruthie?" my mother asked, tucking me under the sleeping bag the night before.

"You didn't say good night last night," I lied.

"I know you're afraid. I'm here now."

"You left us alone last night."

"I'm here now. Don't be silly."

THE TWIN PALMS Motel was a Spanish-style stucco with a red barrel tile roof. The walls outside had been touched up so many times with peach paint that they looked as if there were shadowy blooms, though there was nothing but sand around.

The clay roof had been salted white with sea spray. Outside, the window boxes, painted turquoise to match the front door, were filled with dried cacti atop an inch of sand. The shutters were turquoise, too, and askew. I couldn't take my eyes off the bougainvillea that seemed to be crawling before me.

Cascading from the roof and creeping down around the front door were huge succulent blossoms—the deep purple Brasiliensis, the pale pink Easter Parade and Rosa Preciosa; the brilliant pink Temple Fire, Texas King, and La Joya; the deep red Mahara Magic; the orange petals of Rosenka; and the yellow of California Gold and Golden Glow, all of which I would learn to identify from a tattered magazine, *Ocean's Green Thumb*, which I found in the bookshelf of the motel lobby, and which Dr. Brownstein, the owner, had slipped into the front seat of my mother's station wagon as a gift.

"No, Mom, we can't stay," Dolly whispered on my behalf.

"Now, Ruthie, I know you're afraid, but we don't have a choice."

Seagulls cried out from hunger, circling the parking lot in search of food, making noises that sounded like a baby's cry.

Inside room 21, Dolly and I slipped under the covers with my mother and agreed to wait out the storm. As I watched my mother sleeping, I felt no anger; rather, I felt its absence. I told myself that there were gnomes outside, guarding our door, protecting us from the huge ocean waves and whatever else it was that had been out there, and now, I was sure, was trying to get in.

WHEN I WOKE up a few hours later, all was still. I noticed the framed painting of two large palms on the wall above our soft queen-size bed. Two lamps with tissue-thin shades stood atop worn wooden night tables. The bathroom was clean, and tiled pink, with a white claw-foot tub and a fresh stack of white washcloths on the vanity. I imagined sinking into that tub, picturing bubbles on my kneecaps like two islands, just like the Calgon lady in the commercials.

Our bodies were warm against my mother's naked body, with Dolly and me on either side of her, pretending to be asleep, recalling how the wind had shaken the windows behind thick green drapes. Appreciative of such a large bed, I pulled the palm tree–patterned comforter over my head. I rarely felt this close to my mother. All I wanted was the sound of her breathing to disguise the waves. I tried to make friends with the ocean. I closed my eyes and imagined the waves leaping up into a burning hillside, covering it with water and putting out the fire. I felt intoxicated by the smells: the musty traps of the drapes mixed with Chanel No. 5 perfume from a former guest; the dampness of the gray carpet beneath our feet mixed with the scent of laundry soap; and fresh-pressed linens.

I told Dolly I was happy to be here. "You're adopted," she said in a loud whisper, propping herself up on her elbows. "This place is a dump."

"I like it here," I whispered over my mother's back.

"It's so obvious we have different fathers," she said. "I look like Mom, you look Irish, like the milkman." She had been named Dalia, after our mother's grandfather Daniel. My great-grandmother Ruth was my namesake.

"Sisters don't have to look exactly alike," I argued. Dolly was dark, with small angular features and crimson hair, an odd shade. I was big-boned, taller than Dolly even though I was younger, with pale blue eyes. Dolly affectionately called me Moose. Some called me fat. I had been born with a head of curly red hair like my great-grandmother's, something that proved my lineage. I wore glasses with thick pink frames and frequently donned polyester bell-bottoms that I knew were ugly when I picked them.

Our mother said that according to Jewish tradition, you had to name your baby after a dead relative. You also had to stay away from bacon, unless you wanted worms.

It never bothered me, though Dolly and I looked and behaved nothing alike, that we had different fathers. No one on *General Hospital* had the father they thought was theirs, either. I would never know mine. I never wanted to. My mother and sister were all I needed. I didn't want to open what my mother called a Pandora's box, to know about anyone causing my mother pain, which I was certain our two fathers had done if they took after any of the men on television. There were no real men in our lives.

THE NEXT MORNING, the motel room at the Twin Palms was dimly lit, with a thin curve of light spilling from between the curtains. My mother reached across the bed and picked up the black telephone receiver. She dialed and pushed her hair from her eyes. I imagined the man on the other end of the conversation was wildly in love with her. I could hear his laughter. As she carried the phone into the bathroom, where she sat on the edge of the tub to shave her legs, nestling the receiver under her chin, I pictured her words creeping into the sky, burning with the stars, and becoming dust. Magic swirled around her, as though hot flames. I was certain her magic made everyone fall in love with her—men, women, and children. Someone was always waiting for her, and she was always excited at the outset, before she grew bored. I could tell by the way she drew on her eyebrow pencil that afternoon, creating extra-thick, dark brows, and the fact that she plucked her eyebrows, bewitching Dolly and me, in the flicker of the television. *The Brady Bunch* was on, and I was certain Mr. Brady, an architect, would be the perfect partner for my mother.

"I may not be back for a while. You have everything you need. Play games, okay? Use your imaginations. Be creative."

"What time will you be home?"

"Go to sleep after *Johnny Carson*," she said.

Who was my mother going to see? Why couldn't he come to the motel to bring us food? We were hungry. My mother ran down to the snack machine and bought us Pop-Tarts and pretzels. Our car was still underwater. The phone rang an hour later, and my mother hung up and took off her bra. He couldn't get through the storm, whoever he was. We finished the peanuts in the minibar. To distract us, my mother told us her favorite story, "The Most Beautiful Lady in the World." She had been telling us this story since we were small, and we never tired of it. It was about a young boy who gets lost while shopping with his mother in a market. He asks everyone where his mother is, but he is a stranger to this place. When people ask him to describe her, he says, "My mother is the most beautiful lady in the world." The police search the area, questioning all of the most beautiful women—girls with large black eyes and lustrous long dark hair, girls with thin waists and full red lips. Still, none is the right one. "Is this your mother?" ask the police. Each time, the boy says no. They continue looking for days.

One day, the boy sees a woman in a crowded market. He runs to her and she throws her arms around him. "My son! Where have you been?" The old woman with bloodshot eyes smooths the pleats from her wide yellow dress. Her hair is thin and short, and when she smiles, her mouth is empty of teeth. "My son. Thank you for finding him." The most beautiful lady in the world walks away with her son.

That, my mother said, is how a child should view a mother, whether anyone else thinks her beautiful or not.

WRAPPED IN BLANKETS, we took in an episode of *General Hospital* and then *The Partridge Family*. My mother had quit talking and started drinking, emptying the minibar of tiny bottles, keeping her back to us in the bed. I imagined my sister felt the same way about her, wanting to bridge our mother's silence with our bodies as her moods turned dark. There was too much we didn't know, and yet her whiskey love carried her away from us even further. She wanted something. What was it? She was hungry for it, but she didn't eat. She smoked three Winston Lights and then locked herself in the bathroom to take a hot shower.

She was trying to burn.

Our two fathers had somehow remained a part of the hidden tapestry of our lives. They informed my mother's actions, her drinking, those things I did not understand. It was easier to imagine that they, and not us, were the cause of the tiny bottles of whiskey in her purse, beneath the car seat, in the glove compartment. It was better just to love her. I wanted to protect my mother from the pain I was sure men had caused her, from the fact that her life as a single mother—caused by us—had not been easy on her. This made me hang on the rare sound of my mother's laughter as though it were a life-rope, just as my mother hung on the stories she told us about the full moons, thinking that if she could make us believe, then perhaps they would come true.

WHEN THE POWER went out in the motel, I closed my eyes, wishing the storm would last forever. I had made peace with the ocean by this point, or had become infatuated with it, at least. Not it as much as the closeness it created, its suffocating presence that somehow forced my mother to see me. Who in their right mind would want to be holed up in a weather-beaten motel for this long? I did. I tried to absorb everything, pretending we were never leaving. There was no worrying about the future or the past in this place. No one would be left. Here she was, snuggled into bed, all ours. I could sense someone else near, even back then when I was just a child of six, keeping me company in my mother's shadows.

My mother said this could happen with familial empathy— that a very sensitive person could feel the enormity of emotions of those who had not yet been born into a family or those who had already passed on. Perhaps that is why I had feared the ocean: because my ancestors had come by steamship to America, a difficult trip.

And because I would have a daughter who would fall in love with the sea.

By the time the lights went back on that evening, we had finished up the snacks, along with some oranges and apples, left outside our door by Dr. Brownstein.

Dolly complained that she was hungry again, now that the storm had died down. When she opened the curtained windows, my mother tensed up.

I HADN'T SEEN much of Long Beach during our escape through the rain. I had hardly seen the parking lot. But when I heard the loud barking, I ran to the window. I speculated to Dolly that it might be a dog. My mother was sleeping off a hangover. A few hours later, the barking had stopped, but it was all I could think about. Perhaps an animal had been trapped, I told myself.

"My hair is on fire!" I yelled, but no one heard me. Dolly was in the bathtub. I snuck out of the room and sloshed through the parking lot in my bare feet.

I adjusted my glasses. I could hear splashing. Beside the yellow Volvo, I saw a shiny wet boulder.

It moved, its eyes focused on me. They were deep brown pools above a pointed doglike snout. Its ears perked up aside its crested head, and I could see the light catching on its whiskers. Its dark skin had begun to dry, despite the slick patches. It was vocalizing, barking. Was it grieving? Hurt? Somehow, I was not afraid, which worried me. I knew I should stay away, but something drew me nearer. I kept walking, my hands open, showing I was not a threat. I had seen this done on television. Whenever somebody approached a stray dog, they opened their hands.

Suddenly, the barking turned into deep, loud utterances of dominance. He moved toward me, as big as a car.

I didn't mean to scream.

Sea lions are similar to their seal cousins in many ways, but for the fact that they have protruding ears, and for the position of their hips. While both are pinnipeds, "fin-footed" mammals, sea lions' hips are not fused, so they can rotate their hind flippers under their bodies, and shuffle or "walk." California sea lions can move quite fast, rather than heave their bodies along, as seals do. Though fairly private, they could be fed. They liked the plethora of fish in Long Beach harbor. There were many reasons they might be territorial.

I knew the word "help" but could not say it.

"Child, what in the damn-ass are you doing?" Dolly cried, yanking me back.

Suddenly, we heard a *pop*. Two shots rang out. Blood splattered across our bare legs.

We looked up.

Dr. Brownstein stood on the balcony. She had spotted the sea lion and would later tell us that she had been trying to protect us, not knowing whether the creature was a threat. At over eight hundred pounds, he had most likely become disoriented in the changing current. Though most of the sea lions usually stayed on the white buoy cans that marked the fishing lanes, or floated on the platforms of oil rigs, this one had come in with the storm. In distress, he had climbed onto the beach, seeking refuge or food.

Now, blood spilled across the wet floor of oyster shells, near the yellow Volvo.

Dolly and I began to cry. Dr. Brownstein ran down the stairs toward us.

"Girls, are you okay?" she said. She held a blanket from one of the rooms and threw it over the animal. "Go, hurry on, now. Get going," she said.

My mother stood open-mouthed in the doorway, her hair blown back, her eyes rimmed in dark coal. She stared at her crying daughters and the wet heap beside the car. She ordered us inside.

I stood there for a moment. I imagined how we looked from all angles, from a stranger's eyes. Dolly and I, the sea lion lying in a blanketed hump, and Dr. Brownstein. My mother in the doorway, holding her head.

Within minutes, she was frantically packing our things, stealing motel sheets and towels, shoving them into our station wagon, and sweeping branches off our windshield with her hands. Dr. Brownstein watched from the lobby, holding the telephone to her ear. My mother screamed at us to get ready, for ruining her life, for costing her a new job as the motel housekeeper, which she hadn't even applied for yet. "You could have been killed, Ruthie!" she cried, as we peeled out of the parking lot, leaving Dr. Brownstein alone with the sea lion. "No job. No cash. You girls will not be satisfied until you have ruined my life," my mother cried.

Dolly slammed into me, her hot breath on my neck. "She's going to crash this car. Get ready to jump out, open your door. I'll say when."

I held my breath and shut my eyes. We had grown used to this, careening back and forth in busted seat belts. I knew to have my hand planted on the door handle, ready to jump.

"Damn fool, just like your father. Do you want *them* to take you from me? You'd never survive without me. This is why I try to protect you. You could have been hurt. Is that what you wanted? For *them* to try to take you from me?"

"I thought it was a dog," I whispered. She would leave me again. Now I had to wait for it.

I knew who *them* was, the people we avoided. Dolly and I had to talk to *them* after I fell out of a two-story window into a pool. Dolly and I had been chasing each other around, and I had tumbled right through the screen. Someone had called Social Services, and my mother had to go to court. All I remember is that she bought a navy suit from a thrift store and put her hair up in a bun with black bobby pins. That's when the story about homeschooling originated, and after, our instructions to carry book bags whenever we left the car, which she filled with old tattered schoolbooks from garage sales.

"Who walks toward a wild animal?" Dolly hissed. I slumped into the backseat as we watched the people on busy Second Street. Life had continued here, just a few blocks from where we'd been holed up in the motel, pretending life had stopped, an excuse not to keep moving. People were sweeping water and debris off the sidewalks. Some were riding bicycles. Others were shopping. The ice cream shop was open, and two young boys sat on a bench, staring at Dolly and me as we slowed at a light. "It's so sad," Dolly said. "That animal probably had a family to support." I knew she was just angry, thinking that perhaps my mother would have gotten us ice cream, had it not been for my mistake.

"What will happen to it?" I pressed my face to the window. "Will somebody bury it?"

"They'll probably want to make a coat out of him," worried Dolly.

I nodded, winding my hair around my wrist, gazing at the nape of my mother's neck, at her large Jewish-star charm that slipped back and forth along the chain, beneath tendrils that spilled from her hair, pulled up now in a bun.

When she reached for a bottle from the glove compartment, one hand on the wheel, I looked up. As our car swerved across Second Street, nearly clipping two bicyclists, she said that few people were mensches and that it would be best to find some family. Close friends could become *mishpachah*, family. When she turned on her cassette player, blasting the melodious voices of *Fiddler on the Roof* through the windows, I looked over at Dolly. "What are you staring at?"

WE DROVE ALL day, until nightfall. When my mother finally stopped, we were in the desert. We got out and examined the car, each of us taking a turn to shine the flashlight while the other ran her hands over the nail in the tire. The tiny orange flowers that dotted the cacti were just closing. We followed my mother across the sandy earth for an hour as she clutched her bottle of whiskey, her gait wavering. We were nowhere. Lost again, with nothing and no one around.

"Would you girls like to pick some flowers?" my mother asked, but by this point I was exhausted. I fell in a heap on the hard cold sand, barely able to keep my eyes open. The stars blurred in the sky, as did the sounds, but I could hear her voice lilting in the cold dark waves of the desert. I knew she was drunk. It had been some time since she'd been this bad. I knew the only thing to do was to be quiet and wait.

The air would be warm soon. The desert never stayed cold for very long.

"A calendar, a calendar! Look in the almanac; find out moonshine, find out moonshine," my mother said, tripping over her feet in the moonlight, reciting a line from Shakespeare's *A Midsummer Night's Dream*. She waved her almanac in the air.

I looked up at the waning moon, now a less than perfect circle in the night sky. I felt guilty for my own thoughts, which I was sure I would be punished for. No matter how anyone wanted to sugarcoat it, the fact was that some people were never meant to be mothers.

I buried my head under the orange sleeping bag, imagining the sea lion cutting through a circle of bubbles, its large brown body floating out into the cold dark desert, then taking me with it as it dove beneath the black water.

Chapter Three
1975

I F THE HEART were a book, its lovers would be the chapters. A girl's book begins with her mother, who is her real first love. What happens between them will likely determine the direction of words on all of the subsequent pages. Next, she will fall in love with her first best friend, and her first lover will follow, essentially as the third act. Depending on how the heart is tended during these beginning chapters, its capacity will be reached, or never at all. That is the only goal. No one can say for certain whether the heart will wither like petals near seawater, or whether it will be strong, resilient, able to stave off the elements that will likely befall it. We had to go all the way back to my great-grandmother to find a love story that we could all reference. One that we knew we could go back to again and again, as one does the right book. No woman in our family had gotten it right since 1895.

My mother liked to tell this love story sitting on the hood of the car, filling us with hope. Our ancestors were from Grodno. My great-grandmother Ruth and my great-grandfather Daniel grew up together and fell in love when she was just fifteen.

They spoke Yiddish at home. Daniel came to America first, fleeing anti-Semitic rule. Once he saved up enough money, he sent for Ruth, who had flaming red hair and worked in a large tobacco factory, as well as his sister, Rivka. The two young women boarded a steamship in Hamburg at the turn of the century. My mother kept a black-and-white photograph of them, two refugees waiting on the crowded dock in Germany, collecting a final memento of their former lives. Ruth and Rivka are wearing long white dresses with high Edwardian collars; their flowing bodices are pouched, and below, cinched with sashes at the waist. Their wavy hair is swept up to the top of the head, twisted into a knot. They look hopeful and expectant, as though they are leaving for a grand dance.

They were poor. Once on the ship, they crowded into the steerage compartment—below the main deck, used sometimes for cargo. This was the lowest fare. Rarely cleaned, the space was dank and the air thick. Temporary partitions separated the men from the women. Hundreds breathed putrid air from overflowing washrooms. They would try to sleep while the noisy walls vibrated from the steering controls and engines. They would brave their fears of the sea, existing for a time—maybe a month—their nostrils burning from the aroma of orange peels, herring, and disinfectant. They would sing themselves to sleep in narrow bunks, atop canvas mattresses stuffed with seaweed, holding fast to their dream of a new land and the man who would save them in America—a brother to one, a lover to the other.

Ruth and Daniel's marriage lasted seventy years, up until her death at eighty-six. Before her burial, he draped his body across her casket and pleaded, "My partner, my partner." A tear would fall from my mother's cheek when she retold this part. She had seen it.

"My grandmother Ruth," my mother said, "your great-grandmother, got it right, somehow, at fifteen years old. What's happened to us since?" She said in those days, life was so hard, a husband and wife had to be equal partners. "It sounds dreamy, doesn't it? To be like that with a man? That's how it should always be. A partner. Everyone needs a partner. I always dreamed I'd marry a shopkeeper. We'd have a little grocery store together. We'd work all day together, and before closing up shop, we'd dance in the aisles after everyone had gone," she'd say, staring up at the sky.

After Ruth arrived in America, she and Daniel were never apart for more than a day until she passed. He had a stroke and died six months after she did.

My mother said in those days they called it having a stroke. That's what they said to explain a broken heart.

RUTH HAD NEVER lost her love of the land, her connection to tobacco, and her fear of the ocean. She passed it all down through cellular memory. That, my mother said, was the reason I clung to land. I had, it seemed, inherited all that my great-grandmother had felt on that ship, how she both hated and needed the ocean to carry her to the love that awaited. It was the only way to get from here to there, across the sea, and so she had to make peace with it, to know it, to breathe it in and let it become a part of her.

Tobacco calmed me. I liked the burnt scent of it on my fingers. Often, when I'd find a half-smoked cigarette on the ground and if no one was looking, I'd roll it between my thumb and forefinger so that the remaining tobacco spilled out.

My mother said we all came from the earth. She was reclaiming her roots by connecting to her family this way, through her Farmer's Almanacs.

Relationships ruled everything, even in science.

DEPENDING ON OUR circumstance, my mother said the moon was the child, the sibling, or the spouse of the earth. If the weather was uncooperative, she said the moon was Earth's child. When moonlight helped us navigate our path and find extra work, she said the moon and Earth were siblings, formed at the same time out of a whirlpool of swirling materials in the solar system. Whenever there was a spurned lover in my mother's life, or if she had fallen prey to one, she made mention of the Marriage Theory, which asserted that somewhere else in the solar system, the moon was formed, but it was pulled into Earth's atmosphere by Earth's seductive gravity and then captured. The latter was a sexist theory of planetary creation, my mother said, telling us too much and never enough.

She didn't hate men, just what they did sometimes, but also what some women would do to other women.

Since we were all made from the same material, I imagined there was a piece of moon and earth in us. Everything was, in effect, connected to everything else. It followed, then, that men and women, adults and children, were more connected than we realized. I didn't understand why there was always so much distance.

ONE NIGHT, AS we set up our campsite, my mother made a discovery. The planets were aligning, according to her almanac. "We can pick all night. Heaps of moonlight," she said, pointing at the large Hunter's Moon. "I've been thinking. If we can just get a little leg up, I'd like to get us a house." After the incident at the motel, we had realized we needed to make a new plan. Money was not puddling up from the ground. I was barefoot, noticing the soft dirt under my feet and the holes in Dolly's blue Adidas sneakers, which had come just this way.

Dolly and I dared not look at each other. A real house, the type she often spoke of, never materialized. Oh, to dream of it, though, of running through the bedrooms and down hallways. We could race from room to room. We would make our beds, keep clothes folded in drawers and leave them there, so that we didn't have to grab whatever was on the surface of the mess.

Perhaps one day clothing would be just for wearing, and not for pillows, tables, and seat cushions.

With the whole night in front of us and a full moon to give us extra light, we could just keep driving. She wouldn't say where.

DAWN ROSE OVER Los Angeles, radiating streaks of orange and pink light from behind the thick clouds as the moon faded. We drove north into Ventura County, past the sand beaches, the white dunes, the deep wetlands, the sparkling creeks, and the Santa Clara River. I rubbed my eyes, trying to push away my fatigue. In the distance, I could see the strawberry fields my mother always spoke of, with their alluring neatness, a grid of alternating rows of long muddy trenches and puffy green plants dotted with tiny white flowers, extending for miles, it seemed. We were nearing Oxnard. It was October 1975, strawberry season, and my mother was of the mindset that if there was work, we would go and worry about sleep later. Dolly and I were fatigued, but after a breakfast of hash browns and egg sandwiches, we felt more human.

Strawberry picking was hard, our mother had already told us. But we never complained.

The towns near the coast were blessed with fertile soil and mild onshore breezes, perfect for growing the delicate strawberries, whose skin bruised with the slightest wind, whose tiny white flowers could wither from a single raindrop, and whose berries could grow misshapen when touched by a tiny speck of dust. If a berry was marred in any way, it was less desirable, which meant it was worth little.

The Takahashi Strawberry Ranch was located in the western part of the Oxnard Plain and had the best strawberries in California, according to my mother. "*La fruta del Diablo.*"

"What's that?"

"The fruit of the Devil, because they're so hard to grow, and even harder to pick. They ruin the spine."

We had tried to pick strawberries once before, but an entire crop had been burned in a heat wave.

My mother explained that each strawberry had to be carefully tended, from flower to fruit. Picking strawberries was an art form. If you were good, they'd keep hiring you back. It required delicate handiwork and a strong back. Strawberry plants, at four or five inches tall, required bending at the waist for many hours, for weeks at a time. I just wanted to keep my hands busy, imagining all the things I could buy if the money were as good as my mother said.

I thought about a doll I'd seen on television, a Tiffany Taylor fashion doll with a rotating scalp, whose waist-length hair could be changed from white-blond hair parted in the center to brunette hair with bangs, all by rotating her scalp. She wore a gold lamé swimsuit and green mule clogs, and she could change from being a starlet to a librarian if you put her in the attachable green floor-length skirt. The doll had wide-set eyes, real lashes, and a full face of makeup. Dolly and I had been singing the jingle for weeks: "She's what you want her to be." It came with a sheet of hairstyle instruction tips.

I was nine years old, and eager for a chance to become someone else entirely. My mother said that we could each make about $20 a day or more.

She knew the farmer, Lou, from a past life. Finding reincarnated lovers was possible, she said. They had worked together at a small cannery one summer when she was young, before she abandoned him for the open road. He was a generous guy who had never gotten over her, she said.

We arrived at 6:00 AM, when the fields were still cool. The green berries would turn from white to red in three days, which is why you had to pick them at just the right time. They wouldn't ripen once they were picked. Hot sun was bad. Cold was bad. There could be high winds that withered the leaves, and a gray mold called *botrytis* that could ruin all the berries in a basket. There could be spider mites, too. There were so many things that could go wrong with strawberries, it was amazing that any made it into the basket at all.

The Takahashis' ranch grew resilient berries. It was a family business, and my mother said that was important to her, as if it said something about us.

I had long, agile fingers. I could weave a braid in seconds. I knew how to be delicate. Dolly did not. Finally, I thought. A way for me to prove myself and win my mother's favor. She wouldn't leave me if I was indispensible.

HER BEAUTY HAD something to do with her navigational system. There was something about my mother and men that I could never place. An entire conversation of innuendo would occur in front of me, but I couldn't understand it. Still, it made things a little easier for my mother. Her resemblance to Elizabeth Taylor may have had something to do with it, I imagined. Because of these conversations, we were able to get into or out of any situation my mother desired. I learned how powerful beauty could be. To be saved from harm or given a break, like the women on General Hospital so often were, all one had to do was look pretty and perhaps talk and laugh a little bit "infectiously," a word I'd just learned that applied to laughter and not illness. Certainly, the character Brooke knew the language, too. She'd married the same man three times.

As we pulled up to the strawberry ranch, my mother stopped next to a silver truck. A tall Japanese man in a white button-down shirt and jeans looked up and waved. He was setting up large fans that would remove the field heat from the filled baskets until they were taken to the market. He had small dark eyes, like Dolly's, and a tanned creased face. Wrinkles shot out from the corners of his eyes when he smiled at my mother. She got out of the car, smoothed her blue jean skirt, and walked toward him in her wedge sandals. I heard her laugh as they embraced, and for a moment, I felt a pang of jealousy. My mother belonged to the world, not just to me. "If only the little birds didn't swoop down and eat my strawberries," Lou said, walking toward us. "Remember, you can't stuff berries into a silo like a wheat farmer does. You need to arrange them neatly so customers will think they look good in the basket. Work carefully, most important thing with strawberries."

He looked at Dolly.

"You, little girl, look like you know all about this. Want to scare away the birds today?" Dolly shook her head no. She'd rather pick berries, she told him. He stared at her, hesitating.

"She doesn't mean no," my mother said, quickly. "Dolly's my obstinate child. Don't know where she gets it from. Don't worry, she's a team player. She'll do whatever you want her to do. Won't you, Dolly?" Dolly nodded. My mother smiled. I noticed how Lou shifted his weight onto his right leg, just as Dolly did.

He turned his gaze to me. "Look at you. A big, healthy girl. You grow pretty girls, Diana. I always knew you would."

"Well, it's genetic," my mother said, putting her arm around Dolly's shoulders protectively.

"The girls know about the berries? No berries with white or green tips." We nodded. We were picking for market today, and people cared about the color and shape of the berry. Satisfied, Lou gave my mother a squeeze around her waist, in a way that made me uncomfortable.

The good thing about farm work, I was coming to see, was that people didn't ask questions. It wasn't just single mothers who wanted a job. Men in button-down shirts and cowboy hats gathered near the truck, waiting for picking cards. There were families living alongside the farms in shanties, or sleeping in their cars, like us, ready to work on a second's notice. Their children ran wild in rumpled, torn clothing, just as we did, and they worked alongside their parents, too. Finally, we were with people like us. Finally, we could stop pretending.

"That's what it feels like when you are home. You can stop pretending," my mother said once.

A young boy in a ripped green shirt rolled a ball at my foot. He looked about my age. I caught a flicker of fear in his eyes. But I could be trusted.

"I'm Ruthie," I said, handing him his ball. I noticed that it had a decal with a picture of *Jaws*, the shark movie I had wanted to see. My mother had said I was too young for such horror. My sister and I usually ran around with our backpacks, pretending we had been at school all day, and nobody questioned us. It wasn't the case with Felix. My mother later told me he and his parents were *sin papeles*, "without papers."

"I belong to them," he said, nodding toward his family, now gathered against a small blue car with missing taillights. A large German shepherd came bounding up to him. Felix smiled, seemingly eager for a playmate. "He's friendly. *Mira*—you can pet him."

"She's afraid," my mother said quickly, putting her arm around me. "That's okay, honey. You just wait for me here. You've had enough problems with animals lately."

While my mother followed Mr. Takahashi to the truck for our picking cards, we talked. "Do you even like strawberries?" Felix asked, holding his hand out. He had a large, bright strawberry in his palm. "Go ahead, you should know what you're picking, how to tell the good ones from the bad."

Dolly nudged me. "Take it. Don't be rude."

I picked up the strawberry and bit into it. My tongue curved around the sweet meat, its juice escaping down my chin. Felix and I both laughed.

"Other strawberries are picked for canneries. They're watery, or like straw. These are good ones," he said. I pictured myself dipping strawberries in chocolate, which I'd seen on television once. A man was feeding them to a woman, while picnicking along a river.

"Your hair, it's called strawberry blond?" He had a wide face. His black hair was wavy, if not a little long. I imagined us friends. We were so very much alike, I could tell already. I would not have to explain anything to him. Something about him made me relax, even if I did tower over him by a few inches. And he seemed much more interested in being friends with me than with Dolly, which made me a little happy and Dolly a little irritated.

"She's only nine, okay?" Dolly whispered loudly to him.

"I'm nine, too," said Felix. Dolly put her hands on her hips. He walked away, leaving Dolly and me to gather our picking carts.

"What did you do that for?" I asked.

"His parents, I think, are worried about getting caught," Dolly whispered, as she turned me around. "Lets just hope they have a good day." Felix had said that the farmer was paying at a piece rate today, which meant that fast, careful workers could make more money by filling as many boxes as possible with the best berries, rather than just getting paid for the number of hours spent picking. "Be careful and you'll make money," Felix had said.

The first thing I thought of was Dolly. We were at that competitive age, both on the brink of adolescence. An air of anxiety hung over the field, as if the morning dew were heavier here than anywhere else on Earth. The workers were anxious to get started, shifting their weight as they eyed the plants like cats stalking their prey. Would there be enough of the best berries to make money? Would Dolly and I each have enough? Enough strawberries, enough kindness, enough of my mother's favor? How long would the picking last before the skies turned dark and the rain came, turning the field to mud? A storm was coming; I could feel it in my bones.

I could see Felix on the other side of the field. More children straggled behind his mother, grasping at the hem of her brightly colored skirt. My mother didn't like the word "illegals," which she announced when Mr. Takahashi called them that. "Well, my grandparents were Russian Jews. My grandmother hid under the deck of a boat to get here," she lied. "She arrived in this great country of ours upside down. Home is where you live, not only where you're from."

I reached up and took her hand, trying to quiet her.

Mr. Takahashi looked annoyed. He stopped shuffling his pile of picking cards. He could hire and fire workers without explanation. He handed us each a picking card and walked away.

"Well, shall we, girls?" We joined the rest of the in-betweeners, those for whom this strawberry field was both a haven and a purgatory, the place between homes where some could never leave.

My palms were sweating. My neck itched underneath the collar of my red sweatshirt. I looked down at the mud. Something jumped up from a leaf, and a perfect ripe strawberry fell out. I decided it had been a frog. If my mother had the moon to conspire with, then I would have the help of my imaginary friends, too. I gazed at the long furrows, at the lines of workers in dark blue shirts and pants, bent over their picking carts, so low that their blue caps almost touched the ground. They looked like gnomes, moving up and down, pulling shoots and runners, tossing rotting strawberries to the side. There were people everywhere. This was good, because I so often felt alone.

"Hurry," Dolly announced, standing in the furrow next to mine. She adjusted the green basket.

"Work carefully," my mother said, before she turned away. I saw her reach up toward the sun and then flip her hair back. She checked the drip-irrigation system, and I lost sight of her. I looked at the number on my yellow card. It would soon be covered with punched holes, one for each basket of berries that I delivered to the truck. Soon, the paper, like my hands, would be stained with red juice. Within hours I wouldn't be able to read the number.

I put my card in my pocket. I scoped out the plants in my row. My eyes searched for the green, well-attached stems that would lead me to the best fruit, just as Felix had told me.

I moved quickly, focused on the berries, careful to avoid the white or green skins, picking the best berries that were unmarred. I tried to be gentle so I wouldn't tear their skin, but all I could think about was my new friend and the fact that my mother's back was probably aching from the cold damp morning.

Within an hour my pants were wet, my hands freezing, and I was imagining a warm beach bonfire and the smell of whiskey.

My eyes blurred as I moved quickly down the furrows, pushing my cart. I pushed, scanned the plants, and then bent over, brushing away leaves to my left and right, picked the berries, placed them in baskets, checked the plants, and moved on, all in one fluid motion. I took care not to pull but to twist the berry off the stem, leaving the green leaves on the fruit. I selected only berries of the proper size, firmness, shape, and color, arranging them neatly in baskets to catch the shopper's eye. Once my baskets were filled, I rushed to have them tallied. Then I rushed back and began the process again.

Dolly was ahead. She had more holes punched.

I picked up speed, not straightening up once, thinking of the money we would make today.

"Be careful or he won't pay you." It was Felix. He had made his way over to me. He plucked a white berry from my basket and held it in his dirt-creased palm. He tossed it away.

Dolly whistled from the furrow a few feet over. "Hurry up."

"Don't look up. Don't watch her," Felix said. Then he was gone.

I may have picked a few white berries, but I counted on the fact that Dolly would probably go for the largest, over-ripe ones.

I tried not to watch her. Each time I looked up at her, she seemed busy, flicking bits of leaves. Then, when I kept my eyes focused on my own plants, I could feel her eyes on me. I forgot to be careful. Strawberries fell; some stems broke. I crushed a few berries under my feet and kicked them aside with my sneaker. Something darted in and out, bending the stems, showing me where the ripest, reddest berries were. Perhaps it was the wind. I kept reaching for more berries.

Suddenly, there was a scuffle. I looked up. About twenty feet across the field, Felix was shouting, "*La migra.*" You could see hands trembling in the fields now that the border police had arrived. You could see the strawberries falling from the workers' hands, all through the field, little red triangles falling onto brown mud.

Two uniformed men took Felix's father away, leading him through the field. I watched Felix and his mother run, hugging him. I saw them talking with Mr. Takahashi and counting money. Then the police car drove away with the father in the back. Felix stood in the middle of the road, watching. He had been left, too.

Then he disappeared.

"Keep working," said Dolly. I tried to tear my eyes away from Felix's car, now just a pile of dust.

"How can they do that? How can they let that happen?" I asked.

Mr. Takahashi walked over to me. He plucked a berry covered in brown streaks from my basket. He held it up to my face, so close that I could smell his sweat and the coffee on his breath. I could see every tiny rip in his skin. He turned to my mother. "Diana, you don't like the way I run this ranch, I think? Not good enough for you?"

I dropped my basket. Bruised strawberries spilled out across the ground. He glared at Dolly and shook his head. "I keep saying no to you, but you don't give up, Diana. You want to be free, so now you're free, eh?" He reached into his pocket and pulled out a pile of cash.

"Walk, girls—don't look back," my mother said. "Just act normally. No, not that way. Faster." I climbed into the car. "He's still in love with me," my mother whispered, her knuckles going white on the steering wheel. "So, that's that."

I pulled my hood down over my face.

I still thought about the sea lion, the one I'd left to die in the hot sun. And about Dr. Brownstein, who had protected us when she could have walked away. I fantasized about a different ending to the day, about sitting around with the workers and their children, about making real friends. This was the first place I'd ever felt at home, and now I was forbidden to ever come back. In my fantasy, my mother took out her guitar to play, and everyone thought her extremely beautiful and talented, begging her to sing the Hebrew prayer Shalom Rav and the Spanish "Malagueña." Because of her, they would think I was special, too, not just a big-boned girl with pink Coke-bottle glasses, with a sister who was mad at everyone. They'd see that I, like my mother, was someone worth knowing, too.

"What are we going to do now?" Dolly asked.

My mother started the car, her eyes welling up. "Don't know. I'm not sure I can keep going like this. We're down on our luck."

It was time to head back to the civilized world, she said, where the real people lived, away from the in-betweeners. It was time we had a stable life. "We're never coming back here. I won't humiliate myself again with that *farkakte* man." I started to cry.

"What's wrong, Ruthie? What is it?"

"Can I come back to see Felix? He was my friend."

"You didn't even know him," said Dolly.

"Ruthie," my mother said. "Don't make me do this. We're both too old, and soon you won't want me to come back for you."

She explained that we would do something fun now. We could become pirates.

Dolly cheered.

I suddenly thought about the child I would have, my Naida. I asked my mother how long I'd have to wait for her.

"She'll be ready when it's time, don't worry. Children always are."

I noticed that she didn't say, "Mothers always are."

Chapter Four

I T WAS EASY to become night pirates, casing the streets in the rich section of town. The waning moon, which rose like a great orange ball in the sky, would bring us a productive and protected night of trash picking. The moon's position in the sky made it appear larger, looming, as if it would be traveling right along with us.

Grateful to have left the fields, we drove into the city, passing the streetlights and the dank smells that filled the alleys between the crowded apartment buildings. My mother, undaunted, kept driving. Within a few minutes, we hit the part of town where people left their undesired belongings in bags at the end of their driveways. So began a night of plundering trash for treasures. This, we knew how to do. We had done it before so many times.

We folded bandannas and put them around our heads. We slashed wet plastic garbage bags with pencils, groping for good finds, our hands spilling strings of fake pearls through our fingers. It was free to anyone who drove up and could fit a toaster, a wicker basket, a lime green beanbag chair, or a pile of vinyl records into a car.

Dolly reached into a bag full of old clothes and pulled out T-shirts covered in rainbows and peace signs, and one that had KC and the Sunshine Band on the front. She slipped it on over her undershirt and slapped on a straw hat, torn at the brim. My mother retrieved a set of neon green plastic patio dishes and matching cups. She also found a bag of costume jewelry that contained three plastic bangles. "No one will buy those, Mom. They're cheap plastic," said Dolly.

"Oh, really? Where's my 409?" my mother asked, sliding a chunky carved red bracelet over her wrist. "This, I'll tell you right now, will make us very rich. This is at least thirty dollars right here. Bakelite. Bangle. Bracelet. There's probably more," she said, spilling the contents of the bag onto the hood of the car. "This is a deco black and yellow, and this one is a paprika-and-cream-corn zigzag. Girls, we've hit the jackpot. A ring, too," she said, wiggling her fingers in the moonlight. "I almost don't want to sell it. But of course I have to." Dolly grabbed a bottle of 409 from the back, along with a Q-tip from the box where we kept our toiletries. Dolly shined a flashlight on her lap while we sat on the curb and my mother tested the jewelry. She sprayed 409 on the inside of each bangle and rubbed it with a Q-tip. "Nicotine yellow, girls! It's all real Bakelite, which means we'll be dining at Sizzler in Culver City a lot."

It would go to whiskey and bananas.

I looked up at the moon, pressing my palms together in thanks. I knew the moon was happy with us, providing all this light for us to do our work, to harvest our goods. I thanked it. Abundance was everywhere; at least it would be for the next couple of days. I couldn't imagine anything as good as this lucky night.

The scent of onion and garlic wafted from the open windows of a large house, blowing the palm fronds so as to cast feathery shadows across the street. By the end of the night, after four more streets, I had found two Monopoly games with all the pieces intact and an old red Oriental rug so full of dust that my mother had to pound it with my sneaker before Dolly and I rolled it up and stuck it in the car. I also found a white satin blouse with covered buttons, a pair of women's black riding boots, and an old pair of red-tag Levi's, two sizes too big, which I knew my mother would say I'd grow into. Dolly collected T-shirts and two silver crucifixes and then went to sit on the curb to pout. She was tired and knew we would keep little for ourselves.

This was, in some sense, a tease for us all. We would take most of our treasures to the pawnshop and junk collector, Mr. Ott, and make some real money. Just before we left, my mother found a tin box, and inside, a miniature dagger with a bible, old and cracked. She shut the lid, shoved it under one of the car seats, and forgot about it. She also draped a necklace with an amulet of St. Augustine, which she said she'd just found, around her neck. But she lied. I'd seen it before.

I looked back at the long line of driveways, holding bags of riches in my hands. My mother said she felt like an outlaw, a queen, like she had been reborn. She had snagged a burgundy Danskin dress and strappy shoes. Indeed, we were moving up in the world now. By the time the moon had faded from the sky, my back ached. When we pulled up to the pawnshop the next morning, my mother sold our things. My sister had passed out in my lap, hand on her forehead, wearing a yellow Bakelite bangle that she had begged my mother to let her keep.

Chapter Five

WE WERE FINISHED with farm work and trash picking, my mother said. The cool dry winds confirmed her feeling about it, making her back seize into what felt like a line of tiny fists. La Niña had followed on the heels of her brother, El Niño, conspiring against the crops. I was thrilled we were moving on. Seasonal work with fruits and vegetables was too strenuous, and trash picking too unpredictable, my mother said, especially while chasing her own moods, which had been erratic since she had started drinking again. We sat at an outdoor café in Malibu, sipping orange juice and watching her circle job postings for a housekeeper. Finally, she smiled. Music to her ears: In-law. Apartment.

She walked over to the phone booth, leaving it open a crack so she could motion to Dolly and me. "He's an executive at an oil company in Long Beach!" she whispered, one hand over the receiver. She hung up. "He's not married, either. That's why he needs help. Not sure where the wife is, but I'll find out. He wants me there in twenty minutes for an interview."

Dolly and I followed her into the café bathroom, where she drew a fake beauty mark on her chin with a pen and Dolly teased her black hair with a fork. She slipped into the tight burgundy dress and slapped on her black strappy high heels. "Well, it's overkill for an interview, but it looks good, right?" she sighed.

"Elizabeth Taylor's sister," Dolly said.

Off she went, marching down the slate walkway toward the large house, swinging her arms as Dolly and I waited in the car. The scent of desert evening primrose wafted through the air, its bright purple and white flowers shifting in the breeze. We eyed the huge magnolia tree that covered the patch of grass, with its thick shiny leaves and heavy rope swing. Papery white blossoms spilled from a rusty spray of tiny flowers near the crook of its branches. The house looked like one of those castles I had seen only in books, with a row of neatly trimmed hedges under the windows.

Our mother landed the job. She would be a live-in house-keeper. We would live in the apartment above the garage. She'd put us in school.

Not only that, but we would have a new friend. The place was home to a seven-year-old named Tiffany, with thin stringy hair and a small pink mouth. She wore Levi's jeans with Levi's checked shirts, infinitely cooler than either Dolly or me in our Toughskins and T-shirts. I imagined she didn't know about trash picking or half the things we did. She reigned over a beautiful purple bedroom built of lilacs. A huge white comforter flowed across her canopy bed. "Wicked," Dolly whispered, assuming, like I did, that we would spend most of our time playing in Tiffany's bedroom, and not in the in-law apartment, which was covered with soot and filled with car fumes. Still, our mother fancied herself moving up in the world. With a little elbow grease, she'd get the place sparkling in no time, she said. The problem was that she loved to clean. She'd spend one day on a single room, not practical.

"Did you lose a bet?" was the first thing Tiffany said to me. I was wearing my straw hat and shiny red shoes with the purple high-water pants I had found trash picking.

"Lose what?" I asked.

"How old are you? I'm seven."

"Us, too," Dolly lied. "We're twins. But not by birth."

Tiffany looked confused. "Well, you look older than your sister," she said to me.

I took off my glasses. My shirt was orange and black, with the words "President of David Cassidy Fan Club" on the front. I had my *Partridge Family* lunch box in my hand.

"She's a little runt, and you're sort of a fatty," said Tiffany. "But I'll let you play with me, seeing as you're our help."

"Big boned," I heard myself say. I felt my cheeks turn red and tears begin to spill.

"Do not cry," ordered Dolly.

Tiffany smiled. "Don't bother," she said, and skipped off.

"Ignore her," my mother said. "She's just jealous."

I ran inside and changed my pants. I put on Dolly's brown corduroys. They were too small, but anything was better. "Look at her. Like Tiffany's so great," Dolly said. "She's got a face like a prune. That's because she's mean inside. I thought being pretty was hard. Both are. Stay in between so no one hates you, Moose."

MY MOTHER SET out a canister of roses that first night. She placed it in the center of the small butcher-block table. She took out her guitar. She was tired from mopping all the floors in the house, but her sweet voice filled the apartment. Dolly and I looked on, thrilled that she was so happy. Surely we were turning over a new leaf.

A few nights later, she decided we should get to know Tiffany's father better, given that we were all living under the same roof. She put on her paisley minidress and black high-heeled boots, touched up her eyebrows with pencil, and painted her lips with frosted lipstick. We stood beside her as she knocked on the door of his study, where he liked to sit in a leather chair reading *The Wall Street Journal*. There were toy ships on the bookshelves and photographs of the ocean hanging on the walls. "Would you like to join us? We thought we'd play a little music," my mother said, holding up her guitar.

He laughed, rubbing his gray beard. My mother's face turned red.

"No. No, thank you. The bosses threw a little party for us last night down at the beach. Big old mansion called Weathering Heights. I hope you don't mind," he said. Behind him, a woman in a wrinkled peasant top and bell-bottom jeans looked up from a chair, holding a half-filled wine glass. "Charlotte," he said, motioning to the woman. Then he turned back to my mother. "It's Dana, right?"

My mother looked surprised. "Me? No, it's Diana. Diana Gold. I apologize. I didn't see a car, or I would never have—"

"That's okay," he said.

"Wait, I know you," said Charlotte, getting up. "I was admiring your beautiful house last night. It's the yellow one on the corner, right? With all the rosebushes?"

"No, I live here. Why do you ask?" my mother said, somewhat flattered.

"Because you were standing in the lawn in your nightgown last night, cutting down all your roses."

She'd been drinking. "What? No, that wasn't me," my mother said. She smiled, wiping her eyes as we walked across the grass, her skirt swishing in the moonlight. Dolly and I kept a safe distance behind her, worried about the aftermath. Humiliation. Though we understood its source, we also knew it was the straightest path to fury.

She set her guitar on the grass, waved us away, and got in the car. She shut the door. I knew she had a bottle of whiskey in the glove compartment. She sat there all night, drinking and smoking Winston Lights. Smoke filled the windows to the point where I couldn't see inside anymore. "She is trying to smoke herself to death," said Dolly. "I'm going to check on her again. She wouldn't leave us now. She needs us."

When Dolly went to check on her, she found an empty car. My mother was gone.

THERE HAD BEEN an incident once at the Santa Monica Pier. Dolly and I were little, no older than six and four. We were hot and tired from sitting in the heat, watching the seagulls crash into the waves. People were throwing money into a musician's straw hat on the pavement. We were whining from stomach-aches, corn dogs, and popcorn, which we had been living on. My mother picked up a tambourine and began singing. Every so often he passed her a brown bag. When the crowd thinned, we followed them down to the beach, where they continued to drink. My mother began to roll around in the sand, saying she was a mermaid. She pretended she could not walk, struggling with her tail as the breeze captured her hair. People laughed at her. Dolly and I fell asleep, curled against the guitar case. When we woke up, she was gone, had left us, swum out to sea. We ran across the parking lot in bare feet, broken glass biting into our soles.

That is the only time I remember letting myself be furious at my mother.

SHE HADN'T COME home.

Dolly found a bottle of whiskey in the coat closet and another underneath the bathroom sink. My mother had seemed upset, disappointed, and less interested in doing her job, as always happened eventually. What did we expect?

"What do we do? She can't get fired," I said, pouring a bowl of corn flakes.

"Act natural. Pretend nothing is going on." We dressed ourselves and then went to sit outside on the swing under the magnolia tree. We kept quiet, watching the road, expecting to see her in the distance, walking up over the hill.

"Play with me!" Tiffany begged. "Ruthie, please. I'll let you play with my Tiffany Taylor doll. You can change her hair if you want."

She picked up the coveted doll. With a flick of the wrist she rotated the doll's scalp. "Ta-da!" she said, waving the doll's long blond hair. "She's a dancer. My father's girlfriend buys me presents so I'll like her. But I know she hates me. I'll let you keep my doll until tomorrow if you race me. You can use my red bike."

"Motherfucker," whispered Dolly. I shot Dolly a look. She was only supposed to swear in Yiddish. Dolly was to be feared, with her straight-arrow red hair, tight shoulders, and filthy pink mouth.

I didn't want to cause any strife. After I agreed to ride bicycles with Tiffany, we rode around in circles in the driveway. Tiffany stopped. Her face wrinkled up, and she fell onto the driveway, one pant leg caught in the bike chain. Pinned under the glittery red bicycle, she screamed, her bicycle wheels upside down, spinning.

"Leave her there," said Dolly, trying to grab my arm.

"Help me, please. Ruthie, please!" Tiffany sobbed.

I reached under the wheel and tried to twist the fabric free. I felt ashamed for Tiffany, who had snot running down her lips. When it was clear I couldn't help her, she shouted, "Get my daddy, you pond licker!"

I ran toward his study and flung open the door.

He looked up. "Firecracker. What can I do for you?" When I told him what had happened, he glanced at his watch. He sighed, tossing his newspaper across the floor. Without a word, he unhooked Tiffany and ordered her inside.

"No one calls my daughter a pond licker," my mother said. She had returned, disheveled in her paisley minidress and boots but bolstered by her anger.

"Please accept my apologies, Dana. It's been hard for Tiffany since the divorce," he said to my mother.

"Diana," she said. "My name is Diana."

We drove away with three months' salary, a paid apology for Tiffany's behavior. I remember feeling relieved upon our release from indentured servitude. Years later I would bristle whenever someone called me Firecracker. As we burned down the highway, headed for nowhere, Dolly tried to make me feel better. "It's good we got outta that place. I hated it there. Ruthie did good."

I froze. Damn Dolly for drawing attention to me. The car began to sputter.

"No. This can't happen. Someone stole our gas?" said my mother as the car rolled into the breakdown lane and stopped. "I just put gas in this car last week," she said, banging her fist on the dashboard as we climbed out.

No one had stolen it. We'd been driving for days, right into November.

My mother got out and looked around. There was nothing but desert for miles, and one Joshua tree. We were in a place surrounded by huge looming boulders, prehistoric debris. She leaned back against the car door, raking her fingers through her hair. She looked up at the sky. "Hey up there, does anybody give a lick about my life?"

My mother fell to her knees, wrapped her arms around herself, and rocked, her face now streaked with black mascara. "Everything was fine. I don't know what happened so suddenly."

Dolly put her arms around my mother. "Don't worry, Mom. You have us," I said.

My mother laughed through her tears. "If you only knew. You kids have absolutely ruined my life," she whispered. She pushed Dolly away and sat there for an hour, talking to herself. It scared me. Even Dolly looked nervous. Dolly brought her the bottle of whiskey from under the seat. We walked away, across the sand, pretending to be interested in the cacti and the Joshua trees. Finally, my mother got up and grabbed her almanac. She paced while she read. Dolly handed her a pen from the glove compartment, and my mother scribbled a note. She drew her finger across the right-hand page and landed on something. The moon and sun had conspired to create a solar eclipse, which we'd wait for. This was something spiritual. "Someone does give a lick about my life," she said.

A few minutes later, we watched the moon blot out the sun's blinding rays, darkening the daylight for a few minutes. My mother stood up suddenly. "Someone get me my lipstick. I want everything perfect when I tell you where we're going next."

I ran to the car and rifled through the glove compartment. I found the silver medallion of St. Augustine, pictured with a flaming heart. I had shoved it in there months earlier after a nun put it in my hand. I would later learn that St. Augustine was the patron saint of brewers, and this medallion was sometimes given to folks struggling with addiction.

We watched my mother gulp down the last of the whiskey. "I don't know if Jews are supposed to wear patron-saint medallions," she said. Still, I hooked the silver chain around her neck. It dangled beneath her Jewish-star pendant.

"He's the saint of a good-luck life," Dolly lied.

My mother peered into the side mirror and applied a layer of bright red lipstick. Beauty—it was her greatest vice.

She gazed out at the sprawling desert. "Do I look okay?" *For what*, I wondered. We were all drenched in sweat. "No one's gonna steal my husband from me again. Ruthie, run back and get my guitar. I don't want to leave it in the sun."

I ran back and grabbed my mother's guitar. Sometimes she called it "the husband" because she liked to curl up with it at night.

"Well," said Dolly, hands on her hips, "there's no one on this *farkakte* road, so we can't hitch."

"You girls," my mother said, passing us with her guitar case, her pink muumuu billowing in the heat.

That afternoon we walked for ten miles, until we hit a gas station. As we passed by the cacti, dirt, and rocks, I imagined a hillside of burning Joshua trees.

Our beautiful mother met a mensch. We had watched his wife get out of their red Camaro, stamping off to the side of the gas station to smoke a cigarette. She had kicked off her black high heels and leaned her back against the wall. She blew her cigarette smoke out in a long straight line. My mother said it was a hot day to be wearing that heavy red suit. And in heels, no less. "She not happy. I'm going to talk to her."

She was an angel, my mother.

I could see the woman running her fingers through her straight brown hair. I ran over to my mother, who had bummed a cigarette.

"It's not that we can't afford that car. He got a deal—he says—from a friend. You know, he doesn't make squat as a health inspector. It's just that he spent all our vacation money on that car but he can't scrape together two nickels to take me out to a proper lunch. One vacation, that's all I wanted, and he takes me to In-N-Out Burger for a Double-Double. It's all the way in Baldwin Park, the flagship store with two drive-thrus. I said, 'Take me to the Sands Restaurant, for the love of God. I want to sit in a nice dining room with cloth napkins and look out at the ocean!' Is that so much to ask?"

My mother's ears perked up. "Health inspector, what a fascinating job."

"I wouldn't want to do it. By the way, my name is Sasha." She shrugged and took a long drag of her cigarette. "I'm sorry. I just unloaded all this on you, poor thing. You go on. I'm going to smoke another cigarette and figure out where I want to go for my vacation."

"No, no. I completely understand. My husband is the same way. Hamburger joints. Fancy cars. Men, you know? Anyhow, I've got to get back to my girls. He owes you that vacation. Don't forget it."

My mother brushed the hair from my eyes. "What am I going to do with those bangs?" she said, as we walked back to the car.

My mother smiled at the woman's husband.

"Gorgeous," she said. "A 1970 Chevy. I've never seen one with a convertible top like this," she said. Her pink muumuu was now drenched under her arms. I could see her bra was wet, too, and the outline of her nipples showed through the thin cloth. She looked vulnerable and weak.

He nodded. "That's because they don't make them like this anymore."

"Oh, the convertible roof, I mean. It's really something. Must have cost you a fortune, I imagine, for a custom job like that?"

He glanced at his wife, rifling through her purse for another cigarette.

"Convertibles are standard for Camaros. Not so special," he said.

"Funny, they stopped making Camaro convertibles a few years back; 1969 was the last. Yours is second-generation. Round taillights, right? Which means this convertible roof was made special for this car. That, my friend, must have cost you a pretty penny. By the way, your wife needs a vacation."

"You wouldn't tell her about this."

"No, of course not. But I would love your number. Work phone is fine. I like to have friends around town."

He glanced at his wife as he pulled a business card out of his wallet. "Sure, lady. You just call me if you need a favor."

My mother shooed us away and we sat on the curb, eating a bag of Fritos and drinking Coke as we stared at the oily pools in the dusty ground. I never knew what they talked about after, or how my mother got people to do what she wanted. But within half an hour, we were riding in a red Camaro with Sam and Sasha, back down the highway to our station wagon. He filled the gas tank and told us to take care. "You keep this nice lady happy. I'll call you for lunch, Sasha," my mother said. My mother gathered her hair into a bun on top of her head. She grabbed her almanac from the dashboard and paged through the charts in the calendar section. She scribbled something across the side of the right-hand page. When she was satisfied, she kissed the cover. Then she propped it back up, and we were off.

"Where are we going now, Mom?" I asked.

"Oh, Ruthie. We're going home, sweetie. We're finally going home."

We were headed back to the only place my mother was sure would have us.

It ended up being the perfect place for us.

Chapter Six

M Y MOTHER SAYS that when she was pregnant with me, she used to swim every day. There was a colony of sea lions at the tip of the peninsula in those days. One morning, while she was swimming alone, a sea lion swam right up beside her, so close that she could see its shiny black eyes and its flared nostrils. "It was huge," she said. "Like a large bear under the sea. I looked right into its eyes. It was a rogue male, I was certain. It just raised its head and then dove back underwater, disappearing. I swam like crazy back to shore. The ocean is their terrain. Best to keep a safe distance," she said. Though sea lions are massive, they can slip in and out of view as if they were simply apparitions, diving silently into the deep without so much as a splash, making you wonder if you had seen anything at all, she explained.

Some folks will tell you that although Long Beach has had its share of illusory changes, certain things will always rise to the surface. Before the digging of oil even began here, before one of the largest pools of oil in the country was discovered here and systematically siphoned from the earth, marine life and birds would show up, dying, on the shores, covered in the dark liquid. Children who grew up in the area used to take them home and try to revive them. Dagmar Brownstein said she couldn't even count the number of animals she found while walking down the beach with her daughter, Sasha. The oil had already been leaking out on its own, flowing everywhere it shouldn't have. Some folks say that once the oil rigs were built and the siphoning began, no more oil-soaked animals were found along the beach.

Today, if you are standing on the shore in Long Beach and gazing out at the sparkling Pacific at night, you might see floating cities, a mass of white skyscrapers, appearing on the waves. Hues of red, green, and yellow fan up from the water, bathing the buildings in an array of colors. These lights fall upon the deafening forty-five-foot waterfalls nestled between the scrapers and palm trees. If you look more closely, these islands appear to be part of a tropical resort filled with fig trees, irrigation systems, and wildlife.

But all this is just an illusion, still, a trick of urban camouflage, a by-product of theatrical design meeting genius engineering. The skyscrapers are actually skins that cover massive 175-foot oil derricks. Painted white with green and blue faux balconies, they are part of a plan, carefully constructed in the 1960s by the creators of Disney's Tomorrowland, to allow the oil industry to flourish while preserving the scenic California coastline. They disguised the oil drilling activity with man-made waterfalls that buried the noise of the pumping and digging, and they brought in hundreds of palm trees to give it a tropical ambience. Huge boulders quarried from Catalina Island were positioned around the edges of each artificial island to keep the soil in place.

Today, the man-made drilling platforms are known as the THUMS Islands, named for the original field contractors: Texaco, Humble (which became Exxon), Union, Mobil, and Shell.

The natural world absorbed the artificial in a show of dominance. The islands, along with several free-standing oil rigs, became artificial reefs—home to a plethora of marine mammals and thousands of fish and birds, including herons, falcons, and even parrots.

An illusion, as pleasing to the eye as a carnival, which was the point.

Beneath the surface of these rigs, sea lions could be found diving through the silvery bubbles created by millions of swirling fish, spinning turrets beneath the blue-green water. If you are swimming or kayaking off the coast, chances are, you might run into one of the cows or bulls. Though gentle by nature, they are territorial here. The drilling platforms are their home, the reefs their turf.

Throughout the city, massive prehistoric flamingos appear to rise out of the ground, dipping their beaks in. These are well pumps that siphon oil from the earth, in plain sight. Once the oil industry began to flourish, revitalizing the Long Beach coast, oil executives would sometimes throw lavish parties to keep their workers entertained. One year, a teenage boy who had been swimming in one of the canals discovered the body of a young woman floating in the water, clothed in a fancy dress and still wearing her high heels. She had been a guest at one of the parties, had gotten drunk, and had fallen into the ocean, people said. No one had followed her.

WHEN DAGMAR BROWNSTEIN opened the Twin Palms Motel in the heart of Belmont Shore back in the late '60s, she never dreamed that her entire life would be governed by things she could not see, oil as well as millions of animals.

Dagmar said that nearby, there had been a factory that crushed oyster shells for road cover, before asphalt was the preferred material. She loved the history of the quaint neighborhood with its Spanish-style buildings and beach bungalows.

Built in the 1920s and '30s, these were modest homes made for workers in the area, the train conductors for Pacific Electric, the school librarians, and the folks that worked in the oil industry. The houses had small garages—no one really needed a car back then, given that most people traveled by Red Cars, which were part of the railway system.

To look at Belmont Shore now, you'd never know that the area was once all underwater, but the past can never be completely hidden away. Now and again, when the tide is high, a locker room in the Belmont Shore Athletic Club will fill up with water. This is the result of an oversight by workers, who tossed rocks and concrete into the rivulets. The one they missed reminded people of what went on before.

Dagmar actually bought the Twin Palms because of the breakwater, a huge rock wall rising out of the ocean. She figured it would protect the coastline from the twenty-foot waves of El Niño.

The motel was originally constructed as a two-story beach house. It is the only structure in Belmont Shore that sits directly on the beach. Surrounded completely by sand but for a public parking lot on one side, it provides a view of Veterans Memorial Pier, as well as other sights. From its upper balcony, you can see far into the ocean, including those colorful, silent apparitions floating on the water at night.

Though the breakwater mitigated the waves, there was still enough activity for the kite surfers, swimmers, and kayakers to keep business thriving, if only the red tides didn't pool up and creep onto the sand, occasionally suffocating the fish and making the sea lions sick.

Long Beach Harbor was one of the busiest container harbors around. Once, a whale found its way in and became lodged between the boats in the marina. From the panoramic view of the Sands Restaurant, which rose three floors above the harbor, you could see it.

THE SANDS IS where Sam and his wife took us for dinner the night we met them at the gas station. We didn't know what my mother was planning, but when she said, "Well, time we headed home," Dolly and I pretended there was nothing strange about that statement—we had no home—and we got up casually from our seats. We hadn't had as good a meal in months, even if my stomach felt queasy from the sea air and the endless expanse of ocean all around me.

Still, when we said goodbye to our new friends, I couldn't wait to get back to our campsite and as far from the ocean as possible. Dolly pointed to a huge dome known as the Spruce Goose, where Howard Hughes kept his plane. I focused on the huge ship docked across the bay. The *Queen Mary*, a 1936 art deco ocean liner, was permanently docked in Long Beach. It had recently opened to the public, as a hotel and restaurant.

"It's haunted," Sasha said.

"Don't tell the ghosts that," Sam said. Dolly rolled her eyes when I shot her a look. If he only knew.

"Well, that's what I believe, anyway," Sasha said, and winked at me.

I stared out at the looming ship, and then at the huge floating skyscrapers, and felt my stomach resisting the buttery lobster that I had just eaten for the first time. I tried to keep my eyes focused on the Breakwater. The huge rock wall made me feel safe, an end point that abutted the waves, the only thing that was solid enough to stop them when nothing else could.

MY MOTHER SEEMED anxious to get us into the car. I relaxed in the warm breeze, listening to James Taylor on the radio. I almost didn't notice that she had pulled right up to the Twin Palms Motel parking lot.

"What in God's name are we doing back *here*?" Dolly asked.

"The sea lion," I said.

"You keep quiet and do as I say," my mother said. I stumbled along, nauseous and dismayed that I wasn't going to see my beloved campsite. Sleeping under trees on a back road seemed infinitely better to me than any other place. Even sleeping in the parking lot near the pier seemed doable.

We followed my mother into the lobby of the peach stucco building. I hid behind her. Dolly stood, feet apart, hands behind her head. It was dark, and even if the sea lion's blood had stained the oyster-shell floor, it had washed away by now.

Dr. Brownstein eyed us suspiciously from behind the counter and straightened a pile of vacation brochures by the cash register.

"Well, if it isn't the hurricane of 1939," she said. "What can I do for you ladies?"

My mother smoothed her red patchwork skirt. I knew Dr. Brownstein was right. I felt exactly like that, a natural disaster that had returned after decimating a landscape. "Really, what are you doing here?" she said.

I glanced at the two six-foot plastic palm trees in wooden basket-weave planters filled with fake soil on either side of the room. Though we had spent two days in room 21, I had never seen the motel lobby. I would have remembered this.

"Shall we talk in your office? Best to speak privately," my mother said. I glanced at the rack of miniature paperback copies of the Gospels by the window.

After hesitating, Dr. Brownstein motioned for my mother to follow her. The sign on the office door read ENTER IF DISTURBED.

The room was dimly lit. Large leather-bound books filled the shelves on the wall, and a cat calendar faced us on the desk. The month of December featured a hairless kitten with wrinkled pink skin and a large wedge-shaped head with bulging eyes. The cat hung from a tree branch, looking terrified, I thought. The caption read, "Just Hangin' Around." My mother cleared her throat. "I'm here to see about a room."

"I'm sorry," said Dr. Brownstein. "See the sign? NO OCCU-PANCY." She pointed out the window to the wooden sign hanging from a chain.

"It's just that I've been thinking about that terrible night. About that poor animal. Worried, I guess is a better way to describe it. Worried about my girls," said my mother. "I know you wouldn't want me to file a complaint. Or get a lawyer. About my girls being put in danger when that poor animal was killed. And the broken air-conditioning system. This place is a hazard, let's face it."

Dr. Brownstein's eyes widened. "Suits me fine. But truly, go on. I'm all ears."

"I had the idea that it might not be safe for children. My girls were somewhat traumatized by the shooting."

She peered over her glasses. "And yet you want to stay here with your traumatized children. Darling, I've been around the block once or twice. What exactly do you want?"

My mother folded her arms. Her eyes fastened on the room keys dangling from the key rack on the wall. "A key."

"This is the end of my workday. I am drowning in paperwork."

"What I want is one of your rooms," my mother said.

"I told you we don't have any. Listen, Mrs. Gold."

"Diana. *Miz*. There is no mister. Name belongs to me exclusively."

"Fine. You should get one of the nice apartments around here. I'll make a phone call for you. I've got a friend over at the Queen's Bay Apartments. How about that? Try to find you a nice place for cheap. Nothing wrong with needing a little help." She picked up the receiver.

"No, I want to stay here," my mother said. "And not just for the night."

"Mrs. Gold, we don't—"

"For a little longer. Maybe three nights. Maybe seven. Maybe longer. I really don't know."

"We don't take long-term residents at the Twin Palms. We never have, and I'm not about to start now. How about the Long Beach Rescue Mission? They've just opened. Nice folks, they've been out here a few times to collect old bedding. I think they do a good job. Food, shelter, spiritual guidance for the homeless and less fortunate." She glanced at my mother's necklaces, her silver medallion beside a gold Jewish star.

My cheeks burned. "We don't take charity," Dolly said, moving her hands so as to cover the hole in the elbow of her striped T-shirt.

My mother shook her head. "We're all set with the spiritual aspect of things."

"Clearly," said Dr. Brownstein, looking at my mother's bitten-down fingernails, something she was always embarrassed about.

My mother slid into a vinyl folding chair. Dolly ran her fingers across the kitten calendar. She looked at Dr. Brownstein and held up two dusty fingers. My mother tried not to smile, pulling down Dolly's arm. "We won't be going anywhere. You need a housekeeper, and I can clean. I'm your woman. You need me."

"I would help you. I can hardly afford to keep up with repairs, let alone lose money on a room that is not being filled by paying customers."

I watched my mother swallow hard. She was desperate. "I'll register a complaint. I swear I will," she whispered. Moonlight fanned the half-drawn window shade. "I'll make sure to tell my friend Sam Jackson all about what happened to us here. That my daughters were nearly attacked on your property, and that this place should be shut down because of the disrepair and inhumane treatment of animals. I'm sure he'd be very interested to hear what went on."

"You know Sam Jackson?"

"Known him for years."

Dr. Brownstein sat back in her chair and folded her arms. "You want to see the Twin Palms shut down?"

"I really don't want to report anyone. Only if you force me to."

"So, it's money, is that it?"

"No. I don't want anything for free. I want to work. You don't have to pay me a lot. The girls and I, we'll stay in that same room. Room 21. It's our lucky room. And I'll work hard. God knows, you need someone to help keep this place clean and manage what's all going on here. I'm good with people, and my girls are hard workers, too. They won't bother anyone. They are good girls. Not like some girls."

Dr. Brownstein offered Dolly and me a dusty bowl of miniature chocolate Easter eggs, each wrapped in tinfoil. Dolly took one, and my mother shot her a warning glance. "No, Dolly. Chocolate makes you crazy hyper. Put it back, please."

My sister unwrapped it anyway and popped it in her mouth with a smile.

Dolly's act of defiance turned the tide, somehow creating a bond between Dr. Brownstein and my mother. Most women understood what mothers went through with their daughters. No one, it seemed, would have wished herself on anyone else during her teenage years. When a mother was struggling with her daughter, it was an act of universal healing to help out. It somehow absolved one of one's own sins during girlhood.

Dr. Brownstein, taking pity on my mother, leaned forward. "I had one of my own. Raised her alone. Made it through by the skin of my teeth, and it got dicey. I know what's coming around the bend for you. That is why I'm going to help you. Not because of your threat."

My mother pulled her purse strap tight over her shoulder and got up. "I'd never call Sam about this place. You were very nice to us last time. It's just, the girls and I, sleeping in the back of the car. They're still so young."

"This is the luckiest day of your life, Diana," said Dr. Brownstein. The Twin Palms Motel was ours.

B'shert, meant to be.

"We really have to stay here again?" asked Dolly.

Dr. Brownstein leaned in. "I know you probably don't have the best memories of this place. But that sea lion didn't die. He was rescued and let back out into the ocean."

My sister smiled at me, and I threw my arms around her.

"What did the police say about the shooting?" said my mother.

"I simply told them that the woman who shot the sea lion got away in a green station wagon."

The Twin Palms Motel would be our home for a while, one of the happiest times in my young life.

Chapter Seven

T HE TWIN PALMS was a fine place to start a new life.
Over the next two years, my mother worked her way up
from housekeeper to manager.

By 1977, Dolly and I, at thirteen and eleven, were in middle
school, happily accelerating. We loved going to a real school
and having a dependable schedule. We walked home from
school and kissed our books, just as we had seen our mother
do with her almanac. We did our homework without anyone
telling us to, and we cooked our own meals. My mother felt
buoyed up, too. While she was out, we snuck down to Second
Street at night and practiced smoking cigarettes. She never
knew. Dr. Brownstein kept a watch over us all. One morning,
she put a blue, almost translucent moonstone in my pocket
before school, for luck, she said.

In 1979, the first full moon of the year, the Wolf Moon,
loomed over the Pacific. My mother said it signaled a time of
reaping. This meant that all her hard work would pay off. She
bought a new Farmer's Almanac at the garden shop, just as
she did every year. She slipped the leather cover off of her old
almanac and put it in a cardboard box in the storage room.

The motel had been revived. Dolly and I had helped plant flowers and cacti around the small patch of grass in the front, and we bought new plastic cups, candles, and sachets for the drawers from the Long Beach Drive-in Theater Swap Meet. The motel regained some of its popularity and started bringing in enough money to let Dr. Brownstein think about retiring. As a thank-you gift, she gave my mother the key to the one-bedroom "master" suite, a signal of a fortuitous time to come. My mother now had her own bedroom, and Dolly and I slept on the large pullout couch.

Now that we had a stable home and my mother had become financially and emotionally independent, the next step was to find her a good man for companionship. She had always enjoyed the company of men, she explained.

We deemed it the year of the Dating Moons, a time when all the full moons throughout the year would conspire to help my mother in her quest for love. As if she had scripted it, in no time, she had a fan club of older gentlemen who frequented the motel, engineers and oil executives. At night, before she left the house for a date with a man in town, I'd roll her thick black hair into a bun and then coil a few tendrils, taking special care to wrap them around my pinky just as I had seen my mother do.

"Wish me luck!" she'd call, before leaving.

"Luck," we'd answer, our words fluttering into the warm night air.

We'd microwave TV dinners and do our homework, spilling our books around us on the gray carpet in front of the television. When our homework was finished, we'd play *General Hospital* and act out scenes starring our new heroine, Genie Francis, who played a teenager named Laura Baldwin. Laura was beautiful and had suffered in her young life. Everyone loved her, including her heartthrob boyfriend Scotty Baldwin, despite the fact that she had already murdered someone, her former lover, who was secretly in love with her mother.

We were called "latchkey kids," for the strand of colored yarn we wore around our necks that held a house key. We arrived home at 3:00 PM, just in time for *General Hospital*. After school, while our mother worked at the front desk, kept the books, welcomed new guests, and did the laundry, Dolly and I watched the lives of the people in Port Charles unfold, keeping alive our mother's ritual.

We wanted to help her, but she wouldn't let us, now intent on giving us a childhood filled only with schoolwork and beaches. She had lost interest in soap operas, claiming her own life was full enough. Ours, however, was not.

October 1979 marked a time on the show unlike anything we had seen before. Dolly and I raced home to watch the romance between Luke and Laura play out. Luke Spencer was a bad boy who owned the Campus Disco, where Laura worked. Luke had blond curly hair and wore pants that pulled at the groin and flared at the bottom. He was from the wrong side of the tracks but was easily soft-spoken; plus, he owned the coolest dance spot in town. Dolly was bewitched.

I much preferred the shaggy Scotty Baldwin to Luke, even though they both were in love with Laura. We sat, transfixed, in front of the television each day, eating popcorn and drinking Dr Pepper. There was a problem brewing between Luke and Laura. He'd had a crush on her for a while now. But she wasn't having it. She was in love with Scotty.

But Luke would have her. We watched the red strobe lights flicker as he pulled her down.

By the time my mother returned that night of the Hunter's Moon, we were half asleep on the pullout couch, wrapped in each other's arms. I woke up in the middle of the night panicked, not remembering who I was.

"Dolly, will we always be together?" I asked.

She patted my back. "The moon is right there in the window. You can see my face in it, can't you? Count your heartbeats backward from one hundred and go to sleep."

As Dolly counted backward, I squinted into the dark corners of the room, heavy with guilt for a reason I could not name, and full of sadness for all of us—Laura, myself, and Dolly, at the same time.

MONTHS PASSED AND we were happy, watching the lovers stroll down the pier, arm in arm. Dolly and I always celebrated our birthdays with Dr. Brownstein and my mother. Though I still had not learned to swim, I grew accustomed to the sights and smells of the beach, absorbing it all just as I imagined my great-grandmother had done. Belmont Shore in the '70s had been rife with activity. We learned to skateboard, to do tricks on our bicycles, and to play the drums on tin cans. We roamed around in terry-cloth jumpers and flip-flops. At night, we'd bike down to Second Street, where we'd get pizza and ice cream, with as many toppings as we wanted. We'd sit on a bench on the sidewalk and watch the lovers walk by, and we'd talk about how lucky we were to be living in such a wonderful place.

We spent afternoons kicking around in the sand, picking through the seaweed for shells, making headdresses of washed-up fishing ropes and hats from Styrofoam cups. Beach rats, we were called. We stopped brushing our hair, and it hung in tangles spun by the salt air. We sprayed Sun-In across our heads and let it turn our hair orange in patches. Our skin peeled, and we didn't much care. We woke up to the feel of sand in our sheets. We covered ourselves in baby oil and iodine and let the sun bake our skin. We smelled like Love's Baby Soft perfume, like summer all year long. We were tanned, with freckles across our noses. I still carried a moonstone in my pocket. My hair streaked with blond. Dolly's breasts grew, seemingly overnight.

—◄○►—

THE SALT GOD'S DAUGHTER

DOLLY AND I had time on our hands to fantasize and create, to conjure and compose, to experiment and dramatize, to create a world experienced wholly in the imagination. We'd frequent the pier, our bare feet slapping the wood slats as we played chasing games we were far too old for, while anglers let droplights fall into the water, plugged into the electrical outlets on the pier's overhead lights, in order to capture the attention of small fish that swarmed near the top, led to their destruction by their need for the bright light.

When I returned to Belmont Shore years later, the outlets had been removed. They encouraged fires, I learned, set by itinerant campers who had no other choice when trying to stay warm. I would always look for those who were homeless, boundless, and in chains. There would always be a piece of me there.

One evening at dusk, Dolly and I were walking through the hexagonal midpoint of Veterans Memorial Pier, aiming for the canteen at the T-shaped end. Dolly, who wasn't afraid to talk to anybody, was spotted by a fisherman sitting on an overturned bucket, watching us girls. She had begun to draw male attention, I noticed, already wearing a bra and possessing a sort of approachable dreaminess. Her features had become more defined, making her appear older than even her fast-talking mouth did.

"Can you girls help me try this out?" the fisherman asked. Dolly nodded courageously. He let her share his light and use his fishing wire, and she caught a small white croaker within minutes.

Afterward, he took us to dinner, pepperoni pizza at Salento's. He asked if we'd like to see the new movie people were talking about, *Saturday Night Fever*. We loved the Bee Gees, and the song "Stayin' Alive" played on the radio constantly. Dolly and I knew we shouldn't be going to an R-rated movie. But we went anyway, thrilled by the promise of buttered popcorn and the excitement of rebellion, no matter how trivial.

There we were, sitting next to a fisherman whose name we didn't know, watching a movie that we'd only ever heard about. We watched John Travolta, Tony, try to fool around with the woman he liked, Stephanie. Why was he so pushy with her? Luke had done the same with Laura, only Tony let his love interest go. We watched Annette, the woman who liked Tony, get so drugged up that she did things with two men. When she realized what was happening, she started screaming. It reminded me of Dolly when she'd woken up to the mudslide years before.

As we drove home, I noticed the glowing blue-capped waves. The stranger told me that the bioluminescence was a trick caused by poison blooms. When we got back that night, my mother was on the balcony, smoking a Winston Light, paging through her almanac.

"Where were you girls?" she asked in a rare moment of maternal angst, tapping a crinkled cigarette pack with her foot.

"Getting ice cream," Dolly lied. "Down on Second Street."

"Just remember," said my mother, "I was worried. Next time, why don't you invite me? I'll buy you a cone. Maybe we could spend more time together."

I WAS ALREADY far away from her. On weekends, my mother slept or worked. Dolly and I made our way across the sand to the shops near the marina, passing the women in bikinis, who danced backward on roller skates. They looked so carefree, like the world followed their every spin, a world that Dolly and I were only beginning to dream of.

DOLLY AND I grew more daring. We'd walk along the beach all the way to the *Queen Mary*, but we'd never go in. We couldn't be satisfied with safety, though. Our favorite activity was bicycling in the dark.

My mother had met a nice guy; an old boyfriend from another past life had come back to town. She met up with him almost every night throughout her summer of love, 1980. We didn't meet him. We didn't miss her anymore.

I had dreamed of flying. But now I was doing it.

We loved the way our hair would blow in the wind as we sailed down the streets under a moonlit sky. I loved the feeling of flying, the only danger being the errant piles of sand that could appear on the sidewalks, especially at the turns. We'd lift our feet and sail over the bumps in the road. We'd ride through the streets of Belmont Shore at dusk, when the eclipsed things might have come out. Perhaps we were one of them, I thought. No one ever stopped us or crashed into us. It was because we had become invisible, hanging out in the threshold between childhood and adulthood. Maybe we had always been. People faded away from us, Dr. Brownstein among them. She was traveling, my mother said, enjoying her life on a pleasure cruise. Or visiting her daughter. That was what one did when one earned the right to enjoy life.

As always, we ran home from school to catch Luke and Laura, who had run off on an adventure to save the world. We lived vicariously through them. At this point, I was thirteen and Dolly fifteen. They were almost the only thing we knew of love.

We never met my mother's new-old boyfriend. By the time we asked, they were over. She went to see him one last time. She didn't return.

Early the next morning, as we were getting ready for school, Dolly spotted her. We had been up most of the night waiting and worrying. "She's back!" Dolly cried. I tore through the sand. My mother was sitting in the surf without shoes, her long black hair strewn across her shoulders, her face pale, streaked with mascara. Her low-cut Danskin dress was torn at the shoulder, soaked. She seemed lost, unable to move, letting the waves foam up around her, her hands fluttering at her sides like tiny fins.

She had a bruise on her neck, which made her wince when I tried to reach for her. "Mom! It's us!" Dolly cried, holding her face. She looked at us with bleary eyes. As the waves splashed up foam, pooling in tiny circles, we lifted her. We walked her back inside, her feet scraping along the sand. I asked what had happened, but she just shook her head, and I grew quiet, noticing the mustard-green edge of morning beyond the palms. She just needed to sleep, she said. I kissed her on the cheek, and she wished me a good day and slipped underneath a pile of blankets, shivering. She had been swimming in the ocean for hours, she confessed.

We stayed by her side that next afternoon, noticing she had not moved. We skipped school the next day and tried to nurse her back to health. But she didn't get better. The last guest had checked out of the motel. We had already turned the sign to FULL OCCUPANCY so no one would bother us.

"What should we do?" asked Dolly.

"Don't make her mad," I said. There was no one we could go to. Dr. Brownstein was gone, and my mother was incredibly secretive and didn't want anyone to know what was going on, for fear they would take us away from her. Dolly and I took turns running to the corner to buy her Canada Dry ginger ale and saltines. I played the guitar at her bedside, singing Shalom Rav and songs from *Fiddler on the Roof*, as Dolly held my mother's feet and gave her a massage.

My mother refused any calls from her admirers. We didn't hear from the new-old boyfriend. She trembled in her bed, fighting bouts of fever. I changed her sheets, listening to her labored breathing and the rattle of the ocean inside her lungs. Outside the wind spun turrets across the waves and howled so loudly it filled the apartment with an empty sound that made me shiver.

"What if she dies?" I asked Dolly the next night, sitting on the carpet, my back pressed up to the bathroom door. Dolly was inside, silent. She had been pulling her hair out in secret but leaving it everywhere. A tiny bald patch had appeared at the back of her head.

"Don't talk like that! It's bad luck. Go away!" she yelled through the door.

When Dolly came out, I pulled a blanket over my knees.

"You're blocking me. Will you move out of the way?"

"Not until you do something."

"She's not sick from the red tide, dummy. It's called withdrawal from whiskey."

I no longer noticed the smell of it on her breath, I had become so used to it. I looked down at Dolly's feet, noticing her purple painted toenails. There was dark red hair on the bathroom floor separated from a pile of red nail polish peels. I tried not to stare and moved out of the way.

The next morning, several Belmont Shore residents, while putting out their trash, saw a green station wagon driving itself out of the Twin Palms Motel parking lot, no one at the wheel. They watched the car wavering to the right and the left, stopping abruptly in front of Ripples Dance Club for no apparent reason, before it eventually turned left on E. Ocean Boulevard, then right, and then disappeared. I was at the wheel, set on a pilgrimage to get our mother Robitussin, Triaminic syrup, and a box of Benadryl that we assumed would restore her to health.

"You'll be fine, right?" I asked my mother.

"Of course," she whispered. "I'm an outlaw."

I grabbed her almanac, which I had brought in from the car. "What page?"

"What's the moon doing?" she said, barely able to keep her eyes open. "What's it say?"

I opened the almanac and began to read. "It says this month is the Health Moon."

"Apple doesn't fall far. You're a liar just like your mother," she said. "Now you'll understand why I lied to you girls all these years. It was always for a good reason."

I understood her stories of the moon.

MY MOTHER LAY in a hospital bed for eighteen hours, her face as pale as the sheer hospital curtains, her voice only a whisper. Her cold had turned into pneumonia. She now had an oxygen mask on her face and an IV stuck in her arm. Next to her bed, a small monitor blinked and beeped, flashing with red lights and numbers. She could barely open her eyes, and no one but us knew she had already given up. I stayed by her side, counting her every breath. Dolly wandered in and out, preferring to hedge in the doorway or give the silent treatment to the hospital social worker in the waiting room.

When the nurse left for a moment, my mother pushed up her oxygen mask and reached for my hand. "You're my favorite," she said. She had never spoken so kindly to me. I looked around for Dolly; surely my mother was speaking to her.

"Mom, it's me. It's Ruthie."

"You're the one with the red hair, right?" she said, forcing a smile.

"We both have red hair," I said.

"Well, then, it's a win-win." She was now more lucid than I had seen her in months. "Thirty-six years. It's enough. Your sister, not so tough. Take care of her," she said, her eyes moving from my face to the bedside table. "You're a good girl, Ruthie. I wanted you to be that way. I'll see you sometime," she said, drifting off. Her eyelids fluttered, and I bent down to hear her better. I listened to my mother's breathing, a gurgling sound. I watched the fall of her chest, each time doubting another breath would follow. When I called for help, two nurses pushed into the room. They gruffly put the oxygen mask back on my mother's face. The social worker took my hand.

When the doctor walked into the waiting room and motioned to the social worker, I got up from my chair. Standing in my blue jean shorts and fringed blue tank top, I peed myself. Someone mentioned a do-no-resuscitate order, and Dolly fell on the floor. The social worker said that our next of kin had been called and she was on her way.

The lights flickered. The ribbon of grief caught me around my ankles, making it impossible to walk. The room darkened. I could focus only on the bright globe in the ceiling.

Now, we were the motherless daughters I'd always believed us to be. But this was different. We finally felt her presence. My mother had been here.

"WHICH ONE OF you ladies plays the guitar?"

A giant of a nun with bright blue eyes burst into the waiting room. She was wearing a scarf, with a black sweater and slacks. "Is it you, Ruthie? Or maybe you, Dolly? My, the last time we met you were only little things." Her voice trailed off when she met my eyes. "Ruthie. I'd never forget your red curly hair."

I had little recollection of this old nun, but as I looked into her eyes, I thought I saw hope there. She put her hand on my shoulder. "It's okay if you don't remember me. I'm Sister Mary. I was a friend of your mother's. Everything is going to be fine now. Let's get you a change of clothes, shall we? We have lots of clothes for girls your age."

Sister Mary firmly took my hand, and Dolly's, as we turned to leave. Dolly sloughed off Sister's hand on the way out, but my grip remained firm, unwilling to let go. I hardly noticed the eclipse, the threshold that I knew my mother had somehow been waiting for, the in-between place necessary for an escape. How else could she get out of this life and call it a coincidence?

Chapter Eight
November 1980

THE BEAVER MOON signaled a time to set traps to ensure warmth for the coming winter. The story fit well into my mother's formula—which I wouldn't understand until years later—which was to combine deep-seated neglect with stunning moments of maternal protection. It was this dichotomy that she hoped would protect us. It made it confusing for everyone, most of all Dolly and me. Years before, my mother had made sure we'd be cared for in the event that anything happened to her. She had once begged Sister Mary to take us in, knowing that we would need warmth in the winter.

Years before, Sister had given us a medallion of St. Augustine. She had talked to my mother for an hour as Dolly and I waited in the foyer, knees tucked to our chests, staring up at two large golden angels on the gilded mirror. "They're *meshugenah*," Dolly had whispered.

On an inordinately humid November day, Dolly and I walked through the heavy wooden doors of the Bethesda Home for Young Girls in Long Beach, a privately funded residential home run by three nuns. "Bethesda" meant "house of mercy." But the secret was that we were the ones offering mercy. The nuns needed us as much as we needed them. The Home was fenced in by fuchsia bougainvillea bushes with the hugest blossoms I had ever seen. I fixated on the succulent petals, naming them. *Afterglow*, I thought to myself, oddly calm given the weight of loss I felt. I preferred not to feel, instead focusing on how these flowers forced open their petals. I recognized the heavy bloomer with little foliage that climbed thirstily along the fence of this strangely familiar place that would be our new home.

Dolly and I held hands in the foyer, staring at the mirror with the two angels sculpted into the frame. I now recognized archangel Michael, who looked down on us ominously with wings outstretched, waving a sword of protection. And next to him, archangel Gabriel, holding a bouquet of lilies, a symbol of purity, chastity, and innocence.

I remembered these angels from before.

After the shooting at the Twin Palms, our mother had frantically rushed in, thinking this a church, and begged Sister Mary to take us, just temporarily. Though Sister refused—the home was not equipped for little girls—she talked with my mother. It was on that day that my mother wrote up guardianship papers. Sister Mary, when she heard we had no family to speak of, promised to be "next of kin" and to keep us together if anything should happen to my mother. From that day forward, we belonged to a nun we would not meet for the next several years. My mother never updated the papers. Sister Mary never imagined that the overwhelmed young mother with the crazy sea lion story would take her up on an offer made wholly in haste and purely out of sympathy.

"They need serious help," Dolly whispered.

"Where to begin?" I whispered. Dolly smiled through her tears, sobbing then into her arm. I willed myself not to cry.

This group of three nuns were peculiar-looking, foreign creatures that smiled, lips pursed. Next to Sister Mary, Sister

Zora stood with folded hands, wearing a hand-size leather bag around her neck—a hippie nun. "Welcome," she said. Sister Elizabeth, who sat in a wheelchair, never smiled. I noticed that the style here seemed to be to smile without ever showing any teeth. Sister Mary waved her fingers as she spoke about the rules of the Home.

"We're Jewish. We can't live in a church," Dolly said, as Sister Mary led us from room to room.

"This is a home. Our home. God's home. And now your home, too."

Crucifixes hung askew on every wall on brown flowered wallpaper that peeled up in the corners, revealing chipped patches of color, aqua in some rooms, peach in others.

"Should we tell them about our ancestors?" I asked Dolly. I could picture them rolling over in their graves, all of them, Ruth and Daniel, now my mother. Under the kitchen cabinets, canisters of flour, sugar, and different-shaped macaroni lined the gold-flecked Formica countertop. Amid the crowded mess, there were baskets of bread and crackers, bowls of overripe bananas, strawberries, and mangoes. There were other ingredients I didn't recognize, jars filled with angelica root, crushed lavender, and chunks of brown-red rock called dragon's blood. Labels had been pasted across the glass, with smeared blue handwriting. The kitchen had no garbage disposal, and the windows were so dirty it was hard to see anything through them but blurry shapes.

"How soon before we get out of here?" asked Dolly, hiding a banana and two mangoes in the back of her underwear drawer. Habits from our previous lives on the road remained.

I did my homework, read ahead as many pages as I could, and after dinner, I'd curl up in my twin bed under a pile of quilts, staring out the small glazed window at what I knew to be the full moon, hoping it would finally deem me worthy, despite the fact that I no longer believed. I no longer kept a stone in my pocket. I wished for the belief I had once had. I wished for an aching memory. I felt nothing. I cared for no one.

The nuns taught us to do the waltz. They made sure we had clean clothes to wear to school and that we kept our hair in tight braids, though we unwound them as soon as we sat down on the bus. Though we were too old for them, we packed our *Partridge Family* lunch boxes full with cans of V8, bananas, hummus with carrots, and turkey-and-bean-sprout sandwiches. The Fritos and TV dinners of our past were gone.

There was one small television in Sister Zora's room. I would see her sneaking in there to watch her favorite programs. I got her hooked on *General Hospital*. Sister Mary warned that nothing good could come of TV, but it was all we wanted. I took Sister Zora to movies, to Kristy McNichol and Tatum O'Neal's *Little Darlings*, about two fifteen-year-old girls who make a bet to see who will lose her virginity first.

Dolly had told her it was just about two girls who go off to camp. Sister Zora nearly died when she saw it. We took her to see *Blue Lagoon*, with Brooke Shields and Christopher Atkins, a story of two teenagers stranded together on an island. It was a beautiful story of first love. Sister had fallen for the same trick twice, thinking that it was a Disney movie. Our mother had let us run free, and yet here we were being corrupted by those who knew nothing about corruption.

"I miss Mom," I said to Dolly one morning, as we sat at the table eating cinnamon oatmeal with six other girls. It almost didn't matter. I never spoke to them, unless directed by the nuns to do so. I spoke mostly to Dolly, and usually only in our bedroom at night when the drapes covered the moon, eclipsing the light.

Dolly shook her head no. "Don't you know what 'do not resuscitate' means? How can you miss a person who didn't even want to be with you?" She flipped her hair back, digging into her oatmeal.

Whenever I woke up in the middle of the night, my sister was not in her bed. I'd get up and look for her. I'd find her curled up on the floor—in the library, in the kitchen, or on the marble floor in the foyer, as though she had been searching for our mother in her sleep. On the night she began menstruating, Dolly locked herself in the bathroom and sobbed, deep sobs that finally let out her grief. It was quick, and it eased my mind. It had been a long time coming.

"WE'D LIKE IT very much if you young ladies would cut your hair," Sister Mary said one day. We stood in her office, bathed in the blue haze of the stained-glass window. "And the swearing has to stop. In Jewish or English."

"Jewish is not a language. Hebrew is. We don't speak it. But we can swear in Yiddish, from the old country. Our women never cut their hair." Dolly took my arm and pulled me out of the office.

"I'll cut my hair. I don't care; do you really care this much?"

"Sister Mary is full of shit, Ruthie," Dolly said later. "Do you trust someone who moves her lips when she prays but never makes a sound? Doesn't she believe what she is saying to God?"

"What are you saying to God?" I asked. "I don't know why you always have to fight everything, anyway."

"Well, you don't fight for anything. Why do you always give in so quickly? You didn't fight for Mom."

"What?" I whipped around. "Don't ever say that."

"Well? What are you going to do?"

"Don't try to make me hate you, Dolly. I can't." I turned my back to her but didn't move.

WE WERE LOSING each other.

Life had been brutal with us. I had learned that the best way to face it was to adopt the strange habit of the bougainvillea, here at the Bethesda, to push into the pain. Hadn't their blossoms folded up before a rainstorm, and then suddenly, as if in a moment of doubt, opened wide as it all came rushing down on them?

This is what I did with every situation that tested me. I pushed into my life, open-mouthed, arms outstretched, waiting to take on the pain, all of it with eyes wide open, ready to bear it.

Dolly grew her hair in rebellion, her dark red bangs sticking out in all directions, almost covering her eyes. I let mine grow, too, and it fell into a curly mane down my back.

What could the nuns do? We were two Jewish adolescents living in a small, dysfunctional residential home. Suddenly, we had even more freedom than we'd had with our mother. But we were more dangerous now. We had no one's love, and without that, we were vulnerable.

To hold on to each other, we did what we knew. We ran wild at night.

Sometimes after dinner, Sister Elizabeth put a cassette in the tape player. Sister Mary pushed the coffee table and chairs to the side of the living room, and Sister Zora rolled up the red Oriental carpet. Then Sister Mary would put her hands on Sister Zora's shoulders, and with a nod, the music began. "One, two, three," she'd call. "One, two, three. Can-ta-loupe, can-ta-loupe, can-ta-loupe." We'd chant "cantaloupe" as the music played and the nuns waltzed us across the floor, crossing back and forth in sweeping diagonals as though gliding, their habits puffing out. Sister Zora maintained a solemn expression, though her face flushed whenever she tripped.

We played along, and danced a little.

By this point, we called the shots. We stopped doing the waltz. We started dancing on tables. No one said anything as long as we came home.

We never cut our hair. We grew it out and flung it wildly in the rain. We painted yellow streaks in our hair with Jolen

Creme Bleach, snuck out of bedroom windows, wore too much navy blue eyeliner, fought each other, made each other cry, made mistakes and fell down again, and ran, untethered to what and where we could not have known.

We had inherited our mother's impulsivity and desire for freedom. But there was something else—the gene for hyperfertility.

Chapter Nine

1981

D OLLY LIKED TO joke that she could just look at a guy and get pregnant. She said she learned more about sex from living at Bethesda than from anything else, including movies or soap operas. In our years at the Home, she made two trips over the border to "take care of things," forbidding me to come along.

I kept mostly to myself now. Sister Zora had a crush on *General Hospital*'s Luke, played by Anthony Geary, and we eagerly watched the wedding of Luke and Laura. I couldn't imagine being more excited about a wedding, unless it was my own. For days, we had talked about Laura's dress. Dolly, who now had a boyfriend with a truck, rolled her eyes at us, calling us delusional, saying no girl would ever marry her attacker, accusing us of living in a made-up soap opera world. But for me, that world had become something. My sister was gone, just as my mother had left me when I was six, and before that on a beach in Santa Monica.

IT HAPPENED TO me under the Cold Moon, December 3, 1981, a night when the sheet-metal moon parted the deep blue skies, rife with chunky clouds, signaling the longest night of the year. At fifteen, I was convinced I'd never find anyone to love me. I had never kissed a boy, let alone been touched by one under my shirt. The day before, I had met someone. It was a cool beach day atop some rocks, where he found me reading *Flowers in the Attic*. I had agreed to meet him under the Bougainvillea Castle, a massive cluster of spiny vines full with succulent blossoms—purple, pinks, and reds—cascading from trees in the midst of a grassy field, five miles from the Home. This was the thing about California—gang fights amid tropical flowers, blood in a strawberry field after a rainstorm, spilled from the nose of a little boy who had thrown fists at a farmer one day and ended up locked in the back of a shed, bereft, still angry at the farmer for not saving his father. After all this time, I thought of Felix. I thought of his clear dark eyes as I rode up to the Bougainvillea Castle on my bicycle. The flowers looked toppled over in effigy, their petals torn after a storm, with the slight white cast of mourning. That is what I thought as the dry Santa Anas warmed my face, my purple feather earrings dangling against my neck. It might have been these winds that I mistook for the sound of women's voices crying out for help. I did not know they only wanted to speak for me, for my voice would soon be lost.

The boy, much older than I, had said we would be going to a big party and to wear a miniskirt. But when I arrived there was no party. He'd shown up with two withered pink roses in a plastic grocery store wrapper, and a bottle of tequila. Still, I sat with him on a white woolen blanket under the sheet-metal moon so that he could give me alcohol and kiss me.

The sky was spinning as I looked up, faint, the branches swirling against the deep blue. Within seconds, he was on top of me, groping and clawing at my clothes like a hungry dog, and he whispered into my neck, again and again, that my skin was so soft and did I like it.

I floundered, slipping away, my voice lost as he held me down. I stared at the roses on the grass. One stem had fallen onto the blanket, its thorns stuck against my bottom, tearing my skin as the boy moved up, and up.

You might think I should have cried out from the pain as he pushed my thighs apart and jabbed into me, again and again. But I didn't. I had already learned how to be quiet, to count back from one hundred. I shut my eyes and gritted my teeth and my hands grasped the edges of the blanket. I pulled myself along by counting my own heartbeats. I had learned long ago how to bear things by squeezing my eyes shut and counting. Ninety-nine. Eight. Seven. Faster. Six. There. I left my body. I was watching myself from up in the tree. "Look at me," he whispered, in between his moans. "Look at me!" he ordered.

A thin trickle of saliva dangled from his lips. He met my eyes, just for a moment.

"I'm looking," I whispered.

There are things a girl never forgets when her virginity is stolen. To an outsider it's really nothing more than an old tree—a mess of branches hung with stories, with images from soap operas and movies, about a love she might find and a life she might live. But it is a tree wholly hers and hung with her most secret wishes, the ones she let herself imagine on long summer days, when the sand stretched on for miles of possibility. It is a tree with dreams patterned in its bark. It is a tree that, in a moment, can become ash.

It can engulf a person in flames, if she is standing too close.

These were the things I would remember: the whisper of branches scratching at the sky; the fluttering petals of bougainvillea caught in the wind, streaking hues of scarlet; my mouth open without sound, despite the pain as he pushed into me and asked if I liked it; the feeling of being conquered, branded, of being won; the coarse fibers of the wool blanket where a thorny rose stem tore across my bum; the burning pain in my vagina; the trickle of blood that would run down my thigh and into my high-top sneaker; the sight of smashed roses in the grass after he rolled off of me. And when he was done, the sight of him pulling up his pants, and the rose petals beneath his sneakers drying like blood.

But it was the shame and the humiliation that lingered most of all as I watched him speed away on his bicycle, knowing I'd never see him again. And the self-loathing that followed, the slow and painful slogging through grief as I knelt on his white blanket, stained with my blood, hands covering my face. I would begin walking the never-ending path to forgiveness, trying like hell to figure out how I could have let this happen.

Maybe I had caused it. Maybe I had wanted to be changed. I would struggle with self-blame. Because from the age of thirteen, when I'd first arrived at the Home after my mother's death, I had envied the sensuous blossoms of the bougainvillea, furious at my body for not developing, convinced my breasts were locked up inside me, unlike all the other girls around me, who had already become women.

Now, I had given myself up to a stranger. Had I done it? I had trouble fathoming that it had happened at all, and yet I knew I would always have to live with it. I crawled into the grass. I looked down at the thorns of that single rose stem. I picked up the stained blanket and threw it into the bushes. Most of all, I remembered not being able to say the word "stop."

THE MOON FOLLOWED me as I walked my bicycle back to the Home that night, aching, my clothes stained with grass and grief. I imagined all the girls who lived at the Home were crying as well, tossed in and out of their sleep, taken over with the despair of smoke, as Sister Zora huddled on the fire escape like a gnome, puffing on a cigarette. I imagined the girls waking up suddenly with the dim memory of what they had done and what they would do.

A violation. That's what the nuns called the loss of virginity. This is what Sister Mary said when she washed away the blood between my legs and then handed me a tube of antibiotic ointment. Dolly, weak after a fight with her boyfriend, asked Sister Mary to leave us alone in the bathroom. How carefully my sister washed me in the bathtub, letting me cry. Her normally indelicate hands floated over my body. She did not once tell me to stop, but rubbed my back in hypnotic circles with a wet washcloth. After, she helped me into a clean white nightgown. We lay on my bed and I refused to look at her. She kissed my head and stroked my hair as I wept. She rested her cheek on my shoulder as I stared at the wall.

"Moose, I'm so sorry I let you go by yourself," she whispered.

"Don't take the blame. Don't you dare," I said evenly.

The next day, Sister Mary drove me 140 miles across California to the high Mojave Desert of Joshua Tree National Park so that I could empty myself of my grief, so that my tears would dry up in the sand. I remembered the Joshua trees, with their spindly outstretched limbs that Mormon pioneers once believed pointed to the Promised Land. Some people never returned from this desert.

I'd heard stories of hikers lost in canyons, their footprints disappearing in the dust. Was Sister Mary going to leave me here? I thought about my mother again. I could see myself standing in a puddle on the side of the road and defying the darkness, holding my breath, waiting for the glow of car lights. Now, my eyes followed the abandoned things strewn across the sand, the dented silver fenders and the chalky strings of animal bones. I stared at the rock formations until my eyes found animals in their shapes.

It didn't matter. I could not have cared less about being left.

It took me forty-five minutes to empty myself of words, of tears, with Sister Mary sitting in her gold Chevy with the statue of Jesus on the dashboard, waiting for me as I knelt on the desert floor repenting, spilling out all my sins until I had nothing left.

"If you left me here, I probably wouldn't come back. You'd have room for one more girl," I said, half wishing she would tell me I was right and then at least we would know what the other wanted.

"I don't leave girls. I find them," Sister said.

CHARGES WERE NOT pressed. I didn't fight him. I hadn't even screamed. In those days, in the early '80s, few girls pressed charges, especially when they had gone with the guy willingly, as though lambs to the slaughter, like I had done. People called it consensual. It was about the physical struggle, what you had done. Would it matter if you hit or punched? Would a knee to the groin make a difference? What if you spit in his face, clawed at his neck?

How long did you allow yourself to be choked? Did you choke back? What if you just lay there, doing nothing, motionless, lost from the shock or the alcohol? What if you didn't struggle enough? What if you had wished only to kiss him?

Did you want it?

Girls cried themselves to sleep for their mistakes. Hung their heads low. The older nuns kept their secrets, soaked up blood with towels, drove over the border for cheap abortions, took some girls who were further along to midwives to be checked for pregnancy, which the nuns considered a curse and a blessing. No one talked about what virginity meant, or how its loss could affect a girl. I'd never spoken to anyone about it, not even Dolly. Over and over, as the midwife examined me, poking and prodding, she asked, was this okay? Did this hurt? It reminded me of how the boy had asked if I liked it as he pushed into me. He hadn't stopped, even when he glanced down at my blood on his penis. When it was over, when he was done with me, before he took off, he picked up one of the smashed roses and thanked me.

I'll never forget it: I actually took the rose.

The next day, Dolly cut off my long red curls, almost to my ears, just as I'd asked. I looked like a boy. I had no desire to groom, primp, or adorn myself in any way. I gave back her Bakelite bracelet, the one she had let me borrow. I threw away my Love's Baby Soft lip gloss and eyeliner. I rifled through the pile of old ripped clothing in the charity bag, and I wore baggy pants made for boys to school. But Sister Mary, despite her own deprivation, was wise about the ways of lost virginity. She told me I should not hide my femininity in clothing made for men, nor should I silence my words, because it would strain my soul at its roots. She said I needed to speak. Right now. At exactly this time. I was in between the places I knew, and my voice might be lost forever.

"Speak, Ruthie. As often and as loudly as you can. Keep speaking it," she said.

At the age of fifteen, I learned to speak. She said if I let myself disappear, I would end up like Sister Elizabeth, who had once been raped and never spoke a word again, and was now imprisoned by her own silence, not to mention her wheelchair.

SISTER SAID THIS happened to others. She had seen it a thousand times. Why didn't girls know that some flowers were never meant to be given?

"Slut." Someone whispered from the hallway when I was organizing books on my shelf. Her tight black eyes met mine. I could smell cigarette smoke on her clothing as she stopped at my doorway, out of breath.

The girl startled when Dolly jumped her, slamming her face against the floor. Sister Mary said one more offense like this, and Dolly would be sent away for good.

In the days that followed, Sister Elizabeth was the only one I wanted. I didn't want people fighting for me. I just longed to disappear. With desperation, I sought her out. I needed to be near her in a way I could not explain to Dolly. She was the only one who understood. Her bright hazel eyes flashed with secrets from behind thick glasses, her small delicate mouth hammered into silence. I volunteered to be her aide, a job no one else wanted because she smelled from lack of washing, sometimes defecating in her pants while struggling to reach the toilet. It didn't bother me. Each morning, I brushed her long gray hair and wove it in a braid. Each night, I lifted a plastic chair into the shower so I could bathe her while she sat comfortably. Taking care of her somehow brought me healing. I could not care for myself, but I could care for her. I cared for her in the way I wished my mother had cared for me.

I still cried, but my tears lessened with time, as things do.

I wasn't sure I would ever be able to stop entirely. I tried to keep my tears limited to the shower and the bedroom that I shared with Dolly. Sister Mary was growing frustrated, worried this might never stop.

So one night I stopped. As I stared at the tree in the front, I felt a tug from deep within, or perhaps it came from a universal source outside me, and then a voluminous energy poured into me, insisting that I open up to it. And I did, because I knew how. I had watched the bougainvillea. I had seen my mother in despair, something I had promised I would never repeat.

At that moment, the despair of all the virgins who had been tricked or deceived, or who had deceived themselves, was drawn into one girl. I sucked in my breath, waiting. The bougainvillea were silent for the first time, as if a coffin had been shut.

I imagined my tears held molecules of grief and took on an uncommon energy, that they drew the moon across the ocean so it could be seen and felt at this moment by every girl who, for one reason or another, hadn't been able to say the word *stop*.

My mother had spent all that time looking to the moon to guide her. Now I was guiding it. It was the Rape Theory of Creation, the one we hadn't learned about, the one in which a shifting planet captures another, absorbs it, and they become one, leaving no trace that, once upon a time, two planets existed.

My hands flew to my sore breasts.

I ran outside. The tree was on fire.

Chapter Ten

E VEN ILLUSIONS WERE predictable.
Refusing to see a mirage required enormous effort.
You could drive right through it, back and forth, over and over, to disprove it, and yet, just standing a few feet away, you had proven it. If you were a person who preferred land, once you knew there was oil underneath, you might never be able to see the earth. For you, the ground, in fact, becomes the swirling black liquid. Sometimes a sea lion is really just a star, a meteor of light and bones, visible only for a moment before disappearing into water. Not everything leaves a shadow. Sometimes when the star streaks across the sky and knows it will burn out, it will change into something quite different.

When flames rise up into the night sky, you know that the trees, with their reborn leaves and coal black branches, will fade into the blue, and then grow, then catch on fire, then uproot with floods and disappear, making room for new growth. I remembered waking up in our campsite when I was a child. I remembered a time when hot sand burned my neck as I curled up against a stranger's guitar and slept. Is it an illusion that life cycles on after a tragedy, or is it really that tragedies cycle on, allowing you to call this life?

If you wish it so, you can capture most things, interrupting their cycles. If you watch yourself healing, you may prevent the healing from occurring. How, then, to move on? Everyone you ask will mention the word "forward." Moons move forward in cycles. They are effortless, as automatic as breathing.

Each month, when I was growing up, a new full moon always waited. This was my mother's gift to me. This was the constant I didn't see. It was the only thing that was still faithful, its rabid changeability still finding me wherever I was and leading me not to a new promised land, but to the land I'd already been promised.

Sister Zora got to the fire first, dousing it with the garden hose. Sister Mary warned Dolly never to see her boyfriend again. He had, after one of their fights, taken a stack of newspapers and lit it on fire near the front door. The wind had blown it into the tree. Sister made her an amulet of protection to wear around her neck, a wood carving of Lilith, the seductress from the Bible, with swirling hair and a fire between her legs, who refused to be subservient to Adam and was called "demon."

My pregnancy was confirmed three weeks after the violation.

The nuns moved me through pregnancy, pressing me not to talk about it with anyone but my sister. Dolly bought me a snow globe with a strawberry inside, so I would think of Felix, a nice memory. She never mentioned my child, as though she didn't want to cause me pain. I obsessively thought about what the baby would do when it was six months, one year, five years old. I bought baby books and read them in secret. I stayed away from the girls who smoked, forcing clean air into my lungs. I planted a small garden and grew herbs and carrots, things that were easy for me to care for.

I stared out at the burnt tree in the yard, hoping it would come back to life. I prayed for it.

One day, I asked Sister Mary if I could become a nun. I meant it.

She said it was only right, out of respect for my mother and our Jewish ancestry, that I look into something else. At that time they needed nurses in Long Beach, so Sister Mary advised me to become a nurse. "Strawberries are Sister Elizabeth's favorite food," she told me. And then she thanked me.

"So you'll be able to come back and take care of her and the rest of the nuns when they're old," said Dolly. "In fact, why don't you just stay here forever and become a nun?"

"I asked."

It was because Sister Mary knew that I had been born for care-taking. I had pulled Sister Elizabeth out of a puddle of her own feces the week before. I had been at the Long Beach Swap Meet all day, and when I returned, I found her trapped on the floor in the back bathroom, her blue nylon pants tangled around her ankles. She had remained there, soiled, unable to move, unable or unwilling to call for help, for an entire day. "I'm your friend," I said, touching her shoulder. There wasn't a thing anyone could tell me about her that would make me turn away from her. Her eyes pleaded with me. "I'm going to help you. Don't be embarrassed."

She raised her eyebrows.

"You have helped me, you know. More than I can say," I told her.

She nodded; she trusted me. I bathed her and then helped her slip into a warm flannel nightgown. As I pulled a blanket around her shoulders, she leaned in and kissed me on the mouth. I let her.

I said nothing. I, like my mother, was for everyone.

And yet I would have to learn to keep myself.

That night, I heated up a rice-and-beans dinner the cook had left in a Tupperware container in the refrigerator. I lit two white candles, washed a handful of strawberries, and set out dinner. I spent the evening with Sister, reading to her from her Bible. When I tucked her into bed, I hummed her Shalom Rav. My mother had never sung me a lullaby, but I sang it in a way I imagined a mother would. I sang it as softly as I could, to both Sister Elizabeth and my unborn child. I wondered, could this be the soul that had been waiting for me all this time? I didn't recognize it, though I struggled to. Sister Mary walked by. She backtracked and slid my mother's blond guitar over the threshold.

I sat on the edge of Sister Elizabeth's bed, letting my fingers find the chords my mother had played. I pressed my fingers into the strings along the bridge, and I picked through the strings as my mother had.

Sister Elizabeth smiled. Beautiful teeth.

I tucked her into bed and said goodbye.

Months later, on a cold May morning, I felt contractions and was whisked off to the hospital. There was little discussion but for a short nominal warning from Sister Mary, who, with the help of a lawyer, had already located a deserving family "in the Midwest" that wanted a healthy white infant.

Healthy. White. Infant.

But I would keep my baby. I hadn't planned on giving it up. Now, loaded up with a healthy potion of anesthesia, along with painkillers afterward, I remembered virtually nothing of what happened during my labor or after. The pregnancy had been an apparition. The whole thing happened as if in a dream. No one spoke of it after my child was taken, just as I was gaining consciousness. The nuns and doctor didn't want to know how I felt, and so I began to scream. My job had been to grow a healthy baby inside me.

In all the years I was at the Home, I would watch three other girls do the same. Dolly questioned why the nuns looked away from our tight T-shirts and long bare legs that stretched from under our miniskirts before we'd sneak out to drink beer and meet boys. The nuns handled our wild ways with a strange mix of freedom and admonishment because they were hopeless against us. Against girls like us.

I was told never to think of that baby as a person, for if I did, I would never be able to move on, Sister Mary said. My life had stopped for six months in the in-between place until I delivered my child prematurely. Only Sister Elizabeth had met me there, for she lived in the threshold. Now I understood.

I never learned the gender of my child. Some time after the birth, I sat on the porch, listening to the women's voices rising in a chorus from the bougainvillea. It had begun again, or perhaps the sound was coming from my lips, or from the crowded apartments down the street. I was sore and groggy. Dolly ordered me into bed, but I couldn't move. I was held there by the singing and crying, and the way those petals appeared such a soft blue in the moonlight; they looked like my baby's skin. I had caught a glimpse of it the second before it was whisked away. I didn't hear a single cry, not at first. But a moment later, maybe it was there. Just a small cry, like the sound of a kitten trapped in a tree.

A beckoning.

They thought it wouldn't matter to me anyway whether the baby was a boy or a girl. It was over. When I asked, I was told that if I continued to ask questions, I'd be sent to a foster home far away from my sister. Suddenly, Sister Mary didn't want to hear my voice. But I continued to ask. I was different now, no longer threatened by abandonment. Sister Zora whispered to me it was time I had a relationship with myself. It was important not to let myself down. I had to know I could be my own protector.

Dolly overheard one of the other girls say that my child had been stillborn. I had dreamed of flying among blue petals falling everywhere as trees tumbled off the side of a mountain. Above me, there was a red sun. Dolly grabbed me, waking me, catching me before I jumped.

After the swelling went down, they tried to pretend that it had never happened. A few days later, I snuck off to the local cemetery. I covered myself in wet leaves and mud, beside a small fresh unmarked grave.

THE SISTERS PRAYED me through the recovery.

Still sore, I walked across the cold marble foyer and glanced up at archangel Michael, wondering if my life had just begun or if it should end. I dabbed at my bloodshot blue eyes and told myself never to forget. And yet, how could I? I'd wake up twice a night, peeling the thin soaked fabric of my nightgown from my breasts.

Years later, I'd see a child, big-boned like me, with a shock of bright red hair like mine, and I'd have to keep myself from running after it and tapping it on the shoulder. Of course I was told my medical file was closed, then lost. It was best to forget. For a long time, maybe years, I couldn't forget the pallor of my baby's skin. I had memorized the sound of my baby's first cry. A woman never forgets that. All these years later, the gulls that flocked to the beach on Belmont Shore reminded me of that sound, for in their calls I heard an infant crying. Perhaps that's why I would return, so I wouldn't forget.

I LIVED AT the Home for two more years. It was hard for me to be still. I couldn't bear it.

There were always more girls waiting. I couldn't even name them. One would go; another would take her place. Then the same morning ritual, an introduction that everyone would soon forget. Don't touch my barrettes. That's my favorite pen. I like to be called by my nickname. Please don't talk to me in the morning. I like to do my homework while listening to the radio. Sherri, Maria, Madeleine, LaVerne. Hello. Goodbye. Shalom. God forgives you. There but for the grace of God go I, go you. We were interchangeable. I understood that now, as one does with the perspective of time. I succumbed to Dolly. I was bereft.

I dreamed of the ocean pooling in my footsteps. I dreamed of flying, while in the midst of the flames.

AFTER SHUTTING OUR bedroom door at night, Dolly and I waited until everyone was asleep before we crept out the back by the kitchen. We snuck into bars with fake IDs that she had made using the laminating machine in Sister Mary's office. We were hungry, alive again. We jumped on our bikes and pedaled furiously through the rain, burning past glorious sunsets at dusk as the huge white flamingos dipped into the oily ground. When the colored lights glowed across the floating skyscrapers beyond the marina, we cased the bars, where the air was heavy with the scent of beer and Old Spice cologne. We sometimes hurt ourselves, sat in cars with boys we didn't know, sometimes hated ourselves.

We suffered under judgmental glares, withstood the word "slut." I had already ruined my only chance at a first time.

We drank whiskey and smoked Marlboro Lights and danced on tables. We licked our lips and we shook our hips to "Purple Rain," and we tried to forget our past, all the people we had been. We fell and got up again. Mostly, we tried to ignore the fact that there was no future waiting for us.

Dolly had it in her mind that she would become someone, one day. She talked about becoming a social worker so that she could protect girls like us. In the midst of self-destruction, she was thinking about protection, much like our mother had. The dichotomy.

Each time Dolly traveled across the border to "take care of things," she swore she'd stay away from men. She never did. She told me I was smarter than she was, and to think about college, too. But by this point, I had become too anxious to sit in a classroom all day. Work was the only thing that settled me. Helping people was the only time I could feel my own presence in the world, and

I knew that space had to be walked through before I could safely become a part of everything. Maybe I didn't want to. Not yet.

Memories crept back and asserted themselves into my life without warning, reminding me I was once a person who was raised by books. Thoreau. Shakespeare. Even the Farmer's Almanac. I looked at the moon and asked my mother to tell me her stories. As far as I knew, the box of old almanacs was still in the storage room at the Twin Palms. We hadn't retrieved it before we left. Bits and pieces of those pages fell across my eyes, images I put together. I could decode them one day.

I preferred to keep moving because I didn't have to think. Besides, Dolly and I had no money and no guidance, and neither of us knew what we could become.

The nuns could not bother with girls once they left for good. It wasn't their fault. Too many girls needed a place. A herd of young women waited by the fence of bougainvillea, craving everything, needing as much as we did.

The nuns could not risk the whole for one girl. That's why Sister Mary slipped a bus ticket into Dolly's hand along with a pile of $20 bills. She had found Dolly's boyfriend's note threatening to burn down the Home unless Dolly spoke to him.

Sister Mary told Dolly not to look back, not even at me.

Heads bowed. Hands folded in laps after the decision had been made. "You'll see it's better this way. You girls need time away from each other. How will you each discover who you really are?" Sister Mary asked me.

Dolly called me a few days later.

"I'm in San Diego. I'll send you a bus ticket as soon as I can. I promise. Remember, outlaws. I love you, Moose."

"I'm not your responsibility." I blew her a kiss after hanging up the phone.

AT EIGHTEEN, I left the nuns and forgot all I knew, and I married a man who didn't know me. A district attorney, sitting by a pond in a park. To him, I was a trophy, a collection of body parts that looked good together despite being disparate pieces. He told me I was beautiful. I had grown to my full five-foot-eleven, and my hair reached to my waist. On my wedding day, the day on which I was to marry the man I thought would give me a new life, I poured my body into a tight white chenille dress I had purchased at a thrift shop during a Halloween sale, pinned up my hair in a bun, threaded some baby's breath through my curls, and slipped on flat leather sandals so I wouldn't be taller than my groom. I looked forward to a waltz. But there would be no waltz, my betrothed told me on that day. I bit back the tears, trying not to ruin my eye makeup, a thin blue line blurring beneath my eyelashes, where Dolly brushed her thumb.

"Poor Ruthie. It must be hard being so damn ugly," Dolly laughed, trying to cheer me up, her cream-colored pantsuit illuminating her olive skin. She did make me laugh, just for a moment. I noticed how her newly dyed black hair glistened and that her eyes were painted with bright lavender eye shadow that matched her fingernails. A foot shorter than I was, she was now so busty she appeared as if she might tip forward. "You sure you're ready, Moose?" she asked. She grabbed my hand and ran it through her hair, messing it into tangles.

My only relative stood up for me. It had been a quick courtship, and it was an even quicker marriage. My shiny new husband with his impressive job would have been our late mother's pride and joy had he not come home sobbing for his clients and, after a few drinks, toppled the apartment.

He broke all the kitchen plates, our front door. He said he could beat "the pretty" out of me. According to him, it had never done me a lick of good anyway. What did I ever have to say that was of any value? Was I contributing to society in any meaningful way?

Standing at the front door after the last time, I drew in my breath. I was nineteen now, and I knew that if I didn't act,

I would end up like Sister Elizabeth, in a wheelchair with a mouth hammered into silence.

That is why I held a pan of boiling oil in my hands.

That was the last time he threatened me.

I put the pan down and turned around. I pulled up the hood of my sweatshirt and walked across Artesia Boulevard, through the pouring rain, with $55 in my pocket. I crossed the grass, headed up the main drag to Broadway as water rushed around my ankles. I didn't look back, even after the storm.

I MADE A promise to myself on the night I left him. If I ever had a daughter I would raise her to be strong, smart, self-protective. If she wanted to hurry things up, I would make her wait, even though she might not want to or think she needed to. I didn't care if I had to lock her in her room. I would be strong enough to let her hate me. Even if she shouted and kicked holes in the walls, I would stand firm. I would brace my back against the door. I would push up against the door as each full moon beckoned her, and I'd wait for minutes, hours, days, years, knowing that her mind needed more time to catch up with her body before she let herself get lost.

I would do all this. This was precisely how crazy I would be.

I would wave burning bundles of sage around the corners of her bedroom to protect her. I would cover her head with a scarf, hiding her hair.

Because if she suffered a bad loss, if she was harmed or even harmed herself unintentionally, it could create a condition of colliding events worse than any El Niño. It would create a series of catastrophes in her life. She could become a woman with empty eyes, a woman who allowed herself to be stolen, again and again, who never protected herself because she had never learned her worth, a woman for whom the ground beneath her feet would easily slip away wherever she stood, leaving her terminally unsure, paralyzed as to where to go next. With no place to call home, she'd always feel lost at sea. She might even become a mother accidentally, if only for a second, one split second.

It was not too late for me. Nothing was. I still had the promise of my Naida. I knew she was coming. Soon.

PART TWO

Chapter Eleven
1986

I T WASN'T A home that you'd fall in love with. Homes, despite their ability to seep up the spiritual essence of lives, and their tendency to absorb and contain the energy of joy and grief, were just glass, brick, wood, and mortar. They were constructions, welded with nails and glue, like muscle and bone knit together with sinewy straps, according to a plan. No, you didn't fall in love with a home. You fell in love with the stories you told yourself about what had happened there and what you imagined could happen. Any good realtor would tell you that. Just like any good matchmaker would tell you the same about a soul mate—you didn't fall in love with him. You fell in love with the stories of who you imagined you'd be when you were with him. The feeling of having dreamed of him long before you met him was like invisible ink written on your skin.

It was a leap of faith to try and ascertain what good things might be coming into your future if you zigged in X or zagged with Y. Most people trusted "the feeling" they got about certain places, just as they sensed things when they met certain people. Everyday people with no particular inclination toward spiritual things noticed the signs that seemed to thrash across the ether before a big decision was made. Wherever you were, most everyone could agree on the bad omen of a bird flying into a window, breaking its wing.

Homes, like certain people, would be blamed, too: That place was bad luck; I'd never live in a townhouse again; I had to move and change my life.

Some places were so magnetic and full of energies that they drew the same people back, again and again. What you had in common with these people, you could rarely put into words, but you knew you shared something: inescapability. If you were like Dolly and me, who'd lived on the road for stretches at a time, you might think of your first real home as the beginning of your real life. That's why I returned to the old motel on the beach, despite my lingering fears. I remembered it as a safe house, a communal space, a spiderweb by the sea that trapped wanderers for their own good. Somehow I knew it would still be there. And then, there it was.

With no one around, I tipped my head back and opened my mouth, letting the rain wash over my face, staring up at the dark blue and then at the bright blue door. The weathered salmon stucco still had clusters of bougainvillea spilling across its walls. The vines, I would soon see, hid the loneliness, the monotony, and the ache of the aged with their lush petals as they climbed across the rooftops, across buildings and telephone wires. Gulls still flocked to the beach, and in their calls I still heard an infant crying, a parachute of sound floating above everything. A signal of my return. I'd been running for years.

Dr. Brownstein threw her arms around me when I walked into the lobby. I hadn't expected such an outpouring of emotion. I forced myself to relax in the scent of her Charlie perfume. This was the way a mother would welcome a daughter. I wanted to drink in every last bit of maternal love that I'd missed. I closed my eyes in the soft pillow of her embrace.

The Twin Palms had become a retirement home, now called Wild Acres. I got to know each one of the residents: Mr. Takahashi, whom I'd met a long time ago, and Mrs. Green. Dr. B., as I now called Dr. Brownstein, began to call me "kinder." Her hands trembled, but her eyes were hooded with the same powdery blue eye shadow. The night I'd arrived, she'd opened the snack machine in the lobby, telling me to take whatever I wanted. "Come, child. Tell me everything." She'd smiled and then pretended not to notice how quickly I ate. Her tanned skin. Her leathery hands. Her failing eyesight. The smell of her perfume. The moonstone in her hand as she handed it to me. All were familiar.

"If you're like your mother, you have a unique combination of skills," she said. I could fix a leaky faucet in seconds flat. I had large, stony hands. My mother had shown me everything. This would prepare me for her residents, the likes of which I had never seen. She wiped her eyes with a lace handkerchief when she told me her daughter, Sasha, had divorced Sam. All Sasha wanted was a nice vacation, my mother had said.

By the time we moved permanently to the Twin Palms, Sasha and Sam had moved to Rochester to work for Xerox.

"She liked your mother an awful lot. Said your mother was the reason she got to go to Hawaii. But that's a story for another time. She blessed me, your mother did. Hard worker. There's been no one that I could trust as much as her. I only ever gave her a key. Do you know that? In all this time, only your mother."

She now had a new parakeet, Tick Tock, the third. But this bird could swear in Yiddish, bleating out, *"Kush mir in tuchas"* at random times, making everyone smile. She kept him in the lobby, next to a couch and coffee table, where the residents could be entertained, often falling asleep watching the bird.

Wild Acres was true to its new name, full of mood swings. The residents suffered from varying degrees of dementia and aching bodies. Dr. B. provided a safe home for them, for their memories shifted like Teutonic plates underneath the surface of daily life. This was a dwelling built for transitory things—memories, spirits, last chances caught in the threshold of this plane and the next. For Mrs. Green, the sight of a fishing net washed up on the beach invoked an image of a rash on a screaming baby's chest, the sandpaper burn of scarlet fever under the child's arms. For Mr. Takahashi, the sadness of a good book ending could recall the heavy rains that wiped out an entire field of strawberries in minutes, or the memory of Pearl Harbor, when he happened to go onto shore for a date, unknowing that his ship and all eighty-one men in his division would be lost within hours.

I would come to understand trembling hands that reached over balconies as if to catch lost lovers from falling. I would find tissue paper covered in lipstick kisses and blown over the sand, or handwritten notes on napkins placed in Coke bottles and buried. I would rehang drapes that were tugged down daily to be washed with sunlight.

The first paragraph of a letter would be repeated three times, and we'd find half-eaten sandwiches, a birdcage left open, a faucet running, the wrong pair of shoes, no shoes. I adored Dr. B. for taking people in. But it wasn't just charity. She felt this was her purpose. Lives must be driven by something, she said. My mother had rewarded Dr. B.'s goodness with friendship and a reprieve so that she could spend time with Sasha.

"Be forewarned," Dr. B. told me. "They like to travel." On many nights throughout the halls of Wild Acres, I might find residents in the corridors, disturbed by the full moons, collecting blankets and leaving them in different sections of the hallway and on the fire escape. Their only wish: to be told, "You exist. Go back to sleep." Sometimes being in the wrong place was the only place people would see you.

Mr. Takahashi would appear in the crook of the magnolia trees, in the back of the ice cream truck, discovered and driven back home by Paulo, the ice cream man. He'd show up on the side of the highway five miles away. No one ever saw him leave. I'd find him most of the time. And the others, too. Some, like Mrs. Green, had to be caught as if by a net. I would find her racing into the waves with a suitcase in hand, calling to her husband who was dying of cancer and had just been moved to a nearby hospice, though Dr. B. took her there each morning, when he was most lucid. In her mind, she was always late to meet him. When I spoke to her, she listened. She trusted me. There might be value here, I thought. In me. They valued me.

"Everybody wants to be found," Dr. B. said when I asked whether Mr. Takahashi was really trying to escape.

But of all the things they had lost and found, their slippers meant the most. Outside of each green door, there was a dark rubber mat for slippers—faux-fur pink slip-ons, slipper boots with soft lining you could wear outside the house, knit slipper socks with leather soles sewn in, soft moccasins with beads. Slippers were coveted by gift-toting guests, by relatives looking to exchange guilt for comfort. Cold arthritic feet could ruin Mrs. Green's day, could make it impossible for her to stand at her easel and paint, or to rake the gray shag carpeting so that all the piles fell in the same direction. Tying a shoe could ruin Dr. B.'s back for weeks. Despite the traction of rubber grips, steps were still misplaced. People fell on the sidewalk. Tripped in the kitchen. There were broken hips, bandaged foreheads, pieces of bloodstained gauze that flitted amid the crushed shells in the parking lot, caught up in the chaos by the winds that followed the ambulances back to the emergency room at any time of day or night.

"I'll do a good job," I told Dr. B.

"Ruthie, I know you will. I have absolutely no doubt about it." I already knew I didn't want to disappoint her.

I had been anxious to see our old apartment. On my first day of work at Wild Acres, I recognized Mr. Takahashi standing in the hallway, though he didn't recognize me. Lou, as Dr. B. called him, was bald now. His face was creased, his skin mottled. His dark eyes were the same, and he hunched over and talked too close to my face so that I could smell the coffee and mints on his breath. Dr. B. said he had come here years ago looking for my mother, but we'd been long gone by then. "We get ten calls a day from people looking to place their parents," she said. "I can't take everybody, and even now I have too many. He was one of the first. I told him he could visit room 21. I've never seen a man break down like he did that day. He didn't want to leave. What could I do when his son asked if we'd take him?" The place where my mother once lived held more meaning for him than the farm he'd built up for decades. "His son runs the farm now. You know, Lou never talks of strawberries. Talks of everything but. Anyhow, of course we always have fresh strawberries. They subsidize us."

I noticed his wrinkled white shirt, briefly recalling my discomfort at seeing him touch my mother. Despite all her dating, he was the only man I'd ever seen touch my mother in that way. "Mr. Takahashi, do you remember me? We picked strawberries at your farm. You were very kind," I lied.

"There was that one summer, Diana. We didn't eat or go out much. Where have you put my door?"

I glanced at Dr. B. "I think he remembers you," she whispered.

"I had to hide who I was. They'd have never let me serve. One day, a great bird flew up from the water, lifting right off the waves. We didn't expect that one or the rest that flew over. Torpedoes. I was supposed to be in my battle station in the radio shack."

"You were lucky, Lou. You had a lucky angel," said Dr. B., taking his arm. She turned to me. "We need to paint the doors different colors. They get confused by all the green. Maybe you could start with that, Ruthie. Come inside—see, he likes his brown chair." I followed her into his apartment.

"I remember you, Ruthie," he said, rubbing his eyes. "You're a looker, just like your mother."

"You caught a white croaker off the pier," said Dr. B., trying to impose a memory to get him off his current track. "The pier was all lit up with lights. A million tiny lights on strings across both sides at night."

"Not anymore. They shut it down early because of the vagrants."

"I caught a sand shark and threw it back," I said, to assert my place.

He nodded, but I could tell he was far away. Dr. B. pointed to his door. "The one with the bells." She said his hearing was going. She'd wrapped a bell collar around the door handle to alert him when someone was coming in. I asked if I could fluff his pillow. I made a show of it. I wanted to offer something, to begin to become a part of things. "Yes, yes, that would be fine," he said. "That's my Diana. Her picture is on the wall there. What a beauty."

I stared at the photograph of my mother, with the signature "For my favorite farmer. Love, Diana." It had been taken on our day at his strawberry farm in Oxnard. Dolly, dressed in blue shorts, gathered herself in my mother's skirt. My mother stood next to Mr. Takahashi. Dressed in his signature pressed white button-down shirt, he had his arms around my mother's waist and was staring at the camera with a suspicious half smile. Dolly looked so small, her hands on her hips, her knees knobby above high white tube socks striped blue at the top. I remember talking to Felix by the side of the truck when one of the workers took out his camera.

"Did I tell you my son has a boat? What has Fay Green done with my slippers?" Mr. Takahashi asked, turning to Dr. B.

In the future, he would tell me bits and pieces of my mother's life, the reasons she had done what she had. Every life, it seemed, was just a domino stream of past lives, which is why a person's life was not a predictable curve upward. Life was a jagged line. That's why when you looked back, you'd often think, *That was another life entirely.* Or *I was a different person then.* Because, in fact, you were. Certain cells in the body died every day. More than half of the neurons formed in the embryonic state would die before birth, which possibly meant that you'd had months of memories that you couldn't access. Certain things, like memories, could feel like the only things that linked you to the many selves you had been. If you were like Mr. Takahashi, caught on the Teutonic plates of your past, you might cling to your strongest memory of love to ground yourself.

It was hard to believe my mother had so many other lives. It bothered me to think of her life as so full at one time, and then empty for long after. What had she done to deserve that? Had she just given up? I thought of Mrs. Green. Every Friday night at sundown, we'd sit in the courtyard near the small palm tree that we'd rescued from a demolition site. Mrs. Green would say the prayer over the wine, the kiddush. Dr. B. would say the blessing over the bread, HaMotzi, and tear off a piece of challah and pass it around our makeshift shtetl. Though Dr. B. wouldn't categorize herself and Mrs. Green leaned somewhere between Reform and Conservative, this cobbled-together version of Judaism created a perfect harmony. Making the Sabbath made me incredibly wistful for what I never had, and yet there was the pull of roots and the promise of rest, a time to receive the bride of the Sabbath, the Shekhinah, who would flourish in the ease of kindred spirits, Dr. B. said. Mrs. Green seemed so comfortable leading the prayers; it was hard to reconcile her strength with the shadowy figment that rushed into the waves with a suitcase. The mind, it seemed, was a trolley, its doors opening and closing at different stops, and too easily trapped at some. "Fay, you've outdone yourself again," Dr. B. would tell her over the dinner that she'd cooked for us, chicken soup with matzo balls and fresh challah. After, I'd sit on her plastic-covered couch, calmed and reassured as I listened to their voices.

"We used to go to the supper clubs," said Mr. Takahashi. "It's where I met Diana. She'd lied about her age, but she wasn't too jolly. We'd find oil on the birds some days on the beach, Diana and I. Not anymore. You know Pearl Harbor was a fight over oil? They don't tell you that. I'd swim in a red tide anytime. All these lip flappers crying about hives and headaches. It's just algae," he said.

In the months that followed, Mr. Takahashi would convince me that I had never really known my mother. She had been running from something, but from what? It made my hands ache to think about all that happened to her, that we could have happened to her. "I've given up my life for you girls. I've sacrificed everything," I remembered her saying. And yet, perhaps her life might have ended up this way, too, even if she hadn't had us. Perhaps the blueprint of a life remained the same even if the place and people were different.

Within weeks, I found myself interjected into the narrative, the comfort section, I called it. "Ruthie is the one who fluffs my favorite pillow and leaves it for me. That's what I like. Every day while I'm on my morning walk. Redhead. Always has a smile. She makes lettuce-and-tomato sandwiches and cuts off the crust. Strong. Can lift my chair. Doesn't flap her lips. Why doesn't a pretty girl like Ruthie have a husband?"

As time passed, I learned Mr. Takahashi's likes and dislikes, as well as those of Mrs. Green. She made wonderful challah on Friday mornings, and she preferred overcast days to sunshine. She loved to paint, loved chicken soup, and soft-boiled eggs with the whites scraped out and mixed with salt. Mr. Takahashi liked his things arranged just so and could get out of sorts if something was moved. He loved ice cream, vanilla, and his navy slippers. I fell into a routine surprisingly easily, grateful to be needed again. I wrapped Mrs. Green's thin gray hair in warm oil-coated towels to condition it. I massaged Mr. Takahashi's hands. I visited and I chatted. I fished rings from drains and delivered and charted medication, counting out pills. We played Rummikub and took walks, telling stories. Dr. B. had been doing most of the caretaking, and she was tired. She needed to be taken care of, too. I knew a person could starve from lack of touch. There had been times during my marriage when I was so alone, with Dolly in San Diego. I'd go to the Mane Attraction hair salon just to have Theresa, the owner, put her soft hands on me. Theresa would wash my hair and tell me all about her grandchildren. I'd sit in a chair covered in torn red vinyl as if it were a throne and drink Sanka out of a Styrofoam cup as if it were a silver goblet. For forty-five minutes, I would watch *General Hospital* without sound, along with the other women sitting under hair dryers and staring at the black-and-white television bolted in the corner. I would listen to the soft lilt of Theresa's voice as she spoke to me as if I were someone.

Touch was the beginning of life and the cataclysm. I could give someone back a connection to the rest of the world.

"It's an uncommon gift that you have with the aged and infirm," Dr. B. told me after my first week. "I watch you anchor a spirit into a body when it has other plans. Your mother called it a 'passion for compassion.' That's what she said about you," she said.

"She said that?"

"Of course, child. Didn't she ever say it to you?"

The tears that once accumulated inside me had become empathetic pools.

Happiness was like an escaped wheelbarrow rolling down a hill. You needed to control it, to tie it with a rope and to pull it along with you. It was the one thing I knew how to do well, hold on to that rope for people who'd lost their grip. I'd had enough practice.

My ex-husband had tried to tear it from me. In time, I forgot the way he'd stare at me without blinking. Yet I'd always recall how it was all about getting up and walking away. Then, it was just a matter of how many seconds it would take me to reach the open window, to open the cupboard and stick my head in, to take deep breaths in the backyard as I hung laundry. This is how I lived for a year, pressing my mettle between my lips. I became a very still and very quiet person. By the time I was nineteen, I knew how easily a person could falter under a stillborn sky, even when she had once been independent and strong. Yes, that was another life, and I was another person then.

Many times abandoned, I now spent my life trying to hold on to people.

Wild Acres was my transition, my threshold of invisibility. I still donned a baseball cap and sunglasses, my hair pulled back tight in a ponytail, adequate camouflage. I'd gotten so good at disappearing that I thought nothing of spending my days cleaning, taking the residents on walks, helping Dr. B. with paperwork, buying groceries and extra pairs of slippers. In those days, you weren't expected to be more than a shadow if you weren't in love.

I told myself that caretaking could consume me. But the bougainvillea here were wild, spinning hope into my eyes. Within just a short period of time, I'd watched their brilliant pink petals and remembered I'd once been a person with dreams. I had dipped in and out of life's peripheral vision for years. But the residents of Wild Acres changed all that. They needed me. They saw me. They brought me back. They found me.

ONE MORNING, MY beeper went off. Mrs. Green had fallen. She grasped my hand as if I were a life preserver as I pulled her up. After I put ointment on her knee, I made her a nest out of the brightly colored afghans she'd knitted. She sat on the gold couch. Her hands were shaky, her voice tremulous. I made her drink some orange juice and checked her medication. She sighed with relief as I put cream on her hands. Then I combed her hair up in waves, so as to cover the spots that had thinned, just as I did every day. I sprayed hairspray over the whole thing to hold it in place. "Beautiful. Stunning, as usual," I announced.

"You're good to me, Ruthie. I know you have other things to do."

"We're friends," I told her. She smiled, her large brown eyes welling up. I felt like a warrior for good. She took my face in her hands and told me I was her angel. Yet Dolly maintained that it was time for me to fly.

I walked down to the pier after everyone was asleep. I was lucky to be back here, I knew. It was a homecoming. I'd found good work, but still it was hard to be here. Here was where my mother had died. Here was where the sea lion had been shot. Here was where a childhood had been captured, if only to be released. I missed my sister. Even though I felt I was making great strides, there was a loneliness that ate away at me. That is why Dolly insisted that I join her at a bar the next week for New Year's Eve, to celebrate the good things to come. Almost two years had passed, and it was time I stepped out, she said. And that is why I now walked barefoot across the cool wood, all the way to the end of the pier, where I imagined a wedding canopy knit of stars. I wrapped my arms around myself as I stared down at the rough black water, curling my toes over the edge. Under the chuppah, a bride traditionally circled the groom seven times, just as the world was built in seven days. Seven signified wholeness in Judaism, something that neither person in a marriage could attain separately. I wanted it for myself.

Here, I let myself cry. Here, no one would notice. I watched seven of my tears drop like quiet stones into the moonlit water, without causing so much as a ripple.

Chapter Twelve

December 31, 1987

WHEN I LOOKED at this man for the first time, I knew how our relationship would end. I knew how my sheets would crease with sand in the afternoon, and where he'd want to be touched. I knew what he'd want for his dinner and how he'd roll over in the middle of the night and whisper in my ear. I knew how far he'd push me beyond comfort, and how I'd come to crave the scent of the ocean he'd leave on my skin, on my pillow, on my green curtains. I knew what he'd say when he lied to me about when he was going to return, and I knew the fifty-seven ways he would break my heart.

Still, I shook his hand, feeling the strength of his thick callused fingers grasping mine like a soft plum.

"Graham. Scottish," he said. In the flicker of the disco ball, his lips were pewter, his skin a placid dove gray. Shifting his weight, he seemed the slightest bit nervous, which I appreciated. I watched his dark hair fall in finger-pulled clumps down his back as he let go of my hand and turned to reach across the bar for his glass.

"I'm Ruthie. Ruth, biblical," I said.

"I'm the blasphemous sister," Dolly said.

He laughed, emptying his glass, his pale green eyes fixed on mine. They were tinged with the color of the sea during a red tide, I noticed. Dolly kicked me under the table. Hours earlier, she'd said love was coming. The small bag of jasmine that she carried in her waist wallet had spun things all around, and couldn't I sense it in the wind? For two weeks, she had been casting love spells from a book. She said our dreams of being wives and mothers were already written in the book of destiny. It would happen one day. But in the meantime, stop falling in love with the wrong men. Stop confusing love with pity.

This is why I wore the necklace of rose quartz that Dolly had just given to me.

I couldn't even swim when I met the father of my child, Naida. Not at first.

Hours earlier, Dolly watched me pulling a towel through my wet hair and then draw on blue eyeliner. She said she felt love in her bones.

"You know you don't need to do that," she said, when I put on my wire-rimmed glasses as if to take all the air out of things, apprehension and possibility.

"Leave them off, Moose," she said. "You look Amish."

No. I kept them on. Dolly put on a white tank top and miniskirt. I slipped on the plainest and most comfortable thing I owned, a black cotton sundress, long to the ankles, my calm belied by rivulets of sweat rolling across my freckled chest and down my sides, dampening my dress in splotches.

When we arrived at the bar, she leaned up against me. I could tell she'd been missing me. The more clipped her speech, the more she hurt. We had been used to physical closeness. Now, even when in a large room, we took up no more than a cubic foot of space, as if we were still back in that station wagon. It hastened the ease with which we settled into a new experience or moment.

I grabbed her hand in the flash of the red strobe light and pulled her onto the dance floor. "No, Moose. What are you thinking?" she called. Whirling our bodies with abandon, our long hair streaked with light, we danced to rap music. We faced each other, holding hands crossed at the wrists, and leaned back. We spun around as fast as we could, pulling against each other's weight to keep from falling, our feet moving fast, our hair whipping through the smoky bar as faces blurred by. Dolly had always been my counterbalance. I looked at my sister with her lovely dark eyes and her fast-talking ways. I wanted to hug her, all the vulnerable and forgotten parts of her. I circled Dolly seven times and told her I'd never leave her. As we danced, we flung our hair back to remember the girls we had been.

We kicked our cowboy boots up on the empty chairs, confident there was nothing to be saved from. We were doing well, both of us working, I at Wild Acres and Dolly as a bartender at night while in school for social work in San Diego, never having the time to visit me enough. We were not holding our breath, hoping to be found. We had climbed out from under the weight of our childhood. We had already won.

We wanted to be not like some girls. We wanted to be all girls, all those who would come after us, and all those who had come before. We wanted the questions asked by women generation after generation. We wanted to hold the labels in our hands, to turn them around, to take them apart. The need to label was the need to diminish. Supplicant. Seductress. Slut. You could only be one thing. That was the rule. You had to choose. Or it would choose for you. We'd been raised with the need to know where we stood. We wanted to draw lines, and yet our spirits bucked at the thought. We craved what dwelled inside the circle, and we craved the circle itself, to cross it, and to be that lovely curved line that found itself where it had begun. We ached to capture the essence that was ours, to run like mad with it, holding it like a kite with colored tails in the air. We wanted to feel the light of youth under our feet as we ran.

They were probably thinking us loose girls, with our blue eyeliner and damp red hair, the women at the table next to us, the ones with the long hard stares.

That burning tree. That apple orchard. That strawberry field. That stone with wings. That girl. The one you sneered at. The one you judged. The one that might be you.

Moonlight shimmied up the craggy rocks, escaping across the docks near Alamitos Bay. I glanced at the foggy window, following Graham's silhouette. Despite myself, I wondered if he'd come back. I had seen it before, the way a distancing silhouette could shimmer with a silvery hue, making it appear abrupt and close. Now, as schools of tiny fish darted around the concrete pilings beneath the pier, frenzied by the lights spilling on the surface as if kicked from an open paint can, the beat of drums thumped with finality beneath the docks. I fixed my eyes on the light, noticing the way it defined the shape of the past and illuminated the present. Life would plow forward, regardless of whether you refused to move on. There were shouts and whoops. People partied on their boats. I'd seen some swimming out to the oil rigs while pushing floating thermoses filled with wine, casting out the sea lions from their home. I'd imagined the sea lions would wait in the water, watching.

There were people finding each other right now, coming together, making love on the docks, some who would later stare up at the sky perhaps with regret, praying the new year would come fast, bringing them a clean slate. Or perhaps not, perhaps they'd be amazed they'd found each other just in the nick of time on a night when last-minute mistakes could be made without worry, when strangers could arrive and disappear almost unnoticed. And yet somehow they'd captured something quiet and permanent.

"May we always find truth in books," I said, pulling my mother's 1979 almanac out of my bag, pressing its worn yellow cover and wrinkled dog-eared pages to my chest in the smoky bar.

"Oh, Moose. I haven't seen that in years. Read what it says about today?"

I closed my eyes. "What do you think Mom would say about the moon tonight?"

"She'd say the red tide and the Blue Moon were conspiring to help us. That the blue represented the past sadness and the red represented the fire that would bring us renewal, just as the forest fires brought new brush. Something along those lines."

"Perfect," I told her, slipping the book back into my bag.

Our mother always had a story after she'd disappeared, one that brought us back to life. People would always try to hold on to you, to keep you in myriad ways. They'd walk across the oceans and stand watch in the trees.

I watched Dolly down her shot of whiskey, swearing 1988 would be the best year yet. When the countdown began and the patrons cheered, Graham reappeared; I dropped my glass. Streamers cut through the air in the frenzy of confetti and bleating horns. People kissed. Strangers hugged. Graham knelt, trying to gather the shards in his hands. Callused hands from life on a fishing boat, he would tell me.

"Let me," I said. I dropped a cloth napkin over it. He moved out of the way.

I handed him the covered fist of broken glass and followed him out onto the patio to see what he was doing. He was a fisherman, his arms stained with salt marks. He was an eagle who now flew across the sand, silvery, holding the glass in his talons. I waited, watching him standing by the ocean. He whipped the napkin back, scattering pieces of glass, capturing light like the flash of fishtails against the darkness.

Maybe this was never broken glass at all.

The Blue Moon was a time for reversals. It created an open seam in the universe and allowed in things that existed in a state of unrest. Mistakes could be undone. In-betweeners—the girls, the boys, and certain animals that had wandered into unknown places, confused by storms and the changes in the earth's magnetization—could find their rightful path home. And the moon, too. The moon had been made smaller by God so it would not rival the sun, because God thought that two queens could not share a crown, Dr. B. had said. One day God would return the moon to its rightful size.

Dolly looked flushed when I returned with Graham. Graham pulled up a chair and ordered another drink. "You littered the beach," Dolly told him.

"Glass turns back to sand," Graham said.

"Oh, please," she said, and then a stranger reached around and started kissing her, tugging on her necklace. It made me mad that she was smiling. She drifted across the room like a ribbon in his arms, and I didn't see her again all night.

I brought Graham home that night, filled with the anticipation of impossible things, floating skyscrapers, and white strawberries that never ripened. I had called my sister, who said she'd left with the guy she'd met. She was at his apartment, and they were going for a night swim. I said I was worried about her. She said I should worry about myself; she was fine.

Graham's eyes were rimmed with red. I gave him the ninety-nine-cent tour of my apartment on the beach, the Murphy bed that pulled out of the wall, the walk-in closet that housed my guitar and a futon for Dolly's rare visits, and the pink-tiled bathroom with its glorious claw-foot bathtub like the one my mother had loved so well.

We sat on my porch. He crossed his long legs, his black boots resting on the railing. Hands folded behind his head, he leaned back and glanced at the sky. I'd never ever seen such a pomegranate of stars. He was from an island off the northern coast of Scotland, loved the ocean, everything about it. Loved to fish. Love to swim. Had never married. Had come close twice, and didn't regret anything. Was friends with his exes. Feared birds, but didn't know why. This seemed backwards to me.

"Are you a good swimmer?" he asked.

"Not in real life. Is that important to you?" I asked, and imagined taillights receding into the darkness. He held my gaze, his green eyes warming. I felt my cheeks flush and had to look away. He reached out, his hand resting for a moment on my thigh.

"I'm not going to sleep with you," I said.

"I didn't ask."

"Then why are you here?"

"Loneliness," he said, looking straight at me.

GRAHAM WANDERED THROUGH my apartment on that first night, touching everything, my guitar, the snow globe of the strawberry that Dolly had given me, and my palm tree curtains, the last memento of the old motel. In the lunar glow of the full moon, his skin was pale, glistening, would always be moist and warm, and smooth, his body covered by a layer of downy hair, I would discover, but for the whiskers on his face. Something was different about him, different from other men I'd known. I could feel it even then. As I listened to his stories, I became keenly aware of what I had always known, that a woman could love herself into anything. She could tell herself to see things from a new angle, to get a fresh perspective, to step away from the situation, but it was just a reprieve from what she knew in her gut. That first night and after, Graham's world reached into the darkest, deepest parts of my mind. If he spent most of his time out there in the ocean, wouldn't it make sense that some of the fury and roar of that ocean would return with him and pour into me? His body was large, his shoulders wide, and his stance wider. Yet he moved with precision. I watched as he peered at the one photograph on my wall, a black-and-white of my mother. He took an extraordinary amount of time examining it, tracing its outline with his fingers.

I kept my walls intentionally bare but for that one image. Somehow it seemed right that it would be only her. In the picture, she is sitting on top of our car with her almanac in her lap and her guitar at her feet. She had signed her name, fancy, in red pen, "For Ruthie, from your favorite mother."

I told him the story of The Most Beautiful Lady in the World, about the little boy who had lost and found her. Why else would my mother have told me this story other than to teach me how to see her?

"All mothers will fail their daughters."

"Why do you say that?" I asked.

"Because a mother is her daughter's first love," he said.

HE ASKED IF he could teach me to swim. I didn't answer, and I appreciated that he let this go. Graham was tender with me in his own way, in a way I needed and in a way that no one else understood. He was always unshaven, but that was part of the attraction, too. I stared at him from the other end of the couch, my legs tucked underneath me, the afghan around my shoulders.

"Do you like me?" he whispered, tugging on the blue fringe.

"I've never brought a man home from a bar before," I told him.

"Well, how is it so far?" He could always make me smile.

I leaned over and kissed him. He pulled me on top of him, and we continued to kiss. It was in brushstrokes, mostly, in whispers, our lips drifting together and apart, over and around the shape of shadows, just that way for hours. We slept and woke easily, lying there on the carpeting. He transported me with descriptions of old Viking ships off the coast of Scotland, deserted stone beaches, frigid gray waters, tall

Stone Age monuments that reached into blue skies. I imagined the lush green hills, craggy rocks, and resplendent stone cathedrals that rose up from the mountains he spoke of. A box of colored pencils, which I sometimes used while Mrs. Green painted, spilled from his hands. In blues and greens, he sketched a scene of waterhorses that haunted the coast of Scotland, ridden by the Finmen, territorial creatures that cut the fishing lines of mortal fishermen and rowed invisible boats from Orkney to Norway in just seven strokes. I taped it to the refrigerator.

He could see I was a person who could get carried away by stories.

Almost a year. That's how long Graham eclipsed my world and reintroduced me to the glow of the full moons. He had little interest in practical things, and most things that measured and gauged time. He brought gifts—shells, starfish, and tiny seahorses. He could not have cared less where things were put away until he needed them, at which point he needed me. Things like an ironing board, a lightbulb, even a needle and thread.

Each time he came to visit, he'd toss his wetsuit onto the porch, spreading it to dry over the white patio chair beside the baskets of bougainvillea.

That first night, he walked over to the bookshelf and picked up one of my old encyclopedias. When he opened it up, the dried rose from my violation fell onto the gray carpet.

"This is your past, yes?" he said. I nodded, trying to appear calm.

But he remained quiet. He was removed from meaning. This was a breath of fresh air for me because I was born a person who was empathetic and superstitious, and who assigned meaning to everything, and because of it, I probably suffered more than I should have. The rose petals dissolved when he picked up the stem. I watched the dust tuft into the air.

"DO YOU THINK the divine comes to whiskey-addled mothers in green station wagons who drag around two little girls and teach them to obsessively watch the moon?" Dolly asked.

She'd come to a prayer group at Wild Acres. On Wednesday nights, I attended a small prayer circle led by Dr. B. and Mrs. Green. Though some wouldn't use a tallith at night, Mrs. Green wore her husband's long white woolen tallith over her shoulders, its corners tied with specially knotted fringes. She carried it with her wherever she went, back and forth to the hospital and later to hospice to be with him.

We met in the lobby after-hours, our notebooks open on our laps, our pens scrawling words and pictures as we talked. Mrs. Green would kiss the prayer shawl and fling it up and around her shoulders like a cape. Then with arms extended, she'd let it drape over us to create a spiritual canopy as we gathered underneath it, a safe space that announced we were crossing the threshold of the divine, preserving a holy place where our prayers would be magnified. We'd offer prayers of love, trying to elevate ourselves and our thoughts. We'd welcome the Shekhinah, the female essence of God, the divinity that dwelled in the space of connection, dropping down onto the earth when called by certain prayers, by music or art, by a husband speaking lovingly to a wife, by the harmony that filled a home on the Sabbath, by those who were sick or suffering. This was a whole other sort of Judaism than the backseat version I had grown up on, and yet it spoke to me.

Pulling on her long black sweater, Dr. B. told us to imagine a female God reaching down to illuminate ordinary things that humans could do, little things that could create boundless peace, drawing soul mates together, filling a home with warmth when a wife promised fidelity in loving whispers and meant it. And perhaps that is what my mother meant when she said, "Blessed be the moon."

The full moon represented the reappearance of the Shekhinah, I learned.

"Some say whoever recites the blessing over the new moon welcomes the Shekhinah," Dr. B. said. "And yes, Ruthie. Your mother knew that, too." I recalled how they'd talk on the porch, how they spoke of the men who cheated and the daughters who would one day run the country. My mother wanted to keep the promise of the Shekhinah alive for us, to stand in, as if an apology, like a piece of pink ribbon wound around our ankles, a reminder that the divine flourished among those who were lost, which we so often were, and those who practiced mitzvoth, good deeds, which we so often did. A reminder of redemption, it fled when there were actions harmful to others. A karmic rubber band would not always snap back immediately, but the time would come. There were wrongs done when people abused the power they had. "There's magic for that, too. But that's a discussion for later," said Dr. B. The Shekhinah came, also, to lovers in kisses. Kisses were the beginning of all love. Binding attachments.

I'd been looking at Dr. B.'s books in her massive office library. The divine had been pictured as a stone with wings, as a great eagle, as a mother, a pregnant woman with a glow, a daughter. She'd been represented through time as a healer and a warrior. The dividing line between men and women, believers and nonbelievers, and the separation between people of all walks and beliefs, created all the ills of the world. Mrs. Green would pray about this, insisting on life when she went to sit by her husband's bedside most mornings. Graham would teach me to claim it as my own, the separation, before we could heal it.

TREES FLASHED BY. Puddles caught fire. The stars lit the way as I pedaled to the Bougainvillea Castle. I saw the single rose stem. I was dreaming of that night. Graham had covered me with my blue afghan and was staring at me when I opened my eyes. I pulled my knees in to my chest, just as I always did when I'd grapple with what had happened, going over and over it in my mind, forcing myself to assign blame. I needed to figure it out, to pull it apart like strands of yarn, to examine each separate piece. I needed to know where I stood.

I told Graham the story of my ravaged virginity. I knew I could tell it with the distance and authority of a news reporter. "I was called a slut," I said, letting the dark word pierce the air, vulgar and hungry, its wings frayed. "Some said I got what was coming because I wore blue eyeliner." I looked away. He reached out and brushed my cheek.

"You were a kid, Ruthie. Just a kid."

"You should probably run like hell," I said. "I would if it were me."

"No, Ruthie, you wouldn't." Graham pulled off his white shirt, turning slightly so I could see his back. It was covered with a road map of deep scars. Illuminated in the moonlight, pale pink, brown, and silvery grubs had melded torn flesh. Scars were my first language, stories that pulled me in with their history. A battle fought, won or lost. Scars drew my eyes like black ice, or the glow of blue-capped waves.

"Girls used to call me Sea Monster. I grew the beard to hide the acne marks on my face," he said. My ache for him was visceral.

I sank onto my knees. These were tangible things I could put my hands on. "It's just skin. Not good or bad. Just skin," I told him. He took off the silver chain with its gleaming dragon pendant and placed it around my neck.

My throat tightened as my tears began to spill across his back. My fingers instinctively knew what to do. I circled the scars with my hands, moving my fingers up each vertebra, one by one. As the rain pummeled the uncovered patio furniture,

I pictured the bougainvillea opening up wide, as though swallowing all of it. My grief was somehow deeper, or perhaps I was just feeling the depths of it. I pushed my thumbs between his muscles, moving them in and out. Outside, the wind swept across the windows. Ruthless weather. I leaned down and pressed my cheek against his back and listened to the rise and fall of his breath, trying to memorize the drumbeat.

He turned over and pulled me down onto him, keeping his hands pressed on the small of my back. At once, our lips met perfectly. Graham held me on the carpet, his fingers weaving across my body.

"Do you always ask for the opposite of what you want?" he said. I touched his lips. Then I drew back my fingers. He took my hand and placed it over his pants, and I cupped my hand over him. Then he slipped his hand between my thighs. Graham untied the straps of my dress and pulled them down off my shoulders. He kissed my breasts, and moved to my stomach, and then down around my belly. He pushed his face between my legs.

"Wait," I said, sitting up.

"I'll go slow," he whispered, peering into my eyes. "You can say stop."

I nodded. Slowly, I eased back, keeping watch. I felt his shoulders bumping against my inner thighs and the warmth of his mouth as he kissed me. I felt myself taken by the sky. The whole expanse of it, mine. Before, I didn't have words for what this was, the colors of lost virginities, the gold-green hunger, the pale blue expectation, the burnt-orange fear, the blistering red desire, the white of forgetting—now the colors swirled above me, braided together in one long rope held by the Shekhinah, as she held out her arms, letting the rope untwine and escape through her fingers into a burgeoning fire, rimming me in flames. I'd never felt this. I wanted to name it, to call it something corporeal— lust, bright and intense—but it wasn't only that. Not bad, not damaged. Life-giving. Let me be damned for experiencing this body. Graham felt me as I held on to him. Then, slowly, as I curled away, trembling, he gathered me in his arms on the carpet. I shivered against his warmth, his beard scratching my cheeks as he kissed me.

WHEN I WOKE up, I moved his legs off me. Flesh was so much heavier in the morning than at night, I thought. I folded his jeans and white shirt and made a pot of coffee. I heard the waves lapping at the shoreline as I listened to him breathing. I sat at my small butcher-block table and watched him from across the room, trying to burn the image into my memory, the trail of water his long brown hair left on the carpet, the movement of his hand opening and closing into a fist, capturing and releasing. I was already letting him go.

As I stood in front of the bathroom mirror, I wiped away the smudge of blue eyeliner and let the mirror reveal me. Pale, freckled. Big-boned. I had put on weight. My once small breasts were spilling out of my bra. My hips were fuller. I had gray-blue circles under my eyes. My lips looked raw, bitten. My red hair appeared a pale gold, hollow like straw. I had brought a stranger home on the first day of the year, something I never did.

"Morning, Ruthie-Ruth," Graham said, leaning up against the doorway.

I startled. I grabbed my glasses from the vanity. "I have to go to work. I'm glad we met," I said. I offered him coffee, but he said he had to go. Suddenly in the light we were strangers.

After he dressed and gathered his wetsuit in a drawstring net, he pointed at the window. I glanced at the rainbow as I untangled my curls with my fingers. He picked up his net and told me about an old Scottish superstition, about rainbows and how they were celebrated on certain occasions. A rainbow was a sign that a baby was about to be born. The rainbow would end at the home of the birth. *"There's abrig fur a beuy barin."*

"What does that mean, exactly?" I asked, watching him in the mirror.

"There's a bridge for a boy child."

I put on my glasses. "Happy New Year."

THAT NIGHT, AFTER he'd gone, I fished Mrs. Green's house key from the drain. Then I walked down to the ocean with an orange pail in my hands, my heart pounding. As the water ebbed around my ankles, I bent down and ran my fingers through the waves. My dragon pendant reflected the moonlight across the water. Water had memory, held the shape of every place it had ever been. Love, like grief, could travel within its crystalline molecules, filling every new shape, making it appear as if it had come just for you. I scooped ocean water into the orange pail to pour it into my bath. I was beginning to need the ocean.

For nights after, I would dream of Graham walking toward me through the burgundy hallways. In a state of half-wake, I'd get up and run through my apartment in my dark blue night-shirt, thinking I heard his knock. But there would be no one at the door, no sound but the gulls, diving for bits of plastic toys that washed up on the beach.

Perhaps his fear of birds kept him away, I told myself. I'd wake suddenly, and I'd move over in the bed to make space for his body.

That single rose appeared in the patterns of my drapes whenever the moonlight crept through. The vines outside crawled over everything and opened up—to me, in what would soon be my newly in-love state. They would reek of the whispers of bodies in heat, of sweating bodies tumbling over one another in motion, and of the abundance that somehow appeared in my life. To the residents they would mark tangled memories. The bushes relished humidity, but more, it was the way they'd climb across the sides of certain houses in Belmont Shore and not others, the way they'd shimmy up and over certain rooftops, ruthless, all-consuming, sometimes even climbing over cars that had not been driven. It was clear what they spoke of.

Chaos. The blossoms fed on what was whirling inside and the vibrations in the air all around. It was the perfect place for me.

Chapter Thirteen

1988

D R. B. TOLD Dolly and me a story once, after we'd returned to the Twin Palms for good when we were kids. It was called "The People Who Would Hide in the Skins of Animals." They were a distant tribe. They lived in a faraway place in the ocean and would come to you in secret. They would rise out of the water, shedding their animal skin, and become human. They could make you fall in love with them. They'd make you think you'd never loved anything or anyone before. You'd never know where they went when they left you. Only that they had escaped your love again. Only that unlike you, they lived in two worlds. Sometimes if you had their child, they'd return and bring the child a skin that held the magical powers of the ocean.

Sometimes, you might be one of them but just not know it.

Then, when they'd come for you, you'd change, your body no longer the body you knew. You'd swim through the waves, fast. Your every movement, every decision, ruled by instinct, as if breathing, as if the orbiting earth.

You'd know the ways of the fish and the habits of the giant green waterhorses that tried to drown you if you suddenly climbed onto their backs unannounced, their tails like wheels. Your body would become large and powerful, your skin as sleek as fur. You'd be afraid of nothing, your heart drumming beats, your blood thick like rushing rivers. You'd know the signs of white skies, the direction of the wings of the seabirds, and the invisible places where the emerald pools stilled on the floors of coral caves. The magic of sea mist would turn your eyes to the future, allowing you the gift of second sight. You could begin storms, rescue swimmers torn from the saddles of waterhorses.

You had to be careful. If you accepted their animal skin, you would always be torn between two worlds, land and sea. You'd never feel completely at home in either. You would always miss the place you were before, the place where you no longer were now, and the ones who loved you in that place, who couldn't go with you.

"What would you do, Ruthie? Would you take the animal skin?" Dr. B. asked.

"She would. I wouldn't," said Dolly.

I'd been hiding. "Would I be able to still see my sister?" I asked.

ON JANUARY'S WOLF Moon, I woke up with the taste of salt on my lips. Just weeks after I'd met Graham, I marched down to the ocean and waded out up to my waist, farther than I had ever gone. I had only ever walked into the Pacific up to my ankles, to leave fish for my sea lions, and on rare occasions to my knees. I was alternately drawn to and terrified of the water. Still, the waves piled up. The undertow bucked. It kicked up sand, trying to knock me off balance. But I resisted.

Not the smartest thing to do. Not the safest thing to do. None of it was.

Everything appeared captured, or perhaps it was I who was captured by everything. The red tides had come, turning the sea into a red noose by noon, now haunted by glowing blue caps. Prey was scarce. Hunters would wade through empty landscapes, swearing they saw animals in the storm clouds. Light could engage emotion, causing you to read messages in the random spill of driftwood across the beach if you felt abandoned. The moon could warm the waves when you were feeling as if the world, and everybody in it, had frozen you out. The tips of palm fronds could appear burnt as if holding on to the memory of daylight. You might think, if only for a moment, that the glowing waves had been caused by your need for a greater sense of power over your life. Then you'd see it was only water.

On this night, the waves swelled up lace on the beach, pooling in my footprints. This bioluminescence was the effect of single-celled organisms that formed toxic blooms. When disturbed by a wave, a fin, or a swimmer's kick, they released an enzyme that appeared as a luminescent hue.

"Swirl it," I told Dolly, after she'd captured some of the water in a glass jar. We put it on my porch, swirling it every so often to create enough light to read by, just as our mother had used the moonlight for this very reason.

I steered clear of the teenagers on the beach sitting around a bonfire, who were smoking pot in hooded gray sweatshirts. I walked far enough away that the scent of marijuana dissolved into the salty air and my image was unrecognizable. Now, I took my clothes off, hands clasped behind my head just as Dolly and I used to do while riding bikes with no hands at night. This is how I entered the sea. I knelt so that my hair was soaked with seawater. I had done this before and would do this after this night, time and time again. On nights like this, I swore my hair grew longer. I stood in that water, watching the light play upon the waves, and I pictured Graham's profile, the slope of his neck and the width of his shoulders, and I tried to trick myself into thinking that I could see him. But all I could see were little jellyfish floating on top of the water like moonlit snowflakes, and the sea lions thrusting up through the skin of water, spilling white foam.

The longer I stayed out there, legs numbed to my thighs, the stronger I felt.

"He's not coming back. It's a one-night thing," Dolly said over the phone. "Let it go."

I told her I would not.

Now, I recognized a hazy figure in the ocean, the waves swirling around his shoulders. So one could say he was, indeed, a fisherman. One could say his boat couldn't dock here in Long Beach, with its crowded marina. One could say it had dropped him off far from shore so he had to swim in. Some boats were hard to dock at night.

I jumped up and waved, but he didn't see me. I called his name, and the image disappeared.

Later, as I sat on my porch, shivering, letting the whiskey burn my throat, I spotted the animals.

Three female sea lions were watching me from the waves, their brown bodies tumbled on the sand, revealing spotted bellies. Their noses were sharper, finer than the others I'd seen, their eyes a soft black. Huddling against the winds, they reminded me of Dolly and me as children, always keeping an eye on the rogue parent. From this night on, they would pile up like tossed blankets, folding and unfolding. Sometimes they appeared as boulders, and then other times as clouds, their coats drying to a bluish-purple hue. They'd bundle against each other, bodies overlapping as if there were not enough space, as if they were trying to ward off what was coming, when really there were miles of ocean and beach, and yet I—and Dolly— understood the natural inclination to be close.

I named them the Sisters, for they never strayed too far from each other. Female sea lions would gather in groups to pro- tect each other from competitive males looking to mate, Dr. B. would tell me, watching them from my porch. I'd rush down to the beach, creeping across the sand to kneel a few feet away, watching to see how they could do it—remain together.

Night after night, they slept beneath my porch. While Mr. Takahashi and some other residents complained about the high-pitched barking, I secretly relished it. Their noise crowded my loneliness. Some renegades would even leave fish for them.

No one knew it was me.

They would ward off storms and danger with their flashing dark eyes. They'd watch me as I carried clean sheets and fresh towels from room to room, as I'd climb up and down stairs. Each day, I'd pull sheets from the clothesline strung across the courtyard, peeling nightgowns from the salty air and tucking shirttails into drawers. The residents would check their reflections in the freshly washed windows when they forgot themselves—I gathered the reflections of my people and the Sisters, both at the same time.

I was not afraid of hard work. I patched holes in the cracked cream-colored walls, steamed the wall-to-wall gray shag in all the apartments. The Sisters grew frenzied when Wild Acres became a revolving door. Too many new people, pieces of furniture, stacks of books, framed photographs, and old records tossed around. The residents—with knotted fingers pressed to their thin white lips—had become my family. I knew them well. I would fill in their words for them when they forgot what they were saying, like sand into canals. They could not get enough of me, even when I wanted to disappear. Each time one of the nighttime "travelers" escaped, they'd trip the new alarm system Dr. B. had installed, which would call me out from hiding. I'd race out at night to capture them.

They said I was their lucky angel.

I took Mrs. Green for long walks, her large white hat and sunglasses warding off sunlight. The Sisters retreated into the foam when I set up Mrs. Green's easel on the beach, watching the swoop and arc of her sable brush across the waves, her gold bangles sliding down her wrists. The Sisters would look up suddenly, as if called by an inaudible voice alerting them to escape. They came and went, always without warning, attuned to their own drumbeats.

I painted each door a different color so the residents could find their places. Just as she'd done before, Dr. B. put a moonstone in my pocket whenever she thought of it, telling me it was for protection. I never asked against what. I never knew I could paint. I never knew I could stand next to the ocean without wanting to run, without thinking of the desert.

"Ruthie, you can do anything you can imagine yourself doing," Dolly told me over the phone.

"You sound like Mom," I said, and yet I was grateful.

With a paintbrush in my hands, I could make things up. I gave Dr. B. a yellow-gold door because she held the lasso that kept people from getting lost. Mr. Takahashi's door was painted white, to help him sleep. Regal purple for Mrs. Green, because she could forget all she was.

"Ruthie, I've never seen you as happy. Do you know you sing when you paint?" Mrs. Green stood a few feet away as I knelt on a drop cloth in the hallway, clutching a wide thick brush covered with blue paint. "I have a surprise," she said, the gray feathers of her hair wrapped in a flowing pink scarf. She hooked her arm in mine as we walked out to the beach, her scarf whipping crisply in the wind. My eyes focused forward, concentrating on the gift in front of me.

Two easels stood, side by side. "Let me have my joy," she said. My cheeks grew flushed. "I don't even know how to paint."

"It's another language, Ruthie. A fine one, if you can learn it."

"What if I'm no good at it?"

"You have a good teacher," she said. She would teach me to trust the currents of my own imagination, to navigate my thoughts. She'd teach me to paint wet on wet and wet on dry, both ways of interacting with the paint. When you understood a thing, it gave back to you, could bring you energy though you believed you were expending energy to do it. The paint would fight you unless you understood it, just like the weather. Just like people.

She'd teach me that the old master painters made calculations about light and shadow. Mathematical. Precise. They added and subtracted depth, she explained.

"See here, the hairs of these brushes should be stiff and snap back into place," she said. She had brushes and palette knives in cups. Flats would create sharp edges, and filberts, rounded strokes. Her "favorites" were two size 12's, two 6's, and two size 2 small ones. "Do you like it?"

I nodded. "No one has ever given me anything like this," I whispered.

In no time, my kitchen was filled with boxes of paint supplies—rags and turpentine, gesso, and tools. I became a collector of colors—Ultramarine, Viridian, Cadmium Red. Each had a temperament and would take to the canvas differently.

No matter what, you had to know at what point the paint would refuse you. I worked on my canvases, splashing dabs of crimson, desire; white that kept my secrets; and blue, which deepened into sudden careful thought. I liked a shade of soft lavender that wanted both to be seen and to remain quiet.

Mrs. Green showed me how to scrape away paint with the end of the brush when the colors would mix, turning to brown. "Slow down, Ruthie. You can't learn everything at once. Take your time. You're still just a baby."

"Twenty-one," I said.

I sat alone with the paints at night, learning which colors liked each other and which would create a sharp hedge. What would my mother say about all this, I wondered, about the ladders I drew in the waves, making them reach into the clouds? I imagined her leaning up against the car in the hot desert sun, smoking a cigarette and staring at the heavens.

Mrs. Green called me her protégé as our relationship deepened during afternoons of painting together. We were living parallel lives, both of us waiting and not waiting for someone to return from a distant world.

My car broke down by the side of the road, a white Honda that Dolly called Little Ugly. I was almost grateful to be free of it. While it was in the shop, I traveled by bicycle. My own muscles would carry me, making me aware of my strength. Each evening, I biked beyond Belmont Shore into downtown Long Beach, to a noisy little haven called Sheet Metal Moon Café, named for the metal furniture with its scoured patina. There, the tall palm trees with their feathery fronds reached over the buildings as the oil well pumps lifted toward the bright stars. Beneath the steel and cement forest, the Teutonic plates shifted, and a green waterhorse raced through emerald labyrinths, roiling the earth with its tail like a wheel, I'd tell Dolly.

The Sheet Metal Moon Café became my home away from Wild Acres, a painted-gold respite. At any time of day or night, a group of children gathered outside on their bicycles. Maybe they liked the huge picture window that was always strung with Christmas lights, or the round metal tables that made tinny sounds when drummed. I'd sit at the same table, sipping coffee and reading from my mother's almanacs, which I'd recovered from the storage room. The calendar pages contained charts for each month, long narrow columns filled with planetary symbols, times of high tide, rising and setting suns and moons, full-moon names, and other astronomical and planetary data. My mother had marked up the pages with notes and hand-drawn pictures. Her scribbles streamed across the columns. I deciphered her notes, trying to correlate them with my memories of my past. Had I finally captured her? Beyond what I saw as a child, beyond what had appeared so random to me?

There were fifteen almanacs in all, the first, 1965, skipping 1966—the year of my birth—then from 1967 through 1980, the year of her death. The more I read, the more I saw certain scribbles repeated in several months and through different years. These included but were not limited to:

Good moon-Bad man. Or the converse: *Bad moon-Good man.* And then: *Good moon-Good man.*

In her 1972 almanac, she'd drawn two palm trees and written *El Niño storm—Twin Palms-Sea Lion.*

Her 1975 almanac was the most marked up. She'd drawn a strawberry at the top of October's page, circled and *x*'d out—*Lou's farm.* Following that, she'd written a list, marking what I gathered were her feelings about the divorced almost-husband, when we lived in the in-law apartment. She wrote:

A list of what my Name is Not: Dana, Dara, Danna . . . MY NAME IS DIANA. In the November pages, she'd drawn little Joshua trees, and a note: *Lost in desert. Where is my True North?*

And then, *Joshua Tree.*

If the almanac's covers reflected historical events, my mother wove them into her story. She was resourceful. The "1976 Bicentennial Issue" correlated to a man whom she called The Wanderer. *REVOLUTION—The Wanderer—Do not go back to him.*

In 1979, when we were given our one-bedroom apartment, she wrote: *A Room of Her Own*, with a smiling sun.

In 1980: *The Wanderer Returns.* She'd made a fancy in-love W inside a heart. What had happened to turn things around? I wondered.

Then, her tiny scribbled note: *"Heads," he leaves again. "Tails," he leaves again.*

Followed by: *Good date! When will I see him again?* with tally marks adding up to eighty-nine days, right up to her death that October. The Wanderer was also mentioned in her 1970 almanac, with the words "Santa Monica Pier" and her drawings of music notes over the symbol for water, three scalloped lines, one beneath another, all in a heart. It appeared she'd been riding the waves of a long, tumultuous love affair.

"Did she keep almanacs from the year I was born?" I asked Dr. B. She said she didn't know; 1966 had probably been lost or destroyed.

I LIKED HOW the stiff yellow covers featured wood-engraved black illustrations and lettering. In 1968, it read: *Price 50 Cents* and *Weather Forecasts for All of the USA*. It had a circusy feel, as if designed by Barnum & Bailey. The font was balloonish. There was a small portrait of Benjamin Franklin and, on the right, a portrait of Robert B. Thomas, listed as the almanac's founder.

The main cover design was an oval surrounded by a cornucopia of plants—fruits, grains, grapes, pumpkins, and other foods, along with a farmer's tools. The page was bordered by sheaths of wheat and curling leaves. The title page illustration featured an engraving of Father Time, with angel wings and holding a scythe.

Written along the right-hand side of the 1968 almanac: *Planting Tables, Zodiac Secrets, Recipes, Etc.* Fifty cents was a small price to pay for a map of the universe, I thought. My mother's circled words, arrows, and wrinkled, marked-up, and worn pages told me more than I had ever thought possible. The full moons—their dates and names—created the map of our lives.

Tonight, there was the Snow Moon.

Parking my bike against the palm tree, I looked around and then wrapped my chain lock through the back wheel and the frame and around the gray trunk.

"Hey, lady," I heard someone say. There was nothing but the wind in the nearby alley. White feathers scattered across the sidewalk.

I locked up my bike and started to head inside, reaching for my mother's almanac in my purse.

"Lady. Buy a story for a dollar?" said the voice.

A young girl stepped out of the shadows, wearing a red bandanna around her head. Hands planted on her hips, she was no more than twelve, small for her age, with wide brown eyes and glistening dark skin. She wore a tan trench coat, dirty across the sleeves, her sneakers unlaced. I'd seen her before, hanging out at the pier just as Dolly and I had done.

"Call me Eddie, or Edna. What kind of story do you like? I have all kinds—mysteries, fairy tales, anything," she said, tapping her chin. She smiled, revealing the gap between her two front teeth. A swarm of children on bicycles crowded us. Their black leather jackets reeked of sea air and car exhaust, of nights tucked into the breeze on the beach. They wore necklaces woven with seaweed and copper wire. They held the same sort of fierce determination in their eyes, glazed as if by smoke, by the sort of tumult that seemed too adult and contagious. They'd seen too much of their own futures. Not quite beach rats, not quite city slickers.

Edna sidled up to me, close enough while remaining distant. She leaned in, whispering, "I can stop those kids. You can get me some chili." I nodded. Edna waved her hand, and the children backed away from us, from my bicycle. She lifted her chin, as if we shared some secret language or were on the same team, connected. Old friends. My mother would have liked her, would have called her an in-betweener. I wondered if she disappeared from school and reappeared two months later, two inches taller, with the same too-tight pants, with the same forced-up shoulders. "It's safe. Don't worry," Edna assured me about my bicycle. She held open the thick metal door and followed me into the café, into a cacophony of piped-in music, the grill of voices amped up over the espresso machine. She joined me at my usual table near the window, sitting down heavily on the red velvet seat as I ordered us bowls of chili.

I kept my eyes on the children, their blond hair spun in dreadlocks, their black hair in Afros, their brown hair in stringy brown straw, in auburn curls tufting from underneath bandannas. I could hear the excitement in their voices from all the way in here, over the sound of grinding beans. Laughing and hollering too loud, they kicked up energy everywhere. They broke windows, bones, chain locks on bicycles. They broke away from everything, the sooty beach and the sunlit city streets, their two worlds. I knew they were always hungry. They'd scramble into the street for lit cigarette butts and fill up on smoke, forgetting about food. They slept on the sand and knew the secrets—where the sand still bubbled up with oil, where the blood had been hosed off from the sidewalk, what was said, and what nobody did about it. They started rumors as if setting wildfires. They knew the borders. They could chart the signs in the sky, and they knew about the flurry of white feathers that lifted off the sidewalk, I'd learn. They crowded the sentry palm near the empty lot as if it were a mother hen, its trunk slashed three times with red paint, a symbol of home.

"They're always hunting," Edna said, her eyes stony, reminding me of Dolly and me and the suspiciousness of childhood—what happens to the eyes at around eight, when the trusting baby becomes the little old person. We'd been thieves, too. Of sneakers, bags of chips, water, love, and whatever else we could find.

She told me first of her parents, how she was their American dream. Edna was the good daughter, she said. Her parents told her she was lucky and smart, and so she grew up lucky and smart. A lucky girl, she'd never believed anything different was possible. She said she once jumped like a cat into a garbage can during a drive-by shooting in front of her house, which her mother said was quick, clever thinking. Born lucky, her mother said. All she had to do was not do something stupid and ruin her goddamn life.

She had a knack for adding things up—people, knowing what they wanted. She could also add up stacks of bills that poured into her mother's life—receipts, and numbers written and rewritten over miles and miles of paper bags. Adding things up was her hobby, she said.

"I already got you figured out. You want a story? One dollar."

I placed the money on the table and picked up my mother's almanac, wondering how long Edna would stay. She noticed the cover and her expression changed. Quickly, I put the almanac in my lap under the table and sipped my coffee, watching her relief as she wolfed down her chili. I wondered what Edna would say, and whether her story would have an ending. I remembered how Dolly used to fall asleep with the ripped spiderwebs of stories on her lips. We always fell asleep before the ending came.

Pressing my palms together, I glanced out the window. They tracked a circle around the tree, wolflike. "Those kids. I can't concentrate," Edna said.

She got up, her coat fluttering open, revealing the lining of stitched pockets that held feathers, army knives, stones. She turned and walked outside with one hand in the air, shooing the children away. She was their leader, she'd tell me after. "You'd better get a better bike lock," she said, sliding back into her seat. "You ready for your story?"

I nodded. "Go ahead. I have time."

"Once upon a time, there was a lady who lived by the sea. She was lonely and cried seven tears into the waves. This made a sea animal take notice. The animal came from an island far, far away. He already knew the way here, to Long Beach. He liked the oil islands, him and the rest of his tribe. They would get confused by all the colored lights," she said, nodding at the window, as if at the THUMS Islands. "It looked like the colored lights in the sky where he grew up. The animal peeled off his magic skin and came onto land, becoming a man. The lady fell in love with him. But he always went back to his home in the ocean. It made the woman sad. He was gone, but she had his baby and that made her happy again. Just like always, years passed. Then one day the man came back with a new magic skin for the child. He wanted to take his child away forever to a home in the sea. The child was like him, lived in two worlds though she didn't know it." Edna sat back, satisfied. "How do you like my story so far?"

I was on the edge of my seat. "What was their home like in the sea?"

"An island way up north," she said, holding up her plate. She gestured above it. "There are no trees. It's rocky, and there's a cold wind there. You feel like you're holding an ice cube in your mouth too long."

"Do they all have magic skins up there?" I asked, stirring my chili.

She leaned in, holding the plate in front of her chest and gesturing below it. "Only some. Not the birds. Not the fish."

"Does he come back?" I asked.

She nodded. "Only on the full moon. Only for a few days at a time. Then he has to wait. He might have to wait a month to come back. Maybe a year."

"But you said he would always come back," I said, shifting in my seat.

"Yeah. For his kid. To take it away."

I drew in my breath.

"But the lady fought him every which way to Sunday. A mother will always fight for her kid. He finally went away. Back to the sea. The end."

"A happy-sad ending."

She nodded, rubbing her eyes. "I have all kinds of stories."

I recognized some of the details of Edna's story as being similar to Dr. B.'s story, or what Dolly said about the people who hide in the skins of animals. I wondered if this was an ocean version of an urban myth, a story passed around by word of mouth.

"I need to get home, Edna. Your story was worth the price."

As I stood up to leave, the ground shifted.

My coffee spilled across my lap, staining the pages of November 1979, blurring my mother's notes. The floor tipped; everyone started screaming and rushing around. I caught the shock in Edna's eyes, then her fingers gripping the table. Plates clattered to the floor. I grabbed the back of my chair and sat down, covering my head, peeking out beneath my arm. The glass window quivered like a sheet on a clothesline. The string of Christmas lights knocked against the glass. Stacks of cups bumped against the walls behind the coffee machine, toppling over. Edna crouched under the table, along with the others.

Then it all stopped, just as suddenly.

Slowly, Edna climbed back onto her seat. "What a little tease," she said. She lifted her chin at the window, at the moon behind it, now creeping up behind the palm fronds in the sky as if it, too, had been crouched low. In Edna's yellow-brown eyes, I saw a strange twist of humor, an awareness of her own intelligence, her circumstances, and her desire to play with it, to make something good from it.

"Get a lock that's too much trouble to break," Edna called after me as my feet kicked a tuft of feathers on my way out. When I got undressed that night, I found a blue moonstone in my jacket pocket.

THE NEXT DAY, Mrs. Green told me the trick to seascapes. You had to be disobedient with the clouds. First, you had to learn form and order, but then you could attack. You could thin them with linseed oil, spin those clouds off cliffs. You could forget lines, even forget symbols. Then you could speak in terms of what really mattered. You could turn those clouds into animals, into buildings, if you wanted.

Nothing was as it appeared. You could meet a thief who wanted to be a storyteller. A sea lion could fall upward into the night just like a young girl, leaving a bunch of drifting feathers.

"I saw him go. Your friend. He's tall. Must be six and a half feet, at least," Mrs. Green said, catching me off guard. "There was sand in the hallway. I cleaned it up. It was no trouble at all. Boots trap sand in the tread."

"That won't happen again. He's not coming back," I said.

"If it's meant to be, it will work itself out. You never can predict love."

Here she was, assuming love. I could make someone love me, she believed. But what was *meant* to be was a story. This sense of *Right* and *Not Right* was supposed to make you feel better, relieving you of your problem, hopefulness. No one would insist on something that was *Not Right*, as much as they wanted what they wanted.

Mrs. Green was right, though, about what she said.

Chapter Fourteen
1988

THE GREEN WATERHORSE expelled sea mist across the sand and onto my porch. When the Hunger Moon came in February, the waterhorse kicked up driftwood, whipping its black mane across the waves. It had conspired with the moon to set things right. The bougainvillea were strangely fragrant on this night. Their sweet scent trickled over the bodies of the animals on the beach. This is what Dolly and I imagined in the parking lot of Wild Acres. We were sitting on the roof of my white Honda, which I'd gotten back the week after I met Edna.

We held a flashlight over my mother's 1972 almanac. We glanced up at the bank of moonlit clouds, as opaque as a blanket of feathers, as though one thousand doves had opened their wings, blocking out the moon and stars. "Look at the Hunger Moon," I said.

"Snow Moon," she said. "That's what the almanac calls it."

"Mom never used that name. She always used 'Hunger Moon.'"

"I know, we didn't have snow. But do you see how wrong this was? Mom made up some moon names to fit her purposes. You can't do that. She should have chosen one language and just gone with it. If she'd been consistent, it might have helped. She bent the rules of the universe. That's why we always had trouble."

Dolly had not read through all the almanacs, as I had. I now had some insight. "Do you watch the moon when you're not with me?" I asked her.

She drew her knees to her chest. "I could say I didn't. But I'd be lying," she said, her long ponytail flowing soft and loose over her right shoulder.

"I like knowing. Otherwise, the past was all a waste," I said.

"You can keep what she taught us. But not the stories. Moose, I don't want to see you get hurt."

"I won't. That won't happen."

"The moon isn't going to bring him back to you. I know you're waiting."

"Don't worry about it. I know he's not coming back."

Dolly had been wholly opposed to Graham from the beginning. She said the cycle of his comings and goings reminded her of our mother's, and that I was caught up in our mother's whirling escape hatch. I was still manning the threshold. I had somehow become the keeper of the in-betweeners. She said I was confused as to my role in the family, and in the world. But I wasn't. I had never been clearer.

My body knew. That morning, I'd woken up sweating, my cheeks flushed, as if I'd been running all night. That morning I'd known he was coming back.

"I have a friend at work who's out every night. I can't keep up with her. She just got a divorce."

"What about you? Have you met anybody nice?" I asked.

"I like being alone right now," Dolly said, resting her head on my shoulder.

Hours after she left, I heard a knock through my hazy sleep.

My fingers hesitated on the door before I opened the chain lock. "Ruthie-Ruth?" His voice was low, distant.

"You came back," I said, trembling.

Graham stared at me, hesitant, his chapped lips, parted. It had been two months. His hair was damp, strewn across his white shirt. His jeans were torn at the knees. He handed me a bag of shells. I hugged him in the doorway, as if another earthquake had hit.

"I wasn't sure if you'd want to see me again," he whispered against my neck.

"Come inside," I said, pulling him in.

"You have no idea how good it is to see you. How much I wanted to come back here." He pushed me gently back against the doorframe, kissing me roughly, his hands on my breasts. I could smell whiskey on his breath, and I tasted the salt on his chest as my robe opened. It was as if no time had passed at all. Somehow, I felt I'd known him forever, as if we'd grown up together, like I'd been kissing him forever. And yet it all seemed new.

"I can't believe you came back," I said, sliding my hands up under his shirt, feeling his warm body.

"I had to." He picked me up and pushed the door shut with his foot.

He put me on the bed. "Wait," I said, pushing him away.

"What's wrong?" Through his unbuttoned shirt, I could see his clavicle, the muscles in his neck, his Adam's apple moving as he swallowed. This was comforting, somehow. His humanness.

I pulled up the blanket and covered my legs. "You really scared me, you know. You didn't call." He reached over and smoothed my hair, pressing away one of my tears with his thumb. I hadn't realized it.

"I'll always come back to you," he said, his voice low. Tears, he said, were just energy, not good or bad—the winds and the oceans could pick up this energy and carry it, and some people, when they were close, very close, could feel this and take it on.

Certain animals, too. All things that were sensitive, plants, too, could feel things on a different level. It was then that I noticed the bruises on his neck. He had what looked to be the beginning of a black eye.

"Gifts from the ocean," he said, as if an apology.

"Tell me what happened, please. Whatever it is, just tell me. Where did you get all those bruises? I promise I won't judge you. Not at all. Just be honest."

He looked worried, or sorry. "It was a difficult trip. Storms. Big squalls." He winced slightly, as if he hurt. Then he got up and walked over to the cabinet, where he poured himself a glass of whiskey. He glanced at my easel and then leaned over the stack of canvases, sorting through my paintings like a deck of cards. He examined my seascapes, setting them up across the floor. "You paint the ocean so beautifully. Why not swim in it?"

"Those are mine," I said, getting up.

He drew back his hand. "I just wanted to see what the ocean looks like to you."

I explained that I'd been mostly teaching myself how to capture movement—birds flying, animals swimming, the way the waves looped and made circles for miles, and even how the air looked like it swelled over the beach sometimes.

"What does it look like to you?" I asked.

"Different. The ocean is dangerous, Ruthie-Ruth. The animals are hunted. I don't want to talk about it."

"What about the good things?"

He nodded. "What I saw as a boy. 'Orkney' means 'Seal Island.'" He talked about sea anemones off the coast and starfish floating in shallow pools. Barnacles and sea gooseberries. About "groatie buckies"—rare snails that made you lucky if you'd found them. There were otters that hid in caves. Flurries of arctic terns could block out the sunlight momentarily. You could be lucky enough to see porpoises and dolphins if you were crossing in a ferry.

"The grays—gray seals, I mean—they don't get on too well with the fishermen. They have no fear, eating the catches. You can find them everywhere, thousands of them, and in October and November, with their pups. These are the pups that have the white pelts," he said. He looked away then. He said you could float around them in an inflatable workboat, and they'd come up to you in the waves. "Everyone who visits wants to hear the seal song. If the wind blows in the right direction, you can hear the sound. It's the wind, mostly. That's what you notice: strong, cold. Few tall trees on the islands because of the wind."

My equivalent of that was the sound of women's voices rising in the bougainvillea, which I rarely heard now. And which I was certain no one but I would want to hear.

"Tell me about all this," he said, pointing to the brushes. I explained the different kinds of brushes, and how I preferred flat to round because you could pile more paint on top. I showed him how I toned the canvas so as not to have to paint on stark white, which could make everything appear too dark. I explained the use of shadow and highlighting needed when painting a face.

He liked this, my excitement. If not my paintings, then the fact of me painting.

"I'm just learning," I said.

"You're good, Ruthie."

I met his eyes. "I don't even know where you live."

He sighed. "I keep a small room here and there. I'm away too much to need anything more. I have no phone. Yes, I know that sounds strange. Just never needed one. But I was out there in the middle of the ocean, and all I could think about was you. I came as soon as I could. There's nothing I'm hiding from you." He walked over to the window and stood there for a moment, looking out at the purple and blue streaks just above the horizon. "What can I do to convince you?" he asked.

"I guess it will take time. To find out who you really are," I said, offering him a smile.

His eyes softened. He took my palette from my hands and held it up to the moonlight. Then he opened the glass door to the porch and walked out to get a better look at it. I noticed the way his faded jeans crinkled up in the backs of his knees, and how his bare feet left prints in the rug. His shoulders hunched slightly, curved over the palette. The light caught the hair on his arms as he turned around, and walked back in.

"What do I look like to you?" he said, handing me back the palette.

He was so battered; I nodded, and I took out a canvas.

He pulled off his white shirt, letting it fall onto the carpet. Then he unbuttoned his jeans and pulled them off. He sat in a chair, his leg muscles boxy.

He turned to face me. The bruises on his chest appeared darker in the moonlight, and his body appeared to be fading right into the sky, the purple welts now merging with the clouds.

From his chair, he watched as I lined up the brushes in plastic cups—the round, flat, bright, filbert. I ran my thumb lengthwise across the tip of each brush's bristles just like Mrs. Green did, trying to figure out which one I should begin with. Up until now, I had painted only landscapes. At night, I'd curled up with art books.

I recalled how my eyes had followed the swanlike neck of a ballerina, the pink blossoms on her flushed cheeks, the rest of her captured in strumming white-gold strokes. Below, a rectangle of light on the hardwood floor, and the barre, touched with gold, too. The ballerina's lips would part slightly, her finger caught in that space. I'd examined a certain dark lavender hue, deciding that a flat brush had been used. I defined form in terms of instruments used to create it. As I paged through books, I hunted for patterns and repetitions, just as I did with my mother's almanacs. A blue-lavender hue might trail above a fire near a hearth, and also make up the iron tub where a different woman hitched her foot and unrolled her stockings before she stepped into her bath.

I PULLED OFF the paint caps and squeezed the tubes, forcing the paint up onto my glass. I poured turpentine into a cup. I'd not start with flesh colors. Rather with violet and green hues. As I began to paint, I imagined scaling the cliffs in ballet slippers, holding on to the slippery rocks and feeling the jagged edges below. I had never fallen, not once.

Faces required you to first draw shadows, particularly for the eyes. A face would not make sense until you painted all the colors around it. You could mix Viridian Green with white to make a man's body.

I held up a charcoal pencil to sketch him first. I had never painted a man before. My hands shook too much. No one would understand my pull toward Graham. I'd stopped trying to explain it. I picked up a round brush and toned the canvas with Burnt Umber. I painted in the lightest skin tones first, Creamy White and Burnt Sienna. I used Ultramarine for the midtones. You could imagine a different ocean than the one in front of you. But what color to paint a man?

"Without eyebrows your face is going to look silly. Be prepared," I told him. Dry lips. Sleek dark hair. Pale green eyes. A long straight nose. Flared nostrils. A face was nothing but form and texture, just like those cliffs of my childhood. I opened the curtains to let in enough light to bring out the edges of his face. Mrs. Green had told me that while painting her husband's portrait, she had to turn the canvas upside down in order to reboot her brain. She finished the portrait that way.

Graham's long hair fell across his shoulders but appeared too viny on the canvas. I wanted his hair to be a soft ash brown. "Don't move. You're doing extremely well. You're exceptionally good at being painted," I said.

He raised an eyebrow. "Handsome, right?" Highlights were not white. Shadows were not black. None of this would work unless you built up the color with different hues. Every color was made up of other colors. Water was made up of seven colors, not just blues and greens. There was no such thing as pure red or pure yellow. Nothing was wholly bad or good.

Each dash of color would have its own territory and history—a record of a moment, that millisecond when you placed it on the canvas, when everything around it became eternal, each brushstroke significant. I painted his shoulders stony. I wondered if my stony hands could paint only stony bodies. His stomach caved like the sunken hull of a shipwreck. As I painted his hair back from his neck, I revealed rope burns.

I'd hardly gotten anywhere when he stood up, spilling the light and shadows, ruining everything. He walked toward me. He didn't care.

"Go back," I said. But of course now he couldn't find his exact position. We'd have to forget it. He parted my hair, drawing it down over my breasts.

He put his hands on my shoulders and leaned in so that our foreheads were touching. He was sweating, his eyes glistening. "Now, your turn."

I put my brushes back. I was shy, self-conscious at first. But I lifted my sweatshirt and drew my arms up over my head, letting him see my full chest. I knew I was bigger than before, my breasts fuller. I didn't mind it, nor did he. He lifted my chin and kissed my forehead, then my cheeks and my chin. It was the most exquisite display of tenderness I'd probably ever been shown. The attention he gave my body captured me. As I unzipped my flowered skirt, letting it puddle at my feet, I regretted my bad knees, those had been passed down from my grandmother. I knew they knocked just slightly. My flesh pillowed beneath my navel. I'd stopped policing my body.

My skin was not a perfect canvas, not white as the driven snow. It was covered in freckles, uneven. But I summoned all my courage, showing him I had missed him, that I trusted him. This was a fair exchange. He'd offered his body for my magnified exploration.

His hands grasped my breasts. He bent down, letting his lips linger on my belly. When he picked me up, my legs wrapped around him instinctively. "Is this okay?" he asked. I couldn't look at him. He carried me like that, his breath coming fast as he laid me back on the blue embroidered tablecloth and drew apart my legs. My arms drifted back over my head so that my fingertips brushed the curtains, stirring the fabric.

LATER, IN BED, he glanced over at me. "You won't cut your hair, will you? It's a beautiful color. Uncommon," he said, unwinding my curls.

"I don't make promises," I lied.

I noticed his wetsuit dripping on the porch and remembered my sister once splashing into the ocean at night when we were young, the arc of her arms sweeping across the waves. "Ruthie, don't be scared. Just come in!" she'd cried, but I'd refused, remaining safe on the sand.

"I'm tired," I told him. "I haven't been sleeping."

"Should I be worried about you, Ruthie-Ruth?" Graham said, propped up on one elbow.

"Sleep is for amateurs," I said, deadpan, but he didn't smile. "Should I start asking you questions?"

He closed his eyes and rolled onto his back. Silence. Yes, we'd keep secrets.

THE NEXT MORNING, we played on the beach, watching the animals. I was twenty-one years old, and happy. I wanted to be fifteen, too. Just for a while. I knew I could be that with him.

He was so unassuming. It had been such a long time since I was free. Never, perhaps.

This was a different life entirely than what I'd known, a lucky life. I had never had such fun with anyone. He was the second man I'd been with, but the first I'd made love to. I'd never imagined falling into bed with a man so accepting, who tickled and nuzzled me, rubbed my feet and hands, massaged my neck and thighs. These were the delicacies of the lovers' table, one that by some stroke of good fortune, I was now sitting at. The fact that he expected nothing, and was never disappointed, didn't alert me to the fact that he'd never think I'd be disappointed either.

"Swim with me," he said. My muscles tensed as he took my hand. Everyone I'd ever known was afraid of weakness. What would he think of me? I decided I'd have to be brave, no matter what.

"I don't swim. I don't know how." I ran back across the sand, back to the safety of my apartment. Graham followed.

"Ruthie, don't ever be embarrassed with me."

I buried my head in my hands. "What kind of person lives near the ocean and can't swim?"

He pulled me against him, kissing my forehead. "We need music. I miss that."

I felt my throat tighten and shook my head no.

"But you have a beautiful voice."

My mother's fat-bellied guitar was in my closet. A street musician had given it to her back before I was born. It had been a long time since I'd played. I kept the nylon strings a little loose, and I changed them when I thought of it. Graham's eyes caught me, their green placidity. "If you don't sing, I'm going to start. That won't be pretty."

"The lesser of two evils," I said. When I opened my closet where I kept my guitar, I sucked in my breath.

Clusters of tall grasses, heaps of shells, and wildflowers still with their roots tumbled out of the closet. He was teasing me with the extraordinary.

"Where did you find all these?" I asked, gathering the flowers, brushing the soil off. My fingers were clumsy. I put the flowers in a vase. Then I couldn't find my old pick, but my mother's capo was in the case. We sat on the porch and I managed something, Cat Stevens's "Wild World." My fingers remembered the progression: Am, D7, C, F, Dm, and E.

The Shekhinah. Perhaps she had come back.

I cleared my throat and started again. After a few rough starts, I found my voice. I played the song again, my voice fuller and my fingers finding the chords easily.

"I was terrified. That's the last thing I ever planned on doing," I said, setting down the guitar.

"You're very brave. I didn't realize until now."

I glanced down at the animals looking up from the waves, their dark eyes fixed on me. A few balconies away, Mr. Takahashi looked at me and clapped.

THAT NIGHT, GRAHAM told me that some souls found each other life after life, like some sea animals would always return to the place of their birth. It was an instinct that called living things toward home. Sometimes home was a place. Sometimes home was a person. No one could explain what made it home to one and not to another. It was a combination of chemistry and memory that created resonance, that which allowed a thing to be recognized.

Suddenly, I glanced at the window. She was coming to me again, from out of the blue, my child. I could feel her presence, her energy like the waves, pushing me toward him.

She'd already captured me, my daughter.

Graham pressed his forehead against mine. "I can't believe I finally found you," one of us said with relief.

He carried me into the bath. "I can walk," I laughed. He said he wanted to feel my whole body in his arms.

I was taken with his precision, noticing how he tested the temperature of the water until it was perfect. We were the same in that way, our exacting need. Yet everything, for me, was good or bad. For him, a thing like temperature, hot and cold, was not good or bad. He unfolded the towels, waiting for the bath to fill. I imagined him caring for our children one day, how he'd let me sleep in on Sundays while he got them up and gave them breakfast. I let myself get lost in a life I imagined we'd have. I imagined who I'd be with him. I didn't want to be lost in my own stories. But that's what happened.

Graham took my hand and led me into the tub. I reached up and turned the light off.

He was different when he was in the water, more at ease, and he touched me gently, kissing the backs of my shoulders and the space behind my knees, the parts of my body that I never thought about. Baths became our ritual. How the water made his skin glisten. It made him lighter, happier almost. He smiled more, kissed me more, and drew me to him in a different way—a way that felt more like lovemaking than like a rough exchange between animals. Perhaps he was just trying to get me used to the water. Still, I was not a swimmer. Not yet. But I loved the water with him, and it was always while bathing that I felt closest to him, that I felt I knew him, and that I knew I was falling in love with him.

Chapter Fifteen

I STARTED CALLING GRAHAM the Salt God because that
is how I thought of him—both as otherworldly but as possessing the material qualities of the sea. Mostly, I thought of
him as something not possible. Each time he came back I was
surprised. From that first night on New Year's Eve through the
months that followed, I wanted the taste of salt he left on my
skin, in my hair, that would take days to get out. He would
always return on the full moon, staying only a few days, depending on his gauging of the weather conditions as he stood on the
porch and looked across the ocean.

I tracked storms. I checked the weather reports on the radio,
tuning in to the coast guard channels, made nervous by the
storms of El Niño, hurricanes and dangerous squalls, and the
plumes of sulfurous soot that trailed after the massive cargo
ships that motored into the busy port of Long Beach, with its
oil rigs and breakwaters.

I evaluated tide charts and the patterns of temperature and
weather. I worried about whales flung onto land. Fish turned
over on their bellies and floated up in the ripples of the red
tide. Sea turtles struggled onto the beach, caught in fishermen's

nets. The Sisters came and went, their skin appearing battered, a lighter shade of brown, mottled with shadows.

I told myself he was not coming back. I waited for him, poring over old almanacs on my porch. My new almanac didn't comfort me as much as my mother's old ones did. Hers was territory already crossed. I knew the ending.

I found Mr. Takahashi crouched in the stairwell in the storage room. Mrs. Green spent more time at her husband's bedside as he lost his strength, caught on the threshold of "any day now."

Things could be drawn not only by their energetic alignments but by their misalignments. It was difficult to hold the motions of forward and backward simultaneously, of love being given and then taken back, again and again. Everything alternated between periods of movement and rest, but the fact of another person leaving and then suddenly returning was not an easy one. As soon as my mother had pulled up in her car and let me in, I imagined climbing out of the car. I prayed for taillights to appear in the darkness, and when they did, I imagined them receding. This is how I prepared myself.

"I don't want to talk about him," I told Dolly over the phone. Then I stopped answering her calls. She drove up from San Diego to confront me.

"But I'm your sister. What are you hiding, did he leave you again?"

"You already know he did," I said.

People could get caught in energetic whirlpools, losing themselves in the momentum of millions of molecules of swirling energy, as if in a school of fish. You'd find yourself being pulled into the darkest caves, going deeper in your search for light. To distract me, Dolly spoke of waterhorses, of fairies and water sprites. "Did I tell you? I bumped into the gnomes at the post office. They've just moved back to the 405 after summering on the East Coast. Damn snowbirds," she laughed, meeting my eyes.

"What about you?" I asked.

"Never mind."

"You don't have to try so hard to make me feel better," I said.

"I do, Moose. I always will."

ON THE NIGHT of the Worm Moon in March, lightning flashed, stirring the roots of the trees, awakening the new spring flowers and the souls of lost sailors. The Worm Moon would help the earth and all of its living things reclaim a life worth living.

"I told you I'd come back," Graham said, soaking wet at my door in a puddle of rain, his hair dripping. He was covered in bruises. I brought him towels and blankets and made him Campbell's chicken noodle soup. After he ate, I crawled into bed with him, trying to still his shivers by laying my naked body over his. His cheeks were too pink, his eyes dim. "Just sleep," I told him. He pulled me onto him. We made slow simple love that night.

I flicked on the light. "Why do you come back?"

"Happiness," Graham said, looking straight at me. "I'm just as afraid of something going wrong as you are, Ruthie."

I wondered if that would always be true.

"Ruthie, tell me what you have always wanted," he said, drawing his finger up the spine of my stomach and letting it rest on my chin.

"This," I said.

In the morning, he was gone.

The taste of salt burned my lips.

WHEN HE RETURNED on the night of the Pink Moon in April, the beach turned the color of phlox, one of the first spring flowers. Graham and I woke on the beach at dawn and then escaped back to my apartment before anyone saw us. I combed out our hair with my fingers, and he predicted the time of high tide, based on the direction of the clouds, the appearance of an oncoming storm, and the time of day the animals came back from the ocean and settled on the beach. We left things unsaid. We let our shoulders burn and our skin peel. We left our footprints in the sand, knowing that the sea could not stand an empty space and would fill them. My questions drummed back into the earth as we made love. I didn't look back.

There were more than seven thousand known languages spoken in the world. There were others that no one could chart because they included words you couldn't conceive of. You could teach animals your language. Monkeys, dolphins, and gorillas could learn to sign. The northern mockingbird, the parakeet, and many others could imitate a plethora of sounds. Sea lions communicated through barks and trumpeting sounds. If you were diving, you might hear them, but the sound might just appear as bubbles floating off in the distance.

You had to know when a thing, vast in intelligence, was using meaningful language, not just telling you what you wanted to hear. You would have to learn its language in order to figure this out. I would learn his.

I imagined the Sisters, who could communicate both above and beneath water, calling each other in a language I could not understand. Dolly could find me in a crowded room. Even if she whispered, the recognition cut through all the background noise and made everything else just fade away, all the *Right* and *Not Right*. All the hope and hopelessness. I could capture the sound of my sister's voice like a stone in my hands, and I'd find myself pulled out of the darkness. Dolly could remind me of who I was, where I'd been, my history.

I had walked down a sea lion. I'd continued to love my mother. My third act: I would stop waiting for Graham.

You could teach an animal to learn your language, but you'd be missing the point. The point was to learn its language. Only then would you understand.

During Graham's visit in April, I returned to Mrs. Green again and again, checking to see that she was still there. "Enjoy the time you have with each other," she said. Her hair had whitened, and her fingers were covered with white paint. Her head was wrapped in a blue paisley scarf that drifted down around her shoulders as she painted the waves. The hem of her blue smock was torn open, and her pockets were overstuffed with paintbrushes. I told her I would sew the hem. Her lips parted just slightly, as if in a thank-you, as she focused back on her canvas. I noticed the Sisters, their slick broad backs glistening. In her painting, three women are sitting on the beach. They have soft brown eyes and long sleek brown hair and features that are somehow too heavy, animal.

In the middle of the night, Graham sat up suddenly. "A bird just hit the window." He got up, racing to the porch. I followed him, telling him that it wasn't an omen, that we were safe. That nothing had happened. There was no bird lying in the sand and everybody was fine and he should go back to sleep. He shook his head. "Someone died."

When my beeper went off the next morning, I kissed him and rushed out of bed. "See you in a little bit," I said, leaving him sleeping.

Mr. Takahashi stood in the hallway, barefoot, his black pants rolled up to his knees. Dr. B. was behind him on her phone. "I don't know how much longer I can do this with him. I just don't know if he can stay," she said, after hanging up. I didn't want to let him go. I'd brought him back too many times, and he didn't trust anyone but me.

Mr. Takahashi's eyes burned red. "My slippers. Diana, that thief." He was time-traveling again, his slippers flung off the balcony in a fit of rage. He glanced at the door to the storage room.

"I bet I know where they are," I said. He followed me into the storage room. I noticed the boxes and suitcases had been rearranged. The room was toppled with abandoned chairs, upside down, piled onto one another, forts made from torn mattresses. The Easy-Bake Oven was dusted with fingerprints. Dolly and I had played with this oven as children. We'd acted out dinnertime scenarios that were not ours, but that we'd seen on television. We'd melted crayons in pie tins. We'd said, "Thank heavens" and, "Please pass the margarine." Neither of which my mother ever said. Her almanacs were still in that box by the old card table.

"Where are my strawberries?" Mr. Takahashi asked. "Diana. She's the only one who remembers."

"You grow the best strawberries in California. In the world," I said, handing him his slippers from atop my mother's box. I pushed the box into the shadows. Back in his apartment, I fluffed his pillow and read him an article from *The Wall Street Journal* until he nodded off. I neatened up the newspapers on the black leather ottoman before I left.

Walking back down the hallway toward my apartment, I focused on the blue rectangle I'd passed through, morning, noon, and night. What was the worst thing that could happen? No one had promised me anything.

When I opened the door, I drew in my breath. I pulled off the tightly tucked blanket on the bed, as if I would find him. I rushed out onto the porch, hating the certainty of sunlight. He'd gone.

All signs of water had been scraped away.

In my mind, I made it halfway up the Jacob's ladder before I heard the knock on my door. Graham walked in with a bag of groceries and flowers. Dirt fell across my carpet as I took the bouquet of yellow wildflowers from his hands, roots still weeping. I put the flowers in a tall silver vase, added some sugar to the water. I set it on the kitchen table. Graham took out the avocados, peaches, and oranges and lined them up on the counter, satisfied. "I know you like avocados," he said.

"If you're going to disappear, would you leave me a note?" His expression fell as he put the fruit and avocados in the bowl.

"I was trying to surprise you." He poured a glass of whiskey and walked out onto the porch, closing the sliding glass door behind him. Turning on the faucet, I pushed my hands into cold water. I reached in further until I was wet up to my elbows. I leaned back against the refrigerator and shook off my hands.

That night, I sat up in bed, stilled by the sight of him dreaming, the twitch of his closed eyelids, the strength of his hands folded on his bare chest, the rise and fall of his slightly bowed stomach, the dark line of hair curling beneath his navel. "I've never asked anything of you," I said out loud. I said it again, this time louder. But he didn't hear me.

We woke at dawn, fingers twisted together; the walls that we'd created had come down. We held each other, arms and legs entwined as though having found, for a few minutes, that which got us through the separations and the loneliness. He faced me, staring through me in a way that had excited me at first, the night I met him, but now seemed a replacement for the true bond I imagined. He kissed my forehead and lips and rubbed my shoulders and my hands and gazed into my eyes and told me I was the most wonderful woman in the world, and that he wanted nothing more than to make me happy. But I knew. I nodded and closed my eyes. With his heavy legs slung over mine, I let myself fall asleep. When I woke, I was alone in the bed. I ran to the balcony. I didn't see him. It was pouring rain. I grabbed my raincoat and ran outside, looking for footprints. I waded into the gold-gray water, the bottom of my white nightgown soaked three inches from the hem. He hadn't left a note.

The beach was empty. There was no one here, not even the Sisters.

DOLLY SAID I shouldn't worry that she would say, "I told you so." "I've got your back. But see, this is what happens when you walk among the regular people."

"Outlaws," I said, without enthusiasm.

It was a combination of chemistry and memory that created your tipping point. You would feel your heart racing, as if escaping from a lion in the jungle, or running behind a car that was driving away. That image of your sneakers in a midnight puddle on the side of the road would be forever etched in your memory. Dolly, who knew about the science of trauma because of her work, said that in the midst of a trauma, your brain would take in every detail: the smell of gasoline in the rain, the scrape of tree bark against your palm, a particular shade of lipstick. This was a survival mechanism, whether you were a caveman, a librarian, or a beauty queen. If you suddenly had to run, you could count on the fact that your body was prepared to defend your life.

If you were raised in the back of a station wagon, the paths to excitement and fear were the same, becoming your one-way highway. It was not unusual to have trouble saying "stop."

I STILL WORE my plain gray sundress when Dolly dragged me out "to look. Just to look." My hair grew curlier, lighter, a honeyed shade of red-gold. I cut low bangs across my eyes. I wore my wire-rimmed glasses religiously. According to Dr. B., beauty was in the expression of self-acceptance. Graham had "the eyes of a storm," she said, and he wasn't much for small talk. She'd run into him in the hallway the last time he'd left. Not that anybody was interrogating me, but it was all they could do to keep quiet this long.

On a Friday night before sundown, we gathered in Mrs. Green's apartment for Shabbat dinner. We stood under the tallith as she welcomed the Shekhinah, closing her eyes and whispering, "Thank you for all of this. My friends. My sweet Saul is still with me. Life is good."

She'd made broiled chicken, the skin buttery and crisp, soaked with paprika. A thick pair of men's glasses was pushed back in her hair. The glasses were large and square, with big black plastic frames.

"Is something burning?" I asked.

"My oven. I've cleaned it three times this month, but I can't get rid of that burnt smell," she said as she quickly reached up, retrieving the glasses and tucking them into the pocket of her apron, next to two paintbrushes. "Isn't this silly? I wear Saul's glasses sometimes. I walk around this apartment wearing them when I can't remember the sound of his voice. It helps me."

It bothered me that she thought she had to explain herself to us. I didn't want her to. "Understandable, Fay," Dr. B. said. "How many people survive two more years after being given six months? You're both brave."

"We're only brave for each other," Mrs. Green said. Each morning, she'd return to her husband at the nursing home. Then she'd come home in the afternoon to paint her way back into her other world. She had figured out how to live in both worlds.

As she said the prayers over the wine and the bread, I glanced at my sister, whose hair was pulled back tight in a high ponytail. With no makeup, Dolly looked like a child. She wore my mother's Jewish star and a plain black shirt with black jeans. Her olive skin appeared tan, healthy.

"Is your relationship with Graham exclusive, child?" asked Dr. B. over dinner. "Are you his; is he yours? As in, you don't go with other people?"

"Let Ruthie get some nourishment first. Before she has to answer all these questions." Mrs. Green nodded at Dolly and poured herself some Manischewitz.

"What am I doing here?" I asked Dolly.

"Welcome to your intervention," Dolly said, lifting her glass.

I looked at each of them. "You're kidding, right?"

"Ruthie, can we invite him for supper one night? Nothing fancy. I used to have eighteen people for dinner on the high holidays. What does Graham like to eat? I'll make his favorite dish. Dolly, you'll bring a guest, too."

"You've never brought someone home, that's all," said Dr. B., touching my arm. "We'd like to get to know him, Ruthie."

"He's a fisherman," I said. I glanced at my sister, and she looked away. Dr. B. asked, "What type of boat?"

"A fisherman's boat," Dolly said, when she saw my hesitation.

"Nobody is easy," said Mrs. Green. "Do you understand what I mean when I say I have a good marriage but not an easy marriage?" I nodded, lifting my glass to my lips, though I didn't understand.

"We're glad you met someone. Ruthie. We just hope he's nice."

In that instant I saw in Dr. B.'s eyes what I knew to be true. "I promised your mother a long time ago I'd watch over you."

"Ruthie thinks that everyone who loves her is good. It's not her fault," Dolly said, meeting my gaze, saving and abandoning me.

"Why don't you be quiet?" I asked her.

"I won't, Moose. He'll be with you until there's another you at the next port."

"That's a cliché," I said. "No one really does that."

Mrs. Green got up from the table. A moment later, she stood near the porch. "Ruthie, could you come here for a minute? While I'm thinking of it, I've been meaning to show you this." Gratefully, I got up. She unrolled a print of a Winslow Homer painting called *Jumping Trout*. She told me that years after Homer's death, they had x-rayed his work, trying to dissect his calculations with infrared light. There was much to be unearthed, to uncover all the plotting and thought that had gone into this work. Some artists were scientists, this one in particular. Beneath the fish is one dab of bright red paint, a caster's fly. A dab of Cadmium Red on top of a mixture of browns that placed the entire painting, she said. The dash located all the angst and fear, the wanting and escape of the hunt, the rapids behind the fish, the speckles and bars on its lower half, its ferocity, all movement and energy in that one single red note, in that perfect as-if-an-afterthought flick of the wrist.

"It's time for soup," Mrs. Green announced, rolling the print back up in the canister. Then she whispered, "Only you know what you have with Graham. No one else has to understand it. But you do," she said, squeezing my hand.

Dr. B. would try to assuage me with stories of a failed love affair. Her first love would have been the perfect man if not for the fact of a wife in another place. When she found out, it was like getting hit by lightning, she said. "I fell hard. It was difficult to recover."

"Ruthie falls hard for wounded animals," said Dolly, resting her chin on her palm.

"Because I am one," I said.

Mrs. Green pulled her long gray sweater more tightly around her. "It's freezing in here. Is anybody else freezing?"

"You need to know who this man is," said Dr. B. Dolly nodded.

Mrs. Green patted my hand. It startled me, as if I had been splashed with cold water.

ON THE NIGHT of the Grass Moon in May, Graham came back. We sat on my porch, talking about how the *Queen Mary* was haunted. I recalled the times we'd strolled through the cabins and the restaurants on board and he hadn't said a word about what he knew. She'd been built in Scotland in the early 1930s, he said now. "In World War II, she was called the *Gray Ghost*. They painted her like a battleship," he said. I remembered Sasha and Sam at the Sands Restaurant when I was a child. I remembered her description of the blurry discs that floated over the heads of travelers, that people tried to capture them. I wondered why.

The next day, I brought Graham to the Sheet Metal Moon Café, where we ate chili and listened to music and the coffee machine, amid the shouts of the children who congregated outside. I never saw Edna, but I always expected to. It always seemed like she should be there, but she never was.

We drove up and down the coast and cased the beach towns. Venice, Huntington, Laguna. We drifted by the street peddlers' baskets of jewelry, the silver and turquoise bracelets, coral rings, and copper bangles. We had dinner on the garden porch of a restaurant, where metallic trees sprayed mist across our table to cool us. We talked over mariachi music and sipped cold glasses of syrupy red drinks, chunks of pineapple or cut strawberries on the rim. We filled up on nachos and salsa and let the alcohol go to our heads. We did what other couples did, or what we imagined they did.

One night, just before dessert, Graham reached into the pocket of his jeans and retrieved a coral ring. He lifted my hand from my glass and placed the ring on my finger. "How about that? It fits perfectly," he said.

"I didn't even see you buy this."

"I wanted to surprise you."

I wouldn't ask what it meant.

We watched a sidewalk artist sketching a sunset across the cement in colored chalk. When he was finished, the artist plunked his beach chair in the middle of it and sat, put on his sunglasses, folded his arms, and leaned back as if taking in the scenery.

It was that easy, what you imagined, or had dreamed. Everyone would say you were "brave." This caused you great worry. You knew you were headed for disaster.

"You're a good woman, Ruthie," Graham said one day.

When he said he was not a good man, I assumed he was referring to his ability to be a provider or protector. I didn't need that, as self-sufficient as I was.

"There's been danger in the ocean lately," Graham told me, standing on the deck of the Queen Mary. He looked so at ease here.

"Are you afraid you won't make it back?"

He shook his head no. "Maybe so. Maybe that's true," he whispered a moment later, circling his arms around my waist and pulling me close.

That afternoon, as we walked out of the ship, I saw a young girl sitting cross-legged on a white blanket under a palm tree, her red bandanna tied around her head. I grabbed Graham's arm. Behind her, there was a cardboard sign that read STORIES FOR A DOLLAR. A woman knelt in front of her, listening.

"That's Eddie, the girl I was telling you about," I said. Edna looked up, catching my eyes as if she'd heard me. She smiled. Then she looked at Graham. She quickly reached for her sign, turning it over.

THE STRAWBERRY MOON in June could not have come soon enough. The sky was pink, full of possibility. I'd lived through this before. I remembered it from the Home—an oppressively hopeful sky, a sky that made a person think that if she just waited long enough something big would happen. It was a sky that held a person hostage with hope. It was a sky that, like the sentry palm, never changed.

I'd been missing him. That morning, I packed a picnic basket filled with cold chicken and homemade french fries. I smoothed a new white blanket across the sand. I put the canteen that I'd filled with his whiskey next to me as I stretched my legs out on the blanket, paging through my mother's 1975 almanac, waiting for Graham. Every so often, between deciphering my mother's notes, I glanced up at the waves.

The cool night winds unfolded as if a rope ladder, its top rung lit by ragged stars. Every once in a while, I checked my watch. No Graham. My eyes burned from searching the darkness. Exhausted, hours later, I sighed with relief that he wasn't there. The sand had cooled beneath my cheek through the blanket. As the first rays of light rose, the sky swelled into a gray-green. The animals had begun to wake up. I had remained, waiting.

He didn't come back in June. I was certain he was gone for good.

ONCE, IN THE gallows of our green station wagon, my mother had spun an orange ribbon into my hair, attempting something complicated, to weave it in a braid. She rarely touched my hair. Hardly able to contain my excitement, I'd made the mistake of a simple "ow," which made her let go. She'd let the ribbon fall on my shoulder. I'd known it had all been lost just then, by what I'd done. Dolly had braided it back into my hair, and I'd gone skipping off, pretending not to be destroyed. I had wept loudly at the edge of the forest near the campsite, standing in my blue Dr. Scholl's sandals, the morning air billowing my purple sundress. I'd howled into the trees. I'd almost caught her, my mother.

"I THINK BETTER when I paint," said Mrs. Green. She wore a yellow scarf around her head, and it fluttered up against the air as she waved her paintbrush. I clung to her steadfast predictability.

"Ruthie, when you are together, does it seem like there's no one else? As if you have your own world?"

I nodded, wiping the sweat from my neck. I muddied the image of a child's yellow plastic duck that had washed up on the brown sand.

"Are you feeling okay, Ruthie? You don't seem like yourself."

"I'm fine. I've got everything under control," I lied. I knew that things that appeared suddenly could disappear just as suddenly. I hadn't even said goodbye.

Chapter Sixteen

IN TIME, YOU would learn where your light was meant, Dr. B. said. It was meant for here. You would need to take it in so that in times of doubt, you'd remind yourself. You would be able to do this. You knew you were needed here, and that you needed to be here, and that your purpose was meant for this place. You would come to the knowledge by way of your struggle. You needed to know that you were meant to work here, on Earth. It was irrelevant where to land. The purpose was to shine your light. You would do this wherever you were.

There were angels, some said. They would take the form of people and of animals. Some were already on the Earth.

LUCK AND GRATITUDE went hand in hand. Rarely would anyone wish for a lucky death, but everyone would be grateful for one: *She died doing what she loved. He went quickly without pain, thank God. He died in his sleep, having made peace with his brother after all those years. It was almost as if she knew she would go; she'd tied up loose ends.*

A good death could make everyone feel better about your life.

When Saul Green died, Mrs. Green tied a light blue ribbon around the thin green trunk of the sentry palm in the courtyard. Those who passed by it would recognize the symbol of a gift, a sign that reminded you to notice the gifts all around you, mostly the ones that faded into the landscape of your life. Mr. Green considered himself exceptionally lucky, and he told his wife that every day. This, she said, was the mark of a good marriage—when both partners considered themselves lucky because of the other. But more, when they acted on the gratitude they felt. This had nothing to do with giving presents. This had everything to do with the gift of awareness. If you could do this, your partner would always feel as if your life together was a gift.

They'd raised two healthy sons who had done well, and who were happily partnered. They'd survived inflations and recessions, distance and closeness. They'd enjoyed good friends and California, the most beautiful place on Earth. While Mr. Green's last years were spent either in the hospital or in hospice care in a nursing home, he still recounted a lucky life. Knowing that he had a wife who could go on without him was the gift of a lifetime, he said. This offered him immense relief. This was why she worked so hard at her art, making things meaningful and beautiful.

When Dr. B. called me from the nursing home on the morning Mr. Green died, she said Mrs. Green wanted me to bring his favorite articles of clothing. She had refused for his body to be taken away like this, insisting that he be clothed first. He hated to be cold. He should have his favorite light blue robe, the one that matched his eyes. His soft blue socks should warm his feet. Everything that was to touch him should be blue. In the final weeks of his life, even a sheet had burned his skin. His Timex watch had scratched his wrist, his skin like tissue paper.

I let myself into their apartment, feeling like an imposter. I had never been alone in their bedroom before. The air was too musty and warm, not like I'd remembered it during our Shabbat meals.

Mrs. Green's painting supplies were in boxes in the living room. Her paintings covered the walls in the bedroom. Every single spot was covered, creating a view of one large sea mosaic. Swirls of blue and crashing waves tipped with white foam. Gold streams of light cascaded over cliffs into the sea. Burnt Sienna and Cadmium Red streaked over Ultramarine Blue, like oil spills that had caught fire in the water.

In the corners of the dresser mirror, a cluster of old photographs had been pressed under the wooden frame, fixed in place, the images now faded a pale blue. I glanced at one of the Polaroids. Mr. Green is smiling, unencumbered, his arms around a jubilant Mrs. Green in front of the Wailing Wall. It was labeled in the lower white border, "Israel Trip, 1977." She would tell me of their pilgrimage, the site of the Holy Temple's remains, which marked the place near the gate of heaven. They'd written down their prayers and wishes on slips of paper and pushed them into the wall's crevices. One million notes were pushed between the rocks in the wall each year. Somehow her wish had come true.

His light blue silk robe. His blue socks. His brown moccasins. His blue pin-striped suit with the white lining. That favorite light blue tie, his lucky tie. The one he'd proposed in. The one he'd opened his first store in. The one that had matched his eyes. These were the things I would carry back to her. The threads of a life.

Reaching into his closet, I noticed the slippery grip of the wool suit. Pushing the row of suits aside, I felt their weight, heavy, made of steel. Below, the shoes stood like matchsticks, black wingtips with gleaming toes as if freshly polished. I pulled out a suit and placed it on the bed. I cased his closet and his drawers, searching for his light blue robe. I started to panic, knowing that panic would just make me late.

Where was it? I pushed all the hangers to one side and started again, sifting through them, one by one. Perhaps the robe had been lost in all the shuttling back and forth to and from the hospital.

I hunted everything else down and put his things in a small suitcase I'd brought. I couldn't leave without the robe. I'd checked the closet thoroughly. Suddenly, I recalled Mrs. Green wearing his glasses. I delicately opened the door to her closet, noticing the rainbow of silk scarves dripping out of an open drawer. I spotted the robe then, a pale blue pool of silk on the floor in the corner. I set it on the bed, recognizing the scent of an onion, the scent of a life finished. Then I went back into the closet. Here, hidden next to her shoes, was a canvas I hadn't seen. In the painting, a woman is diving through the ocean. She wears a wetsuit that is open to the waist. She has long red hair that swirls in the currents made by the ten or so sea lions that encircle her. They all look the same, all in pale blue hues, the only divergent colors being the woman's hair, her parted pink lips, her pale green sea glass eyes. I shut the closet door. I hurried out.

Dr. B. was waiting for me beside the long rectangular foyer mirror when I rushed in the door. "I managed to get everything," I said, out of breath.

"She's been fixated. Not doing well," Dr. B. said. "I'm almost done with his arrangements. Why don't you stay with her. I'd feel better knowing she has you here." She pointed to a room down the hallway.

"It's me, Ruthie," I said, knocking on the door.

Mrs. Green came out, thin, frail. She closed the door behind her.

My job had been to catch her, to keep her on the planet. But things would be harder now. Even though he'd not lived at Wild Acres since I'd been there, Mr. Green had been a grounding presence.

"This was not his life," she insisted, her hands drifting to his thick glasses in her hair, now matted on one side. She pushed her gold bangles back up over her tiny wrists, trembling. I opened the suitcase on the table in the hallway. She pulled out the items, one by one. One day, I would help her pack up all her husband's belongings into one box, and she'd remark that it was strange that a life as big as his could be contained in one box.

Carefully unfolding the suit and the tie, she took a deep breath. She looked at me, then at Dr. B., who stood a few feet away, holding a notepad, her gray hair pushed back in a red headband. "Do you need something, Fay?" Dr. B. asked.

"This morning, I made banana pudding, his favorite. I made it this morning as soon as I got here. He didn't touch it," she said, shaking her head. "It didn't matter. I got into his bed. I must have fallen asleep. I'd never done that before. I slept better than I had in years," she said, her eyes pleading. When she woke up, he had passed. "He loved light blue because it matched his eyes." Her face grew flushed as her hands searched the suitcase. "His silk robe. Where is the robe? My husband needs his blue robe."

I pushed the robe into her hands. She drew it to her lips and closed her eyes. "I just don't know whom I'll wake up for every day," Mrs. Green said, wiping her eyes. She searched my face, touching my cheek. "You are a good girl, Ruthie." As I hugged her, small bird cries escaped from her lips. If it was possible to call the Shekhinah, her spiritual essence, I wanted to do that now. I closed my eyes, thinking the sounds outside too brash: the sudden splash of water from a tangled garden hose, a blaring horn, a siren, the squeak of hinges before a shuffle through the front door, the echo of a tennis ball tossed against the apartment next door. None of these sounds seemed the right one—the sounds of life whirling on.

"Come, Fay. Let's go to him," said Dr. B., placing her hand on Mrs. Green's back.

I didn't follow them. They escaped into the room, and I imagined Mrs. Green's fingers sweeping a comb over the tufts of his silver hair, then carefully dabbing his cracked lips with a cool washcloth.

During the funeral, I stood next to Dolly, watching Mrs. Green.

Her two sons stood on either side of her, holding her up, each with an arm hooked in hers. They'd flown in and would leave again in a couple of hours. I was already trying to imagine how I would catch her, taking her to places where she'd see that there was more of life to be lived. "She doesn't look good," Dolly worried, nodding at her.

Fistfuls of dirt fell onto the casket. It had started to rain, the mist dampening our faces.

"We never sat shiva for Mom," said Dolly.

Our mother had been cremated, something Jews usually weren't. I slipped my hand into Dolly's, feeling her smooth short fingers, the edge of her squared fingernails. My mother's urn was kept in Dr. B.'s office, on the third shelf in a wall safe, behind the "D" encyclopedia.

"Where's Graham? Shouldn't he be here with you?" she said.

"He's working," I said too quickly, noticing the holes in the toes of Dolly's scuffed gray shoes.

We wore cut black ribbons pinned to our shirts, a sign of being torn with grief. No one from the funeral should bring death back into the apartment. Placed outside the front door: a pitcher of water, paper towels, a small trash can. We covered all the mirrors. We took off our shoes. We sat on low stools to show we were humbled, that we knew we were never far from our return to the earth. We let our hair tangle as we sat for seven days—"shiva" was the Hebrew word for "seven." The number of days we would say goodbye.

After the funeral, we set out a dairy meal of boiled eggs, a symbol of life. I thought no one would come. I feared the quiet.

But people came every day. The old came, carrying memories of youth on their backs. Old friends and strangers came, those he'd done quiet favors for, who'd never paid him back. They brought comfort foods—trays of kugel, chicken soup, brisket, bagels, and fruit. I missed Graham, and yet I was glad for his absence. I sat with Dolly, our shoulders pressed together in our black dresses. My thoughts racing, I asked my sister if she'd dress me after my final hour, if she'd make sure I had my favorite robe, that I was taken care of, that I was resting where I wanted to be. "If there's no one else, will you?"

"Ruthie, you don't have to ask," she said.

On the seventh day, Mrs. Green wiped her eyes and walked outside. Everyone had a story about Mr. Green, and she said she felt like she'd met him all over again. This was what shiva was for, to help the loved ones of the deceased finally know him as he let himself be known by the world. I thought about my own mother, and how I'd never really known her. I remembered how that last disappearance was unmistakably different from all the previous ones.

You would stumble on imagined rocks for days. You would reach for a hand that was not there. You would hear a voice when you were alone. Sometimes you could imagine a door opening. The scent of her perfume would drift by when you unfolded the sheet. Ring marks from a glass of whiskey would appear on the table. Her tall black boots would stiffen on the mat. For weeks, you would tell yourself that the dead refused to leave you just yet. You would run to the sliding glass door and press your lips to it, breathless, believing she could still kiss.

If you were a child, you would jump on your bicycle and pedal as fast as you could, holding your breath, praying as hard as you could that you would get where you wanted to go before the next day, and the next day, and the next, caught up with you.

The only choice: to keep moving.

Several weeks later, Mrs. Green pressed a new tallith in my hands, having buried her husband with his. I stood beside her in the courtyard, listening as she said a blessing to help us begin our day. Mrs. Green mourned something she had lost, and I something I had never had.

"I think of him every day," I admitted. She nodded with generosity and folded her hands.

Inside my apartment, I let in the absence. I rearranged the pillows on my blue striped couch. I took out my oils and worked on a new painting, this one of the desert. I pored through the books I'd borrowed from Dr. B. and brought the big glossy art book over to the couch. I set it on my coffee table and opened it to my favorite page—an oil painting from 1893 of a naiad, a water fairy. The naiads guarded a particular body of water. In the painting, a young river nymph peers through the trees at a young man lying on the bank of a river. There are leaves strewn through her long dark hair. Her lips are red. She is young, hesitant, but not enough to keep her from her investigation. My child, she was waiting.

Early each morning, I walked with Mrs. Green, trying to fill the time she'd spent with her husband.

-◄○►-

What would my mother say if she were alive? I wondered. Would she take my face in her hands and say, "I understand, my love, be strong," or would she throw her hands up and shout that all her suffering was wasted on me, that I hadn't learned a goddamn thing from her mistakes?

During this time no man so much as looked at me. Perhaps Graham's energy, that which he emitted, had traveled across the waves and put a protective fence around me. The whole dance was about defense, about damage, about communication, about rescuing, and about the strength of chemicals emitted from bodies in waiting and those under stress.

I didn't want to see other men. The mailman had leaned in too close when asking me to sign for packages that arrived at Wild Acres. "You like to surf? Swim? Eat?" Every time I saw him, he had another question. I always answered no. "I don't like to do anything. Just work," I told him finally, as gently as I could.

"The more you hang on, the harder it will be, Moose," said Dolly. "Face it. It's over." I wondered if, in his mind, I existed beyond this apartment. Did he think of me at work, as I did him? I took my mother's photograph off the wall and held it on my lap, asking her to bring through a sign, a dream, anything.

There were people who had it much worse, my mother said, over and over. Do you know what your life could be like? You were lucky. You were lucky to have a roof over your head, even if it was the roof of a car, and to have the food you had, even if it was Coke and kettle corn, and to have people around, even if they kept disappearing.

The sky was overcrowded with prayers. The Wailing Wall was packed with wishes.

Hills were still burning in the wake of the Santa Ana winds. Strawberry fields were igniting, and little boys were watching their fathers get taken away for reasons they did not understand. There were girls stolen under trees, who'd return to school the next day, their eyes vacant and their lips swollen. Children were tossed out of cars on the side of roads like empty bags. But you never heard about them, those who could sustain damage and just keep going. They moved forward with their lids at half-mast. They were always tired at school. They wore dirty clothes. You never heard about how they walked twenty miles in the hot sun, choosing their direction based only on the sliver in the sky, the corner of a gas station sign, or a steeple peeking out from the canopy in the distance. You never heard about the children who refused to get into strangers' cars because it wasn't safe, knowing they'd have to continue to walk alone, directionless, into an unknown future.

No matter what had happened, Dolly and I would always look as if we'd just narrowly escaped. We knew we were lucky.

I thought of my child. I could feel her winged impatience. What was she telling me? She wanted to be here, now, with me.

ON THE NIGHT of the Thunder Moon in July, I stood on the second-floor landing at Wild Acres. Gazing down the long burgundy hallway, I sucked in my breath. Graham leaned against my door, holding a vase full of white tiger lilies. I watched him pace up and down the hallway with it pushed against his chest. Then he set it down on my mat. Mrs. Green came out twice. I watched him shake his head no. She spotted me first and waved. Keeping my eyes focused on Mrs. Green, I picked up my bag and made my way toward them.

He stood there, knees flexed, legs apart, feet planted firmly on the ground as if on the wooden deck of a ship. "You have every right to be upset. There was some trouble. I couldn't get back," he said.

"Two tubes of Titanium White, at your service," I said, handing Mrs. Green the bag of paints. She tried to force a smile, but it didn't work out so well. At least she was painting again, working on a still life that I'd helped arrange. A frayed blue fisherman's net flowing over a cluster of bougainvillea petals, atop Mr. Green's Los Angeles Dodgers–signed baseball from 1963. "I'll be fine," I told her. She raised her chin and told me to call if I needed her. Inside my apartment, Graham folded his wetsuit over the railing. "This season was hell," he said, reaching for me. I became a shadow slipping away from him. His hands returned to his pockets.

"Mr. Green died," I said.

"I know," he said. His scent was equal parts salt water, sweat. His thin white T-shirt was ripped, drenched to his chest. "What will she do now?" he asked, putting his hands on my shoulders.

"She'll go on," I said, pushing back from his chest.

That night, I layered myself to safety, sleeping in my bathrobe over a sweatshirt and my nightgown. "Ruthie, are you awake?" he asked.

"A little," I whispered.

"How do we come back from here, Ruthie-Ruth?"

I turned on the light. "You've never been left. I always watch you go," I said. He nodded. He kissed me in a rush, pouring his saltwater lips over my breasts. I hadn't practiced the pattern of anger. It was not instinctive for me.

Perhaps during that thunderous boom of creation that my mother used to speak of, amid the splitting atoms and the collision of gases, there were souls that had split. This was the Split Souls Theory of Creation. Now, these souls with torn edges were colliding, trying to find their beginnings. The odds were not in your favor. The statistics were daunting. But you told yourself that if you just kept moving, you could find yours. For a time, you decided that you'd think only about exceptions to the rule. Mrs. Green was proof that you could find true love, the only person I knew besides my great-grandmother Ruth who'd found hers. Mrs. Green spoke about how she had never believed in the possibility of a soul mate until she met her husband. These were the types of stories that kept us all hoping. This was the type of story that I'd wanted to have with Graham. Not with anyone else. Only him.

The next morning, I left to do my rounds, knowing I'd return to an empty house. Hours later, I found him sitting on the porch, patching his wetsuit.

How dare I make hospital corners on the bed after all this silence, Dolly said, when she surprised me with a visit later that afternoon. Graham had gone for a swim while I made dinner. How dare I go on like nothing had happened. "You're in a love trance. You're suffering from domestic amnesia. There's a welcome sign on your door with a Christmas wreath and a white dove, for God's sake." She assessed my damage, my folded blue afghan on the arm of the couch. My yellow woven place mats set at my miniscule kitchen table. The waiting pitcher of fresh-squeezed lemonade in my refrigerator. The peaches on the counter, freshly washed. It was clear. I had crossed the line.

"None of the Sunshine Family dolls came from Russian stock and had the knock-knees that run in our family, like Mom's, and like yours, too. Don't forget that."

I knew I shouldn't start with her. But she forced me to defend myself. "You're right. I should be a domestic rebel all my life. Since I'm only allowed to be *one thing*," I said.

She was at a loss for words, for once. Sitting cross-legged on the couch, she fiddled with the two gaping holes in the afghan.

"Dr. B. made that. Don't do that."

"Sorry. Well, it's old and ratty," she said. I took it from her and folded it away.

"Dalia," I said, sitting next to her.

"Your relationship is not *b'shert*. Don't even think for a minute that this man is your destiny. Moose, this man will always leave you."

"I'm in love with him."

"Is that a threat?"

"I guess to you that is."

She sat back. "If I loved somebody," I wouldn't care if you didn't like it."

"He doesn't love me. See what happened," I said.

She hesitated, her eyes softening. "Now you'd better fucking look out for yourself."

When Graham walked in, Dolly jumped like a frightened horse. He had that sandpaper look, his muscles taut, his hair strung in wet locks, his skin blanched by salt. They exchanged hellos, and she said she had to go.

Graham stayed for one more night. That evening, we sat on the porch, our shoulders touching. He told me that the animals were being taken from the ocean.

There were always more boats to be brought down, more pirates to stop from pillaging, he said. "The law's useless, even with the bans. There's no law in the ocean. No one knows what goes on. It's a different world there. Different laws. The animals still need protection."

I wasn't sure I believed him. I wasn't sure what I believed anymore. Tails of starlight streaked the waves. My eyes caught the tiny lights that trickled down from the rivers of the blue-black. What rested there in the highest-up, seeds of lightning. You couldn't catch light. By the time you saw it, it was already a memory. Most things you thought you'd caught would not be yours. Not the single-celled organism in the ocean, the one with the microscopic beating fins. Not the girl in your painting, the one who was running. Not the jumping trout. Not the spirit of your unborn child. Not love.

Light, like water, pushed into footsteps.

I got up. Before I could say anything, Graham pulled me onto his lap. We clasped hands. He stayed there, inside me. I climbed off him, my thighs aching. *This is my body*, I thought. *My body.*

I looked down over the railing, letting my fingertips touch the bougainvillea petals. I wanted to recapture the past, as if in a net. To run with it back across the beach to the first night I met Graham, to even before that, and then to spill it out over the sand so that I could relive it.

Chapter Seventeen

M<small>Y BLOOD WOULDN'T</small> spill in August. The Red Moon. This moon signified the end of summer and the beginning of the cool ocean breeze. Graham arrived with a bruise under his right eye. "It's nothing," he said, when I reached for him. I told him we had to go. He knew where.

As we rode through the streets, the wind pushed against my face as I opened my mouth, breathing it in, memory, letting it dry my tongue, my lips, letting my tears drift onto the sides of my face, my hair, my ears, my neck.

The Bougainvillea Castle, still here after all this time, was more lush, more full with blossoms. When I looked up from beneath the canopy, I saw fuchsia, purple, and orange hues spilling across the night.

My heart flitted in my chest like a trapped bird as I gripped my bike handles, my toes touching the earth, one foot down, then the other up, tipping back and forth, letting my weight help me decide where to go. Clusters of vines heaved petals across the air, their buds reaching out ravenously, splaying the biggest blossoms. Into the vines were woven the secrets of all the girls who had gone before and after me. The voices of those girls I could almost hear now. I pushed back my hair, trying to listen.

"Is this how you remembered it?" Graham asked, as I got off my bike. He stood next to me, his hand touching my shoulder. I felt the heat of the white sky pressing down, and the drumming pulse of the flowers. I felt the blood rushing through the veins of the trees, deepening the cadence of memory. I felt the long rain piercing the grass; the heat of the animals breathing in the dark; the quick beat of small hands on drums; the scrape of bird wings across tinny skies, their moonlit tails whipping against the flash of night, passing.

As ever, my own heartbeat. And now his.

My knees buckled. Graham reached out and steadied me. I motioned with my chin for him to look at the trees. He said he didn't see anything. But I saw the leaves parting. The bougainvillea revealed something I had forgotten about all these years, that iridescent pale blue sheen, the petals held in the white cast of mourning.

The wolf cries of the Santa Anas raced across the canyons and passes and dissolved into the skies. Petals fell like confetti through the wind, their edges torn. I shook off his hand and folded my arms, showing him I could stand alone. After all these years.

Leaves quivered in the breeze like ceremonial ribbons as I smoothed my jean miniskirt. As I knelt to untie my old blue high-top sneakers, my purple feather earrings brushed my neck. I'd kept the earrings all these years, never knowing why. Graham took the bottle of tequila from my basket and gathered the bouquet of red roses we'd bought at a small flower stand on Second Street. They had been wrapped in pink paper, which Graham tore off and shoved into a plastic bag. I was amazed at his attunement to the details of my recollection, even if my own memory had faded over time.

Whatever was here, I was ready to claim it. To stand up and say, Here I am.

And, What more do you want from me?

Catching my breath, I pressed my fists against my chest to steady my heartbeat. The grass was thick. The sky was too thin in patches. Graham remained quiet. I looked around. Suddenly, I was overwhelmed by memory. "Let's go home," I said, wishing I were back in my bed and that I could curl up and shut my eyes.

Graham's eyes held mine. "You have to be sure."

"I need a minute." I walked away. I glanced up at the leaves, at the place where I had gone all those years ago when I had left my body.

Up there in the canopy, I imagined the air was cool and all the sounds blended together, no one louder than the other, everything swirling into a murmuring hum. I closed my eyes to remember what I had come for. Memory met flesh. Birdsong. Bicycle tires crushing, leaves rustling. Insects with pulsing wings, tucked within the bark of trees, the sound and wind all greased by my blood, the marrying thread.

The events of my past could be rewritten. Who'd ever heard of such a thing? He wanted me to be whole, to give me back what I had lost. "Because it still follows you, that night. Only you can walk it down," he'd said. "It chases you like an animal in your dreams." That was exactly what it did.

I wanted to take the chance, knowing that it might be helpful. That the body might be able to do something about the mind's unrelenting jaws, locked on this night.

That girl. She was with me. Here, now. The girl who was tricked. The girl who hadn't known. That burning orchard. That girl with wings. The one who was left.

Everywhere, there was curling smoke.

I shivered, folding my arms. Suddenly, in my mind I was falling, my hands tunneling moonlight.

Carefully unfolding the white blanket, I let my hair fall across my eyes. When I shook out the blanket, it billowed up so that a square of light fell over the grass. Graham knelt at one corner, his large hands spreading it out flat until it was smooth. He put the bottle of tequila near the edge of the blanket. Then he stretched out, hands clasped behind his head, starting up at me. Weaving through my memory, I pictured myself as I was back then, a fresh spray of freckles across my nose, my long hair tangled across a white blanket, streaked with summer sunlight.

I kept my shirt on and tossed my jean skirt in the grass.

I stood there in my underwear, as pale as moonstone. My top fluttered up around my bare stomach. I touched the peace sign charm on my old necklace. I knelt on the blanket. I wanted to feel the wind on my face, the sweet breeze. Then I lay next to Graham, my eyes holding his. I moved closer, my stomach pressed to his. "It's okay. It's just me," he whispered, his warm mouth on my skin, connecting me somehow to myself. Looking up, I searched beyond the flower petals for the night stars. Graham reached over and handed me the bottle of tequila. He told me to try and relax. I told him I didn't want alcohol this time—I wanted to be aware, conscious. My eyes teared. I passed the bottle back to him, and he drank and then replaced the cap and set it aside. I tried to relax as the sky weighted deep blue stones on my shoulders. I imagined having left my body, and now looking down as if from the sky, at my body and Graham's splayed on a white blanket.

"Say when," he said.

The liquor spilled from his lips, trickling down his chin and onto my chest. I reached up and wiped his face clean with my hand. Graham reached for my arm, and, lifting my hand to his mouth, he began kissing me. He continued, kissing my shoulder and the inside curve of my arm. Then he moved to the other side and held my other hand. He did the same thing, caressing my fingers and my palm, pushing my hair back from my neck, leaving kisses behind the ears. My body shivered from head to toe. I stared at the bouquet of roses he'd set in the grass.

He let me lie on top of him for a good long while, almost an hour, allowing me to meld into him, drowning in the musky scent of his warm body.

"It happened right after my first period," I whispered, noticing how his gaze remained steady.

"You're safe. Just go at your own pace," he said.

I would decide what happened this time, and I knew I could say anything to him, that he would not judge me, or think me horrid, or stupid, or naive. Or wrong. Graham kissed my neck, starting to move his hands across my stomach. His breath grew heavy.

"Stop," I said.

He pulled away, and sat up. He understood.

I reached for him, clasping my hands around his neck, pulling him down over me. He began kissing me, moving his lips across my neck, burying his face in my hair. My eyes trailed up the line of tree bark, up to leaves and the scarlet hues streaked across the sky. I heard the whisper of branches, imagining the tree of lost virginities, my own name carved into its thick bark, its leaves rippling blue-white in the sky, like tongues or flames.

"Graham," I said. "Graham, look at me."

"I'm looking," he whispered, not taking his eyes off me. I imagined the red tinge of his eyes, the ink spot approaching in the calm clear water.

I imagined a table underwater, covered by white linens and set with silver bowls filled with chocolate ice cream and freshly washed strawberries.

When we made love, I imagined flight.

Gazing up at the sheet-metal moon, I took it all back, everything I had left.

I WRAPPED MY arms around myself. For a little while, I cried. I hadn't imagined I would need to, but I did.

I lay in his arms, watching those memories now whipping across the air—

That, *How could you.*
That, *Why did you go there to begin with.*
That, *Will you ever recover.*
That, *Let me kill him for you.*

As we gathered our things to leave, I picked up one of the roses.

That night, I burned it on the beach.

Chapter Eighteen

O N   T H E   N I G H T of the Blood Moon in October, leaves fell under a sheet-metal sky. The deer were ready and fattened for the hunt, fed by the Santa Anas heat. They kicked up ash as they disappeared beyond the cement walls, parting the tall grasses.

Smoke crept up from the bluer than blue. The ocean swelled. The sea winds pushed enormous waves toward the shore. The Santa Anas rushed down from the mountains toward the sea to meet them. When the two winds met, they created havoc. I had been watching from my porch and was sent running to the bathroom, spilling myself out over the rim.

My hair curled up around my face. My mouth tasted bitter. I wiped my face with my sleeve. I hadn't slept. I needed something to eat, consumed by the thought of bread. My Naida, who was hungry already. She got me up in the middle of the night in the heat, looking for bread.

I vomited again in the bathtub, struggling for air. The weight of my body was enormous. Grasping the side of the counter, I pulled myself up. My reflection in the mirror looked faded. The purple welts under each of my eyes had deepened.

Graham hadn't returned since the Bougainvillea Castle in August. But I had other things to think about now. Dolly pounded on the bathroom door. She'd let herself into my apartment with her key.

"Moose! Let me in!"

She had come to check on me—she hadn't heard from me in weeks. She'd tried calling Dr. B., who'd left on a trip to Greece. Mrs. Green was visiting her son in Chicago. Mr. Takahashi had knocked gently and then gone back to his apartment.

I crawled to the door, reached up, and turned the knob. She knelt by my side, and she put her hand on my forehead. "Do you think you have a fever?"

I hadn't told her what had happened at the Bougainvillea Castle two months before. How I hadn't had my period since.

"I'm pregnant," I breathed.

She nodded. "We need to get you a test," she said, running cool water across the washcloth. My sister smoothed my hair as I crouched once more against the cold basin, my hands pressed like paws on the cold tiles. She held my hair back, and then I fell across her lap. She rocked me there, sitting on the bathroom floor. Just like she had done once before, all those years ago.

IT WAS CONFIRMED. We stared at the blue line creeping across the tiny white rectangle in the pregnancy wand.

"I told you," I said.

"Moose. We'll figure this out together," Dolly said. That night she tucked me into bed. Then she went to sleep on the couch. Dolly left with a promise to return that next weekend and told me to think about what I wanted to do, even though we both knew there was nothing to think about. When Graham knocked on my door a few nights later, I didn't run to open it. I sat on the couch and stared at it defiantly. This is what it was to feel emptied of everything, I thought. You wouldn't care.

Nothing could touch you. The world could be careening out of its orbit and you'd sit here, letting it take you.

This was a night that was not the full moon. I watched the doorknob turning, the fingernail of light scraping my reflection.

I could press on as long as I did the opposite of what I actually felt. This would be my compass. I got up and opened the door.

He smiled at me with surprise. He could tell something was different. I could see the effects of his fatigue pulling at the corners of his eyes. His wrists looked wrong, bony and large. His fingers too heavy as he pushed the door shut.

"You don't look like yourself. What's going on?" he asked, putting his bag down. He was earnest. That's what I noticed when he reached for my hand. That's what I'd seen from the start. "I've been working. I came as soon as I could," he said. "Can I make you smile? At all? For a second? Just a minute? A half of a second?" Then he pulled back.

"What's wrong?" he asked, putting his bag down. He tried pulling me down on the kitchen floor, wanting to wrestle. I leaned back against the counter, my hands covering my stomach. Why was he so childlike now? I slinked down and pushed my back up against the wall.

"I'm eight weeks pregnant," I said. I pulled up my shirt, revealing my swollen belly. "Yes. It's yours."

He didn't say anything for a moment. Then he crawled toward me and pressed his ear to my abdomen. He smiled, his pale cheek against my tummy. I half wondered if he was going to ask me what I was going to do, or even how this had happened, but he didn't. My loyalty had never been in question. Not once.

Later, I tossed off the covers and slipped out of bed. Pushing open the sliding glass door to the porch, I wanted to see the wetsuit. I touched the sleeve. It was thicker than I had thought, lined with heavy fur. Then I heard something. He was calling my name in his sleep. I ran back inside. Kneeling beside him, I put my hand on his forehead. His eyes fluttered open. I leaned over him, my hair falling across his chest. "Where did you come from? Where do you go? Why me?"

He murmured something. I leaned in. "I could really love you."

"Why did you come here?"

"Ruthie, I dreamed about you before I met you," he whispered.

I touched his cheek, noticing the moistness of his skin, then the bruises on his neck that he'd never explain. I wanted to know his people, to see that he existed beyond our relationship. He caressed my face, moving his thumb around my lips, circling lightly, trying to spin this all into love. It was a beautiful gesture, meant to make me feel delicate. But I would no longer accept tenderness in place of permanence, in place of honesty. This was too high a price to pay. I knew the green waterhorse was shifting his weight under the Teutonic plates. I imagined I could feel its drumming pulse underneath my feet.

He was gentler with me now because he realized he loved me. Or perhaps it was because I was carrying his child. Deciding both could be true, I slipped into the bed and pulled the covers up over my face. He pulled me toward him, my body fitting against his. I turned my back against his chest. I didn't want to fit.

"I'm glad," he whispered against the back of my neck. "You want to know. I am."

"Are we going to raise this child together?" I turned toward him.

His gaze fell. "You know I can't."

I didn't need him to hold me, for him to tell me that he'd always be there for me. That we'd always be friends. When his eyes met mine, I knew it was over even though I still felt something. I knew then that I always would. I had to send him away. He got up and started to get dressed.

The earth was cracking open. I held my stomach, watching him. Where was my sister? I wanted my sister, who'd been by my side forever.

This was not what I had imagined. Whatever life he was leading surely couldn't be more important than the life we had created. Did he care? The realization that I was following in my mother's footsteps, that I was going to do this alone, hit me like a wall of flames. I'd been waiting a lifetime for my child, never thinking that history would repeat in this way.

By myself. Become a mother. What if I would be like my mother? What if I could not stay with my child?

"You'll be a wonderful mother," he said, picking up his wetsuit.

"I can't believe this is happening," I whispered. He nodded and said he understood. It was an old story.

Standing in the doorway, he raked his fingers through his hair, watching me. "Some day, you'll meet someone who will love you like I can't. You deserve better," he said. I nodded.

What I knew: We didn't want to be fighting. Neither of us was good at it. We both wanted to make peace. We craved it, that old stillness, all that time we'd sit on the beach in the sunlight and imagine the future. We didn't want the shadows that filled our eyes when we looked at each other, reminding us of the distance that had always been there, of what we had not buried, of the chasm that we had not successfully crossed. We didn't want our words to sound like thunderclouds. We knew we were not unsinkable. We didn't want this moment, or the necessary ending that it meant. We didn't want to have failed.

"I will come back. It's my responsibility."

"Come back because you love me. Not because you have to." I stood in front of him, my hands pressed to my swollen breasts. I had never felt more vulnerable in my life.

"Ruthie, you're more than this," he said.

"Aren't you?" I said, but I didn't know that. Each time I opened my mouth I imagined birds sweeping by and catching my words. There were birds flocking between us now, a whole cavern of them, darting this way and that, curving and swooping. I understood what my mother wanted me to know, that we were different.

I bucked up. I threw my shoulders back. I had never abandoned anything in my life. Not a person. Not a single moment.

This feeling was familiar. I hadn't felt anything like this since she'd died. I missed her. I wondered if I was ready to go on without Graham, knowing I had no choice. I had never wanted to let anyone go. But I would never wait for him again.

Graham put his hands on my shoulders. "I know you'll protect my child, Ruthie."

My throat tightened. "Never come back. If you leave, you can never come back."

"Ruthie," he said, his voice thin, "I shouldn't have come. It's better if I go. You'll see."

He pushed open the sliding glass door and grabbed his knapsack and wetsuit from the chair. When he came back he took out two objects: a small white dagger, its bone handle carved in the shape of a horse, its mane encircling it. Then he took out an old bible with a black leather cover. "These are mine. I keep them with me for protection, but I want you to have them now." I followed him into my bedroom. He lifted the mattress and pushed the dagger and the bible back to the farthest point underneath. "Keep these here. They'll protect you when you sleep. And our child. Will you promise me that?"

I could hear the Sisters barking.

He sighed, his eyes holding mine.

"These will protect you both. Will you promise me you'll keep them here under the bed?"

"I don't make promises," I said. That was my new truth.

He lingered in the doorway. "I don't imagine I'll get over you."

The fact that he didn't want to disappoint me made it that much harder. I told him goodbye.

All was quiet. Things were returning to their rightful places, reversing the mistakes of that first Blue Moon. I had been one of the in-betweeners that night, one who'd been trapped. I had become confused, thinking I'd been found. But people like me, like my mother, too, who couldn't read maps, who made up her map as she went along, would forget the signs and symbols she'd already found. The problem was forgetfulness. Time and time again.

Time could fool you; it could soften the sharp corners of a thing. You might see this as a change in the thing itself. You might think that a soft corner on a piece of sea glass meant that the glass didn't have the potential to break. But glass would always contain within it the capacity to cut you, no matter how it appeared. The same road would always lead you back to the place you once knew, back to the place where you were your most raw, unbridled self, back to the place where you were mostly animal.

Danger would always be danger.

After I closed the door, I removed the dagger and the bible and put them in a box in the storage room with my mother's almanacs. I would never take them out again. I would never take that same road again. Graham was now a part of my past, and so were my mother's stories. I closed the cover of the box and taped it shut, beginning a new life.

IN THE WEEKS and months that followed, my sheets would not unfold with sand. Staring out at the breakwater that abutted the waves, I thought about how the sea always knew where it stood.

"The only way to get over him is to let yourself want him. Want him until you don't want him anymore," said Dolly over the phone. Her sensitivity surprised me.

"We both wanted something." I held the phone under my chin. "Do you think Mom was a liar?"

"Why do you ask?" Dolly said.

"She said I would be a better mother than she was."

"She wasn't a liar about everything," Dolly said.

In my mind, I pictured Dolly as a child, straight red hair, sitting on the bathroom floor, pulling her hair out, leaving it across the tile, and then trying to hide it, kicking it under a towel. Now, here she was, my Rock of Gibraltar.

"Do you want me to come there and bring you something? Do you need anything?" Dolly asked.

I couldn't let her come. I noticed the bougainvillea crawling over my porch railing. It fed on yearning. I had never wanted my mother more than I did now. "I'm fine. I'm going to bed now."

"You will do this. You will do this because doing this is who you are," said Dolly. "I'll help you. Ruthie, you're not alone. I promise you that." She meant it. Helping was her best intention.

Grief could disguise itself as a lover, and before you knew it, you would only feel safe in its arms. That is what Sister Mary told me over the phone when I called to tell her the news of my pregnancy. I'm not sure why I thought she should know. We owed each other nothing, and I hadn't talked to her in years. She'd been my keeper once. That was all. Maybe I had loved her. Maybe she had loved me. Yes, I was certain she had. Somehow I still thought of her as wanting something to do with me. I wanted her to say something loving. I wanted her to bless me, to tell me this would all be okay. She'd been there the first time. "God be with you, Ruth," she said.

"And also with you," I said, after I hung up.

Dr. B. took over my duties. For a brief time, I locked myself away in my apartment. One particularly bad night, I took Graham's shells and spilled them out across the carpet. I wanted to see the size of my denial, to see it spread out before me. I needed to quantify it.

Someone was at the door. "It's us, Ruthie."

"I'm sick," I called, looking at the broken shells everywhere. "Come back later."

"Fay made chicken soup. We have briscuit. Orange juice, fresh squeezed." I sat there, knowing how this would look to them. Mrs. Green would hover over me and pretend there was nothing wrong with me. Dr. B. would fold her arms, staring me down. She would ask where I stood. What my plan was. What I'd decided. I would have to reveal how great my naiveté had been. They'd want to protect me. They'd say things. I'd have to defend Graham, which I didn't want to do right now. "Ruthie, open the door."

I opened the door and sat down on the floor amid the broken shells.

Mrs. Green spread her tallith across my couch, pretending not to notice the litter. It was a relief. I could count on her for always taking the road most generous.

I pulled off the coral ring and put it in my pocket. I told them I was fine, that they could count on me to buck up. Mrs. Green warmed up some soup. I didn't want prayer now. I just wanted to be left alone.

LATER THAT NIGHT, after the air was cleared, to create some space for the new good things to come in, I walked out to the ocean toward the sudden piles of driftwood, chalky in the moonlight.

The water was freezing.

A wave splashed over me. I pushed up through it, trying to catch my breath.

Someone was shouting my name. I looked back. Dr. B. was standing on the beach with a red towel in her arms. Her curly gray hair tufted in the wind as she kicked off her sandals. Her long black dress flounced up around her calves as she came toward me, meeting me halfway, waves sweeping her shins. She wrapped the towel around my shoulders and walked me back inside. She said that this would pass, my morning sickness and my feelings about Graham. "That little spirit is with you now. Motherhood is not about mothers. Now, you get yourself together."

INSIDE, SHE SMOOTHED the blanket over my legs.

I pulled it up over my face. "I don't know how to be a mother," I whispered. How would I be a mother when I had no mother to show me how to do it?

"You have us now. We're your family now. So sit up. Sit yourself up," she said, straightening my shoulders, her voice stiffening. "You need to choose this. You need to choose the life that has chosen you."

I looked into her eyes. Here, I read compassion. Here, I found more compassion than I'd ever seen, more understanding than I thought another person could offer. Perhaps it wasn't there before. Or I didn't need it as much. I felt her strength. Her belief in me. She knew me. She wasn't just giving me lip service, telling me what I wanted to hear.

"Promise me you won't ever turn your back on yourself like this again," she said.

I promised.

I got up. Running into the bathroom, I thought about my child. I splashed water across my face. I took a deep breath. Then another. Then my eyes focused forward again. The map. It was here.

—◇—

DAY AFTER DAY, the animals watched me as I passed by them on the beach. If I would always be scrutinized by the cashier at the grocery store, first eyeing my swollen belly and then directing her gaze to my naked ring finger, I had to become blind to it, to this continued examination of my motives, my choices. Some would feel sorry for me, which was almost as disappointing as being judged. Others would blame me. I'd be called irresponsible, irrepressible. Inexcusable. I would hear "out of wedlock." I would hear "single mother." I would put it all on pause, just as I'd learned to do. Dolly said not to trust anyone. I didn't believe it.

I read everything I could about childbirth. About what to expect. I would be the right kind of mother. I moved through my days, weeks, months, walking the hallways of Wild Acres, my growing belly leading the way. I'd like to say that I forgot Graham. I'd like to tell you about how my firm decision and absolute resolution and newfound strength changed me and made me into someone who had no memory of his voice. But each morning as I waited for the walls to stop spinning, I'd find myself going over every word we'd said to each other, as newly estranged lovers do.

I taped a calendar to my refrigerator and started marking off the days. Then I attended to my people, to my animals. Mr. Takahashi's son had arranged for someone from his farm to drop off fresh strawberries, handpicked, every few days. One night, when I was arranging his towels, he looked at me with a smile. "What is it?" I asked. He handed me an envelope. I opened it. Inside was a keychain. One that he'd given my mother when they first started dating so that she could drive his convertible. It still had the key on it. "This is your child's car. Care of your mother. It'll be waiting in my garage in Oxnard." I hugged him, feeling his wooden ribs against mine, and I thanked him.

Mrs. Green knit baby blankets and hats in a neutral beige yarn. I started to draw, temporarily forgoing my painting, as the fumes could be toxic to my baby. My drawings calmed me. I drew in another language, not blues and greens but reds. I created a series of sketches called *The Red Tides*. Telegraphing my emotions through the waxy pencils, I was determined to turn this all into something beautiful.

I was drawn to those who played flutes, guitars, and drums on the boardwalks and pier. Mr. Takahashi and Mrs. Green continued to argue about slippers. A door was slammed shut. A curtain was pulled tight. A walk refused. Then, all was forgotten.

The little being growing inside me would feel every thought, every whisper. It would absorb the molecules of my emotions in the same way it absorbed the nutrients in my blood. I had never been as careful with myself. Each morning, I sat in the courtyard, focusing on the resoluteness of the sentry palm. My child already wanted things, too. I knew what she wanted most, though. I could already feel it, that butterfly flutter whenever I walked near the ocean.

My mother had ruled the universe with her stories. She had never told me about the Baby Moon. I was glad for that. Glad to be able to make it up all on my own.

Chapter Nineteen

I SWAM IN MY dreams.

Swimming was all I thought of, kicking my feet and floating, letting the sun beat down on my cheeks.

It was time to learn. Five months had passed since Graham left. My lingering fears of the water faded. Dr. B. agreed to teach me on one condition: I would not go further than I was prepared for. Although she was often shaky on land, she was graceful in the water, a sight to behold, a kind and good teacher with a pink plastic bathing cap and blue flippers. My big tummy constantly turned me on my back. I choked back seawater and tried again. I was determined.

"Like this," she instructed, demonstrating kicking her feet back as she floated. She took off her flippers and pushed them across the water toward me. "Good girl, Ruthie!" She clapped for me as I sputtered water. I had learned to float. And within a few weeks, I would learn to swim. Little did I know, my child was propelling me forward because she wanted so much to be in the ocean.

Had I known that, I might never have learned to swim at all.

The more time I spent in the water, the more I felt my child moving inside me. Day after day, Mrs. Green watched from under her beach umbrella, slathering her body with white streaks of sunscreen, as Dr. B. and I swam through the waves together, the Sisters watching. Mr. Takahashi stood on the beach and yelled at us. A pregnant woman learning to swim? How was it that a nice girl like Ruthie had gone and done this to begin with? Why, he'd ask, would I want to learn to swim now? Dr. B. swam back to the shore and splashed him. I had never seen him laugh like that, his white shirt soaked with water. It delighted me.

I DECORATED THE nursery, formerly the walk-in closet. Dr. B. sewed gingham drapes. Mrs. Green and I found some old tossed out window frames. We tacked posters of the ocean behind them and hung them like faux windows. We covered a wall with navy blue felt, and cut palm trees out of green and brown felt, which we then stuck to the navy. We cut out other shapes—fish, sea lions, horses—which Naida would be able to play with, moving them around as she grew. Dr. B. gifted us with a new white crib—a convertible classic that could become a toddler bed, a daybed, and a full-size headboard as my baby grew. The headboard had wainscoting and fluted posts. Mr. Takahashi and I put it together using the tools from my mother's old red tin toolbox.

I didn't know that the moon would make my child swim inside me. All I knew was that its waxing and waning made the baby roll around as though frolicking in the waves. At night, I'd lie awake staring at the moon through the window, letting the palm leaves cast shadows and patterns across my belly. My bedroom was bathed in light. I shuddered as I watched the moonlight escaping down the walls, carrying with it the force to move the tides, to stir my baby.

I craved ice water. I emptied the ice tray and refilled it several times a day, noticing how it just made me more thirsty. My child was a fire burning inside me. My drawings were gold, red, orange. Everything was sharper, clearer.

Mrs. Green left Wild Acres to go live with her son in Chicago. When she came to say goodbye, she told me I had made her feel as if she mattered. She tried to hold me, my belly between us, and she laughed and said this would be her granddaughter, and that she wanted photos sent every month. I promised her I would send them. There was hardly anything that had gone unspoken between us. We didn't need to say goodbye. She was a person who had no regrets. I wanted to make her proud. I didn't want to watch her go. But I did. She had met me in the place I was. A rare friend, she'd never demanded that I be more or less than who I was. I thought about my mother's words, how you would always find truth in books. You could find it in certain people too. Despite all your hiding—your tough acts, your jokes, your makeup, and your remote, hard-to-reach, crumbling ways—you'd see that you could be found, too.

ON NEW YEAR'S Eve 1988, at four months pregnant, exactly one year after I met Graham, I set the table for my sister. Dolly arrived from San Diego with a bottle of sparkling cider, two plastic champagne glasses, a box of Entenmann's chocolate chip cookies, and a bag of balloons. Within minutes, there were balloons everywhere.

Dolly peered into the courtyard at the sentry palm, which still hadn't changed. "What am I going to do about that guy?" she said.

I smiled up at her from the kitchen floor, where I sat folding laundry. "We are too wild and crazy. Look at us on New Year's Eve," I said.

"Bad girls never make good, isn't that what they say?"

"I forgot that's what we are." Dolly said the term was a cliché perpetuated to scare girls onto the virginal path. "It just fosters bad blood between women."

"Remember the girls at the Home? You were so tough, Doll."

"Ruthie, I haven't cried in five years. Nothing comes."

I tossed a pair of jeans at her. She caught them in her lap. "There's nothing wrong with you. The only thing wrong with you is that you think something is wrong with you."

"I want to help you raise this baby. I'm the aunt."

"You'll change your mind once the diapers get here. The midnight feedings? The temper tantrums? Besides, stop thinking you owe me anything." As I reached for a glass of water, I glanced out the window. Dr. B. was walking through the courtyard, hanging colored streamers from the palm tree. "Only good thoughts. Babies can hear everything from the womb, by the way," I said to Dolly.

"You're my little sister and you've got a big belly and you'll need a lot of help. I have vacation time coming to me. I'll sleep on the couch. I don't care. They have me on the road too much anyway."

"No. Don't get trapped by this. This is mine to deal with," I said, facing her.

I heard cheering from down the hall. People blew streamers and danced on the beach. Later, Dolly and I fell asleep on the couch, wrapped in each other's arms.

THE NEXT MORNING, on the first day of 1989, I sat on the beach with a book opened in my lap. I blinked into the sun, hoping love was a thread that never broke. The sky looked whiter than it often did. I sensed my child's spirit reaching for the waves. Suddenly, I had more people in my life than I had ever imagined my life could hold.

My child wouldn't be a shame.

Dolly came down to the beach. She pulled the blue afghan around my shoulders. Did I remember Dr. B.'s story about the people who hid in the skins of animals? She wanted to know. I listened to her retell it, warm and safe on my blanket, watching the sea lions dive into the waves and splash up, disappearing under the water.

NAIDA DIANA GOLD was born on the night of the Blue Moon on May 31, 1989. She was the size of a doll, with thick dark lashes and bright green seaglass eyes. Awed, I gazed at my baby as she slept. Named after the naiads, those sprites that watched over the rivers and streams, she was perfect, a beautiful little fairy with rosebud lips and a headful of black curls they said would fall out but didn't. The rush of love mixed with adrenaline was unlike anything I had ever felt. She was a person now, her cries like that of a lamb, but strong. I placed my hand over the back of her head, her body now unattached to my body. Dolly leaned over and kissed her. Naida latched on to my breast easily and suckled hungrily.

My daughter gazed up at me and her fingers curled over mine, as if by reflex. Eyes that clear, I had never seen. These were brand-new eyes. I had a strange sort of knowing—as if Naida were that one lightbulb that made the whole string of lights work, that one tiny light. Hope. In Russian, *Naida* means "hope."

AFTER HER BATH, my daughter's hair was soft—not matted, caked, or threaded with blood—and her skin had that soft chalky feeling. I ran my hand along her shoulders and her back. This little being captivated me. As Naida suckled, I caressed her face. I whispered, "I'll never let you go." I asked her if she was mine over and over again, as though she would answer. I traced her perfect features, her nose, and her tiny seashell ears.

I told my daughter that she would grow up to be elegant and smart. That she would always know where she stood with me, and when she didn't know where she stood with the world, I would help her discover that. I told her she would be kind and careful with herself. I wondered if my own mother imagined my life the day she gave birth to me, if part of her distance came from her fear that I would be like her, or that she would somehow ruin me.

And then I saw Naida's foot.

FINGERS AND TOES, I would learn, initially developed in the shape of paddles and then separated. At about sixteen weeks, an enzyme would dissolve the tissue in between the fingers and toes in a process known as apoptosis, a programmed death of certain cells. But sometimes this process wouldn't occur completely, and the toes would remain joined.

It could have occurred for any number of reasons. In many cases, it was genetic. The surgeon said that if you couldn't find it in your immediate family, you could often find it if you went back through the generations. You just had to look far enough.

As I read about this condition, I learned of its history in the Orkney Islands. According to lore some families there traced their genealogy back to the selkie-folk, shape-shifting creatures that assumed human form on land and seals in the water.

In the back of my mind, I wondered if I had somehow caused this. If my memories of being abandoned and my need to cling to things had somehow affected her. Perhaps her body had absorbed my fear and created this condition.

Translated, it was failure to separate.

Chapter Twenty

1989

I HAVE AN IMAGE in my mind of Naida on a hot beach day, her mop of black curls tufting in the wind, her steely gaze piercing the sea, cheeks puffing in and out, face flushed as her little arms and legs flailed, scrambling across the sand and into the water. I'd run after her, scooping her up in my arms, only to have her writhe until I put her down.

My arms were always scratched as though by a cat. The intensity of her tantrums worsened when she couldn't go in the ocean. She was like a Tasmanian devil circling in a puff of wind, not wanting to be caught. There was such a fierceness and obsessive excitement in her when I'd bring her down to the ocean that I bristled at its force, knowing I had as much chance to stop it as I did of holding an umbrella in a hurricane. While other mothers clapped, cheered, and bragged about their children's swimming accomplishments, the sight of Naida careening toward the ocean in her pink tutu bathing suit struck me with panic. Preventing her from swimming, playing on the beach, and frolicking in her ocean element went against every good and rightful bone in my body.

I'd let her swim as long as I could hold on to her, doing the breaststroke kick, pulling Naida with me as though already rescuing her from drowning. She'd kick me and slip out of my arms, paddling away from me as quickly as she could, and by the time I'd be able to retrieve her and make it back to shore, we'd both be out of breath as we fell onto the beach blanket, struck by the sheer force and determination of the other.

In addition to warding off the ocean, I became attuned to the other hazards the new mothers I'd meet would talk about. These included but were not limited to: PVC in yellow plastic ducks; acid rain; the deterioration of the ozone layer and the resulting engulfment of the earth in flames; the destruction of the rain forest and the depletion of oxygen; lightning; hormones in milk that would make a child mature too soon; fire; the emotions of animals before slaughter and the resulting release of the stress hormone cortisol, which remained in the meat; Naida falling in love too young; Naida never falling in love; love; the traveling swarm of killer bees; pesticides; the past; the future; and of course there was more. I never figured bullies into the equation, those who would torture my child for being born different.

I could protect Naida from most things in the world. But I couldn't protect her from herself. I couldn't keep her from the ocean, the sand, the Sisters, and her absent father. These were the things she wanted most. I'd developed an indefatigable grip, but nothing scared me more than the idea of someone stealing her. I was haunted by a grocery store scene in which I'd reach for peanut butter on the shelf. When I'd turn back around, she'd be gone. I'd spin around, but all I'd see were blank stares and faces streaking by.

I hardly let her out of my sight. She defied me at every turn.

I never regretted meeting Graham. No matter how I felt, I knew he was the reason I had my daughter.

I would keep her close. Each morning I'd belt an ERGO baby carrier onto the front of my body and slip Naida inside, her cheek on my chest. I carried her all day as if she were still a part of me for the first year and a half, even on my shifts with the new residents. I bandaged heads and fixed leaky sinks and dispensed medication, even as my shoulders ached from Naida's weight. Naida saw the world from that warm pocket for the first eighteen months of her life, and then occasionally afterward, when my fear would take over again and I'd swing her right back into the pouch at twenty-five, thirty-five, even forty pounds.

But I was no match for the ocean; Graham was right. Horrified, I watched her rushing into the waves.

There was no telling how a child would turn out, whom she would take after, what talents she'd have that you'd wished for her. At night, I'd hear the Sisters barking in a way that sounded like longing. I'd bring Naida into bed with me and fall asleep with her clutched against me. When I went out, I wore long sleeves to mask my scratched skin. It was nature against nature. Naida against me. And me against Naida and her partner, the sea.

As Naida grew, it became more apparent that she was more Graham than I had bargained for. She had his pale green eyes, his red lips, his love of the ocean, and she had secrets. Though she hit every milestone well before expected, I worried at what cost. All I wanted was for her to slow down, and then I'd remember what Dr. B. said. "Motherhood is not about mothers. The first thing nobody tells you."

Her foot was not the only thing that was different about her.

When she was three, I took her to a mommy-and-me playgroup, and Naida, dressed in her overalls with the apple patches on the pockets, started talking about the other children and their mothers. During a blustery picnic one afternoon, she walked right up to a woman named Ronnika, who was sitting with her young son, Julio, on a plaid blanket. Naida told her that the little boy had "rocks in the blood." Ronnika laughed at Naida and then glanced at me expectantly.

"Naida, we have to go," I said, grabbing Naida's hand.

Ronnika's eyes grew wide. "Ruthie? What does she mean?"

"I never know with Naida. Probably nothing."

Ronnika picked up Julio, clutching him to her chest beneath the blanket.

A week later, I received a phone call telling me that Julio had lymphocytic leukemia.

No one could deny that Naida was a beautiful child, striking, with black ringlets, and dewy white skin. She had a laugh that sounded like bells and, as she grew, the stubbornness of a battleship and the ability to hyperfocus when she was interested in something.

"Mr. Taki gave me these," she said one day, after I'd pulled a pair of cuff links out of her hands.

"No, Naida. Those belong to him. He forgets things sometimes." I put the cuff links in my pocket.

"Grammy Diana went to heaven. He's going to see her," she said, looking up at me, her eyes bright.

I tried not to appear alarmed. "When, honey? When is Mr. Taki going?"

"The cuff links, Mama. I put them in my pockets."

The fact that my daughter and my late mother were now conspiring made me more than a bit apprehensive.

When Naida was learning to walk, I'd guide her up and down the burgundy-carpeted halls of the apartment building. She wore her pink ballet slippers—her shoes of choice—and banged her flat palm against the doors. Everyone would open their door and smile.

She took after Graham in other ways. She had inherited his fear of birds and his nightmares. She often woke up in the middle of the night crying because of dreams of birds crashing into windows, of owls with sour eyes perched on the tops of mailboxes, and of clicking sounds that were like the ticking of a clock. She'd run into my bed and curl up against me, pleading with me to do something.

She came with me during the day as I did my chores and took care of the residents. At least within the protected walls of Wild Acres, she was welcome everywhere, and I think she got used to people cheering whenever she walked into the room. We spent our days playing games that I made out of my chores. Changing sheets became a dance with wind. Refilling soap containers became a race to see who could pour without spilling the magic oil. I read her fairy tales and taught her to read when she was just over a year and a half. She developed a love of books like I had. We made homemade playdough, built forts out of empty boxes, and drew pictures for hours while listening to classical music, folk ballads, Pink Floyd, and the Beatles. I tried to indulge her creativity. Some children were hitters, others carried smelly blankets, and still others picked their noses. In the scheme of things, Naida's habit of knowing things was not uncontrollable. I gently tried to distract her from it without giving it too much attention. I tried to teach her how to be tactful, how to whisper things in my ear rather than announce them to random people at the top of her lungs—at the grocery store, the Mane Attraction Hair Salon, Home Depot. But tact was not a three-year-old's first language.

Pictures were. Naida drew pictures of a giant green water-horse the size of a house, with hooves the size of cars. She said that when it was angry it would race out of the water, and it would wait for her under our porch at night. "Oh, you mean Bob the horse? Oh, that's Bob, honey. He's just looking for fish," I'd say, trying to still my terror. She'd stare at me, and then a smile would break across her face.

"Horses don't eat fish!"

"He'll go away once he realizes that." She'd go back to sleep within minutes.

"She's telling you something in the only way she can. And you'd better listen," Dolly warned.

All mothers had to deal with the yearnings of their daughters. Still, I was certain that none had a child with a magical glint in her eye, who could diagnose illness, who would rush out to the beach and shriek with delight when thunderous hooves kicked up white foam.

Chapter Twenty-one
1993

THE SISTERS WOKE me, frenzied.

On the night of the Beaver Moon in November, when traps would be set for the winter hunts, I ran to Naida's bedroom only to find tousled sheets, her strawberry blanket puddled on the floor. Pictures of horses filled the room, the floor, the walls. When did she draw all of these? I hadn't seen any of them before, their thick crayon marks signaling an obvious urgency. There was one drawing of Naida riding the horse on the beach, her hands grasping its long black mane. There was another, of my daughter being thrown from the horse.

Shouting her name, I ran through the hallway, down the stairs, and across the beach, kicking up sand. There she was ahead, lying in a shallow pool at the shoreline. Her hair drifted on the skin of the water, flowing like feathered strands of seaweed, and in the dark night appeared to extend the length of her body. I noticed she was holding a blue crayon. Lacy foam covered her pale cheeks. Her lips were pewter, her skin a dove gray. The Sisters drew near, their coats a pale blue under the moon, their black eyes flashing.

"Get away from her!" I screamed, as they retreated. I had to get her out of the water. I picked up her cold swollen body, noticing the bruises on her arms and the scrapes on her chin and forehead. Suddenly, I was running with her in my arms. I fell on my knees. She wasn't breathing. I screamed for someone to call 911. I began CPR on my baby, pinching her nose and covering her mouth with my own, shouting for help between breaths. Mr. Takahashi came running. Then Dr. B. Then the rest of the residents, standing in their nightgowns and robes like matchsticks in the darkness.

I PACED THE hallway of the hospital. Dolly handed me black coffee in a Styrofoam cup. I was barely able to recall the ambulance ride. After several hours, I tried to imagine the guardian angels from Bethesda, whose luminescent wings shielded the young girls who crossed the threshold.

Was Naida with them now? I thought of Sister Mary. She could tell me about angels.

Dolly patrolled me to make sure I ate and slept, but of course I could not do either. At night I watched Naida for any signs of movement as I sat in the worn gray hospital chair next to her bed. I picked up one of the children's books Dr. B. had left. Light scraped my eyes. Dolly had fallen asleep standing up, her back against the wall. As soon as I'd nod off, I'd wake myself up. I'd reach for Naida's face in front of me. I'd see my sister leaning against the wall, her eyes closed, her long red hair covering Dr. B.'s prayer shawl.

With the help of a respirator, Naida existed motionless in a hospital bed for four days as doctors monitored her brain's activity. They watched for swelling, examining films and conducting scans. But still there was no Naida. My baby was gone, saliva dribbling out of the corner of her mouth. I sat beside her and dabbed at her face with a cool washcloth. I spoke to her loudly, and then in whispers. Where had she gone? I couldn't feel her. The nurses told me to go home, to take care of myself, but I could not leave her. What if the moment I left something happened?

Dolly took a photograph of us, my hand resting delicately on top of Naida's head, her dark curly hair flowing down over her shoulders. Words were too much of an effort. Pacing the halls, I spent the next several days thinking far too much about my mistakes. Dolly couldn't pull me out. She came and left quietly, handing me thermoses of Irish coffee with too much sugar and too much whiskey, trying to talk me out of my guilt for not finding Naida sooner. It was the only thing I had to hang on to, the only reason I could find to tell me why God would do this. I was an imperfect mother, but I loved her so. I needed to make sure that her heart was beating, the only language we shared now. I could hear that drumbeat. In my mind, it grew louder. I saw the rushing rivers and the trees falling off cliffs. Here, I could imagine the sand cobbled with clouds that had fallen from the sky.

Dr. B.'s hands trembled as she took the prayer shawl and stood at the foot of Naida's bed. "Pull it over her legs, Ruthie. It will help our prayers be heard," she told me. After I smoothed it over Naida's legs, Dr. B. smiled. She kissed Naida and then she kissed me. She sat in the chair next to Naida's bed and opened the fairy tale book. I covered Naida's limp foot with my hand.

FLIGHT COULD BE telegraphed through water, in fleeing footsteps. The ocean had taken her and only the ocean could give her back. My little girl rested in a place between dark and light, the threshold where bones piled up in the strawberry field, all too familiar. I had to bring her back.

Standing in the water up to my knees, the hem of my night-gown swirling, I walked in seven circles, my tears dropping like stones. The doctors had sent me home to get some sleep.

But my thoughts were kindling, errant pieces of driftwood scattered across the sand. I waited, but there was nothing. As the wind kicked up the worst storm of the year, I knelt in the shallow water, the waves pushing me back, trying to force me down. In the distance, I could see the crest of a huge wave coming toward me. Then the swell crashed over me, dragging me out. Choking back water, I began to fight it.

The undertow, it was here; it caught my ankles and pulled. I felt the sputter and rush all around me, the bitter cold, a swell of iridescent hues covering my arms and legs. The incessant pounding of hooves across water.

The wild horse tugged at me. My voice pooled up under tinfoil skies. One thousand promises made to God. *If just this, then that. Then what. Then anything, everything.*

I had a sense of its relentlessness, its desire, perhaps for Naida, as if it were only doing what she wanted. I fought through it as it bucked and pushed, kicking up sand and salt water, its mane like an oil slick, like sweeps of black seaweed moving back and forth. Mist burned my eyes, taking my breath away. Each time another wave crashed over my head I managed to push myself up. I fought back, remembering Edna's words.

My hands swept across the waves as I drew the horizon toward me.

There was no line between the sea and sky now. No separation between skin and bone.

My cheek hit the sand.

I stared up at the mist rising above the sea, willing myself to reach Naida, letting the harsh wind cut icy picks into my flesh. If her spirit slipped out, mine would go, too. I stayed there like a small fire, choking back the swells of salt water that covered my face, my ears and nostrils. This was how I took her back. With my gripping heart, with my fingers pulling back the blue cover of night. Suddenly, I felt fingers in my hair and on my shoulders. Dr. B. was taking my arm.

"Come now, child. Get up," Dr. B. said, and she tried to pull me from the water. I had bruises on my arms and on my legs. My palms were raw as Graham's had been on more than one occasion, as if a rope had been ripped from them. Noticing my nightgown stained with splotches of red, through ragged breaths I said that it was time to bring my daughter home.

WHEN WE ARRIVED at the hospital, Naida was sitting up, her face lustrous. "I was hiding with the animals," she said. She started to cry, saying that her throat hurt. Later, she would tell me that they loved her.

I took Naida's hands in mine and kissed them, weeping.

One of the young doctors said that for Naida to have found her way back, given the unknowns, she must have really wanted to be here. Her tests were clear. The hospital social worker, in her white button-down shirt and tan twill pants, had been observing me from afar. Why hadn't I been watching my daughter? she now asked. How could a four-year-old child have wandered out into the night during a storm, unnoticed? Why didn't I have a lock on my front door, a baby gate, an alarm system, and a baby monitor to keep her from getting out? I had all those things, but I was so beside myself with relief, I told her what I understood as truth—Naida had only been looking for her father, who was at sea. Luckily, Dolly appeared just then and talked to the woman in the white shirt. Then the woman disappeared. My magnificent sister.

I watched Naida playing with her blue dog. With her hair parted slightly, I could see the only trace of anything different about her, a faint pink scar across her forehead.

EAGER TO MOVE on with our lives and start fresh, I hung wallpaper throughout the apartment, a yellow tea rose print that I found at a Laura Ashley seconds sale. I had almost enough to cover all the walls, but for one spot in the hallway, which I filled using mirrored tiles. I felt proud of myself, of the new life we were creating. We were far from rich, but I had made a nice home. I baked fresh challah a few times a week, and I started having Dr. B. over on Wednesday nights again to pray.

I bought furniture at a garage sale: a shabby-chic ivory couch with a tear in the back that I sewed up, and a small matching chaise. On either side, I placed a standing red lamp with beads. I had refurbished a wooden coffee table that Mrs. Green had kept in the storage room. Dr. B. had given me the one remaining plastic palm tree from the days of the Twin Palms Motel. I put it in the corner of Naida's bedroom. All my books were shelved in white painted bookcases and baskets throughout the house, a few of which Dr. B. had given to me, too.

In the corner of the living room, next to the porch, Naida had an easel and art table positioned so she could paint the sea. Her markers and crayons were displayed in little cups along the sides. I now had two photographs on the wall. My mother's and my daughter's. In the photograph, Naida is standing on the beach, hands on her hips. She has sand covering her cheeks. Her long black hair hangs in salty clumps, falling across one pale eye. She is looking off to the right with the slightest smile, as if pressing a secret between her lips, just as the girl in the painting of the naiad had done.

I bought Naida an entire wardrobe, which included dresses, striped leggings, princess sneakers with a tread that lit up when she walked, sea slippers, and five pairs of ballet shoes, which were still the most comfortable thing for her feet. It would be another couple of years before she'd become embarrassed about her foot, when she saw the reactions of other children.

I had been walking around in the same gauze shirts, faded jeans, and worn leather clogs with busted buckles for years. Now I wanted to burn everything and start anew. I tried on a bright blue dress with heels, turning in the mirror. I had lost some weight over these last few months, and I was catching up on sleep. At twenty-seven, I peered at my face in the mirror, my fingers pressing the skin around my eyes. I'd begun to see the faintest wrinkles in the corners of my eyes and on the sides of my mouth, welcome signs of hard-won battles.

I ate avocados and sprinkled flax seeds over yogurt with honey, and in time my hair recovered its original fullness. Once in a while, I even put on lipstick, a pale peach color that brought out my freckles. I didn't look terrible, I decided.

It was a second chance. Naida had a chance to be just a normal girl.

It was clear what she had inherited from my side, the dominant genes for rebellion, stubbornness, and creative rapid-fire swearing, which she demonstrated while at brunch on her fifth birthday, stunning Dolly and me with the mention of "damn-ass eggs." This had all started with my mother.

I continued to watch Naida for any early signs of trouble.

I saw trouble all over the place.

Chapter Twenty-two

THE FOLLOWING YEAR, under the Lenten Moon in March, the last full moon of winter, a time when the past could return to meet you where you'd left it, I heard a knock on my door. I had been in bed, sick, for two days. I peered through the peephole and sucked in my breath as I stared at him.

Graham, as out of the blue as he'd come the first time.

He looked old, weary, dressed in a black turtleneck sweater, torn at the shoulder, and jeans. His brown beard had streaks of gray in it now, and his complexion was sallow. His pale green eyes were distant. He held out his palms, showing me he had nothing. I grabbed the cell phone and threatened to dial 911. "Ruthie, I have no one," he said, through the door.

"I have company. There's a man here," I lied, hoping he'd go away.

"Ruthie. Nobody's with you."

"Go away," I called.

"I need help."

My fingers unbolted the locks I'd installed after Naida's accident. I left the chain on and cracked open the door.

"I asked you not to come back," I said quickly, noticing how weathered he looked. He was different, not the burly gentle giant of a man I remembered. He had wrinkles around his eyes and a deep groove between his eyebrows. His lips were badly chapped, and there was a gash on his forehead over his right eye.

I shut the door and pressed my back against it. Naida was asleep. That's how I wanted it to stay.

"Ruthie," he said.

Gathering my navy blue robe more tightly around my body, I opened the door. He said nothing. Not at first.

"Thank you," he said, watching carefully. So carefully, in fact, that I was afraid he'd see that I sometimes remembered him. He was carrying his wetsuit, just like always. "I've been thinking about you both."

"You missed your damn window of opportunity," I said, as I watched him set his wetsuit over the chair on the porch, just as he always did. Some things never changed.

"I have a right to see her. She's my child, too."

"You're too late."

"You've gotten tough with age, Ruthie."

In my mind, I slapped him. "What do you want, Graham? Why did you come back?" I smoothed my hair. It was long and curly. I hadn't cut it in years. Now I wished I'd cut it short, that there was nothing about me that even hinted at femininity. But no, of course I would not hide in boys' ripped clothing as I once had. I would not disguise myself. I would not be silenced, or become a watered-down version of myself. Not again.

"I just needed to see her, you," he said.

"I will call the police. I mean it." I stood with my hands on the back of Naida's art chair. Her drawings were now of the beach, or the ocean, or just the Sisters. No longer of the green waterhorse.

My legs shook, and I hoped he wouldn't notice. But of course he would. Graham noticed everything about me.

"You've done a nice job," he said, looking around. "You've made a good home for the two of you. You have no idea how good it is to see you," he said, reaching for me, his eyes hazy. I kept my distance and told him what had happened to her. He had a right to know. "I know you're a good mother."

"No, you don't. I might be a shitty mother. I might be the shittiest mother there is. My daughter escaped into the ocean while I slept. She barely made it back."

I noticed the blood on his knuckles. He had been in a fight. He walked toward me. My body was moving toward him, but my mind was working hard, searching for a concrete thought to anchor me. The table. The easel. The red sippy cup Naida still used and had left balancing on the arm of the couch, with its chewed spout. His fingers dusted my cheek. In my mind I was reaching for him, until I caught sight of the look in his eyes.

"She's sleeping," I said. Before I could get another word out, he put his arm around me. I twisted away. I had not been with a man in five years. It took everything I had not to be touched.

"No. No more. You have to go," I told him. Then, Naida's voice.

"Mama?"

I ran to Naida and picked her up, kissing her cheek.

"Who is he!" said Naida, struggling to see Graham over my shoulder. I couldn't just spring this on her. Of course, it would take time to introduce the subject. I didn't want to think of it. Not yet. Not until I had to.

I told her he was a friend of Mama's from a long time ago. Graham gave Naida a little pinky wave before we disappeared.

I tucked her back into bed for the second time that night. "When did he come? Is he staying here? Where will he sleep? What will he eat? Will I see him tomorrow? Can I show him my tree in my bedroom?" I replaced the red bulb in her plastic horse-shaped nightlight, the reason she had gotten out of bed in the first place.

"That's my daddy," Naida said, as I was getting up to leave. I stared at the red hues spilling across her bed. Her hair fell across her eyes and she pursed her lips in disapproval, just like Dolly. "It is him," she said, folding her arms across her chest. "I know it is."

"We'll talk tomorrow, honey," I said quickly, for Naida could pull me into a conversation too easily. Just as I was about to shut the door, I heard her.

"He wants me to go with him, Mama."

I shut the door.

GRAHAM WAS GAZING at Naida's photograph on the wall. He'd made himself at home, his glass of whiskey on the counter.

"Go now, please," I said.

"I remember," he said, pointing to the wall. "Six years ago, the only photo you had—"

"I know, I know. Now I've got two."

"I noticed her foot."

Defensively, I told him that the surgery was painful. I told him all about the recovery time, and about the chance of infection and more surgeries. We'd already been to two surgeons who both said the same thing: If the benefits didn't outweigh the costs, leave it alone. It appeared not to be a problem for her. She could decide when she was older what to do.

He looked at me with despair and then nodded in agreement. There was blood on his shirt. "The child shouldn't suffer," he said finally.

"The child has a name. Naida."

"Naida, Naida," he repeated. "What kind of name is Naida?"

"Water fairy," I whispered. "Fresh water," I said, in my best "fuck you" tone. "She is my everything, Graham."

I told him to leave. He didn't move. It was a condition that every cell in my body remembered. "Just go. Do you want her to remember this, our fighting? You shouldn't be here."

"Ruthie. There's more to say. Did you keep them under the mattress, the dagger and the bible?" He grabbed my wrist.

"Let go of me!" I said. He did.

"I'm the child's father," he said.

Calm. Feel the ground beneath you. "You left your child and the mother of your child. What kind of father does that make you?"

At that, he hurled his glass at the wall. I watched the golden liquid spill across my beautiful wallpaper, and the broken crystal scatter across the carpet.

He stepped back. "Jesus, I'm sorry," he whispered, his eyes pleading. "I don't know how to do this with you," he said, picking up the glass. He tossed the shards in the trash. I imagined little pieces of hiding in the shag rug, waiting for Naida's bare feet to find them.

I cleaned off the wall and grabbed the DustBuster to vacuum up the rest of the mess. After, he stood in front of me, shoulders squared, feet planted apart, waiting for me to do something.

"Ruthie, I know I didn't give you what you wanted."

"No, neither of us got what we wanted," I said, opening the door.

As he walked away down the hallway, his shadow dissolved into the light.

THE FIRST RAYS of dawn shone through the window. I was a person who had once been superstitious. I'd made meaning from things. I liked it that way, couldn't help it. Somehow, none of it mattered because Naida was here. And like it or not, the threads of first love could never be broken. I had strengthened them with my fear and my hatred, and with my worry. The molecules that existed among those threads, incited by love and by fear, formed the bonds that connected one living thing to another. Peak emotion created waves of energy that remained long after an inciting event. Perhaps those molecules would spread out everywhere, could travel through all matter, carried on the waves of the oceans and in the breezes. They could never be destroyed, only changed. They could change and become forgiveness. I wondered. Had I really drawn him back to me? Stepping back from the mirror, I took off my glasses and set them on the vanity. Then I splashed my face with cold water.

I GAVE NAIDA a glass of milk and sent her back to bed. I put down my glass of whiskey, trying to still the occasional shivers. I heard a noise out on the beach. There, in the sand, a huge male sea lion waited, his eyes large and piercing, his ears pricked. Magnificent, his blue-black body was unmovable, his neck as thick as a tree trunk, his forehead formed of a bony crest. His long front flippers were winglike, made of bones similar to those of an arm and a hand. I turned off the porch light. I kept checking, though, well after I'd put her to bed. That animal, all eight hundred pounds of him, was a mirror image of the sea lion I'd once seen shot in this very parking lot.

He remained on the beach all night. I couldn't stand it, his barking. Mr. Takahashi and Dr. B. stood on their porches, hands on their hips, complaining to each other through the wind. Dr. B. said she'd have someone come get him if he wasn't gone by morning.

It sounded to me as though he was grieving.

By sunrise, he had disappeared.

PART THREE

Chapter Twenty-three

Naida, 1995

THE FIRST TIME anyone ever called me Frog Witch, I was six, with chapped red lips, as if my mouth held a small flame. The humidity was so thick, it coated me in sweat seconds after a shower, convincing me to finally forgo beach slippers. To go barefoot.

The heat wave sank the pink bougainvillea blossoms over Wild Acres, threatening to cave in the roof, causing the sea creatures to stare back with gold-flecked eyes, refusing to leave the ocean. Mr. Taki knelt beside me, scraping a moat around the sand castle we'd just built. My mother lay stretched out on a blue blanket a few feet away, holding a book over her face, her feet tipped in wet sand. Everywhere, people laid themselves out like downed trees on colorful patchworks across the beach. I pushed my wet hair from my eyes and drew a dragon on the side of the castle wall with a stick when Mr. Taki got up to go for a swim.

My hands were blanched by salt. My foot twitched in the heat.

A little girl in a gold bikini wandered up to me. She had short brown hair pushed back in a ribbon headband and a wide smile like her mother, who watched from her blanket a few feet away. The girl crouched beside me, lacing her plump fingers over her knees. She admired my castle and its adornment of white shells. Then her eyes grew wide.

"What's *that*?" she asked, pointing at me.

"So the bad guys can't get to the castle," I explained, waving my hands over the moat. "Because of the alligators in there."

"No, your *foot*. That *frog foot*."

I heard the scrape of waves hitting the rocks as something hard and frozen shifted high inside my belly. It rose up in my throat, capturing my voice. Shadows of blue-black distilled into ivory and lavender hues, fading into the distant sky. I pushed my foot into the sand, burying it up to my ankle.

"Are you a frog?" Her blue eyes held mine, burning, before I could answer. "You're a Frog Witch," she said, matter-of-factly. She said the words over and over as Mr. Taki walked toward us from the water, dripping wet in his white button-down and cuffed jeans. "Frog Witch picks up sticks. Frog Witch has an itch. Frog Witch—"

I started flinging words right back at her in a louder rhyme, telling her she was a *gold witch*, and a *rich witch*, neither of which really sounded like an insult, mostly because in my heart, I didn't want to hurt her feelings, which I knew, even at six, didn't make sense.

"I'll beat you in swimming," I said, to which she said we'd have a race, and yet what if I failed miserably? What if she left me even more embarrassed than before? "Over there to there," I said, pointing from the lifeguard's chair to the blue-striped buoy about ten feet away.

Then, suddenly, I was lifted out of there by my mother. "Why don't we take a break from the castle and have a little lunch? You can come back and play later," my mother suggested, more as a demand, as I buried my face against her freckled chest. The girl ran off with my secret, and my shells.

"What am I? Am I dangerous?"

"No, of course not."

"What about poisonous?" My mother shook her head no and wrapped me up in a thick red towel. I was not beautiful and perfect the way God made me, as the residents of Wild Acres always insisted. That was a lie; I knew that now. The Wizard, who operated the fuse box that controlled the timing and installation of bodies, had ruined me, despite all his metallic circuitry, switches made of glass, and tangled nests of messed-up copper wiring. Why, if the Wizard could part the Red Sea, could part the heavens and make rain, could rip apart the continent with an earthquake, couldn't he part the skin between my toes?

"Sometimes God decides things before we're born, honey. Then she wants to see how we'll do."

"Like a test?"

"It's no one's fault. It makes you different. Special," my mother said. But I just wanted to be like everybody else. She kissed the top of my head. A few feet away, the little girl's mother waved apologetically. I reached my hands around the back of my mother's neck, pulling her close to me. She carried me back inside, waving to Mr. Taki to follow us. "I know it's hard, Naida, but you're beautiful and perfect in my eyes, and you'll always be."

I could already sense that the little girl's stories had begun careening through the ether, taking root like wild raucous flowers, spreading like wildfire. My green foot, scaled like a lizard's. My hoof. My toes like claws. Like a bird's foot. Like a paw. My foot that had a snake's face with a forked tongue. My foot. My difference. The one that didn't make me special. The one that made me the Frog Witch.

—◦—

IT MIGHT HAVE been better to have just pounded my fists in the sand, or better yet to have run away—some moments are better marked in that way, recognized for their significance. Moments such as the one that had just transpired, when careless little hands tore your secret from the air, should not go unnoticed. They should not pass as silently as an eclipse, capable of tricking the birds into thinking it was twilight, or tricking you into thinking your life would continue to move along swimmingly, when in fact your whole life would never be the same. Not everything that had significance made a sound.

Little girls raced each other through the waves, swimming for their lives. Planets raced silently through the galaxy, scraping gaseous edges from the corners of the atmosphere as they halted like freight trains on rusted orbiting tracks, tumbling red velvet seats and twisted chrome bumpers through the air onto land, leaving dented chrome and smoky tunnels. There wouldn't even be a ripple of noise. You might see the sparks fly as if stars and call it a meteor shower. Comets whisked across the night sky, carrying within them the molecules of noise from all those comets that had come before, but you never heard them hit the skin of Earth's high atmosphere. Astral avalanches were somber, silent things, even when meteors left canyons in the earth. Dowsing rods quivered as soon as you stepped into a circle of neolithic stones, where whispers were amplified to the degree of screams.

Those stones in Orkney, the ones I read about so I'd know where my father came from, just confirmed what I knew to be true. Whispers were as dangerous as nasty nicknames, more so, for their energy would go unseen and therefore wouldn't dissipate quickly, and could return years later, having been redirected to the future as if by Earth's magnetic lines, causing things to catch up with you and one day explode. And yet I didn't know that things returned in the way they did, that whispers would boomerang onto those whose lips they first escaped.

THE BOUGAINVILLEA WERE holding us all in place, rooting us to the earth, Dr. B. always said. Each year they grew more lush, capturing Wild Acres in a net of fuchsia petals, entangling us all. No one had ever seen vines as thick as these, which could become full with bees and butterflies.

I'd lived in the glass fishbowl of Wild Acres up until that day when I was six, my bare feet never to be worn outside again. More than what it did to me, I worried about my mother, her guilt. The Most Beautiful Lady in the World had been my universe—my first love. She vowed I'd never feel unwanted, and I hated to be away from her. Trying to pattern myself after her, an unattainable goal, I'd realize, I'd memorized the constellation of freckles across her face, the black beauty mark on her shoulder I once thought of as the earth, a planet around which all the stars revolved. She was a reflection of all that was right in the universe. The Big Dipper constellation on her chest was proof, for it mirrored the night sky, which I had traced from the time she kept me in an ERGO pressed to her skin. But that didn't protect me, not from my own judgments and failings and my ever-shifting need to be distant and then suddenly close. We'd always told stories in my family like the ancients who tried to find reasons for the weather, who found reasons to create gods and goddesses. Somehow we had not been satisfied by thousands of years of revelations and inventions.

The world I now knew held no calm bed of pine needles beneath the trees, the place where the children in fairy tales always fell asleep when they wandered off lost, before they would wake up to a new day, having been found by fairies or by a compassionate woodsman or by a kind princess. No matter what stories my grandmother had told, they could not carry me away.

The world I now knew would be made up on my own. The fine line between a truth and a lie seemed only a matter of consensus, of how many people believed or did not, which seemed irrelevant to me, given the haphazard ways opinions were often drawn or judgments made with little evidence, like those who bullied me about my foot or drew their eyes away from me when they saw me being teased. It was just a hairline, barely visible. But when Aunt Dolly announced that breathing underwater was impossible, obliterating it from my life under the guise of something called common knowledge, a thing that could win you an argument without even trying, I thought she was playing a trick on me. I'd never questioned it or thought to tell anyone about it, for I assumed everyone did it.

"I'm not saying you're lying, Naida. I'm only saying that it can't happen."

"But it does happen."

"Must have been a dream, honey."

"You can't do it, so you think I can't."

"Come on, now. The truth of the matter is that you simply don't have gills."

Gills. I knew what gills were. What did that matter, though? Why couldn't I breathe underwater? If I had a webbed foot, who said I couldn't do other things, too? "I have gills *inside* my chest."

"So do I. They're called lungs," she said, winning the argument and reducing me to just human. I'd let her believe that, at least. But in truth, I still didn't buy it. It didn't make sense to me that the body would stop doing something that worked on automatic pilot, just because of a thing like water. This would be the first of many things I'd mistake for normalcy, like eating cereal for dinner and staying up late in celebration of nothing in particular, when my mother was working and Aunt Dolly was staying with me, her unpredictability making her a favorite babysitter, letting me watch her make a Jell-O mold for a work picnic she was going to the next day, or playing checkers with her on the patio in the moonlight until she'd say she was tired and then dance me off to bed. Aunt Dolly's stories were always good ones, always starring little girls who grew up in a world without adults and had adventures as they struggled to survive without grocery stores, policemen, hospitals, cars, bicycles, and other civilized things like bedrooms and furniture and dishware.

Her rogue honesty both enticed me and infuriated me.

I'd stared in disbelief after she broke the news of breathing underwater. How I wanted to curl up on the bottom of the ocean to prove her wrong. Distraught, I'd snuck into the hall closet to wait for my mother to get home. As soon as I heard the door open, I planned on rushing out like a butterfly, flitting around her, begging to be told I was right and it was true, making sense of all those times I'd taken my time to evaluate what I saw underwater, my sisters and their translucent arms. My mother had always maintained that I remembered everything, which I assumed included some things before my birth. That's how I knew that my father's voice in my head wasn't a dream. The heavy sound waves once made by his words were stacked like bricks in my memory. On nights when sleep seemed impossible, when the sea switched places with the sky and turned quiet and thunder grew from the earth, shaking the ocean as if with knotted arthritic hands, I'd stand on my bed, feet planted squarely apart, and I'd hold my hand to my eyes as if from a glaring sun. I'd replay my father's voice, showing the world and all its creatures that he would be supreme over all, including the planets, the animals, and the weather. All the things he would come back for.

I'd always remember breathing underwater like a fish, even years later when I no longer argued the fact and had switched camps, believing it a dream. That still didn't erase the memory of it. There were many things that people told you never happened but that you still had memories of. I'd think of it every time I noticed my mother's organza curtains billowing up through the swirling blue sky, amid all those invisible kicking legs of jellyfish I could envision on the window. There were times when I'd test it out, sinking down in the water and beginning to draw in air through my nose, and then with the slightest pressure of the oncoming water, I'd give up, renewing my doubt in myself. My father would understand, though. I was certain he could do it, too. I knew there was no point in trying to convince anyone else. As soon as they said it was impossible, my ability was lost.

"Moose, you should have a talk with her. She still thinks Graham's coming back. I watched you wait, and now her," Aunt Dolly told my mother later that night. I watched from the cracked door of the closet in the hallway, standing in my nightshirt, my knees shaking, positive they'd fling open the door and discover me here. I was becoming like Harriet the Spy, my heroine in books.

"Let me get my coat off, at least." My mother untied her stained apron and sat on the couch, kicking off her black leather restaurant shoes as Aunt Dolly perched on the coffee table, facing her in a white baseball shirt with navy blue sleeves and faded jeans. She placed her hands on my mother's shoulders, telling her all about me and what she'd better do to make sure to keep me on the planet.

My mother knew something had to be done, for my connection to my father and the ocean were primal and vital. It had been building for years, my need for him, stronger now after that moment on the beach when my foot had been discovered by others.

She pulled me gently out of the closet and sat me down on the bed. "He'd want you to have this," my mother told me, reaching into her jewelry box, which was nothing more than an old rusted tin box that she'd picked up while trash picking many years ago during one of those times when they had no money and they had to sell garbage. My mother was fond of the box, which also held a miniature dagger and bible. She'd lined it with a gold quilted fabric and edged it in gold trim, which she super-glued and stuck her fingers to the fabric for a few minutes. Otherwise, it was perfect. Now, she took out a silver pendant on a thick chain, which she said had been worn by my father, and which he'd given to her the first time he left. The swirling lines of the animal still glimmered. Its ornate body was made of shiny overlapping circles. She called it a dragon, but to me it looked like a horse. I never told her that, or took it off.

My escape into the ocean always soothed me.

I'd hold up my arms, making myself heavy like a stone, sinking to the bottom. Pushing fast through the water, I'd imagine whales rising like mountains as their flukes carved the breeze. Then, I'd glide among the sea lions, rolling back and forth, looking up as if the sky were the mirror. In my dreams, the people who hid in animal skins could find me like this, at dawn or twilight on the beach. I imagined my own sisters, three of them. I'd come face-to-face with the eldest sister, her long black hair fanning across her breasts, her freckled cheeks and long straight nose like mine, as were her long fingers. She'd gaze at me, her black eyes flecked with silver. Behind her was a smaller girl with silver hair to her thighs, and behind her, a third sister who looked younger than the others, with straight red hair and olive skin like Aunt Dolly's.

Bars of sunlight flashed across their skin as they all treaded water, their hands moving quickly in sync at their sides like fins. My mother's three sea lions, which she called the Sisters, still remained on the beach most times, but never when my own sisters came to visit. Then they disappeared.

The smallest girl held up her hands, showing me empty glowing palms and splayed fingers, the translucent webbed skin tinged with tiny red capillaries like maps. I looked down at her feet, but she was kicking too fast.

All I knew was that her voice had the distancing feeling of an echo. Dipping her chin to her chest, she'd turn her back in a cloud of bubbles and dive into the darkness. Then the others retreated, too. My protectors. My sisters. These were my people, the ones who hid in the skins of animals. The ones who would risk everything for me. The ones who could swim across the ocean to find my father and bring him back.

My mother said the bougainvillea fed on love. But it wasn't love. Something else, uncertainty. I'd see my sisters walking out of the shallow water, one by one, dropping their animal skins in a heap at their feet. They'd stand in thin white nightgowns, the fabric ripped in different spots, pulled apart like tissue paper. They'd encircle me, clasping hands. Then, kneeling in the sand, they'd untie the silvery thread around their necks, each of which held a small drum with the picture of a dragon etched on the skin. They'd tap their drums with fingertips, which made my heart beat fast. In their language, they told me how to tunnel through moonlight. They found me when I hid. They hid me when I wanted to disappear. But they wanted things, too. They wanted to take me away with them. But I couldn't leave my mother, not at first.

In my dreams, I'd huddle with them for warmth. I imagined them tucked in bed beside me, as I used to do with my mother.

The girls could swim like dragons, and I could swim almost as fast.

"Curiosity is natural at her age. She's got to find a way to deflect it," Aunt Dolly said, to explain the incessant questions about my foot.

"But their comments are rude. Naida shouldn't have to answer anything; she's only six. Just tell them you have my permission to say they should mind their own business," my mother said, fiercely protective. I felt as if the sun were searing the canvas of my sneakers, illuminating my stuck-together toes. My mother told me to say, if people asked, that being different made me special, which I knew it didn't, and which of course I'd never say. When Irene and I met up on the beach the next day, we stood a few feet apart, facing each other as if in a standoff, my hands hanging at the sides of my ruffled pink bathing suit.

"Ready?" She nodded.

"Swim from there to there," I said, pointing at the buoys, bobbing on the waves in the roped-off portion of the shallow beach. Irene kicked off her sandals and said she'd swum with sharks before. How I longed to be able to kick off my sea slippers, too, but I couldn't again, even if she already knew what my foot looked like. When she said go, I folded my arms, watching her run off ahead of me, kicking sand, diving into the ocean, and then her arms furiously slicing through the water. I could see the splash made by her kick, all foam and angst. That was my signal. I raced into the waves and dove in. I let her think she could outswim me, but no one could. I dove underneath a wave, disappearing and swimming past Irene with all my strength, catching sight of her face only once, when I looked back as she opened her mouth to take a breath, and in that moment, when water rushed over her face, it was made clear to her that she had no chance, her expression one of panic, with snot running down her lips. When I surfaced, touching the buoy, she was still about three feet away.

"Cheater!" she called.

I started to swim, competitive as I was, back to shore. When I reached the sand, I fell onto the beach on my back, arms splayed out, trying to catch my breath. "Don't think you won," she called from the shallow area, choking back the salt water.

"I won fair and square."

She pushed her brown bangs off her forehead and smiled as she walked by me in the sand. "I'm not the loser here."

WHEN I WAS seven, I developed a habit of climbing into my window after school, my feet swung over the ledge, looping my toes in the vines, pulling the bougainvillea from their clawed place on the stucco, careful not to kick away my ladder. My mother's smile always fell when she saw me, and I knew there'd be a small confrontation, which began with her demanding that I come down. "What are you looking for out there?"

"I don't want to be a kid anymore," I said. Second grade carried with it a sort of desperation, a time when cliques had started to form as if silent torrents over the waves and girls sought frenzied alliances, solidified with notes passed for play-dates after school. I'd no longer be satisfied with my island of a desk, listening to other girls talk of their plans. They'd smirk when I tried to join in their conversations. Once in a while, they said, "We don't have time for frogs" when I joined them on the playground. Then they'd ignore me. They put a sign on their desks that said "No Frogs Allowed." For a time it was better to be alone, staying in my classroom while the other children were at lunch or on the playground. Teachers were paid to be patient with you.

"You don't want to play hopscotch or jump rope? It looks like they're having so much fun out there, doesn't it?" my teacher would ask.

"No, I don't like games so much. I'll just stay in here and read," I'd reply, and I'd lose myself in a book. Sometimes I'd ask for special assignments, like wiping down the blackboard and cleaning the erasers, things I could do competently.

"Only fly away with me," my mother said, reaching for me in my bedroom window. She sailed me through the air, urging me to fling my wings out, making me laugh.

Then her eyes fell to the floor.

Sighing, she put me down on the bed and she knelt, her fingers drifting over the pictures I'd cut out from magazines. A hammock in the grass. A father riding on his lawn mower. A father reading a fairy tale to his daughter in his lap. A father building a tree house in the backyard. Grilling chicken. Holding a briefcase. Who tucked them in. Who took them swimming. Who walked them home from school to protect them from the bullies who would chase them. Who told them where they came from. Who called them by a secret name. Who stole them back. Who made them a foot just like his own.

"Fathers," she said, almost hesitating to say the word aloud. Then, "This is only going to get worse," my mother said, causing a meteor that had been racing through the atmosphere to suddenly halt and explode into sprays of rock, another canyon avoided on Earth.

Chapter Twenty-four

ON RAINY WEEKENDS when I could not find my sisters, my eyes would burn red and watery. I'd find myself drawn to shadows, and to the oncoming storms that billowed up in the corners of the vast morning sky. My mother would tell me to take a bath, hoping I'd be calmed by the sensation of floating and the scented rose oil in the bathwater for a little while. I'd pile my hair up on top of my head and sink down beneath the bubbles, holding my breath, daring myself to breathe. With a mouthful of bubbles, I'd rise up, spitting the soap out, drawing a heavy terry-cloth towel across my tongue. I'd dress quickly, announcing it didn't work. Then my mother would send me out back: "Naida, go get it off your chest." I'd stand on the beach in my shiny red ladybug raincoat with my matching shiny red rain hat and boots, my hands balled into fists, and I'd scream so loud that the seagulls would lift off, as if a curtain of collective shock, blackening the sky. The horizon would light up with silver wire, and all the lavender and golden hues in the sky would slide into the waves as if melted from a wall of ice.

When I was eight, I began to dive off the pier and the rocks at the end of the peninsula. By nine, I secretly began imagining a dive off the rooftop of the Sands Restaurant, where my mother worked some nights as a cook. I'd been up there before, at one of my mother's work parties, and I knew the cool scrape of those roof tiles on the soles of my feet, the roof gripped under me, and I'd dared myself to do it. I'd already checked out the rocks underneath and had found a safe spot.

Day after day, I ran home from school, chased by bullies who threw rocks at my back and called me names. My mother had written a note giving me permission to leave early on account of my violin lessons, which I took for a month and then dropped, when the screeching horsehair bow was just too much for the residents to take. Yet still, no one questioned it when I'd leave a few minutes early, just enough time to fly out the door and trample the football field, getting a head start on my bullies. This was the only thing that saved me.

Night after night, I escaped through my window, climbing down the vines, racing over the bike path, and climbing up the fire escape ladder to the roof, where I'd walk to the end, my toes curled over the edge, my belly undulating from the height. I imagined I'd push off and just fly. But I never did.

At home, I practiced jumping from my dresser to my bed, arms and legs flung out, landing in soft pillows. But fear held me back from doing the real thing. It was too far down. My bare feet would kick up moonlight across the waves, but only in my imagination, and I'd leave the roof, time and time again, invisible somehow, and defeated.

Somewhere around that time, my sisters took a hiatus. No longer able to communicate with them, my voice box quit working altogether. The air was too full of stories, and there was no room left for my wild imaginings. Not only did I have my own memories, but I had those of my mother and my grandmother to keep track of.

"Keep busy. Write down what's bothering you. Write a letter. Anything," my mother told me. She wanted me to know the power of having a tool in my hands. Though she said she didn't have time for her own artwork anymore, it had helped her through a certain time in her life. Her paintings that had once hung throughout the house were reminders of that difficult time, and though she'd taken them down, she never forgot what they'd given her. She pushed a small spiral notepad toward my blue placemat at the kitchen table and pointed to the green magic marker, which she knew would entice me.

I shook my head no. When she narrowed her eyes, I grabbed the paper and wrote: "But I have no one to write to." *My father has no address* is what I wanted to say, but she didn't deserve to have her feelings hurt. I'd rather endure my own pain than cause hers.

"Write to me," she said, crossing her arms over her breasts, a ritual of hope. "I would love to have a letter from you. That would make me happy."

My letter was addressed to The Most Beautiful Lady in the World. She taped it to her mirror above the bureau. Back then, I didn't know why she wrote the wrong date on it—six years into the future. That would make me fifteen. She told me she was saving it for when I became a teenager, when I'd decide I no longer liked her—but I knew that would never happen. Everyone liked my mother. She was naturally likable and never cross, unlike me. Just one more thing I knew I must have in common with my father.

Whenever a thought felt trapped in my throat, I just tore off a scrap of paper and wrote my mother a note, an easy reprieve. Sometimes I left notes for her on her pillow, a replacement for words that had not been spoken. She always looked surprised, pleased, no matter what the note said. Even if I wrote that I hated my foot. As long as I was expressing myself, she'd be pleased. That led to my writing other notes, this time for other people.

That is how I became the *Put*-pocket.

THE PUT-POCKET WOULD slip notes into coat pockets, purses, and the bags of lost or downtrodden travelers. Throwing my hair back in a ponytail, I'd pull on my gray hooded sweatshirt over whatever I was wearing, a black sundress or a T-shirt and jeans, and I'd tip my straw hat forward and slip on my black boots with the big brass buckles that went up the side. This was my Put-pocket uniform. I carried the notebook and marker in my backpack wherever I went, leaving myself reminders about people I saw who needed a good word, who needed a second chance. It would be years before I'd learn that my grandmother did a similar thing by keeping track of her life in her almanacs. My grandmother didn't scare me, nor did comparisons to her. There was no threat that I'd become somebody else. I was, in effect, too much myself. I was keeping track of other people's lives, not mine. I was a rescuer, no longer a person who was just waiting for her father to come back.

I left notes for swimmers on their towels at the beach, for waitresses on empty plates in restaurants, for mothers on benches when they'd get up to push their young children in a swing; some notes were rolled up in cast-off high-tops left in the sand by beach walkers whenever someone raced into the water. Weaving through a crowd, I left them in people's coat pockets, brushing by quickly, or slipped them into open grocery bags in parking lots while people returned their shopping carts to the racks. Put-pocketing required careful planning and people-watching, for only those who needed me most would receive a note. People were always telling you what they needed, in all sorts of languages that had nothing to do with words: in brushstrokes, in sideways glances, in long silences, and in myriad other ways.

The straightforward talkers, like my aunt, were usually the most feared. But most were like me and could forget what was good about them because everybody around them was telling them they were bad, at least at school. I was aware at the time that I needed somehow to do this, to make up for my own inef-fectiveness at solving my problem with my bullies. But I knew this was important and would settle the score for others, bal-ancing out the tipped scales of the universe, tipping people's karma in favor of them, for every disrupted molecule had a ripple effect: If people in general were feeling too weighed down, the whole atmosphere would feel satiated, too full, and off-kilter, making you late for appointments, making machin-ery break down, making you lose things, becoming like a gray-yellow cloud that hovered over the place you lived, a smoglike consistency, like the kind that hung over the Los Angeles basin, not easily cleared, and occasionally moved and carried by the Santa Ana winds. Whenever we'd drive down the 405 toward Los Angeles, heading toward the San Gabriel Mountains, my eyes would burn from the smog, and I'd imagine all those good notes I'd have to write while we were there to try and help the people clear it up.

To the teenager I'd seen coughing at a bus stop and who, after she caught her breath, lit up a cigarette, I'd written a note that said her future children wanted her healthy enough to play with. I'd slipped it onto the bench when she got up to stretch her legs and tried to wave down the wrong bus. She returned to the bench to find it. I'd hidden behind a bush to watch her open it.

"Very funny," she said, coughing. "Hello? Hellooo?" She got up and looked around. I felt like one of the Fairies, those ancient people who first inhabited the land where my father was from, who lived in underground mounds, inside trees, and between the caves and craggy cliffs of Orkney, and who left no written record of a language, mostly hidden creatures. When no one answered her, she looked around and glanced up for a moment. Then she shoved the note in her pocket. But when I came back a week later, she sat on the bench and didn't smoke, instead holding a pencil between her fingers and taking long, unsatisfying drags on the lead.

At ten, I was at the height of put-pocketing power, for it would last only as long as I was still small enough, and whippet-fast, before I had my growth spurt. I'd follow people across the beach, ducking behind garbage cans, waiting behind trees, biding my time for the right opportunity. I had assumed a sort of military vigilance, perhaps to compensate for my mother's free-flowing philosophy when it came to my behavior, and my aunt's determined rebelliousness, which she'd encourage and then quash with a sudden maternal flash. I was smart enough to be careful, and naive enough not to worry about what would happen if I were caught. So far, I'd never been caught, not once, which I was proud of, but which I secretly began to worry would be impossible one day. Still, I was created perfectly for this. I could move through a crowd like a breeze in my gray sweatshirt with my hood pulled up over my chin, my gold ballet dress tufting out from under the sweatshirt, glimmering, like some sort of military ballet nymph, I imagined. During the day, I dressed in requisite pastel sundresses or polo shirts to try and fit in, and yet even in the appropriate costume I stuck out like a sore thumb and was still bullied, called the Frog Witch, asked if I was Aquaman's wife and whether or not I could still guess people's injuries and sicknesses, like I'd done for Julio that time on the beach when I told his mother his blood had rocks. By now, the story had changed, I'd hear later; it had morphed into a tall tale, urban folklore, that I had caused his blood to have rocks.

I'd already left notes for all the residents of Wild Acres and all those orbiting-satellite types, like the mailman and the electrician, but no one ever said a word. Just yesterday, I'd discovered the ice cream man, Paulo, whom my mother remembered from when she was a girl. He'd been slumped under a tree in the park, barefoot. I'd called him "the hatter" in my notes, for people left money in his overturned baseball hat. He'd been there for a week, lying on his side, jacket twisted up under the arms, white T-shirt greased. His pants were rolled up to the knees, exposing the sores on his shins. His stench made your eyes water from all the way over on the sidewalk, a mixture of sweat, urine, and mouthwash. The first time I saw him lying there, I thought he was dead. I crept toward him and noticed with relief that his hand was twitching in the grass, and every once in a while his leg would kick, and I'd wondered where he was running to, what he was trying to catch—whether he'd lost something, perhaps his life—whether he had children, a wife, a runaway job, a second chance. These were the only things I could think of.

I decided he would need a fresh change of clothing, and so I asked my mother to take me to Goodwill, where she'd purchase for me trousers and two flannel shirts, for a supposed scarecrow we were making in art class on account of Halloween. I hated to lie to her, but this was a white lie, a lie meant for good, Aunt Dolly had taught me. The shirts would keep him warm. Excited, I folded them into my backpack, ready to leave them in the grass as soon as I saw him again. It occurred to me then how strange it was that I always seemed to think of the adults I met as not having any families or attachments, unlike any of the new children I met, who always appeared better situated. I'd left one note each day over the last week for Paulo as he slept. That night, I imagined him waking up and thinking he had a lucky angel. That he'd been chosen, and that feeling of being plucked by luck would cause him to turn over a new leaf. I knew I was beginning to break my own rule, that falling in too deep was not okay. This could bind me, inexplicably, to another soul in milliseconds. That was the bargain I'd made with myself: to remain sequestered. But I became so worried about him, I confessed it to my mother, who insisted we go back the next day to see about a shelter for him. That was how I'd spend my twelfth birthday.

Birthdays had special rituals and contained magical powers, especially if you'd stacked up the same wish several consecutive years. That could give your wish more power. Wishes made on birthdays went right to God and did not have to wait in line at the gate. They would get top priority in the snack line, and they were given special consideration if at all outlandish. In my opinion, my wish was something purposeful, not fanciful. It wasn't like I was wishing for straight hair, or for an expensive toy. I didn't care about new stuffed animals, for I'd had the same one since I was a child, a blue dog, and never needed another. Not a new bike or a computer game that lit up, which I wasn't allowed to play anyway because it would make you fall in love with your television and fry your brains, my mother said. No, my wish was the same as it had been since I first discovered wishes. That wish had to do with my foot.

The morning of my birthday, a metal horse lifted its head out of the ocean, a machinelike version of the green water-horse from years ago, but this one's face was conical, its eyes shaped like rusted oily hexagons, his sheet-metal body riveted by iron nails, his fringed hooves scouring sand as he rose. I could see it from my bedroom window as I listened to the clatter of pans in the kitchen and the sound of my mother and my aunt's voices as they cooked a traditional birthday breakfast. French toast with confectionary sugar and fresh strawberries. I worried about the old man under the tree, about moments that changed everything. I imagined my new foot.

People returned on birthdays, too. They'd say things like, "I've been thinking about you and it seemed a fine time to . . . . " or, "How could I forget you today . . . . " This is what I imagined my father saying when he came back for me. Surely he'd return on a day such as this, on a special occasion such as my birthday. Surely there were other changes and surprises in store for me. Just as I did on every birthday, before I lost all my nerve, I drew in a full breath, fully planning on yanking the blanket off my foot and expecting to see a change. I'd worn socks to bed the night before, a ritual to keep the surprise until the next morning. But I let go of the blanket, not wanting to be disappointed yet. Maybe this year would be different. Maybe this would be a year of no disappointments. My mother had said that however you spent the day of your birthday was how you'd spend your entire year, so you had to be careful. Maybe I'd never look at my foot all day. That way, I'd prevent my disappointment and the waves of sadness that came later.

When I saw the horse, I knew my father was not coming. There was something unsettling and stalled about his large, cabinetlike metal chest and his flared black eyes, something cold and unapproachable. Maybe it was a confirmation of extraordinary things. Perhaps my father had sent the horse in place of himself. When I looked back at the horse, there was only just rain out there, all steely skies and gray-silvery water, reflecting glinting hues, like fallen car parts, like tinfoil, like metal leg braces worn by one of the old residents, which I'd found in the storage room one day when I was playing.

Now, in my full-length mirror, I evaluated myself. I scanned my body for any other sign of change. Maybe my cheeks appeared too flushed, my eyelashes appearing blacker, thicker. Maybe my hair had grown an inch since yesterday, curling halfway down my back. Then I glanced down. Who was I kidding? I couldn't keep a secret, not even from myself. My curiosity, like the elephant's child in Rudyard Kipling's story, was insatiable.

I pulled off the sock.

As if not disappointed, I leapt across the room, throwing my hands into the air. I jumped in a circle and threw open my curtains. Grabbing my supplies, I said that yes, this would be different anyway. Adding to this was that in the humidity I felt taller, my bangs curled up too high on the top of my head. I shoved my notepad and pen into my backpack. Was it wrong for a girl—just a girl—to imagine she could do something big in one day? That she could make this day the day that changed everything? Perhaps that was a quantum leap of faith, too big for me. I wondered as I ate a big breakfast and said twelve felt like eleven, only taller. I wondered if I would ever stop wishing for things, if one day I'd have all of my wishes come true and there would be nothing left to wish for. Then I'd be like a nun, only worrying about other people's wishes and greasing the wheels for messages sent up to God. Or perhaps I would always wake up expecting to be different.

"Your grandmother would have loved seeing you so happy, Naida," said Dr. B., joining us at the breakfast table as everyone clinked glasses of orange juice and toasted to my future, which I myself could not see. I hated how they all got ahead of me, bringing up things like college and my wedding, when I wasn't even out of the gate yet. It made me worry that there were things waiting for me that should be worried about, and that this was the reason they had started so early. My mother believed in being prepared. She didn't like uncertainty and didn't like surprises. I ate hurriedly and assured my mother I'd be back for lunch, when we'd have my cake.

I slipped out of the door, intending to race to the boardwalk. Just then I heard my mother. "Hold on. Wait for us—don't you remember we said we wanted to come with you? For Paulo," she said, as my aunt pulled on her jacket. "My old ice cream man, the one you told us about," my mother said, out of breath. "We're going to find him."

"He's gone," I said flatly.

"Did you see him?"

"No, but I just don't think he's still there," I told them.

My aunt glanced at my mother, telling her she thought we should try anyway.

As we walked together down the bike path toward Maiden's Cross Village, I took out my notebook and thumbed through the pages. My records were labeled "man with broken tooth," "woman with red sandals," "smart boy from candy store." In time, I'd have stacks of these notebooks under my bed, heaps of paper, hidden words. Now, as we approached the park next to the boardwalk, I saw the shadow of Paulo's body in the downed blades of grass, but no Paulo. I imagined hidden chambers existed underneath this tree, where a soul could curl up, waiting to climb out on a shaft of light. The shape of absence reminded me of my father. I put my hand on the tree trunk, imagining what it could tell me, all it had seen, and whether it had conspired with the moon last night to disappear Paulo, and my father.

"This is where he was," I said. "Right here. See the grass?" I pointed to the bare patch. "His hat. It was right there."

My mother and aunt walked back home while I stayed to continue my plan. I watched people waltz back and forth across the boardwalk, excitement and worry rising like steam above their heads, trying to see who needed a good word. A runaway boy begged for change. A mother complained that her feet were killing her as she pushed a stroller. As I scanned the crowd, I saw someone familiar. Mr. Taki's back was to me. When he faced me, there was no recognition in his eyes. Then he escaped into the alley behind the restaurant. I tried to follow him, but he disappeared. I hoped he would go home now.

I wrote five notes in an hour. I slipped each note into pockets, purses, and bags. "What do you think you're doing, young lady?" A blond woman in a red suit needed to be reminded of her wisdom. She'd just forgotten all she knew. She gripped my arm, staring at me with pressed lips painted bright red. I could see the layer of powder on her face, and one false eyelash flicked over the rest. She waved the note I'd left in her pocket. "Thief," she hissed.

"I didn't take anything. It's just a friendly note. It's my birthday."

She looked at me strangely and opened the note. She peered at me over the edge of the paper.

"You think I'm wise?"

I nodded. She smiled, wiping her eyes. Such was the magic of birthdays, a common language that everyone could understand. One of the high holidays that made strangers act like old friends and celebrate with you.

"Well, happy birthday to you," she said.

Mr. Taki was crouched under the stairwell when I got home, talking of Pearl Harbor. I offered him my hand and led him back to his door. "Mr. Taki's caught in the past again," I told my mother.

"That's what happens. He's old, and his memory is confused." But she didn't understand. He'd already left. He was like the stars now, just a memory of what had transpired miles and years ago.

That night, as I sank beneath white sheets, I listened to my mother play the guitar, an old Irish folk song about a woman who lived by the sea. I thought about the surprise of an old strawberry farmer, who upon waking would find on his mat a note that said, "You were my true love. Yours, Diana." And then another note, which said yes, the right thing to do was to leave your ship and meet that nice woman for a date on the island. He'd also find a snow globe that contained a strawberry, which my mother wouldn't miss.

-◄o►-

THE FUTURE DOESN'T come to you in lightning-bolt flashes—that's only in the movies. It comes to you as memories, made recognizable by a vague familiarity, of things you have already seen and done. It comes to you through the sound of your own voice echoing in a dark hallway. You wake up with the memory of that which has not yet occurred, sensing the comfort of a threadbare piece of clothing, a faded family photograph, or an old table scratched and worn by elbows. It comes to you in signs, like moonstones in your laundry basket. Or in flickers, in fleeting moments like feathers on the sidewalk. Sometimes it is so delicate it is barely recognizable, almost transparent, as if you were looking through tinted glasses at images superimposed on the present.

My mother thought my gift of knowing things had been extinguished like a fire. That I had woken up in the hospital, at the age of four, no longer possessing any strange abilities. But that wasn't true. My gift was not like fire—more like water, ebbing and flowing like the tide.

It was easier for us not to talk about it. Julio's mother had frightened me all those years ago when I'd said his blood had rocks. I'd seen the way she looked at me. I had then realized that my gift might not always been seen as good. So I'd tried to shut it down.

I'd almost never been able to see my own future, at least not when I had strong feelings swirling around me. Feelings clouded my sight. Visions could sneak up on me, and I'd have a physical reaction. Like this morning, when I'd looked out my window and seen a vision of a metal horse rising from the ocean. The taste of a penny had filled my mouth, as sudden as cold water.

I'd had that tinny taste on my tongue all day long.

Lately, there had been more things—raindrops became seahorses flooding my dreams, piercing the ocean. When I turned on the shower, I'd hear hooves clomping across metal. The images were becoming clearer, or maybe I just noticed them more distinctly now that I was older.

I didn't always understand what I saw. I didn't know that the future was coming for me now.

Time and time again, I'd see an old woman with braids at the door, dripping wet in a raincoat.

Until you could separate your wants from those of others, it was best to stay distant. Or you might get lost. Then your sight would fail and your hearing would become confused. You'd be vulnerable to different things. Other people's futures were like entrances to a labyrinth you shouldn't enter, like the chambers in the Maeshowe tomb in Orkney, where Viking warriors left inscriptions on the walls of underground mounds, scraping thirty runes into the tombs.

At times you'd stumble toward the sea like a small child, too young to be so caught up in a world that wasn't there, called into the waves at night, the night your mother referred to as "the accident," and yet it seemed that it was not that at the time. You'd been drawn there by the horse, quite purposefully, and there had been nothing accidental about him or his wanting you to swim. Most of the people who needed to be saved began as rescuers.

You had to be on guard against things that would steal you.

Now, with the taste of metal on my tongue, I looked back through my books about Scotland, trying to keep myself from getting lost—in a world that had not yet occurred.

MOONLIGHT SPILLED OVER the oil derricks, fake skyscrapers rising from imagined islands while giant machinelike white flamingos dipped their beaks into the earth. If only the stork could swoop down and lift me up and away, across the sea to Orkney, the place of nightless summers, where the aurora borealis performed a ballet of dancing lights. A true aurora was a collision of electrons from solar winds that hit atoms in the high atmosphere and made them explode and then sail down Earth's magnetic lines, appearing as green or red curtains if they hit oxygen, and blue or purple if they hit nitrogen. From far away, they might look like a sun rising in the wrong place.

My books about Scotland told of how Maeshowe held the spirit of a fourteen-foot man. In that tomb with its many chambers, a human skull and horse bones were found. Some said the structure was a calendar that marked the winter solstice, built in such a way as to allow a shaft of light to sneak through the tomb's entrance in the weeks leading up to the darkest time of the year, the only time light would shine in the dark caves. Some said this marked the continuation of life for those who'd died, the entrance of the sun like rebirth. Still others said that the souls that were lost in the tomb could climb out on the shaft of light like a ladder to the heavens. Along with the runes, a fire-breathing dragon was etched in the wall. Some said it was a wolf. To me, with its tail like a sword, it looked like a horse, the same one that I wore on the pendent around my neck, which my father had once given to my mother when he'd promised her that he'd always come back.

I read about the Festival of the Horse, an early-nineteenth-century annual tradition in which children competed in plowing matches on the beach. Boys would pull a miniature metal plow across a four-foot square in South Ronaldsay and be awarded prizes for the neatest and most careful job. Girls dressed in costumes representing the fancy decorations on harnesses worn by Clydesdale horses back in the days of the big plows. The costumes, adorned with medals, were handed down through families and consisted of a colorful headdress, collar, belt, hat, and ankle fringes representing the horses' feathers. Young girls would gather in the square, their costumes jangling, medals glinting, dressed as working horses.

But fairy tales weren't the stories I wanted anymore.

Chapter Twenty-five

FIRE, UNLIKE WATER, liked to have a partner. It liked to conspire with wind, with air, with dry brush and trees, with human constructions, even with water. The strange orange cloud that crept across the sky could burn the tips of the trees, making them appear golden, never again to become green. Now, a black veil of smoke drifted through the air from miles away. When wildfires swept through Orange County, the winds suddenly switched directions, carrying the strange blanket of billowing smoke north to Belmont Shore. Plumes of ash were pulled all the way toward the ocean in a strange change of wind. The instructions would be to stay inside if possible, to close car windows. As I gazed out the window of my science class, I knew I had never before seen an orange sky like this, eerily dark and strangely tempting. My teacher said the particles that traveled all this way from the far-off fires were many times thinner than a human hair and could hang in the air for days. They could penetrate the lungs and enter the bloodstream and could do damage to people who had breathing and heart problems.

I glanced around the room, wanting to see if anyone else felt the way I did. Julio, who liked to make fun of my foot, mouthed, "Blow me" from two rows away. I gave him the finger and quickly averted my eyes back to the window.

He said my mother meant to name me *nadie*, which meant "nobody." He said I was nothing, and that I'd never be anything.

My teacher, Mr. DeFusto, explained a burning sea in different ways. Fuel spilled from a boat fire or a tanker could create flames on the waves. But this wouldn't be the water burning. You could hold a match over salt water and watch it catch fire if you knew how to release hydrogen from oxygen using radio waves. As long as you kept hydrogen molecules at a certain radio frequency, they would burn, making salt water appear to be on fire. The whole thing was about assumptions and whether you were a person who was more apt to accept things that you saw with your own eyes. This proved that what you saw with your own eyes would sometimes fool you, too, Mr. DeFusto said. That, he explained, was the similarity between science and faith. Faith required a suspension of belief, he said. So did science, if you knew enough to question what you saw.

If there were a lack of wind and humidity in the air, causing smoke to bank down, there would be toxicity. Storage tank fires produced clouds of thick smoke. There could be a small fire in the park, he said, making me imagine Paulo and his baseball hat. But the big wildfires always came from neighboring cities, where there were wide expanses of grasslands and trees, where the deer still disappeared in the smoky dawn, where mountain lions occasionally crept down from their beds and showed up with noses pressed to the window of restaurants. We had no wildfires in Long Beach, but we had wildflowers, and we had wilderness. An ocean wilderness, one in which castles grew from coral and waterhorses kicked holes in the walls of caves. That morning, I remembered, my mother had said to be careful coming and going, that the bougainvillea were suddenly thick with bees.

JULIO WAS TRYING to get my attention. I could feel his eyes searing my back, cutting into me, causing me to shift in my seat and finally to turn around and glance back at him. I lifted my chin. This time, he gave me the finger. I gave it back to him again.

"Rise above, Naida," my mother always said. But I was not that godly. Not a saint and certainly not enough of a wallflower, though I wished to be. Lift off like a huge white bird. Float away like a feather, out of reach. Sometimes I forgot, after days of put-pocketing, that in school I was antimatter, a negatively charged space, a shadow. No matter how many times I changed my phone number, somebody would find it. I'd been stupid, gullible, easily tricked by the promise of friendship with Irene. There had been so many years of bad blood, I was eager to be done with it. She'd gone after me for no reason, so I didn't know why exactly I was so willing to be her friend. She'd first stolen the secret of my foot when I was six and had authored a series of stories about my hoof and my claw, had pretended to like me in order to get my phone number. Now, she was almost as tall as our teachers, just a half year younger than I, with a gossiping mouth, a wide smile like her mother's, and long legs. Her authoritative presence made everybody afraid of her, mostly of her meanness. When she saved me a seat at her lunch table, I felt a strange satisfaction at being noticed. Not long after I gave her my phone number, the obscene texts started. It was easier not to have a phone. I shoved it in the garbage and didn't look back.

The bully drills. Those torturous things. There were instructions to walk away, as if away were a better place. To ignore a bully. Not to give a bully attention.

It gets better, they said, though it never did.

I walked away. It didn't help. My bullies followed me. My teachers, they could not help at all. Telling on the bullies made things worse. The bullies would come back angrier, or perhaps satisfied they were in trouble. "Back when you were bullied," my mother would say, always using the past tense. Fourth grade had worried her to the point of insomnia. She had called Irene's mother and other parents, trying to get at the root of things, trying to ferret out any festering insecurities as if they were lint from the dryer trap. People said their children were just curious about me, having heard the stories about my foot, their curiosity a ballooning thing that required answers. But now that I was older, all that was behind me. No more questions, my mother said. And she believed that because she'd said it, the universe would conspire. I couldn't tell her the truth: that the bullying had come back like El Niño, changing every few months, as if I had a sign or a smoke signal over my head that would suddenly flash and alert everyone to gang up on me again.

I tried to ignore Julio. As Mr. DeFusto talked about the distant smoke, I imagined the sea lions roaring, barking under our apartment window. I worried about my sisters, imagining them racing deep under the ocean, frightened by the strange smoke. The principal's voice rang out over the PA system, announcing early dismissal. Mr. DeFusto clapped two erasers together, a plume of white smoke rising up, and told us all to be safe out there. Everyone would have to leave at the same time today, preventing me from getting away. My fear was like a room full of twisted metal. At once, something hit my foot. I grabbed the yellow paper and unfolded it in my lap.

"Witch hunt today after school," it said.

THE HALLWAYS FILLED with thunderous voices, shouts of excitement fed by testosterone, freedom, and the clatter of backpacks slung into lockers. Metal lockers slapped open and closed, high fives were given, plans to meet up were shouted through the corridors. I made it to my locker unharmed but breathless. My pulse raced. I didn't want anyone to look at me, to see how nervous I was. All I wanted was to get away. Today, all I had to do was run as fast as I could. Race across the football field and then dash through the streets.

As I stood frozen in front of my locker, I felt my legs become light, quivering, and I imagined the sound of my boots crunching broken glass, pounding my fear like oyster shells into the parking lot of Wild Acres. I wondered if this would be the day I didn't make it home. I tried to steady myself by imagining I was already home and sinking into the gray carpet. It didn't work. I had to come up with something else, a better plan. Perhaps another door. Another route home. I hadn't scouted any new ones lately. I'd been entirely too busy worrying about my father and my sisters, about my mother and my aunt, and the rest of the people who were somehow always there but never there at the right time, like now, for instance. Today, I needed to be careful. I didn't know what they meant by "witch hunt," but I knew it was not good. The air was unsafe. No one could get away unnoticed.

Suddenly, I could hear the taunts of my bullies, and then a body knocked into me. "Frog Witch," someone whispered, laughing. When something hit the back of my head, my stomach clenched. I reached back and felt the saliva in my hair. My cheeks flushed, and my eyes watered up.

My hands shook too much to spin my locker combination: 25-right, 32-left, 15-right. Breathe. Focus on your sisters, I told myself. On the serenity of the ocean. On the fluidity of graceful arms carving through rippling water. Think of circles overlapping. Better. I could think. I tried again as the sweat slipped down my neck and made dark flowers under each arm.

I wouldn't show fear. They were only trying to get a piece of me. The boys, in their low-riding jeans, laughed into their shirts and high-fived each other. The girls, in their low-cut T-shirts, kept their heads tilted to one side, letting their hair fall forward, covering half their face, smiling coyly at each other. What I'd noticed was that you could never predict or explain your bullies. Some would interpret your shyness as trying to appear tough. Some would think you were tough and would want to take you down a notch. Others would be afraid you'd reveal them. Regardless of all that provoked them, they seemed to share an elevated sense of importance. Everyone knew that bullies were cowards in disguise, that as soon as you faced them and stood up to them, they'd back down. That's what they'd said, at least. I'd tried everything. And I was still occasionally surprised that they continued. I was merely habit for them at this point—a predictable target.

Now Irene brushed by me, her arm around Julio's waist, her cold blue eyes tearing into me when she looked back, her frosted lipstick glimmering against her tanned skin. When I caught her eyes, she stopped for a moment, lips parted, hesitating. Julio glanced back. "Like my boyfriend, Frog Witch?"

That malformed strawberry. That girl with wings. The one you teased. The one you looked away from. The one who made you grateful for your perfection. That girl who was forced to hide. Who was different. Imperfect. Not you. The one who still believed, for no good reason, that she was a little unstoppable.

I TORE THROUGH the hallway, racing against the tide, an animal trapped by fluorescent lights. My black boots pounded the cold floor as a crowd of students clamored for the door. I had tried to call my mother and my aunt to come and pick me up, but neither was home. Now I slammed the door to the girls' bathroom and sat on the floor of a stall, refusing to cry, feeling the chill of the cold metal against my back. I drew my father's name with my finger across the gritty hexagons, waiting. I'd stay in here all night if I had to, wishing and praying for him to come. I sat on the lid of the toilet, stretching my legs out so that my bootheels gripped the door. I was too scared to walk home now by myself, knowing that there was no chance to get away.

My only shot was to wait until everyone had gone. Hopefully, they'd be too busy with their plans to worry about me. I saw my name and my cell phone number written in black marker on the wall. I kicked the door, my hands balling into fists. Ink came off on my fingers as I tried to scribble out my name. I wanted only to worry about other people, about put-pocketing, not about my own survival.

My forehead against the bathroom mirror, I imagined myself doing impossible things. Breathing underwater. Jumping off rooftops. Finding possibility where no one else saw it. I imagined the sunlight creeping in through the entrance of Maeshowe. It was all a matter of timing for those souls to escape, just as it would be for me.

Wait, I told myself. Just a little bit longer. Just a few more minutes, until I was sure everyone had gone.

That's when the bathroom door sprung open. The principal was staring at me, her white-blond wedge frizzled around her large tortoiseshell glasses. I could see Irene's face behind her in the hallway. "Irene, you were right. Thank you for letting me know. Naida, we need to evacuate. Do you have a ride home?"

I pushed through the heavy metal doors of the school and flew outside. The Wizard ignited my muscles. Sirens in the distance. Fire in my lungs. My jean skirt puckered as I ran, my black knee-high boots pulling at my calves. My yellow T-shirt became soaked under my armpits. My backpack slapped my back. I thought of my father, waiting for me in the ocean.

"Hey, Frog Witch! You're going to burn! Stop, Frog Witch!" I outran my bullies, sliding down a grassy mud hill behind a stranger's house.

When my bullies moved on to their next escapade, all jacked up on the excitement of a natural disaster, I cut around the corner and made my way toward my house through the back of Maiden's Cross Village. In the alley, I caught my breath, black soot drifting all around me. I wiped my face and noticed the black streaks on my hands. I whipped around at the sudden noise behind me.

Julio leapt out from behind the Dumpster. "Caught you, Frog Witch!"

He pushed me down onto the asphalt, his sweaty blond hair thick as straw as he hovered. Pain shot through my neck as he pinned my shoulders with his knees. I tried to kick him. I screamed, but no sound came out, my voice trapped by quiet stones. With his right hand, he leaned down close to my face.

I spat at the wind, the scent of the sweat and fire thickened with sea air snaking across my face, soaking my clothing.

When he pulled up my skirt, he laughed at my day-of-the-week underwear. I was wearing Thursday. It was a Friday. That morning, I hadn't been able to find Friday.

He smirked. "Wrong day, Frog Witch."

"Get off me," I breathed. That just made him angrier.

His breath reeked of pot as he peered into my eyes. His red football jersey stunk of body odor. Number 29. He was number 29.

I had begun to conjure my father like my mother told me she used to do. I pictured smoke snaking across the water. I shook my head no, my fingers clawing at the ground.

Let me go before you do something you'll regret, I imagined myself saying, something threatening and wise, something that warned him of the future. But my words became like birds above me.

"Let me go," I said. "I won't tell anyone." There it was. A cloud above him.

"Show me your frog foot."

I tried to kick him, but he dug his knee into my thigh. Sweating, he pulled my boot off, then wrestled off my blue argyle sock. He grabbed my ankle, illuminating my bare foot against the orange sky. Julio's mouth twisted into a smile, satisfied, as if he had gotten to the root of things or had discovered a hidden treasure. A foot. There it was.

"You are part frog," he gasped, a twisted smile on his face. He would suffer for this. His name would be burned in the karmic dictionary under the word "asshole." "Amazing. I actually didn't believe it. Damn right you are a freak." I kneed him, and he started to cough. I rolled away and got up on my knees.

The salty breeze flooded the air, replacing the scent of ash and fire. Julio looked up, coughing uncontrollably. Papers spilled from his backpack and flitted in the wind. "What the hell? What did you do, Frog Witch?" Through my tears I saw him running down the alley, trying to catch the papers caught in the trees. "I'll get you. Freak!" he shouted. I kicked off my other boot and started to run. Julio chased me down the street as the orange sky followed. I ran around to the front of the Sands Restaurant and pounded on the windows.

Why was everybody gone?

I grabbed the metal rungs of the fire escape and scissored my legs, crawling up the metal grate, and Julio jumped up after me. I knew he was afraid of heights. I'd seen him refusing to climb the knotted rope swing in gym class, all his friends around, jeering at him. He'd looked so defeated that day, I'd actually felt sorry for him. I wouldn't feel sorry for him anymore.

When I looked down, he had talked himself into crawling up the ladder after me, looking at me like I was crazy. At the top, I stepped out onto the slick roof. When I jumped off, I always imagined it could be like landing on ice, only worse, perhaps like cement. Now I had no choice.

It would be the end. I would go bravely. Not like a coward. I would fight, making people proud of me.

I knew the pattern of the rocks, every crag and every cave. Lifting my chin, I held my face to the orange sky. I straightened my arms out at my sides, my palms turned up as if this would lift me. Sweat poured down the sides of my face. I heard Julio call, "Crazy bitch." But it didn't matter. Now there was nothing but flight. I could fall straight up into the sky and disappear into the stars, becoming one with them, all caught by the single thread of memory of our beginnings, which was wound through every cell. The waves below were streaked with yellow, reflections of the dirty air. I closed my eyes. There was only the sound of my heartbeat. I drew in my breath, my body wrapped up in the warm wind. No more Frog Witch. No more holding my breath. No more anything that remotely resembled a stalled life. A life spent waiting and trying to hide. My feet pushed off the gritty roof, my body arcing across the glowing water.

Flight.

The dark skin of the waves burned my fingertips.

IN THE BEGINNING, the Wizard made water, not light. The fish came first, then the animals, then came those flesh-covered machines known as human beings. In the beginning, human beings believed they were free. There was a plan for everything. Somebody always knew how to get from A to B. Why, then, should existing be so difficult? Perhaps we'd begin to devolve into animals. Dr. B. said it was because we could pull fistfuls of light in our hands, but that we shouldn't think of it like that—we should just be human.

Water.

I landed in a pearly sea. Splashing into a soft cushion of seaweed, I was far enough out from the rocks. The energy of the sea. Huge. Whalelike waves came in from the atmosphere, tripped up by a magnetic wire gone awry out there, from the silent astral avalanche. Swimming a great distance under the water, farther than I ever had before, I rose up out of it to take a breath. The sea appeared as if on fire, reflecting the sky. Ignited by the emotion of the hunt and the need for my father, I swam faster, letting the waves pull me farther out.

I felt grateful to the Wizard for my body, for once. I had left the old Naida behind. Good riddance, I thought. Goodbye to all the pain of my old Frog Witch self.

When I surfaced, at least fifty yards away, I saw all the hotel windows in stacked rows across the distance. I dipped down and spun around.

Something brushed my foot. I kicked it away. I wanted to keep swimming. The waves pulled me toward deeper waters. The enormous strength of the undertow caught my ankles, the wild horse that had almost drowned me years ago. Now it wanted to play. I began to kick at it, my legs like tiny sticks in its huge jaws. I struggled to right myself. But nothing could rein it in.

Where was my father?

Just then a pair of gold-flecked eyes appeared beneath the water.

A sea lion thrust up through the waves, then disappeared. I dipped down, caught sight of a tunnel made of seaweed, a string of tiny bubbles strung through it like a necklace. Then long black spiraling strands of hair swirled through the water. I had to come up for a breath. The more I kicked in the other direction, the more it pulled me. I was fighting with myself, panicked, wanting to go back.

Where was my father?

I shouted into the distance, my words snuffed out by the crashing waves. I told my father that he'd lied. I screamed that he'd left me. "Where are you?" I called across the hazy sky, my voice dissolving like the sea mist over the rocks. As many obscenities as I hurled into that water, only silence flew back at me with its oily flustered wings, stinging my eyes with salt.

I finally reached the shore a half mile from my house.

Dragging myself onto the beach, I glanced back at the burning sea, all lit up with reflections. I wanted to reach out and push it back, back across the bike path. Back through time.

Back through my own decision to be born. Everyone was right. My father was not coming to save me.

When I reached the salmon arch of Wild Acres, the bougain-villea blossoms were rising, billowing over the sliver of moon that appeared too early in the late-afternoon sky and that I knew had conspired with the vines to draw me back onto land.

My mother stood on the porch next to Dr. B. and Aunt Dolly, calling to me as I realized there was no hiding. They would be angry at my unexplained absence, especially with all the panic of the fires. The deep orange sky cast long dark shadows over the sand. My black hair soaking down my back, I looked at my legs, moonstone blue in the now dimming light.

"What happened, child? Those fires won't come all the way here," Dr. B. said, putting her arm around me. She ushered me into the lobby as if to give my mother a little cooling-off period, or perhaps to give one to me.

"Why are they so mean to me?" I asked.

Dr. B. reached out, her fingers brushing my cheek. "Who's mean?"

"Everyone," I said.

"Surely not everyone. You're very loved. You're a wonderful girl."

"No one at school wants to be friends with the Frog Witch."

She waved me toward the green microsuede couch and offered me a box of tissues as I told her what had happened.

"You know who you remind me of?"

Tick Tock chattered, jumping between perches in his cage. "A lady who was an outlaw," I said. She nodded, and told me my grandmother had been caught in an elevator that was stuck between two floors.

"Things won't always be that way. One day you'll grow up and you won't even remember." I hadn't told her about Julio's attack. Only about the teasing. "This will get better. You can't see that now because you haven't been down that road. But we've all been the subject of gossip at some point in our lives."

"My foot. It's the whole problem," I said.

"You know what, honey? I think if God had wanted feet to be perfect, she wouldn't have invented high-heeled shoes." She raised an eyebrow. I offered her the only smile I could, a half-crooked poor attempt, only because she didn't deserve to worry. "I just hate being different."

She shook her head. "You come from a long line of exceptional women. Different in other ways. Your grandmother, for instance. That lovely woman watched the moon like it was the rising sun, like it could begin and end all things."

"What about my mother?"

"What about her?"

"You said a long line of women. You were including my mother and my aunt."

She nodded. "That's right. Now your mother."

"There's nothing wrong with her," I said.

Dr. B. smiled and glanced at the ground. "Everybody's got something. Your mother would be the first one to tell you she isn't perfect."

"But that's what makes her so normal. Besides, she has no secrets."

"How would you know that?"

She was right. How would I know if my mother had secrets?

She told me my mother had had her own struggles. By that I assumed she was talking about my father. And I knew how my grandmother had raised my mother and my aunt. I knew it wasn't easy. "You know, sometimes people don't even know they have secrets. At least yours is out there for all to see. You know exactly what it is. And I reckon that one day, you won't even think about it anymore. One day, it'll seem so normal to you that it'll be like anything else you get used to, like the color of your eyes. But by then, you'll have other things to worry about."

I glanced at her. "What other things?"

She shrugged. "Life. Your job. Your family. Maybe a husband. Children—they're worth it if you choose."

Why was she talking about all these unreal things when my real life was so messed up and misunderstood? I couldn't see my own path ahead of me. How could she?

"I don't want to get married. Ever," I said, surprising myself. No one in my family had ever talked against marriage. But no one had talked for it, either. My mother never mentioned it, in fact, which had never seemed strange to me, but now suddenly did. I knew all my mother's stories about my father.

"What's so bad about marriage?" she asked, folding her arms.

"I've just never seen it. Anywhere but on television."

Dr. B. laughed and said she hadn't thought about that before. She said that when she was a little girl, she didn't know any adults who weren't married. "I think it's high time you got to know your grandmother a little bit better. The only way you'll know her is to read her own words. Has your mother ever shown you the almanacs?"

I said no.

"There's a box marked 'Diana' in the storage room. You'll have to rummage around a bit in there. It's been years since your mother looked at it, and I've had movers going in and out of there since. But I know it's there. I don't want you in there by yourself, though. You come and get me tomorrow, and I'll help you find that box." She reached out, lifting my chin. "My door is always open to you, Naida. You don't ever have to even knock. I'm always here."

She gave me a hug, and I felt the strength of her arms and the smell of the freshly starched fabric of her faded yellow dress. Then she stared at me and smiled.

"You don't have to get married," she whispered.

"Didn't my mother ever want to?"

She shook her head no. "Did you hear her say that?"

"No, but I just thought."

"Well, you never can tell what people wish for, can you? Wishes change. You'll see that one day. Right now all you want is to blend in. One day, you'll want to stand out. That's the trouble with life, you know. Hard to get the right wishes matched with the right part of your life."

I stood up to leave and crossed the small room toward the door.

"Naida?" Dr. B. asked.

"Yes?" I said, turning around to face her. I almost backed away farther from the intensity of her stare.

"Do you have a good mother?" she asked.

"Yes," I whispered.

"That's important to know," she said.

MY MOTHER STOOD in the living room, her keys clenched in her hand. The new pink silk pillows scattered across the brown couch shimmered in the late-afternoon haze. Her eyes were rimmed with blue eyeliner, and her freckled skin was slick with patches of powdery blush. I hated to be the cause of her worry.

"Naida, I left work and drove to school to pick you up. The secretary said you left an hour ago. I've been worried sick, driving around looking for you. Where have you been? Have you been crying? And of course you're soaking wet."

I glanced at the television. The weatherman was reporting the fires, showing the map of Southern California. "The smoke. Made my eyes water a little," I said. "So the fires are over?"

"Dying down. At least they're under control now. There's been a lot of damage out there. But we're safe, thankfully. I wish those poor people the best."

No one was safe, fires or not. "I'm going to get into the tub," I told her, escaping into the bathroom. I peeled off my clothes and ran the water as hot as I could stand it, letting the memories of Julio circle the drain and disappear.

Later that night, my mother flicked on the lights in my bedroom. She sat down at the foot of my bed, demoralized. "Why? That's all I want to know. Don't you know how dangerous this is? Swimming at all times of day and night. And on a day like today. What if something happened to you out there?"

Something is happening to me out there, I wanted to say. *Something has been happening to me for my entire life.* My promise to stop made her sigh with relief. I rubbed my eyes, which were still burning. My body ached from Julio's attack, and I had bruises on my shoulders, my arms, and my thigh where he'd pressed his knees.

I had stayed in the water too long.

I had been designated as Other, destined for a place no one could reach or measure or contain. If I had any doubts that I was meant to be here, they'd been confirmed now. My father hadn't come to find me. But I wasn't convinced that he wouldn't. Maybe I just hadn't been looking at the right time. It was all timing, as Dr. B. said. Sometimes your life had to catch up with your wishes. I knew the ocean was still inside me, thundering in my ears, causing my hair to become tangled like the girl's in that painting of the naiad. I was certain my mother didn't understand me. Why did she have to argue with me all the time about the ocean? Didn't she know that the ocean was saving my life?

That night, I dreamed I was running through the hallways at school. The bell rang. I counted my breaths, as my mother had taught me. I raced past the hall monitor, the teachers, but they didn't see me. I knew I was invisible. I could hear laughter as I ran. Then I was running across the skin of the ocean, my steps leaving ripples like huge heavy raindrops. I felt something hit the back of my leg.

When I reached for it, my hand was wet, slick with oil.

Black. When I opened my fist, a bird's wing became a dagger in my hand. It had a horse's mane carved into it. It glowed bone white in the moonlight.

Chapter Twenty-six

W HEN YOU ARE lost at sea for any period that is longer than a short while, you will start to find the strangest things familiar. Aching for home, you will find similarities in remote things. Giant cliffs and craggy rocks will resemble sea lions rising up out of the water. A patch of rippling, reflected sky will become the window you used to look out when you woke up to your first backyard. Birdsongs will overlap with human voices and become indistinguishable. You will imagine yourself back home during your loneliest sleepless nights. If you are far from the Orkney Islands of Scotland, your home, on the longest day of the year, you will read a book outside at midnight, holding a flashlight, as you think of your friends enjoying a nightless night. You may even imagine seeing the aurora borealis—the northern lights—in the far-off sky. If you are a fisherman who has been at sea for long periods of time, you'll be so drawn to the colored lights on the THUMS Islands off the coast of Long Beach that you may even come ashore, thinking you're home.

Going against Dr. B.'s wishes, I snuck into the storage room late that night. I just couldn't wait. I couldn't go back to school tomorrow. I had no idea how I would face Julio, or the rest of them. The story of my attack and my dive off the pier was sure to spread through the phone chain and become something else entirely.

I was on a downturn, as Aunt Dolly sometimes called it. Headed for no good.

It felt comforting to be in here, amid the boxes and the old furniture covered with dust, hidden among the stacks of other people's memories, all the forgotten things once valued and since left by the residents of Wild Acres, and even before. Old cameras, telephones, and bags of clothing. Children's toys. A box of old record albums. I sifted through them, hardly recognizing any of the names. Cheap Trick and Michael Jackson. Kiss and David Bowie. Lynyrd Skynyrd and REO Speedwagon. All those things someone once stacked in boxes. The last remnants of a life tossed here or there, slowly fading into worthlessness, when once they'd held so much power, so much value as to make it to the end of a life. Not an easy thing to do. Not for a piece of clothing, a record album, or a person. How many people made it to the end of someone else's life? When I looked around, most people I saw were alone. They had been at Wild Acres, at least. Everyone except my mother and my aunt. They would never part. No matter what. Though Aunt Dolly still lived in San Diego, one day they'd end up back together. They still planned gardens together. They still called each other five times a day. What all was there to talk about? And yet I knew even then that they had something lovely and divine, something I wished I had, too. By this time, the allure of my imagined sisters was fading. Something very frightening had happened, and I had begun to divide things into two camps: *Right* and *Not Right*. *Good For You* and *Not Good For You*. My sisters didn't fade entirely. I was not quite ready to let them go.

What was it about those things so imbued with memory that made them impossible to throw away? Mrs. Green's old easel rested against the wall. An old plastic Easy-Bake Oven stood a few feet away, a box of broken Crayola crayons on top. I picked up the broken crayons and read the labels in the dim light. I remember my mother always loved the names. Cornflower Blue. Teal Blue. Jungle Green. Caribbean Green. Bits and pieces of crayon had been melted in tinfoil cake tins, now covered by a thick layer of dust. The swirls of wax appeared as *National Geographic* photographs of the earth from space. What else had my aunt and my mother captured in a pan of melted crayons when they were little, I wondered. Besides their wanting, their homelessness, their search for my grandmother amid her extraordinary tales. I shoved the old oven out of the way, reaching for the box behind it. I slid an old suitcase back into the stairwell and pushed some other boxes out of the way with my knees. I didn't see anything with my grandmother's name. I scanned the room.

A framed painting of a jumping fish was propped against the wall on a box. At the other end of the room, a blue La-Z-Boy chair held an old radio or weather monitor, I wasn't sure which. Upon closer inspection, it turned out to be an old Panasonic television. I walked over to it, spotting a cluster of dolls held together in a rubber band. A family—mother, father, baby. I remembered my mother talking about them. The mother doll had long blond hair and a flowery dress with an apron and lace collar. The father was tan, dressed in a red turtleneck and khaki pants, muscular. The baby had bright red hair—I'd never seen a real baby as peaceful. I wondered if this was what families used to look like, once upon a time. Back in the old days, when my mother was little.

My gaze drifted. The lighting wasn't good in here, just a bulb swinging from a wire, but I finally found what I was looking for. My mother's old canvases were stacked by the far wall. Red oceans. Piles of red oceans. I looked through them, remembering a time when they used to cover our walls. Now I saw something else. Behind the painting of the fish, a box marked "Diana."

I blew the dust off the top, drawing my fingernail through the tape to open it. My grandmother's Farmer's Almanacs were all inside, just as Dr. B. had said. They were all intact, but with worn yellow covers, some of the pages dog-eared. I picked up the almanac marked 1979, and it immediately splayed open to October. My grandmother had scribbled, *Luke and Laura* in black marker across the top. As I thumbed through the pages, I noticed the words *Bad Man, Bad Moon, The Wanderer* on several pages. Dr. B. would know what all of this meant and why my grandmother had written *Bad Moon* so many times.

Dr. B. called to me from the doorway. "Is that you, Naida?"

"I'm sorry," I said, ashamed I hadn't listened to her. I glanced up. There, in a rectangle of light, she held my gaze. It was late. The lines in her face deepened. I put the almanacs back into the box and closed the top. As I started to leave, something caught my eye, something glowing from underneath the Easy-Bake Oven a few feet away. I went back and lifted the oven. There, I found a dusty blue velvet bag with a white handle sticking out. Dr. B. said to bring the box out as long as I had gone to the trouble of finding it. I pushed the bag into the box.

"Are you angry with me?" I asked, following her down the hall and back into the lobby.

"No, I don't get angry. Disappointed you didn't listen to me. But we are where we are. See here, your grandmother kept everything. For a woman who had no house for much of her life, she was surprisingly attached to certain things. These being some." She patted the box. "Let's see what Diana has left for you." I sat down next to her, smelling her Charlie perfume as the musty scent of old paper and dust clouded the air.

One by one, I removed the almanacs and set them out on the coffee table in three rows, five books in each. I didn't tell Dr. B.

about the glowing handle in the velvet bag. I'm not sure why I didn't. I somehow knew that was just for me.

"She kept a record of everything. She believed there was truth in books. She was very imaginative and thoughtful in certain ways. A lot like you." Dr. B. opened the 1969 almanac, waving her fingers across the pages of charts. I swallowed, my throat aching.

"Does my mother even remember this? I wonder if this is why she was scared of the water all her life." I pointed to a scrawled note about my mother's near drowning.

"I don't know. I don't think I've ever seen that. I never asked her," she said, putting her glasses on. "I remember when I taught her to swim, though. I was a good teacher. She was a good student, bless your mother's heart. Courageous. Lord knows how afraid she was. You know why your mother learned to swim, don't you?"

I nodded. "Because my father wanted her to."

"No, because you wanted her to, honey. You'd roll around in her tummy like you were already swimming, kicking those little legs of yours, and she couldn't keep up. She got over her fear of the water for you. You gave the Pacific Ocean to your mother. That's a fine present, I think."

"What are all those funny pictures. Symbols?"

"The calendar is separated into months. The left-hand page lists the time of the moon's rise and fall. The right-hand page lists the full moon's name," she said, running her finger down the columns. She stopped on a circle. "April. See here, April is the Pink Moon."

Aunt Dolly had been trying to sort through the moon names—colonial Americans had called this the Planter's Moon. To the Celts, it was the Growing Moon. The Chinese called it the Peony Moon. To different groups of American Indians, it was the Flower Moon, or Wildcat Moon, or the Moon When Geese Return in Scattered Formation. "It bothers my aunt that there are so many names for one moon."

"Some people don't like interpretations. They prefer things clear cut. And so it should be for your aunt."

She picked up the 1975 almanac, flipping it open to a chart with more funny symbols and numbers. "Planets. Tide charts. Moon rising. The full moon was what captured your grandmother's imagination. But you know that. I can't imagine how she would have made it as far as she did without these books."

"But my mother said they were sad a lot of the time. They had times when they had no food. When my grandmother left them alone. It sounded kind of scary."

"I'm not glorifying it. Those were troubled times for her and the girls. Diana was the first to tell you that she made her mistakes. Now, Naida, you know the best thing about her almanacs?"

"No, tell me."

"They led your family right here. Twice. Your mother three times. Like a boomerang. Just kept coming back." She smiled. "See, you were meant to be here. This place right here where you're sitting? This has been not just your home but the home of your mother and your grandmother, of my own daughter, and maybe your daughter one day."

"I'm only twelve," I whispered.

She smiled. "Well, I'd like the place to stay in the family, just so you know, and Sasha will never leave the East Coast. She loves the snow, can you believe that?"

I took out the 1972 almanac and opened to the month of September. Seeing the way my grandmother had written my mother's name in big scalloped letters made me catch my breath, the R in big swooping curls. I decided that my mother's sixth birthday had probably happened on a good moon. I decided then that my grandmother had loved my mother. Big flouncy script meant happiness, meant love. I wrote the same way when I was happy. I would remember to show my mother this.

"By the way?"

"Yes?"

"You're a very wise young lady," she said, taking the new note from her pocket where I'd put it.

It was close to one o'clock in the morning when I snuck out of the house with my backpack. The tide glowed with bluish foam. A perfect Blue Moon, signaling a season for paths to cross and certain people to find you again. Footsteps on the beach would be filled with glowing water. Algal blooms feathered the beach. All things changed. Some things let you know they had been moved, torn apart, disturbed. That was actually a gift. Otherwise, how would you know?

I stood on the beach with a glass jar in one hand and my grandmother's 1975 almanac in the other hand. I watched the lacy spills creep over a large piece of driftwood. I reached into the water, covering my hands and feet. From across the sea, I imagined the whispers of a waterhorse, but I wouldn't fall for that again.

Water eased into the jar. Capturing it, I swirled it around. I pulled off my sweatshirt and pillowed it against the log. Stretching out on the sand, I opened to the calendar pages for October and then November. The jar of glowing water lit up the pages. The margins were filled with my grandmother's handwritten notes and tiny sketches. There were Joshua trees with twisted branches, as if hands balled into fists.

Then I unzipped my backpack and took out the velvet bag. Sticking out was a bone white handle. I'd seen it in my dream. I poured the contents of the bag onto the sand. The glow from the glass jar of luminescent blooms lit up the dagger, as well as an old bible with flecked gold lettering on the cover.

The blade was covered in a leather sheath, which held the imprint of the dragon, the same design as the pendent I wore around my neck. I felt my heart race. These had to be my father's. Why hadn't my mother ever told me? Rubbing the handle with my thumb, I revealed the carving of an animal, its mane wrapped around the handle. Exposed. I thought of my mother's stories and imagined hands dropping strawberries like raindrops across the furrows.

When I brushed the dust from the cover of the bible, I felt a shock of energy. My hands felt funny, tingling as I traced the faded gold lettering: Anderson. Anderson. I repeated the name, my name. I opened the bible and stared at the inside cover. All lit up in the glowing liquid, a motel stamp bled through the inside page. *We appreciate your patronage. Grayson Motel, San Clemente, CA.*

This could belong to anyone, I thought. I didn't know any Anderson. I waved the jar of glowing liquid over the bible to get a better look. What appeared to seep through the inside cover, the dragon design, was this time so slight I recognized it only because I'd seen it twice now, once on my pendent and once on the sheath. Graham Anderson. My mother had never told me my father's last name. She'd tell me one day that it was a common name and that she'd known it. There were things that she'd tell me when I was older, decisions I'd have to make about my foot. About my father. But here I was, taking the decision out of her hands. Naida Anderson, I thought. I whispered the name over and over until it felt like my own. I thought about how I took up so much of her life, with my shifting moods and my questions. I loved her, but I deserved a life apart from her. I was tired of always staying on the threshold of my window, in between, never really staying and never really going. This was the moment I'd been waiting for. The silent meteor about to hit my life. There were other things that cascaded through my mind, memories, thoughts, and wishes that I was ready for, and some that I was not.

Secrets were risky, unguarded things if you found them this way, the way I did. How could I do this to my mother? There was always the chance that my father didn't want to see me. I slipped the relics into my backpack and climbed back up the vines, hoisting myself into my bedroom window. This was one of those times when you didn't want to think. When you just did what you had to do. That's what I told myself as I threw a pair of jeans and my toothbrush into a bigger backpack. I pulled on my gray sweatshirt and twisted up my hair into a baseball cap. I emptied out my piggy bank, grabbing all the money in there—$44. The sun was rising as I snuck out. I rode my bike to the bus station and locked it there against the metal grate. Within a moment, I climbed the steps of Bus 1 and set out to meet the man I'd been waiting for my whole life.

I remembered my mother's always saying that you should sit next to an old woman on a bus so that no one else would sit next to you. A woman with long silver hair glanced up and smiled at me as she put on her lipstick. I pulled my hood up, slinking into the seat next to her as if someone would recognize me. All I could think about was what I would say to my father when I found him.

The woman, whose name was Berta, started talking. She offered me spearmint gum and showed me pictures of her grandchildren, two sets of twins. She unwound her purple tie-dyed scarf and folded it in her lap as she described them, all boys, all rambunctious. Then she adjusted it back around her neck, making a full loose knot just below her diamond necklace. It said *Mom*, with a diamond in the *o*. She told me all about her grandsons' sports, and about not seeing them enough. She was going to visit her son, who lived in San Clemente.

We rode the whole way together, talking so that I didn't even feel alone. Every once in a while as the bus shifted down Pacific Coast Highway, I'd glance out at the ocean and wonder if my mother had gotten up yet and about the crests of white foam spilling toward the beach, endless. I told Berta I was going to see my father. That I hadn't seen him in a very long time. She said that must have been a lovely thing to have looked forward to.

"Is he coming to get you? Maybe you'd like a ride?" she asked, as we got off the bus and no one was waiting for me.

I nodded. "If it wouldn't be too much trouble."

She kissed her son, and he picked up her bag. "Who's this? You made a new friend, Ma?" he asked.

"Naida Anderson," I said. I pushed my hair from my eyes and smiled.

AS WE PULLED up to the old beachside motel, I bit back the tears. The white stucco motel was bordered up. There were no cars in the parking lot. The grass was overgrown with weeds, had overtaken the old porch, where I was sure my father had sat many times, drinking coffee or reading the paper, just like a regular father. "Are you sure you have the right place?" Berta asked.

"I'm sure," I whispered, getting out.

"I don't want to leave you here alone. It's not safe."

"Oh, this is the right place. He's meeting me here," I lied. I thanked her and she stared at her son. He shrugged.

"Ma, the kid says it's the right place." Berta reached into her pocket for a pen and pulled out a piece of paper.

"What's this?" she asked. She opened my put-pocket note and smiled as she read it. Then she met my eyes. "Thank you, Naida. Thank you very much. I'll treasure it," she said, writing her phone number down. "You call me if there's any problem."

As I watched their car pull away, Berta didn't take her eyes off me but waved through the window. I took a deep breath and turned my back, not wanting anyone. This, I would do alone.

I walked around to the back of the motel. There was an empty birdcage hanging from the ceiling, all rusted up. When I looked in on the courtyard, I drew in my breath. There on the grass.

A metal sculpture of a horse and plow looked out over a line of tall palm trees on the beach. My father had been here. Of that I was certain. This was what I'd seen in my vision. Something had shifted out there in the ether, or perhaps inside me.

I sat down on the ground by the horse in a patch of hot sun and tucked up my knees. I had never been away from my mother. Not even for a night, not since my accident when I was four. Now I cried, sobbing into my arm. Here was my father. Here was the end of my search. The end of the road. My last hope. My last hunt. It would all end here.

I walked down to the beach. The sand was warm; the water looked inviting. I changed in the bathroom of the Beachcomber Restaurant and swam until it grew cold out. I bought myself a hot dog and onion rings and ate them on the beach, watching the families come and go for what seemed like hours. I'd never felt so alone. I watched the sun set, paging through my grandmother's almanac, staring at the dagger and the bible on the sand in front of me, at the white handle and the curling mane. That night, I tucked myself up in the courtyard of the motel, cold, my face covered with an old newspaper I'd found. I shivered all night in the sea breeze and didn't sleep much.

When the first rays of morning lifted through the palm trees, I was finished. It was over between us, me and my imaginary father. Then I began the long walk home.

The sun burned my cheeks as I headed back down the highway. Kicking the stones with each step, I imagined my mother, all her stories of being left. And here I was, walking alone by choice, thirsty and hungry, a little bit frightened. Perhaps in that thunderous boom of creation, when the planets spun off and the dust formed into bits of water, when light was grown from seeds and planted in the clouds, perhaps after all of that happened, a smaller moon spun off from the larger one. That smaller moon would circle in the bigger moon's orbit, around and around for years, following a gradually widening track.

Then the smaller moon would curve, with each rotation a little farther and farther away, until suddenly it had left the tracks of Earth's orbit. It would spin out and make its own orbit for a while. Perhaps it would even find its own galaxy. Then, little by little, it would come back. When its wheels found its old tracks again, there would be a shift in the atmosphere. Some things would lift off from the water, other things would fall. This, what would be called the Daughter Theory of Creation.

As I headed down the highway, I noticed the oil derricks on the islands. Once you knew the truth, you'd never again see the mask. How much energy and electricity was being used just to create the artifice? This was not the aurora borealis, or anything close. This was a human construction made to look like a carnival, like a circus, like a magic show, like Disneyland.

This, what was known as the Father Theory of Creation.

I stopped into a small grocery store and bought myself a blueberry muffin and a can of V8. I wolfed down the muffin and bought another, and then walked some more, until my legs began to ache. At the next bus stop, I got on and rode home, sitting alone, falling asleep with my head against the window, jarred awake only when the driver shouted, "Long Beach."

I PEDALED HOME through the light rain, keeping my head down. When I reached Wild Acres, just beyond the hill, I could see flashing blue lights. There were two police cars in the parking lot, and my mother and my aunt were standing there, my aunt with her arm around my mother's waist, talking to the police. My mother dropped her phone when she saw me. She held her arms out and cried, hugging me as if she'd been without me for a year. But that's how it felt.

"My baby, my baby," my mother said. Aunt Dolly wiped her eyes and told me never to do this again. I had a lot of making up to do. I hated for anyone to be disappointed in me. My mother stepped back, keeping me at arm's length. "I've tried so hard to do the right things for you. All I ever wanted was to not break your heart. I never believed you'd break mine."

I watched as she walked out to the porch. She leaned on the railing, putting her head in her hands.

I glanced at Aunt Dolly. "What do I do?"

"Fix what you broke. If you can."

I didn't want to force my mother to look at me. I stood quietly next to her. "You didn't break my heart. Not once," I whispered.

When she turned around, I saw a hesitancy in her eyes that hadn't been there before, something I recognized as mine. My lips quivered as I stared at her.

"Don't ever do that again," she said, pulling me toward her. I didn't worry about how long she would hug me.

THAT NIGHT, I dreamed of the desert, the opposite of the ocean, a place I'd known my whole life. I was standing under the open sky at night, surrounded by huge rocks on all sides. Piles of tumbled boulders were waiting for the right light to hit them, turning them into sculptures. Soon the animals would reveal themselves in the rocks and become moving breathing beings that could stampede across miles of sand, dust, and water. Creation was faith, no matter what story or version of it you chose. The details didn't matter. Your particular version didn't matter.

There were others, not only you, finding their way back to each other through the oceans. Everywhere now, there were sea lions made of rock, the largest a gleaming blue-black. In this light I could see the bony crest on its head. I could make out two eyes as big as moon shadows. The eclipse rose, just a few seconds of this particular light from this angle. As quickly, the light faded and the shadows retreated, causing the sea lions to disappear.

Then a golden light spilled over the boulders and across the waves of the desert, drawing shadows all the way back to the sea.

Chapter Twenty-seven

O NE NIGHT IN April, under the Missing Bird Moon, people across the western United States saw a blue-green light with a streaming tail shooting across the night sky. Nobody had thought it a parakeet, though that's how it appeared to some. If you were watching the sky, you might not have known what to call this. The full moon in April had many names, none of which was the Missing Bird Moon.

You'd hear that it traveled from the coast to the desert, rapidly changing color along the way—from blue to green to orange, and then back. Some called it a dead satellite that had fallen to Earth, or a piece of interplanetary debris that had hit Earth's atmosphere and exploded. Or a falling star that just kept going until it was too low to see. Within minutes, residents from Orkney to Orange County reported seeing it, too. Within an hour, people from all over the West were calling their friends and relatives, telling them that the sky was falling. In the end, the glowing bird was deemed a meteor. If you were driving down the 91 freeway, seeing this might have caused you to pull over and call a loved one. If you were on the 405 going south, you would have seen the glowing light in the East.

You might have thought it the searchlight of a helicopter, but then it headed for the ground. This might have made you pull over to the side of the road and make a list of things you wanted to accomplish when your life began. Other people might have thought it part of a fireworks display. Someone in Las Vegas would call in to a radio show, saying that it had landed on the next block, and that the military had roped it off and everyone should head for the hills.

Dr. B. told me Tick Tock had escaped. She'd found an opened cage. I helped her look for him. Together, we walked around the neighborhood, casing the beach, checking under parked cars in the lot. I climbed a tree when I thought I saw him. I reached up and grabbed a branch, swinging my legs over it until I caught a foothold. Then I stood up. The bird fluttered out of the branches. It was another bird, not hers. We checked underneath windows, looking up through the branches and nearby bushes all around Wild Acres. Perhaps he had disappeared into the atmosphere, too, right along with the satellite or the piece of broken planet.

Dr. B. stood back and waved her hand. "My old friend. I've lost him."

She told me years ago that she thought I had an affinity for birds. She was just trying to give me something I could hang on to, something to make me feel connected. Parakeets needed a back wall to retreat to. They would not feel safe without a wall. It was their breakwater, which caused more people than you'd expect to move to this place, feeling as if they were protected. She said a person needed to keep one hand behind her touching the wall of her past, and one hand in front of her, open to the future. She said some people didn't trust things right off the bat, even when they had a reason to. They'd leave you and then come back, if for no other reason than to make sure you'd always be there. No other animal needed to test things like human beings, I thought. Some people would wait for you after you left. Even if you never came back, sometimes they'd still wait. I thought about my mother. About those who would stay with you forever.

Dr. B. said she didn't want another bird.

A MONTH LATER, under the House Moon, Dr. B. returned from her trip back East and called us into the lobby of the motel. I sat next to my mother on the couch, noticing how Dr. B.'s face flushed when she cleared her throat. I'd never seen her like this. My mother held my hand when Dr. B. said she was closing the motel for good. She could no longer run it, and Sasha needed her now. She wanted her mother with her in upstate New York, in the land of snow and ice. My mother squeezed my hand. I hoped she wouldn't cry. I wiped my eyes with the corner of my sleeve, tried to look at Dr. B., tried to imagine what this place would be like in her absence. I couldn't.

"This old bird will soon be a snowbird," said Dr. B. "Never thought I'd say those words, but you can't argue with your child if she says she needs you."

"No, you can't," whispered my mother.

"Now I've got to go tell Lou. I've called his son already; he'll go back home."

"I don't know how I'm going to let all of you go," my mother said.

That night, as I lay in bed, I tried to imagine where we'd live. I tried to imagine myself waking up in the back of a green station wagon, and what I'd see when I looked out the window. Here was the only home I'd ever known. I tossed and turned in bed all night, wondering what window I'd look up at, who my neighbors would be, and whether we'd live at the beach or not. I couldn't imagine not waking up every morning to another horizon, or walking right out onto the sand every day. I couldn't imagine a lot of things. If you had told me that we would ever leave Wild Acres, I wouldn't have believed you. I had assumed my mother and Dr. B. would always be here, unchanging, like the sentry palm. My mother used to say that no one ever left this place. Not ever, even when they tried. Some places would always pull you back.

That night, I snuck into my mother's room. "Can I sleep in here?"

She opened her eyes and asked me what was wrong. "Are you upset about the motel?"

I nodded, crawling under the sheets.

"The most important thing is that we're together," she said. "That's all that counts."

I took a deep breath. I told her about my imaginary sisters, finally letting her into my world. About how I dreamed of green water and sea gardens, of orange coral reefs and black caves where iridescent flowers bloomed in the darkness—all those dreams I had never shared with her about a beautiful world filled with castles of rock, where striped fish darted through the rows of tall sea trees, where jellyfish floated by as if on glass, where girls raced each other across the sea, arms gliding over the chalky bones on the ocean floor.

"I have a secret, too," she said, her voice low and soothing. "I'm going to try to buy this place. Dolly and me. Dr. B. has suggested it. I've never done anything like this in my life. Dolly's got money saved up, and I have a little bit, too."

My eyes grew wide, and I jumped up and shouted into the darkness.

She glanced up at me. "You're so pretty when you smile," she said. "I remember when they put you in my arms. I couldn't believe you were mine. Of all the daughters I could have had, Naida, I'm so glad I had you."

Then I told her, in the quietest voice, that I loved her. She said she knew.

Chapter Twenty-eight

MY MOTHER HAD always said the bougainvillea were holding Wild Acres in place, rooting us all to the earth. That the colors that swirled through the ocean reflected onto the sky, and not the other way around. They flashed across the ether, illuminating the ocean's changing mood, and they were a beacon. That once upon a time she had heard the voices of women in the petals at the Bethesda Home, but here they had always been more like whispers. Still, they'd echoed the chaos and the fervor, the angst and the longing, the elation and the swell of love that was never captured.

But that night while we slept, Mr. Takahashi, distraught over the news of the closing of Wild Acres, cut them all down with pruning shears. In the morning, there was a sudden lightness in the air, as if the whole place could just lift up and disappear into the sky. Vines were strewn across the beach, heaps of fuchsia and green. My mother, Dr. B., and I cleaned them up from the sand. No one could find Mr. Takahashi. When he didn't return after a half hour, Dr. B. called his son and told him to come. There were petals scattered across the water, vines and flowers floating away on the waves. My mother piled the wreckage and blossoms into big green plastic garbage bags. Dr. B. said she didn't care about the flowers; they would grow back. The most important thing was to find Lou. My mother stayed behind while I got into Dr. B.'s black Lincoln, and we drove around looking for him. Suddenly, I knew where to find him.

"I think I know where he is," I said. I remembered seeing him at the boardwalk, disappearing into the alley. She stopped the car.

"Let me come with you," she said. But I knew her hip was bothering her and that it would be better for her to wait. I got out and raced to the boardwalk. When I cut through the back alley, I heard a noise behind me.

"Is that you, Mr. Taki?" I asked, walking toward the Dumpster. I hesitated. Something felt off. "Everyone's waiting for you," I called.

"Waiting for me, Frog Witch?" Julio appeared on his bike, cutting me off.

I started to back up, feeling the scrape of the brick wall behind me. "You don't understand. My friend is missing."

"You don't have any friends, Frog Witch."

"Why don't you leave me alone?" The air in the alley was dank, full of garbage smells. Fish and rotting tomatoes. The stench of rotting food swelled in the afternoon heat. An open bag of bread crumbs lay a few feet away.

"You know you want it," he said, throwing his bike to the side. I started to run, and he grabbed the back of my shirt. He pushed me down, one side of my face hitting the asphalt.

Julio pushed one hand over my mouth. I could taste blood in my mouth, salty, my jaw tingling into numbness. Over his shoulder, I could see the bright blue, then the pebbles and sand by my face, streaked red with my blood. People were passing by on the street, but they couldn't see me behind the Dumpster. A seagull swooped in and landed near my face a few feet away.

Another flitted into the alley, pecking at the torn bread. Julio leaned closer, his lips brushing mine. Each time I struggled, he just pressed into me harder. Fear ripped through me, my heart pounding out of my chest. My body was on fire. The Wizard made my every cell signal danger. Julio's weight was too much for me. His voice grew thunderous in my ears.

You never believed something like this would happen. My mother had warned me never to walk through an alley at night. I had never thought anything would happen during the day.

His face was slick. I could see the whiskers on his chin as sweat dripped off him onto my neck.

"You'll never be anything but a Frog Witch," he breathed, his mouth wet on mine.

Then, I felt rumbling.

There it was again. Back and forth.

The ground jerked out from under us. Julio lifted his hand from my mouth, and I started to scream. Mr. Takahashi, his face flushed and eyes burning as if with memory, was running toward us in the alley. Julio jumped off me and ran out of the alley, leaving his bike and the scrape of his footsteps to settle like the lids of tin cans against the sandy ground. Forcing myself up, I glanced at Mr. Takahashi, pain radiating through my right arm. He nodded and grabbed my free hand, and we walked quickly through the crowd on the street and out toward the beach, watching the palm trees sway back and forth as swimmers raced to shore.

Drop. Cover. Hold, I thought, but there was no time to do that.

We were far enough away from the buildings and any resulting debris. I looked out at the ocean, half expecting a curtain of water to fall across the shore. There had been a small tremor. The waterhorse had come and gone, wanting only to let you know he was still there. Some things wanted only to be told that they were seen.

Mr. Taki held my bruised face in his hands. "Where have you been?" he asked.

"A NICE BOY like Julio, from a good family." That's what some people said about the attack. We would press charges, my mother said, without a doubt. This shouldn't still be happening. It should never have happened in the first place. In time, our school would enforce a new no-bullying policy. But I wouldn't go anywhere alone, not for a long while. There was so much attention on my attack, I knew he would never touch me again. Some older girls, who I hadn't known before, started walking me home. They said no one should treat me that way.

Chapter Twenty-nine

THE PHOTOGRAPH OF my father that had once scraped
the cold winds had been kept in a bottle on an island in
the North Atlantic. But nobody knew this except for the old
woman who was now standing at our front door, dressed in
a black raincoat streaked with salt, her long gray braids falling forward over her chest. I watched as she pushed back her
hood, revealing a blue cap knit with orange circles. She said my
father's name. Her skin looked windburnt across her cheeks, as
she blinked back tears.

It was the old woman from my vision, whom I had seen on
my birthday. She held up a photograph. "I'm not looking for
anything. Just wanted to speak with you."

"He's gone," my mother said, holding her gaze. The woman
nodded.

"Lost at sea" were the only words I heard before my eyes
began to burn. I felt my face flush as if my tongue were fire.
Something hard and sharp rose up in my throat. I reached for
my mother's hand. The sea flooded the parking lot, covering
the sand and oyster shells with a sheet of glass. It was a rainy
Saturday, and we hadn't left the apartment all day. El Niño

had returned with a vengeance, and from the window, cars appeared to be floating islands.

"How did you find us?" I heard my mother ask, her voice catching in her throat.

The woman's watery brown eyes flicked from my mother down to me. "He talked about you often. He used to say you were his family." She said she had worked alongside my father for a very long time. "I'm sorry there isn't more that I can do for you. But at least this."

My mother squeezed my shoulder, the photograph of my father clutched in her hand. The old woman waited in the doorway.

And then, "He was one of the bravest people I knew. There's no law in the ocean, nothing to protect the animals. Only people to protect them from other people. He loved you both," she said, pulling her hood back up.

In the photograph, my father is thinner than my mother had described him, with long gray hair falling over his shoulders, and an almost all-white beard. What struck me more than his hair were his eyes, the way he seemed to measure my gaze, drawing back as if to both evaluate me and capture me. He looks old, close to fifty, I thought. So depleted and aged and utterly human. His navy blue trousers are covered with splotches of white paint. He is standing in front of a boat about to be christened, holding a champagne bottle of some sort, a look of pride on his tanned face. The boat's name, painted in white, is *Naida Hope*.

I imagined I could see the boat that night, out there in the distance. I imagined the blue-green lights of the aurora borealis falling in curtains across the deck, illuminating the faces of sailors, and then flickering red as the curtains billowed over the water, creating a sea of gold as the sea lions rose up, appearing as stones scattered across the skin of the waves. I knew it would never be over between us, my father and me. I had said goodbye once in San Clemente. When I cast him out of my heart back then, I imagined him lost.

I sat on the couch and buried my face in my hands. My mother put her arms around me. "Did he love us?" I asked her, leaving her no choice.

She nodded. "He was just a man," she said. "The Shekhinah, she came to let us know." She pulled me against her and rocked me there for a few minutes as the rain drummed against the porch window and the storm lifted the bougainvillea from their resting places.

My father had been as close as the moon and as far.

You could walk between two worlds, the desert and the ocean. Each would, at times, appear to be the other. You could love that which you didn't understand, and you could hold that which no longer existed anymore. My mother offered me the photograph.

THAT NIGHT, I dreamed of a bird fluttering against my window. In my state of half-wakefulness, I opened my window, but the bird remained hovering. I watched as he passed right through the glass. He flew over my head and dove across the room. A lightning rod of brilliant blue streaked across the air and then circled once as it made its way above our heads. When it fluttered down and perched on the top of the chair, I drew in my breath. I started to walk toward it, but it flew away then and escaped through my doorway into the hallway. I got up and ran into the living room, but it disappeared. I thought it might be the last bit of magic my father had to offer.

MY HANDS SLIPPED from the rusty ladder as I climbed, my chin lifted toward the moon. My feet barely touched the rungs. My toes curved on the edge. I looked behind me, held by the shadows and the flickering lights from the string of Chinese lanterns.

I extended my arms. I caught my breath, letting go of thoughts of my past. Then it all disappeared as I pushed off. I was flying, my body curved across the sea. Sea mist. Red moon. Bad man. Good man. All of it, swirling on Teutonic plates, amid my mother's nighttime whispers of blistering deserts and of her young body stolen under confetti petals, of breezes laden with tears that swept across desert skies and into the wide arms of the roiling Pacific, and then north to another ocean. I kept my eyes open, knowing the waves were rising to meet me; I landed with a small splash, sinking down through the water. I opened my eyes underwater, glancing up at the seaweed canopy and the moonlight spilling through like a tunnel. Suddenly a huge cloud crossed over me, blackening out the moonlight. A floating island, I thought as I watched from underneath. Then, a flicker of light. Animal. A sea lion overhead. In its black eyes, I caught that ribbon of light, that spirit of a thing. Now a rippling image, the sea lion floated away above my head until it became a tiny ink spot in the night sky.

A few minutes later, I woke up breathing underwater. I pushed back my blanket and walked out on the patio.

"Can't sleep," I told my mother.

All things could shift their shapes. Molecules of hate could become love. Animals from a far-off place could huddle like rocks against the cold night winds. The sea turned over from storms, and then the fish came back. Mothers survived their daughters. And daughters survived their mothers. All things moved on. Knowing you had a home changed everything. My mother and I walked down to the beach.

There was something pulling at me, an echo—once filled with stories of rescues, of escapes, of dreams and wishes made on the full moon. Now there was something else. Something that reminded me remotely of me. I dug my heels into the wet sand as the first spray of sunlight splashed up across the rippling water, lifting the clouds.

The assumption had always been flight.

That canopy. That magic. That girl in the back of the room. That animal fading into the night sky. That girl in the miniskirt who got up and could fly. Just a girl. Who remembered that she was loved, and who would remember to love herself. In time.

The blue light that was scattered throughout the ocean, not the atmosphere, gave the sky its color. Sunlight, which would wake you from a cold dark winter, could convince you that your life was something entirely different in a matter of hours, could find you curled up in the smallest, darkest part of yourself. Sunlight, which drew and reversed shadows, illuminated the moon. If you believed that the moon started and stopped all things, you might believe that its presence enabled the sun to begin with. This is something my grandmother Diana would probably have believed. This, what was called the Grandmother Theory of Creation.

All this time. All those stories.

THE NEXT NIGHT, instead of escaping into the waves, I crept down to the courtyard, carrying a brown paper bag. I knelt in the moon garden we'd made beneath the sentry palm, which looked quiet and peaceful in this light, not struggling, not appearing to have struggled. The sentry palm's bark was still green, and it still grew only two palm fronds, the tips golden. We'd planted moonflowers, which bloomed only at night, which loved the humidity. We'd planted tall stakes in a circle around the tree, and the tendrils of each twining vine grew around them, each with seven six-inch blossoms. The blossoms opened so fast in the evening you could watch them, and they lasted through the night, closing with the slightest hint of morning. We planted the common white variation, starting them off as seeds, nicked with a file and soaked the day before. In time, a bright blue blossom would appear. Then another. I would learn that this was the rarest type—the blue moonflower, whose blossoms appeared a striking bright blue and, after closing, my mother's favorite pale shade of lavender. Their fragrance was lush and sweet, filling the air each evening. One day, the vines would grow right along with the sentry palm, reaching up around the trunk of the tree to its full ten feet, petals splayed open at night, opening wider in times of harsh winds and rain.

We hadn't made the garden perfectly round. Not a complete circle. The moon was only ever full for just one night.

I dug my fingers into the earth all around it. Aunt Dolly appeared next to me. "What am I going to do about this tree?" she asked.

Without a word, she sank to her knees and pushed her fingers into the ground, scraping away the earth, clawing a deep trench around the trunk of the tree, careful not to disturb its roots. I turned the paper bag upside down, letting my grandmother's 1966 almanac—from the year of my mother's birth—fall into the mud—each page holding the promise of abundant stories. I had found it in the storage room behind a box of slippers. Across the top, she'd written: "The Wanderer." My mother had refused it when I offered it to her, saying that was no longer her life. My father's death had ended her need for stories.

Now the cells that made up the paper would be joined with those of the sentry palm and become a living, breathing part of it. Maybe seeing these stirrings, these stories of the moon, these words in the margins written by my grandmother, who believed, with every fiber, in the life she could create, would make the sentry palm grow.

Perhaps all this gravity was unnatural. Maybe things were meant to exist in a permanent state of falling. Why else would people have so much trouble staying put? Perhaps some souls existed long before that thunderous boom of creation ever occurred. Perhaps they'd waited patiently, floating like tiny jellyfish through the galaxy, waiting for the planets to just get on with things already and take form. When certain souls were drawn to Earth, some fell together. You would see it as a meteor shower, as a cluster of tiny stones with wings.

Those people would be your family, those you were meant to come into this life with. Others would become your friends, people you traveled through this lifetime with.

You would appear to be falling. At first, it would seem that way. But you would land gently on Earth as if on the waves. You would touch down only for a lifetime, just a millisecond. Not any longer. Then you would lift off.

If you were a person who'd been left, you would always be surprised when the world rose up to meet you like all those crystalline molecules of water rushing in to fill an empty space. In time, you would thank your lucky stars that somehow, despite your trials, you felt mostly buoyed up, that you were driven by purpose, that somehow, despite the darkness, you could always pull light in, holding it with your fists.

Years later, while walking to the boardwalk with my mother, my arm hooked in hers, I'd gasp at the empty outline of a man lying under a tree. In my mind, I'd picture an upturned baseball cap and soiled clothing. Once, Paulo walked by, holding his small granddaughter on his shoulders, dressed in the blue flannel shirt I'd once picked out for him. That little girl wore such a smile on her face, proud of her grandfather for any number of reasons I could think of. He was the universe.

In time, I would learn about art. I would learn that a painter could capture a leaping trout with a single dash of red paint—a caster's fly.

And yet.

Sometimes a caster's fly was only just paint. Sometimes it did not illuminate everything else, creating a story. A thing, less important than its relativity, most importantly wanted to be seen just for what it was. It was almost impossible to do this. Sometimes if you closed your eyes you could do it. Or if you looked underwater, sometimes you could also do it.

And yet.

The disruptive and surprising placement of color, the place where value and form converged to place an entire ocean—you did not need to be godlike to capture it. You needed only to be an ordinary girl. You needed only to draw one blue line beneath each eye and go about living your life. The trick had always been in knowing when a dash was just a dash and when it was something more. Would it ever mean what you thought? You would make meaning from things, from symbols and signs. This form would be in languages. In sculptures. In brushstrokes. In words. If you were looking at a young girl especially, you needed to be most gentle about your calculations.

Sometimes that girl with blue eyeliner was just a girl with a crayon, sitting in her bathroom one night, bored, playing with color. She simply liked the way it made the color of her eyes look. She simply thought it was pretty. Everything that tumbled into your mind, all the meaning you made from it, what you thought you knew about her because of it, would be a mistake. My mother had a right to be shocked by what happened to her when she was fifteen. I swore that would not happen to me. I was lucky.

Because of this, my mother had endured too many judgments. Bullied, as I have been. Because of this people said it was fine that things were stolen from her. She was just a girl with a reputation like me. Reputation, the atmosphere around a thing. The ability to see it for what it was, not to derive meaning from it, was critical. It was easy for me to see why my father appealed to her. He didn't judge her. For him that red dash in that painting would have meant only that. It was red. It was triangular. It was flat. Placed in the middle of brown. It meant nothing. Neither did a line of blue.

WHAT I SOUGHT was what I was capable of. In time, I'd see that. Just as birds would learn that they would not remain in a permanent state of falling, you didn't have to hide in the skins of animals. No one could steal you. Not you. No matter what you imagined they took. No matter what they had wanted, they wouldn't have you. You were endless, could never be destroyed. You and the ocean, you were the same. This, what was called the Salt God Theory of Creation.

The time you came here was the time you were meant to be here. My place, my time, was now, no matter what my bullies would want me to believe about how I was made, about skin, about what I would become.

I REMEMBER STANDING outside Wild Acres a few nights after I'd found out about my father. Three women sat on a blanket by the sea. Dr. B. listened as my mother told a story, my aunt beside her, her legs tucked under her as the waves crashed and the meteor shower silently tore dreams across the night sky. My mother looked up as if she heard something, but it was only the wind spinning glimmers of the last light of day over the waves, taking the bougainvillea petals with it. I remember how the waves unfolded under the pull of the new moon. I remember the sound of her stories—the roar of the ocean, the collision of wind on waves, the hollow strum of a guitar.

It was then I truly saw the future.

The bougainvillea would always come back with abandon.

Epilogue
Diana

I NEVER WANTED SECOND sight. It could make me chase
my tail. Leave me blind to what was right in front of me. It
could capture me. I tried to make sense of things that couldn't
be understood, as if trying to weave threads that could not
be separated, as if my fingers had become the threads themselves. Never enough dexterity with my fingers. They were raw,
clumsy. You can see I was good at saying what I didn't want.

Let me tell you what I did want. I wanted my daughters.

I wanted their freedom.

In the beginning there was music. Ruthie's father taught
me to play my first guitar—he gave me his. I called him The
Wanderer because he came from a far-off place, a place I could
never go. The dust he kicked up because he didn't want to be
tied down carried me back and forth across the night skies,
across deserts and across the ocean. Certainly this clouded my
own emotions, my own gifts, whether anybody saw them or
not. That's what I wanted. I was running from it, what stormed
inside me like the ocean. Under that moon on the beach, where
I first met him, the waves glowed as I took his guitar and felt
my first note of peace. I peeled the peace sign from its belly

and stuck it on his forehead. He laughed, though he'd meant I should keep it.

If I told you I was not afraid of the quiet, I'd be lying. I was not used to it. But I wanted very much not to be caught in the storm. I was used to things much more ethereal than love. Love was not my first language. It wasn't elusive, rather the opposite. It was something I didn't see—a thing too tangible, concrete. But I learned it. A thing real, not imagined. Step by step. Bone by bone. Rock by rock. Ladder by ladder. Child by child. I learned its form.

Dalia had come first, from a farmer, a man of the earth who could reach into the soil and grow fruit. Then Ruth, from this Wanderer, a creature of the sea. A man who'd always escape back into the ocean.

And yet, not just a man.

When I tired of running, when I was ready to face my mistakes, I went back there to the place on the beach, finally to see what was there. All I was. And all I was not. I had to recover what we'd left. Sticks, shells, bones to show where the path had been broken.

And that is where The Wanderer found me again.

I wanted to look him in the eye, to stare down his escapability. To walk it down, as if a curse, an illness, a rogue animal cast out. Begin again, Dagmar told me. Work. Eat. Sleep. I needed to build a life for my girls. A bed they could wake up in. A table they could sit down at. A window they could open. And close. Depending.

We would make curtains. Bread. This, to me, felt like a miracle.

Things would still carry me away. But not as much. No, not as much as they once had.

The Wanderer climbed out of the water, pushing me aside for the last time, his eyes on the old motel covered in vines where I'd made our home. This time he'd brought a skin for my child, his child. He wanted to take her back to the place I could not go, back to his home in the sea. Over his shoulder I saw the bougainvillea wrestling the moon as the clouds and the sea mist flooded across the rooftops where my little girls slept safely.

He didn't stop. We fought out there in the sea. We fought with fists. With words. We fought with shouts, though no one heard us.

If you ask why I didn't see this coming, I will ask you to imagine looking up at the sky and not being able to see the moon because you are standing on it. I will tell you not to fear the silence—silence is not the absence of noise; it is simply the state of hearing too many stories at once. It must be waited out, so each story can be parceled out, heard. I didn't see things on my own course. For a time I needed a map, books. I tried to make sense of what would always slip away.

On that last night of my life, I wanted to see the flash of my own fire on the waves, to recapture myself from that ocean and its moon, to take back all of my stories and for it to leave me, for once, in peace. Nothing should be kept in cages, and yet people built their own. I had built mine, and it gave me something to put my hands on. Cages made you demand your freedom. Until you didn't need that kind of thing anymore to be free.

When the Salt God let go of me, the moonlight whipped back like a tail flashing against the night sky. It disappeared into the waves, taking the moon and all its stories with it.

Back to the place of the animals. To the place before even them, when there were only stars.

Dagmar and I had promised each other that my girls wouldn't know about my mistakes, my choices, my gift, what I did for love. That was the pact we made. There is strength in numbers. If you are part of a tribe, you band together. My girls would stay together. I never wanted them to know my sacrifice. That was not theirs to carry. I didn't want them to know their difference, either. I loved them the same.

Yes, I loved them, imperfectly.

My girls found me near daybreak sitting in a pocket of shallow water. My body was broken, but I felt enormous strength. I had wanted to simply bask in the silvery sky, to watch the full yellow moon sink into the blue-black, and to know that I'd fought for another person, and had won. My last fight had been for love, something real, not imagined. In the end, The Wanderer, Ruth's father, would go. The moon and its stories would fade. My girls would wake up together, and would remain together, side by side, their language one of stories. I used to tell them that nothing in life would ever be as permanent as the words on the page, certainly not the moon, which always changed, certainly not human beings, with their shifting thoughts and their swirling feelings, with their smoke signals, their stories, and their threats of silence and their secrets. Then, I knew I was wrong. I'd become recognizable. When I stopped running.

I made Ruth promise me she would be a better mother than I was. I saw that a child teaches its mother what no one else can. I think this was what we were all doing here together to begin with.

Dagmar would call this the Mother Theory of Creation.

I had given Ruth back her freedom. Devotion, she already knew. Devotion and freedom, they could coexist. But I never had to teach Ruth that. For her, that was instinct.

That morning, as I rested in the waves, I looked out at the sky. *I was here*, I thought. *No more stories.*

Like the waves, my girls came.

A girl. Just a girl. Then, another.

Acknowledgments

M Y GRATITUDE FIRST to my family—to my husband and my three children, without whose love and support it simply wouldn't have been possible to write this book.

My thanks to some extraordinary people: Caroline Leavitt, Joyce Maynard, Louisa Paushter, Marlene Lang, and a fabulous librarian called Retro Doll. For their expertise, thank you to Judi Feldman; Julie Glovin, LICSW; Jessie Pelton, MS, PA-C; and Nancy Kaplan of Temple Kerem Shalom. Lifelong friend and Belmont Shore resident Suzanne Shaheen made California feel like home all over again. To Tracy Winn, Emily Rubin, and the Concord Women Writers, all my thanks for the friendship and wisdom. For research matters related to syndactyly, thanks to Dr. Joseph Upton, Professor of Surgery at Harvard Medical School in Boston. I appreciate the Long Beach Fire Department, the Long Beach Marine Institute, and the New York City Alliance Against Sexual Assault for their research and support.

There are some decisions in life that you just know are right. Not long ago, I put this book in the hands of my talented editor, Dan Smetanka, and never looked back. My thanks to Dan and the fine folks at Soft Skull/Counterpoint Press for their enthusiasm and support of me and this book. And to Sally Wofford-Girand, as always.

Finally, thank you to my wonderful father, Raymond Ruby, for the lucky angel.